# BABYDREAMS

Philip was taller than Stevie by a head. His hair was longish, thick and dark. He wore small wire-rimmed glasses and a playful expression. From the way he was standing, his arms wrapped around Stevie, nearly crushing her in his embrace, it was evident he loved her and was proud of her too. Had anyone ever looked at her that way? Carol wondered sadly. No, never. And Stevie, perfect as ever – was wearing a string bikini that showed off a stomach as flat as a plate and a pair of perky breasts that didn't need the scant support the bikini top offered. Carol thought of the scar running up her midsection like a fleshy pink zipper and her breasts flattened by breastfeeding. It wasn't fair, she thought with a shock of anger. Stevie had everything any woman could want and it had been so easy for her. A college degree, a glamorous career, a handsome, rich lover, a body unmarked by childbirth, the undying love of her very own ex-husband – but she didn't have Lisa. Carol grasped the thought and held onto it tightly. No matter what Stevie has, no matter what she looks like, she is old. Too old to have a child.

# MAXINE PAETRO

# BABYDREAMS

**A Mandarin Paperback**
BABYDREAMS

First published in Great Britain 1989
by William Heinemann Ltd
This edition published 1990
by Mandarin Paperbacks
an imprint of Reed Consumer Books Ltd
Michelin House, 81 Fulham Road, London SW3 6RB
and Auckland, Melbourne, Singapore and Toronto

Reprinted 1994

A CIP catalogue record for this book
is available from the British Library
ISBN 0 7493 0288 7

Printed and bound in Great Britain
by Cox & Wyman Ltd, Reading, Berks

For Arthur

# BABYDREAMS

# Prologue
## 1969

The good thing about having the small attic room at Sigma Tau House, thought Stevie, was she didn't have to share it with a roommate. The bad thing about having the small room was—she didn't have a roommate. There was no warm body in another bed across the room, no studious scholar spoiling the twilight with a desk lamp switched on over a clacking typewriter, no soulmate to pull at her, prod her, until she grudgingly revealed the scary, beautiful secret that no one knew; no one, not even Andy. She would have to tell someone soon, would want to, but right now she only wanted to sit as she was sitting, on the window seat fitted into the dormer window, knees tucked up under Andy's baseball jersey, looking out over the campus and at a fat silver moon rising in the indigo sky.

Stevie took the neckline of the jersey and stretched it over her nose. She inhaled the sexy, sweaty scent of her boyfriend. She wished she were with him right now. She loved him so much. That's what it meant to want to be with a person all the time, to want to turn yourself inside out for that person. Of course, Andy was amazingly easy to love. He was nicer than anyone, so genuinely nice that no one begrudged him his 3.5 average, fantastic looks, and the singular distinction of being the only athlete on campus who had been sought out by a professional ball club.

Stevie unfolded her legs and climbed down from the window seat. She crouched by the bed and felt around in the dark until she found the long, cedar cigar box, then got cross-legged onto her bed with the box in her lap. She turned on a lamp and sorted through her treasures. There were the score sheets from the games, and love letters from Andy that she knew by heart, and a fortune she'd saved from their first Chinese restaurant meal. "Listen to your heart," it said, "and let it guide you." Right. She fingered the slip of paper and dropped it back into the box. She had stripped petals from the bouquets Andy had given her and now sifted the crumbly potpourri with her fingers. She lifted out a photograph of Andy winding up for a pitch, squinting into the sun, and pressed it to her cheek. She put the picture beside her and slid the box back under the bed.

Bending over made her dizzy. Don't do that anymore, she cautioned herself. She leaned back against the wall until she felt stable again, and then gingerly touched her breasts. They ached. They ached all over. She couldn't be wrong. She had never been even an hour late before and now her period was three days overdue. She was sure. Her body was changing almost by the minute. She was pregnant. She was having a baby!

The sudden certainty chilled her and erased Andy from her

mind. She could see nothing, hear nothing, feel nothing but a tingling sensation as though she were suspended miles above earth. What would happen to her? she wondered for the first time. Images of herself, gravid and pale, bloomed then burst before her eyes. She would be expelled from school. She would be sent to a "home," her newborn infant wrenched from her and sold to strangers.

The vision was too horrible. In one swift motion, she buried herself in her blankets. "God, if you help me—" she said aloud, then covered her mouth. How *dare* she ask for God's help now, when if she ever thought about Him at all it was to challenge His existence. There was nothing about her upbringing that led her to believe that God answered prayers. No, it would be Andy who would help her. Andy would fix everything. She wanted to talk with him *now*.

She wished she could phone him, but Andy was on a bus somewhere, coming home from an away game. It was just as well. She shouldn't tell him on the phone. Then where should she tell him? She tried to picture the perfect place. She knew. They could sit on the white wooden bench at the back of the music building, right near the copse of hibiscus bushes where it had happened. Someone had been inside the building that night, practicing a lilting rhapsody on the piano. The music had drifted almost magically out into the night and mingled with the sweet fragrance of orange blossoms. She thought about Andy's arms and hands, so tanned they were invisible in the dark. His fingers had looked like shadows quickly pressing the buttons of her white cotton dress through the buttonholes, skimming off her underthings, shiny and luminous in the moonlight. She had squirmed and quivered under those invisible hands, breathless, dying to love him, wanting him so badly that she couldn't wait, couldn't even think about rolled-up, unromantic rubbers. She had thought instead of how delicious it had been having him inside her all the way, how good and right she had felt to be really a woman at last. And making love with Andy had gotten even better as their love had deepened.

Stevie hugged herself and looked out the window. Full moon. Full Stevie. What would they do? She had a dark thought, an ugly thought. What if he didn't want her to have the baby? What if he wanted her to get rid of it? Fragments and phrases of witchy solutions to desperate problems came back to her; hot baths, gin and quinine, gruesome stories about abortions performed by medical students and questionable doctors in vile places. She closed her eyes hard against black and white visions of humiliation, pain, death. No. She didn't have to worry about any of that. Andy loved her and she loved him. They would get married and move to a little apartment off-campus until he finished school this year. Then they would go wherever his ball club sent them. They'd stay in Florida, probably, or maybe they'd move to New York State. She'd stay home for a while with their baby and then she'd go back to school. She'd take their baby to Andy's games. She could see herself holding a chubby hand, pointing it toward a beloved figure in the center of the baseball diamond. "That's Daddy," she'd say. "Watch Daddy throw the ball." Their baby. Stevie got goose bumps thinking about it. With her ash-blond hair, his gold, they would have a beautiful, fair-haired baby with blue-gray eyes and fat kissable cheeks and a darling little mouth . . .

Stevie heard footsteps coming up the stairs toward her room. Damn. She wanted to be alone. There was a knock on the door.

"Stevie? Are you in there? Phone."

Andy. She knew it. "Coming," she said. "Tell him I'm coming." She stepped into her moccasins and, flinging open the door, raced down the stairs.

"Hi," she said breathlessly, folding her body onto the steamer trunk under the pay phone in the hall.

"Hi," Andy said. There was a crackle on the line, and more. Something was wrong.

"Andy? Are you okay?"

"Wait a second," said Andy over a tape-recorded message, "Please deposit sixty cents for the next five minutes."

Stevie listened to the gonging sounds of the coins falling from Andy's hand into a chute somewhere far away. "Where are you?" she asked when the line was clear.

"I'm still in Baton Rouge," he said. "Stevie, I have something awful to tell you."

"What is it?" What could it be? Let it be that they lost the game, not that he'd been hurt. Stevie focused as hard as she could on Andy's voice, willing him into three dimensions.

"Darlin', I don't want to be telling you this on the phone, but I may not be able to see you for days and I want to tell you before you hear from someone else."

"Andy. I'm dying. Tell me."

"You remember that girl I was dating before we started going out?"

"Carol Wilder?" Stevie asked, tucking her legs more tightly under her. She remembered a thin, gawky girl in her biology lab last year. She'd been hard to talk to and since then Stevie had wondered how Carol and Andy had ever gotten together.

"Yes. Carol. She's pregnant, Stevie. About five months."

Stevie couldn't speak. She listened to every crackle on the line. Two of her sorority sisters hovered, impatient to use the phone. She would not look at them. They braced themselves against the opposite wall and conversed normally as if Stevie weren't precariously balanced on the edge of a precipice. She heard Andy clear his throat.

"Her daddy pulled me out of the game. Right off the field. He told me I could marry her the hard way or the easy way."

"Marry her?" Stevie said weakly.

"God, Stevie. I love you. You know that." There was a long pause as Andy took deep breaths. Stevie heard him slapping the sides of the phone booth. "He literally slammed me against the locker room wall and held a bat across my throat. Said I could marry her today, or he would get my scholarship yanked, break my knees, and then I could marry her from a wheelchair."

"Andy, he can't, this can't be . . ." Stevie wept.

"I know, darlin', I know. I wish I could hold you, Stevie."

Stevie wiped her wet face with her sleeve, and tried to find her thoughts. "Are you sure it's yours?" she asked.

"I don't know. Yes. Yes, it is. God. I believe her. It's mine."

A pre-disconnect sound came through the earpiece. Thirty seconds. "I have to see you, Andy," Stevie said, frightened now. What was going to happen to her? What was she going to do?

"I don't have any more change, darlin'," he said, his voice husky and dry. "Listen to me. I'll be back in a few days, after all this is settled."

"Andy. Don't do it!"

"I have to. I have to give my child a father. But I don't love her, Stevie."

"Please deposit sixty cents for the next five minutes," repeated the cold electronic voice.

"I love *you*," she heard Andy say over the recording.

"Andy, Andy, I'm . . ." Then she was holding a dead receiver attached to a metal wire cord, attached to—nothing.

Even before Stevie numbly replaced the receiver into its cradle she knew what would take her the rest of the piercing, fearful, and desperately lonely night to decide. If she couldn't be with Andy, she could not, would not, have this baby.

# 1

## 1988

The intercom blared. "Miss Weinberger. Your car is here."

"Tell Sal to go out for coffee, Pete. I'll be ready in ten."

Stevie threw open the closet door. What to wear? Cotton jersey pants, silk sweater, linen blazer. She dressed quickly, stepped into lizard skin shoes. She stroked the brush through her hair, slicked pale tints on her cheeks, lips, and eyes. She peered critically into a gilded-framed mirror by the front door. "I'm coming," she called into the intercom. She locked her front door and traveled the distance from it to the street below without awareness until the glass lobby door was opened into the warm summer morning.

"I'm ready, Sal," she called to the driver, who was cracking sunflower seeds with his teeth, blowing the hulls into the wind. The prematurely gray young man was leaning against the street side of the blue sedan. A gust of traffic-produced wind lifted the flap of his jacket revealing his shoulder holster.

"I've got the door," Stevie said, opening it and sliding into the plush interior.

"Here you go, Stevie, ma'am," Sal said, passing a coffee container through the transom.

"Thanks." It was progress of a sort, she thought. It had taken Sal a year to call her Stevie at all. She stared at her reflection in the glass until her attention drifted unwillingly to her upcoming lunch this day with Carol Wilder. And then the image dissolved and she was looking back into a black and raining night. The limousine then had been white, not blue. She had met it in the parking lot of a take-out hamburger place, and she had had with her a thousand dollars in a brown paper bag. Oh, God. She would not think of that last time she had seen Andy. She looked quickly out the window. Change the channel, she thought. Pale pictures of street activity made faint impressions on her conscious mind.

"Last stop," Sal said, swinging open the passenger door.

As she entered her office, smoke and the sound of Ed Warner's voice assailed her.

"Are we moving together?" the executive producer rhetorically asked the assembled crew who were sprawled around the conversation-pit meeting area. "No," he answered himself. "Do we have a clip of the reunion scene? No. Do we know where the gorilla man can be reached? No. Has the thimble lady been replaced? No. Are we taping at five? Yes. Does anyone give a fat flying damn?" Warner tapped cigar ashes into a film can and squeaked back into the secretarial chair. His purplish wattled neck seemed to puff up twice its normal size. "I'm going to die at an early age," Warner said dramatically.

"Eddie, Eddie, it's too late for that," someone said in mock sympathy.

"It's never too late to die at an early age," Warner growled, rubbing the top of his stubbly head. "Nice of you to join us," he added as Stevie stepped over blue-jeaned legs and found her spot at the center of the horseshoe.

"Has the world ended?" she asked, unconcerned, affectionately imitating Ed's rhetorical style. "No. Am I sorry? Yes. Am I forgiven or do I have to drink the coffee?"

"Ha, ha," said Warner.

"What have I missed?" Stevie asked Pamela Friedman, her associate producer, sitting at her right.

"You missed the crummy donuts and most of the ritual chewing out. That's about it." Pam lifted a tangle of dark curls off her forehead for this remark, then dropped the forelock back over her eyes. She took a stapled packet of paper out of her clipboard and handed it to Stevie. Luann, Stevie's secretary, brought a mug of coffee into the room, gave it to the person closest to the door who passed it, bucket brigade style, along to Stevie.

"What happened to the thimble lady?" Stevie asked. "I liked her."

"Slipped a disk," Pam said. "She left this for you."

"Oh," Stevie said, opening a box. "It's Warren Beatty, isn't it? I love it."

Warner cleared his throat. "Very touching. Truly. But we have a show to do, people, and unless that thimble is going to break into song . . ."

"I spoke to the gorilla man last night," Pam said. "He's staying at the Carlyle and will be calling in this morning. I think you should meet him, Steve."

"A messenger just came with a cassette," Luann said from the door.

"Bring it in please, Lu."

"Want me to put it up?" she asked, standing before the video machine. She pushed her butterfly wing glasses up on her nose and looked at Stevie.

Stevie pulled her shoulders back in an exaggerated fashion, her signal to Luann to stand up straight, which she did. "Yes, please," Stevie said. A home-style video tape came on the screen.

"Great, great," B. Willy Foster, the show's director, said to Stevie. "The film is great, but I'm a little worried about how these guys are going to play. I can't understand any of them."

"It's just the background noise, really Will," Pam said to her husband. "They were eighty percent cogent in my office."

B. Willy tapped his front teeth with a fingernail. "Gonna have to fool around with the sound. Drop the level so the Bronx guy doesn't blow out the mikes. Steve, I'm gonna ask you to speak up on their segment, okay?"

"Better remind me."

The door opened. Martha, the talent booker, a stolid grayhaired woman dressed in mint-green ruffles, stuck her head through the opening. "I've got Pete Armstrong from the Stress Institute," she said. "He'll fill in for the thimble lady."

"We can count on him?" Warner asked.

"Affirmative," said Martha.

"You don't look happy, Ed," said Stevie, teasing the producer. "It's buttoned up. We've got triplets, a stress reducer, and what else?"

"Viewer mail," Pam said flatly.

"Right. Mail. We live another day," Stevie finished.

"Luck," Warner said. "Pure luck. Everybody got the line-up for the week?" he asked. "Yes," he answered. "Any questions? No. I'll see you all at four." He rose. Stretching out his neck and shoving both hands into his pockets, he left the room, taking all of the tension with him.

"Bye, everyone," Stevie said gaily. Luann came back in toward her, pushing through the crowd of exiting crew. When they had all gone, she and Stevie pushed cushions back into place, cleared the coffee containers and tobacco ashes into the waste can.

"My perm sucks, doesn't it?" Luann asked Stevie.

"Not exactly."

"I told you it would look sucky."

"First of all, it doesn't look that bad. Anyway, it will relax."

"When?"

"When you stop hating it."

"Fabulous. I'll be ancient."

"Tut tut, and stand up straight. I don't know how you can slump that way. If I had your body, my show would be network."

"If you had my face, you'd be on radio."

Stevie laughed. "You crazy girl. Why do you say those things about yourself?"

"I like to provide contrast to your good cheer. By the way, you've got a meeting with Boobs in ten minutes . . ."

"No, Luann. You may not call her Boobs."

"Sorry," Luann said, chastened but recovering quickly. "You have a meeting with Pam-el-a in ten minutes. Wardrobe at ten. Martha wants to talk to you before lunch. That reporter from *Savvy* will be here at eleven to interview you, and who's this Carol Wilder that got onto your calendar?"

"Old college schoolmate. It's going to be a 'Remember crazy Professor Briggs, and remember when we went to Daytona Beach' kind of lunch."

"Sounds like fun. I canceled your exercise class."

"Uh-huh."

"What's the matter?"

Stevie looked at the concerned face of her secretary. How was Lu able to read her so well? "It's nothing. Curious about how she turned out, I suppose."

"Oh." Luann cocked her head. Flecks of mother-of-pearl imbedded in purple plastic frames winked at Stevie, and she smiled.

"Call the club, okay?"

"Twelve-thirty?"

"Yeah."

"Okay. You've got a meeting with Grunch—'scuse me, Ed— at three, lighting at three-thirty, and then the run-through. Here are your messages. Here are your newspapers."

"Thanks. Wait. Where's the *Times?*"

"Willy borrowed it."

"Lu! Why didn't you tell him no? There's a newsstand downstairs."

"I told him no."

"You did not." Stevie looked at her secretary and relented. Luann's hopeless crush on Willy was so obvious.

"I'll go downstairs and get you another copy."

"No rush," Stevie said. "I'll start with these."

Stevie walked to the far end of the office and up the half step to her work area. Her desk was at the windowed end of the large square room. She sat down and picked up the phone, tapping out numbers as Luann closed the door behind her. "The time is exactly nine-oh-three," said the electronic voice. Stevie hung up the phone. She moved three glass paperweights two inches each. She opened and closed a silver box with rose petals inside.

She was having lunch with Carol, having not seen her in almost twenty years. Hell, if she didn't see her for another twenty years it would be okay, so why, dummy, why had she agreed to the lunch date? Well, she'd been caught by surprise and then she'd been seduced by curiosity, always a failing of hers, but still, where was her good sense? She should have known that when the actual day arrived, she wouldn't want to spend two whole hours with Carol.

Could she still be suffering from the loss of Andy? She hadn't thought about him in a million years. As she considered this, she called up a wavering image of his face and remembered the pain of that sudden, senseless disconnection. They had been so very young but their love had seemed so bright, so pure. Perhaps first love, unhampered by past hurts, went deeper than the subsequent, more guarded kind. But really, Steve, really, she reasoned, that Andy stuff happened an actual half-a-lifetime ago.

Back then, she had been a pretty, well-behaved little girl, so blond, so clean, so good; not a girl who would scrap, or scream, or trap a man to get what she wanted. You were a poor little know-nothing, she thought sadly. Everything happening to you, and no experience, nobody to lean on. She hadn't been prepared for anything worse than a broken date on the night of a big dance. That Stevie had been the product of her grandmother's work. Eleanor, her careless young mother, had delivered her, then ignored her, leaving the spit, the polish, and the upbringing to Nana. It had been Nana, matron of their tiered, stuccoed, jungle-hidden house in Coconut Grove, who had brushed her and scrubbed her and chastened her and nearly convinced her that she was a pretty girl, a perfect girl, and that perfect pretty girls were the only girls worth loving. It had been Nana who had pushed her into sorority life, packed her bags when she had been rushed by Sigma Tau. And hadn't college proven Nana right? For pretty girls college was roses and convertibles, dressy dresses and places to go in them. And dates with the very best boys from good families with money. Like hers.

Of course, she had been smart enough to know her life was

not the real world. Young women her own age were demonstrating against the war, joining the Peace Corps. It was embarrassing to her now to remember how the reality of the outside world had frightened her and how the security of banding with a small group of girls—girls like herself—meant she could feel safe on a big campus far from her home. And, of course, she had been completely involved in her love affair with Andy. But what if she had taken that love affair the final step farther?

If she had married poor Andy Newman from Waldo, Florida, Nana would have thought her insane. Eleanor wouldn't have come to the wedding. She would have had something very ordinary from Tiffany sent by mail with a card written out by the shipping clerk. Granddad would have come and he would have given her away, but in the house her father had left, her grandfather on her mother's side didn't count at all. Not that she could have married Andy. If she could have, she would have. But. There had been Carol. If Eleanor had known Carol was the reason she hadn't married Andy she would have sent Carol something really *special* from Tiffany, possibly given her a shower, Stevie thought wryly. What a great gal her mother was. Oh, they had been so relieved those two, Nana and Eleanor, when she and Andy had broken up, when she had transferred up north to NYU without ever saying why.

What would Carol be like now? Stevie remembered a brainy girl, an attractive girl who hadn't known it, who seemed to work against her own attractiveness. When she thought of her now, Stevie recalled frequent, nervous laughter, unflattering clothes, and a shiny, lacquered, beehive hairdo. Stevie shook her head, disbelieving still. This girl, this awkward girl whom Andy hadn't even loved, had trapped him, borne his child, and snuffed the life out of Stevie's dreams.

She was curious, damn it. How had it really turned out for Carol? What would she look like? She hoped she'd be a dumpy matron with that same goofy smile and lime-green espadrilles.

Carol had said she owned a real estate firm in Chappaqua, so that would fit. What else had Carol said? She tried to remember exactly but it was hard to do. Carol's phone call last week had shocked the actual words right out of her mind.

"It's a Carol Wilder," Luann had said. "Says she knows you from college." She had stared vacantly at her secretary while absorbing what she had heard. When the name connected with a face, connected with a meaning, Stevie found she still didn't know what to say.

"She's called once already," Luann had added. "Should I get rid of her or what?"

Just hearing Carol's name had unnerved her, felt as sharp and as unexpected as an alarm clock going off without being set. She had been unable to even guess why she would call. She was calling to get reacquainted, Carol had told her when Stevie had assembled the wits required to depress the blinking button on her phone. "I watch your show every night," Carol had said. "I'd love to get together and catch up with you after all these years."

Stevie had agreed, not knowing how to say no, never knowing how to say no to calls like these, had suggested having lunch in her club.

Now she turned a silver picture frame so she could look Philip in the eye. She touched the packet of papers with the heading, "Stevie Weinberger On-the-Air." These were her things. This was her show. She loved a fantastic man who loved her back. If only she had known all those years ago that one day she was going to take possession of her life, create her shining, joy-filled career, fall in love with Philip Durfee. But how, at twenty, can one possibly imagine thirty-nine?

She hadn't needed to accept that call. Or she could have spoken with Carol on the phone, said "Nice talking to you," and hung up. Why had she cracked open the door on that drafty corridor? Stevie swiveled in her chair and stared out the window.

# 2

Carol crunched the last ice cube. She wanted a cigarette, but she had promised Lisa she would stop smoking. She could stop. She had done a thousand things harder than that. She tried to think of a few of the thousand but couldn't. She tipped her empty glass toward the waiter, who nodded and brought her another Bloody Mary. The waiter was wearing a name tag on the breast of his red vest. Albert. He had a French accent, so she imagined his name would be pronounced Al-bear. "Thank you, Albear," she said. "Madame," he replied, dipping his head before he wheeled away. Albert looked like a parrot, she decided. He had pouchy skin all folded up under his eyes and a beaky nose.

Carol looked at her watch. She was still early, but she wasn't early out of nerves or eagerness to please, as Stevie might think if she knew how long Carol had been sitting here. She was early simply because she had finished showing Beth Turner's house sooner than she thought she would, had caught the early train after all, and then it was either come here or kill a half hour at Bendel's. A half hour at Bendel's would be frustrating. If she saw something she wanted and didn't buy it because she couldn't try it on she would feel cheated, or more probably she wouldn't try on whatever it was and would buy it anyway and then when she put it on at home, Lisa would say "Ick, Mother, that's so tacky." And then she would keep it so long she could never return it, because she didn't get into New York City enough times to really shop there. So that's why she was a half hour early for lunch, just in case someone wanted to know.

Carol sniffed longingly at a trail of smoke coming from the smoking section to her right. Why was she listening to Lisa? Lisa never listened to her. Other people smoked and didn't die. Beth Turner smoked. Beth Turner smoked her head off, and she looked fine. Of course Beth Turner was the world's most stubborn person. If she knew, absolutely knew for a fact, that she was going to die from smoking, she would still smoke. Thank the good Lord Beth hadn't been standing there smoking and looking pleasant while she showed her house this morning. Of course she'd finished showing the Turner house early. One could not sell a house for six-fifty with an above-ground pool. Real estate prices were climbing as fast as a monkey on a rope, but that still didn't excuse six-fifty for that lump of a dump with a blue plastic pool. The Turners would have to come down at least a hundred if they were going to sell this season.

At five-fifty, maybe she would buy that house. She would love the big south-facing rear yard. Dream on, Carol, she thought. That house would stay at six-fifty until the damned thing was worth it no matter what century that was. Anyway, she *would* like to go to Bendel's. She could almost justify a new suit, but when was there enough time to shop?

Carol opened her date book and scanned her appointments for the day. She had meetings with two clients, the first at four o'clock. If she caught the 2:58 she could make it. She sighed and snapped the book shut. Work, work, work. How come working for herself meant more work than being employed by someone else? She drummed her fingers on the maroon table-cloth. There was a large oil painting of a garden on the wall opposite her table and she stared at it. Wide-eyed hollyhocks, china-blue delphiniums, and something yellow she didn't recognize leaned against a garden wall. In the foreground, a peasant girl held a little spotted rabbit in her arms. The painting looked English. English gardens were at their height this time of year. She needed to get away for a while, she thought. Get out of the country, have a fling with an exotic foreigner, spend some money. But now was the wrong time. Business was good beyond human belief, and more importantly, she needed to spend time with Lisa this summer. There was still a chance she could talk her into leaving that damned riding instructor, Reed whatever-his-name-was. That relationship just turned her hair white. How Lisa had convinced herself to turn down every ivy league college in the country to be near that horse trainer still completely mystified her. Sarah Lawrence College. Sarah Lawrence playschool was more like it.

College kids did dumb things. Carol had been dumb and now Lisa, her heart and soul, was being dumb. Why was it she could sell million-dollar houses and she couldn't stop her own dumb kid from throwing her life away on a married man?

Carol sipped the spicy drink in front of her. She wanted a

cigarette and bad. Maybe she wasn't cut out for cold turkey. Maybe she had to try cold chicken first; wean herself with those low-tar cigarettes. Shit. That would never work. She'd smoke low tar for a while, then she'd be back on the hard stuff. She reached into her handbag and pulled out a compact, then opened it and checked her lipstick in the mirror. She pulled the mirror back a few inches and looked at her face. She pushed a brown, silver-shot wave into place, pressed her lips together, smoothed an eyebrow, and firmly clicked the case closed. She looked okay. Better than she looked in college, God knew. She had looked like an ostrich in college. A ditsy ostrich. This was a good outfit for the meeting with Stevie. Smart, not too dressy. Azalea pink was a great color for her. Would Stevie see that she had changed? Well, hell, she was a little nervous after all. Success in real estate was not the same as being a TV personality. Would Stevie think she was a bore? A suburban drip? Hi, I'm sure you remember me, Carol Percolator, your basic suburban drip, she thought with a broad stroke of self-deprecation.

It was hard to believe that she and Stevie were having lunch now when they had never shared as much as a pack of gum together before. They had been in two completely different social classes in school. Stevie had been what they called "popular," had been in all the good clubs and what had that sorority been called? Sigma something—Sigma Tau—while she herself had been in the lump of dump set. No greeks, no beach parties; there was probably a lot of other stuff they hadn't been admitted to. Still, even in the most desperate times, she hadn't been able to work up a hate for Stevie. Stevie had been so nice to the not cool, not popular, not anybody girl she had been. What had she been? A geek. And a brain, she supposed. And definitely least likely to marry the campus hero. Carol permitted herself a wry smile. The collision of a minuscule sperm cell with an egg the size of a speck of dust had been quite an equalizer. Thought touched thought and then Carol braked her wandering reverie and looked up guiltily. If only she could believe it had been an accident. If only she, the careful math major, hadn't marked off the days in her diary, crossed off the numbers, circled the date that she knew would be the one day that would make Andy hers for the rest of her life. Scrutinizing the results of that microscopic smack-up was like touching ice to a tender tooth. Carol squirmed. She had to have a goddamned cigarette. Wasn't there a spare in the side zipper of her bag. Carol bent to the floor and reached for the leather envelope. She dug around in the contents, looked up at the sound of her name.

"Carol?"

"Oh my God, Stevie. It's you."

"It's me," Stevie said, sliding into a chair. "Am I late? Let me look at you." Even as Stevie spoke the words, she felt her real self, her internal self, recoil. I don't want to be here. This lunch is going to be a charade; phony politeness, kiss-kiss, old chums reunited. Wouldn't it be enough to simply know that she hated this woman in the back of her mind? This meeting was dangerous! What if she accidently liked Carol? Or worse, she thought suddenly, what if her past hatred transplanted itself into the present?

"You wouldn't know me, would you?" Carol asked shyly. Stevie was so pretty. So put-together, and so effortlessly too. Silk and linen, aqua and white, sleek blond hair perfectly cut hanging straight to her shoulders. Perfect, perfect, perfect. Some things never changed. Carol put her hands in her lap to hide the nicotine stains and the ragged edges around her nails.

"Sure, I would," said Stevie. "You look the same but better. And you're still skinny, you lucky girl." Oh, God, I'm going to be nice. It's too crazy. She hurt me once and maybe, if she could, she'd hurt me again, and here's me, so nice, so goody-goody, so wimpy little Nana's girl. Why don't I just slap her in the face and walk out of here? Never say a word. Stevie bit down hard on her bizarre and illogical thought. Look at the woman, she advised herself. In what possible way could she be dangerous? Carol had turned into a suburban real estate broker with streaked frizzy hair wearing an awful pink dress. This woman was not life-threatening.

"Nerves," said Carol. "Real estate keeps you on edge in my town. I call it 'the nerves diet.' No dangerous drugs, no boring exercise, money back if not satisfied."

Stevie laughed, surprising herself. "I don't think it works for everyone. I, for one, eat when I'm nervous," she said, filling her cheeks with air. Carol grinned.

"I've seen you do that face on TV."

Stevie smiled thinly, checking herself. Let's not perform for her, she counseled herself. Let's not be too cute. This is a date, not a relationship. "Would you like another drink?" she asked politely. "What are you having?"

"A Bloody Mary, but I'm just fine with this one."

"I'd like a glass of white wine," Stevie said to the waiter. "Have you been waiting long?"

"No. Anyway, it was be here a little bit early or blow a bundle at Bendel's," Carol said shyly. Stevie doesn't worry about spending money at a department store. She probably gets her clothes for free. "Well, hey, you haven't changed at all," she said, covering her last utterance with a compliment.

"No? And I so desperately hoped I had." Awkward silence engulfed the two. Oh, God, that sounded hostile, Stevie thought. I didn't mean that. "But thanks," she said, retrieving the bad moment. "Thanks for the compliment." Carol grinned nervously and sipped her drink.

"So," Stevie said, smiling warily at Carol. "Cheers." I'm going to need this drink. Why had she called her up? Yes, please, why had she called her up out of the void, Stevie wondered again. She could be back in her office doing leg lifts and eating banana yogurt. She could be lying on the floor bullshitting with Pam. She could be napping, making up for last night's short sleep. What's up? she wanted to ask pointedly. What favor do you need? Let's get this over with. Relax, Steve-o, she heard Philip's voice say in her head. If he said that, he would be right. She *should* relax; look for something nice to come out of this. But how? The despicable teenager Carol had once been had never been confronted, never been punished, yet Stevie had no right to face her down now. In fact—and here was the decision: She would be nice. She would get through this, and then she would retire Carol from her mind forever.

"So, what's new?" she asked, as if she had just seen Carol a day before. The two women laughed with relief. "Can you believe this?" Stevie continued. "I go on camera every night and interview strangers—and I've known you since we were kids and I feel shy."

"I know what you mean," said Carol. "If I go first, I'll just gush. You're the only celebrity I know."

Stevie watched Carol color and fidget. Her public persona had this damned weird effect on people. So now, on top of everything, she was going to have to put Carol at ease. Forcing herself to relax, she heard her television voice describing her job and the people with whom she worked. She talked about the support she had from the staff and crew, and the responsibility she had to them, to stay on top of the ratings, to insure their jobs. "I'm only the one they point the camera at," she said in conclusion. "If those guys weren't as great as they are, I'd be in a state of stark terror all the time."

"They must just love you," Carol said, thumbing hopefully through the index in her brain for something more interesting to say. What she wanted to ask was this: Are you grateful to me for saving you? Because you should be, you know. You should be.

"Well, I hope they at least like me a lot."

Carol shook her head. "I could never do what you do in a million years."

"And I couldn't sell water in the desert. Having your own business must be exciting. What's it like?"

"Sure—bedrooms and baths and new furnaces—it's *so* exciting," Carol said facetiously. She saw the phone with a line of flashing buttons. Cards strewn across her blotter. A double row of desks facing hers, each occupied by a person who needed to be bullied, coaxed, supported, paid, or fired. She saw her ashtray overflowing with lipstick-rimmed filter tips and Lisa going through money like Carol printed it up at night, just taking her soft life for granted. Carol wanted to talk about Lisa, not about Hudson River acreage that didn't exist. Could she talk to Stevie? Her marriage to Andy was such old history, but, still, she wanted to talk about it. She had never told Stevie how bad that victory had felt. Could she now? Her mom used to say, "If you feel froggy, leap."

"No, seriously, Carol, when I knew you last, you were a math major. How did you get into real estate?"

"Oh, I don't know. I guess I have to say it was kind of a lucky accident," Carol said, turning over a fork, smoothing the napkin on her lap. That was the honest truth. Leap. "You know I never graduated?" she said.

Stevie nodded. Carol, taking in Stevie's affirmation, continued. "Well, after Andy and I got married, we moved to upstate New York . . ."

Hearing Andy's name felt like a punch to her insides. Why hadn't she been braced? Couldn't Carol have said, "Get ready. I'm going to punch you now." This woman had been Andy's wife and had given birth to Andy's child. She could hear the sound of Carol's voice but it was a background hum. Stevie swallowed, took in air through her mouth. Andy. She had loved him. Loved him.

"It was horrible, Stevie," she heard Carol say. "My father had called me names I can't say even now and cut off my puny allowance and there I was as big as a boat, the two and a half of us trying to make do on Andy's pitiful salary. I guess we spent half our time in a bus moving from one hokey little town to another. We ate so many of those fifteen-cent hamburgers, I'm surprised we didn't sprout little turrets on the tops of our heads. I swear, I don't know who was the bigger martyr: Andy for dragging me around after him, or me for being dragged. And of course we were doing it for the baby . . ."

*Clang. Da-clang.* Stevie heard coins dropping into a pay phone slot many years in the past. "I'm still in Baton Rouge," she could still hear Andy saying. "I have something awful to tell you . . . Remember that girl I was seeing last semester? Remember Carol?" Stevie looked across the table at Carol. Shocking pink offended her eyes. As if through a haze, she could see a glossy beehive hairdo and a big belly pushing out a shocking pink dress. Andy's baby. The baby *I* should have had, she thought angrily. "We should order lunch," she said in a brusque tone. "I have to get back to the station soon."

"Of course," Carol said, flustered, opening the menu. "I'm talking too much about myself. I have a way of doing that."

"No, no," Stevie demurred, first out of reflex politeness, then from a growing sense of shame. Carol had been telling her the story of her life. Stevie had asked her to and then she had cut her off. Carol couldn't possibly be jabbing her intentionally. Carol had never even known the extent of what she had done. Apologetically, Stevie said, "It's just that they get backed up in the kitchen sometimes . . ."

"Oh, I understand. What do you recommend?"

"I always have the same thing. The chef's salad is really good, but they have an artichoke and sliced chicken breast . . ."

"The chef's salad sounds perfect," Carol said, bending a twitchy pull in the corner of her mouth into a smile.

"Two chef's salads, please, Albert," Stevie said to the waiter. No bears were mentioned, Al types or otherwise, Carol noticed with embarrassment. How sophisticated Stevie was. Maybe she too could have grown up normally, matured, become a woman of the world. If she hadn't been so dumb. If she had graduated. If she had met a man who loved her. If she hadn't been so sure no one would ever love her. If, if, if. I saved you, Stevie. I really did. If only I had known that winning was losing.

"Another drink?" Stevie asked Carol.

"Perrier," Carol said to the waiter.

"Two," said Stevie, and then, "I'm sorry. Please go on, Carol. You were saying about the baby."

Carol cleared her throat and pressed the tines of a fork gently and repeatedly into the tablecloth. "Lisa. Her name is Lisa." Carol looked away and then back to Stevie. "About Andy. We didn't love each other, Stevie. Or rather," Carol softly cleared her throat again, "Andy didn't love me anymore. I was pregnant, you know, when I left school," Carol said, ducking her head slightly, leaving behind a verbal offering.

Stevie nodded. "Oh, I'm sure . . ." she began, not knowing quite how she was going to finish the sentence. I'm sure Andy loved you? No.

Carol spoke into the pause. "My father . . . He almost killed me when he found out."

"I know," Stevie said. "Andy told me." And what had he told Carol? Anything? Everything?

There was a pause which grew into silence which was broken by Carol. "We got divorced, you know. First we had Andy's baseball career, then we had Andy's academic life. One was worse than the other. Boston was okay, but after that . . . try to imagine living in Gigantic-no-place, New York, if you know what I mean. A great big town that's just like every little town you ever knew. And there's Andy teaching gym and me sitting at home becoming a vegetable. I couldn't take being an appendage any more. I tried, but I couldn't. We split up and I moved down to Chappaqua with Lisa and got a job answering phones in a real estate company. The rest, as they say, is history."

Both women beamed bright, forced smiles at each other. Carol's smile collapsed first. "You loved him, didn't you?" Carol asked in a low voice.

"Oh. I guess I did. It was a long time ago."

Carol nodded, relieved. It was silly to think that Stevie Weinberger could still be in love with Andy Newman. That juvenile. That loser. Stevie had been spared for someone finer. "You didn't miss a thing," she said hastily, before she could examine what she was giving away. "He was a selfish little boy and that's the beginning and the end of the story," she added vehemently. "You don't know about baseball players, Stevie. They're kids, every last one of them, and with a baseball player you can take your pick. You can be his mother or you can be a kid like him and hope someone else will take care of you both, but you cannot get him to be an adult married man." What was that expression on Stevie's face? She was looking at her like she had told a lie. What did she think? That Andy was a saint for marrying her? She felt suddenly awkward, as though she had uttered a gross indiscretion. Couldn't she be honest about her own husband? "Are you married?" she asked suddenly.

"No, not yet." Stevie answered distractedly. She tried to imagine a selfish, childlike Andy, but that was simply not the Andy she knew. The Andy she knew had sacrificed their love to do his duty to this woman and their child. Maybe anyone would begin to take after giving so much.

"How did you ever avoid it?" Carol asked in genuine disbelief.

Stevie turned her attention to Carol's question. What had she asked? Oh, why she had never married. There was nothing she would rather talk about less than this. Funny how people would rather talk about nothing more. "My favorite subject," she said in a tone that she hoped would dissuade Carol from probing.

"Really?"

"No. I hate talking about being single. Whenever I'm interviewed for something, that's the subject interviewers zoom in on. 'Stevie Weinberger, the old maid of the air waves.' See? Do I sound defensive?"

"Oh, who wouldn't? Old maid. That's so stupid. I'm sorry I brought it up."

"It's okay. Don't apologize."

"Don't you apologize either," Carol said vehemently. "I'm sure you could have married anyone you wanted to." Uh-oh, an inner voice warned. "I mean, you're gorgeous, and famous."

"No, no," Stevie demurred.

"Well, you are."

Stevie laughed. "Thank you, that's very nice of you to say. I guess I've come close to marriage a few times," Stevie said. Why am I telling her all this? she wondered. This isn't like me. And I don't want to give anything to Carol. "It's just that the world got a little strange for women in the last couple of decades, don't you think?"

Carol nodded. She had read that article in *People* about Donna Mills and Terri Garr being single, and who else? Cher? No, Linda Gray, she thought. So Stevie was one of them. "I know," she said sympathetically. "But you probably didn't want to get married, right?"

"I don't think I did," Stevie said, thinking about it. "Not for a long time. I was working all crazy hours when I was a producer, before I got the show. Then after I got it, I seemed to attract a wide assortment of the wrong men."

"Like what kind?" Carol asked, leaning into the table.

"Mostly people who wanted me to be who I was on TV. Cool, interesting, famous, the perfect business wife. Trouble is, when I'm not working I like to stay home and eat sardines. I like to watch 'L.A. Law.'" Stevie shrugged, hoping to dislodge the memory of those lonely, disheartening days. Talking about dating gave her a headache. She didn't want to go back to that time, not for a minute. It made her think of the users, and the opportunists, and the fakers, and the ones who seemed perfect and then got scared and ran away. And the endless issues that differed from man to man; the power things, Stevie thought tiredly. Who was making more money, whose job was more important, whose meeting was earlier in the morning so therefore in whose apartment they would spend the night. Whose country house they would go to on the weekend. All of it was New York City craziness—manufactured, unreal, neurotic. The whole dating experience had just about worn out her patience and her expectation of a happy ending. But it didn't matter anymore. Those days were over. Philip loved her, sardines and all. Especially because of the sardines, he would say.

"Sure," Carol said, nodding sympathetically. "But I'll bet a lot of men are just intimidated at the idea of even asking you out."

"I suppose," Stevie said with a small smile. She looked at Carol, who was looking back at her with such a sweet expression. Carol had relaxed, gotten normal. Stevie even felt Carol was interested in her, not in some prurient way, but almost as if they were friends. This was nice, she realized. Could she trust it? Stevie took a breath and continued. "I wasn't willing to give up too much either, I have to admit. I hadn't even met anyone I wanted to be serious with in years. That is, until I met Philip."

"So there is someone."

"We've been together for a couple of years," Stevie said.

"Well, what's he like, if you don't mind my asking?"

Stevie thought for a moment and smiled. How could she describe Philip? "Well, he's pretty good-looking," she said, "or at least I think so. I'll show you a picture of him. Here," she said, taking a color picture out of her wallet. She handed it to Carol.

"Gor-geous," Carol said. "What does he do?"

"He's a venture capitalist. He specializes in backing inventors of things like talking bathroom scales, shoes that let you walk on walls." Stevie grinned. "Things we can't live without. He provides the money and if the product succeeds, Philip cashes in."

Carol stared at the photograph. He's rich. She had met enough money to recognize it instantly. She wouldn't be able to say how; but it had something to do with the self-confident thrust of his jaw. This picture was obviously taken in Europe somewhere.

"We took that in Cannes last month," Stevie said. "Philip has a house there."

"Well, that's very nice," Carol said, tilting the photograph toward the light. Philip was taller than Stevie by a head. His hair was longish, thick and dark. He wore small wire-rimmed glasses and a playful expression. From the way he was standing, his arms wrapped around Stevie, nearly crushing her in his embrace, it was evident he loved her and was proud of her too. Had anyone ever looked at her that way? Carol wondered sadly. No, never. And Stevie, perfect as ever—was wearing a string bikini that showed off a stomach as flat as a plate and a pair of perky breasts that didn't need the scant support the bikini top offered. Carol thought of the scar running up her own midsection like a fleshy pink zipper and her breasts flattened by breastfeeding. It wasn't fair, she thought with a shock of anger. Stevie had everything any woman could want and it had been so easy for her. A college degree, a glamorous career, a handsome, rich, lover, a body unmarked by childbirth, the undying love of her very own ex-husband—but she didn't have

Lisa. Carol grasped the thought and held onto it tightly. No matter what Stevie has, no matter what she looks like, she is old. Too old to have a child.

"He's just gorgeous," Carol said, handing the photo back to Stevie, stabbing a bit of food, chewing it.

"The way he looks hardly even counts," Stevie said, gazing at the picture for a moment before she put it back in her wallet. "He's so different from every man I ever knew before. He's funny, and so smart, and being with him is as easy as being with, I don't know who, a girlfriend, I suppose. Do you know what I mean?"

Carol nodded. "You two look very happy together." The man she'd been seeing lately was a contractor, big-bellied, fifty-two; a man whose favorite tee shirt read "Life's too short to dance with ugly women." "So when are you getting married?"

"Oh, I don't know. I think I've embarrassed myself."

"Why? Why do you say that?"

"Oh, because we haven't made any definite plans." Stevie popped a cherry tomato into her mouth. "We talk about it, 'when we're old and gray together,' that sort of thing. I guess, to be honest, I've had fantasies before about getting married to the most wonderful man in the world. But besides Philip, every other man I've thought of marrying, I've had to make big allowances for in some way or other."

"Boy, you said it. I know what you mean," Carol said, groaning. "I think the older you get, the more allowances you have to make. When you're a kid, you don't know enough to know you're compromising."

Stevie nodded in agreement. "Yeah, well, I think I'd given up on the idea of the perfect man for me. Then Philip showed up and in a way it's like all those other disappointments never happened. These days I stand on the porch of my country house and think about what a wonderful wedding I could have with tents all set up in the long grass, and a string quartet in white playing classical music down by the lake, and what a blissful life I could have as Mrs. Philip Durfee."

"Spoken like a woman who has never been married," Carol said, piercing the pretty picture with a knowing smirk.

"I suppose. I know some people who have been married think the institution has been oversold, but maybe when you've reached the age I am, and the age Philip is, you've got enough experience to make a relationship work."

"Well, I wish you luck and I hope you're right. I still hope for perfect love myself."

"Are you seeing someone?"

Carol nodded. "He's no Philip Durfee." Silence fell over the table. "Houses are my thing," Carol said, struggling to free them both. "Where and what is your house with that big old porch, and will you list it with me?"

The two women smiled at each other. "I can't sell my house," Stevie said. "It's just a not-very-fancy Victorian farmhouse, and it's in Connecticut. I've fixed her all up with lace and what-nots and planted her all around with blowsy flowers and now she looks like someone's crazy old aunt."

"How wonderful," Carol said. She could actually feel the blood pounding in her ears. A Victorian house in Connecticut, a dream man, a dream job, a perfect body. Was she just jealous, or would anyone sitting across from Stevie want to murder her? "You grow flowers," she commented in the most neutral voice she could attain. "I'm a gardener too."

"I'm not really. I like plants but my thumbs are brown. I run out and buy a flat of something once in a while but I have a wonderful little Swedish woman who comes and sprays and prunes."

"Oh," Carol said. She thought of her backyard in Chappaqua, facing east, packed with every kind of bloom that could possibly tolerate the weak sun. She thought of the huge maple that if felled would open a sunny patch near the kitchen for vegetables and salad herbs, and how she couldn't bear to sacrifice that noble tree. She felt the conflict every morning. Was Stevie ever conflicted? Did she have a little Swedish woman tending everything? "Stevie, are you older than me or younger?"

"I don't know. I'll be thirty-nine next week."

"Well, hey, happy birthday."

"Thanks. When is yours?"

"I just had mine last month."

"Happy birthday to you too," Stevie said, touching her water glass to Carol's. "How was it?"

"Good. Fine, really. Thirty-nine is supposed to be rough, but it was painless. I don't think birthdays worry women who've had children as much as women who haven't."

"Really? Do you mean me? I'm not worried about not having children." Whoa. Where did that come from, Stevie wondered, reeling slightly. Shit. I made her jealous.

"No?" Carol asked. "You aren't planning on having any?"

Stevie replied emphatically, "I'm too old to have kids. I don't mean biologically, I mean psychologically. I *love* the life I have. I couldn't squeeze kids into it. Besides, Philip has two kids by his former wife and he doesn't want to have children either." Stevie looked at Carol's accepting expression. Does she believe me? She had told Carol what she told everyone, what she thought was true. She didn't want to have children. Or, rather, she had made the choices she had made, arrived at the age of thirty-seven without having had children, and then she had fallen in love, seriously and permanently, with Philip. And so that was how her decision had been made. Why was she even questioning herself?

Carol sipped her sparkling water. Would she have children if her life were like Stevie's? Yes. Lisa was the single most important thing in her life. Lisa meant more to her than a man, her career, her very breath. Look how much she had given up for her. How convenient for Stevie that her whole life had been delivered to her all tucked in and kissed good night. She had never had to sacrifice one perfect second for anyone else. Why did this remind her of Lisa? Because Lisa also had a damned soft life. All those years she had spent mining the stony ground of cold calls and rejection so Lisa could have everything: money, education, introductions to a world Carol had been denied. And now, after all that, Lisa had turned down Brown and turned down Yale and turned down Harvard for dumb old Sarah Lawrence so she could be near that creep Reed. "Mom, I want to be a writer," she had said. "I don't want to go to a nerd school. I don't care how good my grades are, I don't see why I should be punished just because I got good grades." Harvard. Punishment!?

"Tell me about your daughter," Stevie said. "What's she like?" She was flirting with something dangerous now. She knew it, but she did not know its name. "Do you have a picture of Lisa?" Stevie continued, the words flowing out of her mouth as if some other person had spoken.

Carol opened the locket hanging by a gold thread around her neck, and by leaning across the table, held it out to Stevie. "Oh," Stevie said. Carol watched a change come over Stevie's face. She lost her composure for a moment; looked so soft and vulnerable. Not at all the self-assured talk show celebrity. How lovely she was. How natural. She could see how a man, how Andy, would have loved her. What lovely hands, she thought, watching Stevie's fingers holding the heart between them. "Lisa is hardly a baby anymore," she said. "She's almost nineteen and a college brat. That's Lisa at six months." She tapped a carmine fingernail against the glass-covered photo.

Stevie stared at the picture. This was the moment she had feared. The picture was of a fair-haired baby girl, blue-eyed, chubby-cheeked. Andy's baby. In her mind, she heard coins marking their descent with a cacophonous clang. "I have to give my child a father," Andy had said. *But I love you. I love* you. There was a roar in her ears, the sound of rain coming down hard on the metal skin of the car, and a living picture appeared just inside her mind. She could not see Andy in this picture. Her eyes looked straight ahead, looked straight into the watery glass. She thought she could hear the sound of Andy's voice, but not the words. The words were her own. They were, "No. Leave me alone." And her thoughts were, I can't be doing this. I must.

Stevie blinked. Oh, God. It could still hurt, even though it had happened so long ago—loving Andy and hating him. Dreaming of a baby they had made, but never had. Where would her baby be now? What would her baby have been like? Like this baby? Like Lisa? Angry words gathered; stormclouds about to burst. *I* was pregnant too, she wanted to shout. *I* was pregnant *too* and I gave up my baby because of yours! She gazed stupidly at Carol, listened as the roar subsided. She couldn't say this out loud to anyone. No good would come of blurting out a secret she had kept for so long. What could Carol say or do? She'd say, "I'm so sorry, I didn't know," and that would be true. And it wouldn't be enough. "She's a honey," Stevie said of Carol's infant girl, her voice husky and low. "A real beauty."

"Thank you," Carol replied, busy now with her own thoughts, reaching down beside her, searching for her handbag. "I have some grown-up pictures somewhere . . . No, I've left them at the office. Oh Lord, I've been talking about nothing but me."

"No. Please. We're catching up." Had Carol remarried? She couldn't even guess. "Did you ever remarry, Carol?"

"No. I've had two thousand dates with two thousand almosts, not readys, not interesteds, not for me's, and another two thousand I can't remember anymore."

Stevie nodded. "I know exactly what you mean." If dating had been hard for her, what must it be like for Carol; business owner, mother, living in the suburbs. She felt flushed with a sudden warm feeling for the woman sitting across from her. "So you raised Lisa by yourself?"

"Yes. Andy lived so far away, and my mother was too afraid of my father to be much help . . ." Carol thought of the stern face of her father as yet unsoftened by the beauty, the sheer miracle of Lisa. "I really hate my father," Carol said.

Stevie felt shock as Carol said the words. Stevie's own father had died when she was so young she hardly remembered him. She was sure though that if she had known him she would have loved him. What could it possibly be like to hate one of your parents, to be divorced from your husband, to raise a baby to adulthood? What had Carol been through?

"Would you like to see the dessert menu?" the waiter asked.

"Not for me," she said looking up, refocusing her eyes. "Carol?"

"Just coffee," Carol said.

"Decaffeinated, please," Stevie said, turning back to Carol. "My father is dead. He died when I was two."

"I'm sorry," Carol said, looking hard at Stevie.

"I miss not having had him."

Carol nodded.

"I think he must have been a very good man. My mother loved him very much."

"Do you have brothers and sisters?"

"No. It was just me."

"How did it happen?"

"Cancer." Stevie sighed.

Carol ndded again. "How did your mother manage? Did she work?"

"Uh-uh. No. There was money. My dad left money, and my grandparents on my mother's side really raised me. I was always aware that there was enough to take care of our needs. But you must have had it very hard."

"Well, there wasn't any money. Not at the beginning anyway, but Andy stayed in close touch with Lisa. They're still close. But being close and being *there* are two different things . . . Anyway, it's been worth it. A thousand times over. Lisa is the brightest kid in the world, and please forgive my pride, but the prettiest too. She was accepted at every Ivy League school you can think of. All the ones that didn't used to let women in when we were kids."

"Great!" Stevie said, forcing enthusiasm.

"My darling daughter turned down Harvard and turned down Yale, didn't even respond to Brown. Instead, she's going to Sarah Lawrence. Lisa wants to be a writer." Carol sighed with exasperation.

"I don't understand. Sarah Lawrence is a very good school. What's wrong with that?" What's wrong with Carol? she wondered.

"Well what, I ask you, does *writer* mean? How many writers can support themselves? Lisa could be *anything*. She had straight A's in science. And math. She got a three eight from Dunnington Prep. I struggled for so long to get her into the right places." Carol closed her eyes briefly, remembering the canned meals, the discount clothing, the nights on the telephone developing leads so that she could bring in more money than the paltry bits of change Andy kicked their way. She remembered the vacations she'd skipped so she could send Lisa to Europe, the European kids she had taken in for summers so Lisa could have similar privileges in France, England. "This writer crap, excuse me, is just another word for housewife. She's in love with her riding instructor. Reed, his name is. She's sleeping with him."

"Oh," Stevie said simply. Lisa was old enough to have sex! And Carol could be Eleanor talking. "My daughter's in love with a baseball player," she would have said. "A nobody."

"And he can't even marry her. He *is* married."

"Oh."

"She's at Sarah Lawrence so she can be near him. I could kill her. She's messing up her whole life."

"You've tried to talk with her."

"Have I ever? 'I don't want to be off with nerds,' she says, 'getting a degree in ma-ath.' She'd rather be screwing around with this pretentious loser—and believe me, he's a loser—waiting for some miraculous day when he leaves his wife so she can marry him and have his babies. Can you get the picture? Reed training horses. Lisa writing plays and breastfeeding. Do you think I would go to jail for a very long time if I killed him?"

"I think so," Stevie said, smiling.

"I told her I wouldn't pay for Sarah Lawrence. Do you think I'm obliged to keep my child in a school I think is wrong for her?"

Stevie stared at Carol. Was that a parent's role, to force a child to do what you wanted? If Lisa was so bright, couldn't she make up her own mind?

Carol continued. "I've agreed to go along with her for one more year, but after that I don't know." Carol shook her head. "She's the same age I was when I fell for Andy. And look what that cost me. Sorry. I didn't mean to be so self-pitying. I just want better for my little girl. I want her to have a life like yours. Action, New York City, excitement, big business, not some dumb tract colonial in Ossining all wrapped up in a picket fence."

What if I had married Andy? Stevie's perspective did a midair flip. Is this the story I would be telling? Did Carol's baby save me from a life I would have loathed?

"I think he'll get a divorce, that's what I think. That's what I fear."

"Carol," Stevie said helplessly.

"I don't want to make her sound like a bad kid," Carol said earnestly.

"You didn't. Don't worry." Stevie stirred her coffee intently. Would her child be involved with a married man? Would she be trying to hold so tightly to her own daughter?

Carol sighed. "You know, it was Lisa who asked me to call you."

"It was?" Stevie looked up sharply.

"She's entering this contest. 'The Moira Glick Playwriting Competition.' The winner gets his or her play produced in New York City. Off Broadway, of course. Off-off."

Stevie nodded.

"Lisa's entry is going to be a play about a married couple who co-anchor a news show. A comedy. Listen, Stevie, if what I'm about to ask you is an imposition, just tell me. Okay?"

"Sure. Of course I'll tell you."

"Really."

"Okay, it's an imposition."

Carol laughed. "She wants to visit your station, interview you, do some research."

"That's easy," Stevie said. Could she bear to meet Lisa? Could she bear not to? She sipped her coffee. "You know, we sometimes hire interns for the summer. We had a kid up until last week. She got mono and had to leave. Do you think Lisa would be any good at being an office slave? Work around the newsroom, get coffee, do some typing, things like that?"

"Are you kidding? She'd do cartwheels for a chance at it."

"Okay. Just have her call me. I'll have her talk to the personnel department. I'll see what I can do."

"Lord," Carol said. "What an idea! Lisa is a little in awe of you. No, don't look so modest, she is. 'I can't believe you actually went to school with Stevie Weinberger,'" Carol said, imitating her daughter's voice. "You laugh, but you're a role model. You can't imagine what a summer job with you will mean."

Stevie signed the check that was placed in front of her. Was her pulse racing? "Come on—let me guess. Lisa comes to work at the station fetching coffee. She stops seeing the married man. She transfers to MIT and specializes in nuclear physics. The East, knowing the West will win the war, backs down. There is global disarmament. It all starts here."

Carol laughed. She felt years younger than when she had sat down such a short time ago. "Right! That ridiculous picket fence fantasy is going to seem tame after a summer at WON-TV."

"Oh, Carol, really. Don't expect too much. She's going to be hanging wire service copy from bulldog clips. She's going to be running out for Sweet 'n Low. It ain't Hollywood."

"She'll love that. She's not the slightest bit precious. *Au contraire.* My little girl can't wait to get her hands on cloth diapers. No. Watching you. Seeing what you do. Working in New York City. Being in the work force. Reed Creep-o is going to seem mighty dull."

Stevie shrugged. "I don't know," she said doubtfully. "But I'll do what I can to get her the job."

"You're going to like her," Carol said. "And thanks so much for this favor."

Like her? Stevie thought. What would she look like, be like? Would she be anything like the child she would have had if she and Andy . . . "No problem," Stevie said. "I can't wait to meet her."

"Having a kid," Carol said, rising with Stevie, straightening her collar, tucking her handbag under her arm. "You have no idea how much you worry. Little kids, little worries. Big kids, big worries. You can't imagine what it's like."

"No," Stevie said.

"Be glad you didn't have any," Carol said, edging her way around her chair.

"I am," Stevie said, a dizzying thought pushing forward. A chill went through her. Amazing. She was being given the extraordinary opportunity to explore "the road not taken." She was going to meet Lisa Newman! She smiled and turned toward Carol. "I'm glad we did this," she said.

"Next lunch is on me," Carol said, giving Stevie's arm a squeeze. They walked outside into the muggy air.

Lisa Newman, Stevie thought. "Can I drop you somewhere?" she asked.

"That would be wonderful," Carol said. "If you don't mind. I'd love a lift to Grand Central. Oh, Stevie. Do you ever see anyone from school? And do you remember that crazy Professor Briggs?" Carol asked as they approached Stevie's car.

# 3

Stevie squeezed her eyes tightly closed and willed the phone to stop ringing. She was chin-deep in warm water and fragrant, frothy suds. She had been imagining herself a lotus blossom floating on the surface of a scented pond; the ringing phone fragmented her peace. "R-r-r-r-r," she growled. "All right, all right," she shouted. So much for the de-stress exercise, she thought, standing in the huge marble tub. She wrapped a towel around her hair, draped another around her body, and trudged to the bedroom, leaving damp footprints in the carpeting.

"Hello?"

"Stevie, it's Ken," said the deep voice of Philip's sixteen-year-old son.

"Kenny. You're not supposed to pick me up for an hour. Is something wrong?"

"Not really. Um. I can't get to the car keys. Dad's going to kill me."

What was this about? Stevie sat gingerly on the edge of the bed. Her skin was prickling as the water evaporated. "Well, what did you do with them, Kenny? Isn't there another set?"

"Um. The only keys I've got are in the car."

"So, can't you get them out of the car? Is the car locked or something?"

"Not really. I don't know where the car is exactly."

"What? You've lost the car? It's been stolen?!"

"Um. Not really. I mean I know where the car is sort of, I just can't get to it."

Stevie listened intently. Can't get to the car. What did that mean? It was lying in a ditch? No. There were no ditches in Manhattan. Why didn't he say what he meant? She imagined this tall, clumsy hulk of a child switching the phone receiver from one hand to the other, calculating how much he could say to satisfy her questions without saying enough to indict himself. Don't do this, Kenny, Stevie thought. "Kenny," she said evenly, "please tell me what you're talking about."

Kenny sighed heavily. "Nothing really. I mean like it's been towed."

"You parked in a no-parking zone?"

"No. It's like the wheels were locked or whatever."

"I don't get it."

"Well, I backed up over something and I think I hurt the axle."

"*What*, Kenny? You backed over what?"

"Like a hydrant or whatever."

· 50 ·

"Oh, God," Stevie said. She gripped the receiver tightly. She saw the back of the green Jaguar parted, wrapped obscenely around the water plug. Was he hurt, or was this the end of the story? "You're not hurt?" she asked.

"I'm okay."

"Thank God." Stevie unwrapped the towel from her head and rubbed her hair. "Did you call your father?"

"Yeah."

"Good. What did he say?"

"I didn't speak with him."

"Kenny. Stop this. Don't make me drag this story out of you—one, word, at, a, time."

There was a sob on the other end of the phone.

Oh no. Had she been too rough? "Ken. Kenny, I'm sorry. Talk to me."

"His . . . his line was busy. I can't call again."

"You don't want *me* to call him for you?"

"You have to."

"I can't. It wouldn't be right. Listen. I want you to hang up now and call him back. Don't worry. As bad as it is, he'll get over it, you'll see." That was true, wasn't it? There was silence on the phone. "Kenny. Did you hear me?"

"Uh-huh. I can't call him again."

"You can! You have to."

"They only let me have one call."

"Where are you? You're not at the police station?!" Snuffling sounds came over the receiver. "Kenny, it's all right. It's okay. Is there anything else?"

"No."

"You're sure? Nobody was hurt?"

"The hydrant was hurt. The hydrant was totaled."

"Okay. Don't worry. Tell me where you are," she said, scribbling down the adress, the phone number. "I'm calling your dad. Don't cry, Kenny. He'll be there in a little while. You're not locked up or anything?" she asked, making certain.

"No. Not really."

"What does that mean?"

"I'm not locked up."

"Good. We'll see you soon."

Stevie depressed the cradle hook and dialed Philip's number. She heard his voice after the third ring.

"Philip," she said evenly, "don't panic, but Kenny had a little mishap with the car."

"Stevie, don't spare me. What happened?"

"He backed over a fire hydrant and the police are holding him until you come down and get him."

"I don't believe it. How is he?"

"Scared. Real scared. He sounded like he'd pulled his head entirely into his body. Otherwise he's okay."

"Good. Shit. He didn't say backed over, did he? He must have said backed into."

"I'm pretty sure he said backed over."

"My car," Philip said, his voice pained.

Stevie listened to silence. "Philip?"

"Here I am."

"Are you all right?"

"I don't know. The stove. The computer. The car. What's next? What's he going to do next?"

"It was an accident. He was crying."

"Don't side with him. He's a living, breathing poltergeist. Since last Wednesday, Kenny has cost me twenty grand."

"A teeny exaggeration."

"Not by much," Philip grumbled. "What do you think I should do?"

"I don't know," she said. "I honestly don't know. This is completely out of my range."

Philip groaned. "Mine too. Somehow, taking away his television privileges doesn't seem appropriate. The guillotine seems appropriate."

Stevie laughed. "At least. For starters."

"Yeah. Shit. If I'm going to kill him, I guess I'd better go get him. Where is he?"

"Twenty-fourth precinct. It's on one hundredth between Columbus and Amsterdam. I'll come with you. I'll meet you there."

"Don't, sweetheart. It'll be easier if I just go in there, put a ring in his nose, and lead him out."

"Really?"

"Yeah. And I think I'm going to use some language on him he wouldn't want you to hear."

"Okay. But if you change your mind when you get there . . ." Stevie felt a pull to be with Kenny. Wouldn't he want someone accepting and female?

"I shouldn't have let him take the car."

"Philip, you didn't know. You thought he could handle it."

"I knew. I was being a good guy. He wanted to drive us to dinner. He wanted to do something, I don't know, elegant."

"Hmmm. Well, he almost did something elegant. Let's give him points for good intentions."

"No." A long pause thickened. "We're going to be late for dinner."

"It's okay."

"I don't know if we'll make it at all."

"I'm sorry, but it's okay. Bail out your kid."

"I'll call you when I know what's up."

"Take as much time as you need. I'll cancel the reservations."

"Good. Thanks. Steve?"

"Huh?"

"You're the best."

"Sure, sure." She kissed at the phone receiver and replaced

it. Back in the bathroom, she gazed sadly at the flat foam, then reluctantly pulled the plug. Would they end up eating in? Should she run out and get some food? She had steaks. Old ones in the freezer and some cheese, not as old. There was some ice cream, she was almost sure. The Korean fruit stand would deliver salad greens. She could eat a salad if they didn't go out. The constant weight watch. If only Carol's "nerves diet" worked for her.

She shot a sidelong, baleful glare at the bathroom scale. A gift; her nemesis, her foe, her albatross. Philip had brought the talking scale to her show the first time she'd met him, along with the talking typewriter, talking doll, and talking flower pot. The typewriter had been amazing, the doll, charming, but the scale made her twitchy. Could you cheat a talking bathroom scale? Even then, she hadn't thought so. Never mind. When Philip—a man whom she'd thought of at the time as an exceptionally handsome guest, probably married, at least heavily involved—asked her to, she demonstrated the scale in front of the whole world.

"What do you weigh?" he asked nicely.

"Uh. One twenty-two more or less," she replied before she could figure out how to duck the question.

"Is that your ideal weight?"

"I don't think I've ever weighed my ideal weight," Stevie answered. "Not even when I was born."

Philip laughed. "Well let's pretend one twenty-two is what you want to weigh, and let's add three pounds for your clothes, so I'm setting it for one twenty-five. I'm going to tell it your name," he said, turning the sleek black machine over, saying "Stevie" into a grid. Then he fiddled with a knob and put the machine on the floor. "Are you ready?" A warm smile creased his intelligent face.

Could anyone have resisted him? Stevie remembered thinking, this Philip Durfee is brilliant on the one hand. On the other hand, definitely a snuggler. He wore comfortable over-sized clothes, all tweedy and soft, with laced-up shoes and wire-framed glasses which, she would have been relieved to know, he would leave on the set and retrieve the next day. His thick brown hair was medium length and shone under the lights. His eyes were compelling and alive. Stevie had been captivated. She had also felt saddened, even bereft. The show was going to be over soon and someone was going to be snuggling up to this man. She wanted it to be her. She envisioned herself cud-dled up with this man she didn't know, talking to him for the rest of her life. The vision faded.

"I don't believe I'm doing this," she had muttered, kicking off her flats, stepping onto the scale. Numbers flickered, wob-bled, held. Then, an electronic fanfare had tootled out from the scale. "Congratulations," pause, "Stee-vee," it said. "You've exceeded your goal. Your weight is," pause, "one twenty-three and twelve ounces. Go ahead and sin a little." That was then.

Incredible, but true, Philip hadn't been living with anyone. His ex-wife lived in California with their kids whom he never saw, and he was six months post bust-up with a woman who, without two words in his direction, had married her dentist and moved to Scarsdale. Philip told her this at their first coffee date. Some time thereafter he touched one of her fingertips with one of his and told her that from the moment he met her, he had imagined cuddling up and talking with her for the rest of his life. Then he gave her the bathroom scale. Perfect, she had thought. Flowers or champagne would have been too ordi-nary a gift from such a man.

Since Philip had given Stevie the bathroom scale, the sleek plastic gizmo had turned mean. Having been adopted, it could do whatever it wanted to do. It was rude now. Fearless.

"Get ready, you," she said to the scale. She flung her towels onto the towel warmer, then taking a deep breath, got into posi-tion. "Blaaaap," honked the machine. "Sorry," pause, "Stee-vee. Your weight is," pause, "one twenty-two and fourteen ounces. Try to eat smaller portions today."

"Drop dead," she said to the scale, giving it a shove with her toe. This thing was as much fun as a talking wart, she thought. Philip was going to lose money on this little goblin.

Stevie stood in front of the full-length bathroom mirror. She sucked in her tummy, threw out her chest, and turned sideways. Sam, who came to her office five times a week to coach her exercise routine, said her buttocks were getting flabby. Sam said she wasn't taking her exercise seriously enough. Honestly, thought Stevie. I'm not a slob. That's a decent butt. Pretty decent. Is it so awful to mellow gently into middle age? She turned back to the dreaded front view, and cupped her hands over her thighs. Thousands of leg lifts and still she had pudgy thighs. Philip said he loved her thighs. He said her whole body was delicious. If only there were more men like Philip, she thought, women wouldn't make themselves so neurotic.

Stevie slid an extra, extra large Yankees tee shirt over her body and padded barefooted to her dressing room. She sat in front of the rare, hand-carved vanity table. Maple hummingbird wings seemed to flutter in the light cast by the glass-shaded vanity lamps. An artful wooden nymph, unaware that in sixty years or so Calvin Klein would decry her rounded body shape, brazenly draped her nude form over the top of the mirror frame. Stevie turned on her hair dryer.

As she blew her hair dry, she thought about how terrified Kenny must be. His first time in New York, and now he was what? Arrested? She hoped Philip got to him soon and there wouldn't be any real trouble. Kenny and Philip. Stevie stifled a smile. It wasn't funny but it was. After fourteen years of separation, Kenny-the-Kid, as Philip called him, was renewing his filial bonds with his father by clunking through Philip's comfortable existence with his spurs on, shooting up the saloon and spooking the horses. Poor Philip. He'd been expecting to pal around with his teenaged buddy Ken. Instead, he'd gotten a full-blown passive-aggressive, communication-phobic, six-foot-three little boy. Philip was exasperated, but who wouldn't be? How could he know what to do with a big clunky kid he didn't even know, who was too big to spank, too old to change, and a temporary resident at best? And as quiet and as pleasant as he was, could all of these accidents be accidents?

Stevie turned off the blow dryer and brushed her hair off her face, pinning it back with combs. She looked at herself in the mirror. Mysteriously, she was getting better-looking as she got older. Not as gorgeous as Carol had said, but something only a little short of real good-looking.

Did she look thirty-nine? Did she look old enough to be someone's mother? She put a finger under her chin and stretched the soft skin back toward her throat. She removed her finger and the neat little mound went back into place. She put her hands on either side of her face and pulled her cheeks toward her ears, flattening the barely perceptible furrows running from the sides of her nose toward her chin. The slight softening of her face was becoming to her, she thought; serenity and wisdom imposing itself over crazy-eyed youthful shine. One of these days, station management would suggest she surgically tighten up some of the softness. For the camera, they'd say.

Stevie smiled at her reflection. Her relationship with Philip was so good. Would it happen this time? Would they get married? She held her left hand in front of her. She'd never put a ring of any kind on the finger meant for a wedding band. It was superstitious, she knew, but still she held that narrow circle of skin sacrosanct. Unconsciously, she folded her hands in her lap and crossed her feet at the ankles. If she and Philip got married, her life would be completely perfect. Philip Durfee was an entirely grown-up, loving man, who loved *her*, crooked teeth, dimpled thighs, with or without her celebrity, just exactly the way she was. She couldn't possibly wish for more than her life added to Philip's.

But what about what Carol had said today? Birthdays didn't bother women who had children as much as women who had not. Nice shot, Carol. She could have a baby if she wanted to. What in the world would she do with a baby? She wouldn't know how to be a mother. Eleanor Weinberger hadn't been much of an example. Hadn't she known even when she was small that her mother wished she had never had her? Nana, smelling of lavender water, her silver hair sprayed into place, had fussed with Stevie, buttoned her into starched little dresses, smacked her hands when they weren't folded in her lap. "Be good, Stevie. Don't you want your mother to see you looking pretty?" "See the pretty bow I got for your hair, Stevie. Your mother will love you in this bow." Eleanor, her flip, run-around, barely out-of-her-teens mother, widowed at twenty. "Stevie, don't call me Mother in public. I don't like it." "Stevie, make sure you spend some time with Nana. I'll see you tomorrow when you get home from school." Eleanor had been more a sister than a mother. She had dated, and gone on trips, and left Stevie to do the growing up under Nana's very proper wing.

If she had a baby, just hypothesizing now, what would she have to give up? Her job? How could she have twelve-hour work days if she had a baby? How could she keep her show as fresh as it was without spending as much time in preparation as she did? Babies, little ones anyway, needed real time with their mothers, didn't they? Well, somehow she'd managed okay without much real time. Of course, there had been Nana. She tried to imagine Eleanor becoming a "nana" and quickly gave up.

So suppose she were able to hire someone to be a substitute mother while she was working. Already that felt wrong. She wasn't a halfway kind of person. How could she turn that job over to someone else? Stevie rubbed moisturizer into her forehead. She saw small fingers rubbing chocolate onto her Parisian wallpaper. She thought about her sauna and her gray marble bathroom; both were baby booby traps. This apartment couldn't be baby-proofed. If she had a baby, this place would have to go. She thought about the rickety stairs in her three-story farmhouse in the country, and about the steep rocky slide down into the gorge where the brook ran, and the pond, an irresistible, deathly child-seducer. The farmhouse, too, would have to go. And the freedom to sleep late on the weekends, catch up on her reading, make love with Philip anywhere, any time—the rewards for her solid weekly commitment to her career. No, not rewards, her due relaxation that actually made the hard work possible week after week. It would all change.

And in the place of these luxuries would be what? Another Kenny? She clapped her hand over her mouth as she examined the idea. Maybe another Kenny. Or maybe someone small and cute and perfect. The kind of child no one she knew had ever had. Oh, aren't you your mother's daughter, she thought. The phone rang. She snatched up the receiver on the first ring.

"We're home," Philip said, his voice tired, worn out.

"How are you? How is Kenny? Is he really all right?"

"He's depressed. He's not talking. He hasn't said ten words. The car may never go again."

"Oh, honey," she said sympathetically. "Do you just want to stay home and sleep? What do you want to do?"

"Bury my head in your bosom. Have a steak and fries."

"Simultaneously?"

"Yes."

Stevie laughed. "I don't have any fries."

"That's okay. Steak and bosom."

Stevie laughed again. "I've got steak and salad. What about Kenny? Do you think he'll eat?"

Philip sighed. "Near as I can tell, he wants to sulk. God. What a mess. Wasn't I a bachelor not too long ago?"

"You were."

"I'm sorry I'm being such a pain."

"You're not being a pain."

"Thanks. That's nice of you."

"I know, I'm generous as hell. Listen, Philip, grab the kid, pick up some fries at MacDonald's if you want them, and come over. Maybe we'll have dinner in front of the television so you don't have to talk. Okay?"

"Yeah, that sounds nice." There was a long pause, then Philip said, "If he's movable, I'll bring him."

"See you soon," she said, and then they said good-bye.

Stevie went to the refrigerator and, using a can opener, pried three steaks out of the frost-sealed freezer compartment, tossed them into the microwave oven, and pushed Defrost. Then she went back into the bathroom and refilled the tub. When it was full of warm, sudsy water, she got in.

Kenny lay in the bed fully dressed, his arm covering his eyes. Philip sat in a chair beside the bed. The room was dark and silent. Until recently the room had been a library with a pull-out sofa. A clean room. An ordered room. Now there were clothes covering every surface, the sofabed was never folded away, and there were dirty plates and glasses everywhere.

Philip raked his hair back and looked out the window. The river was dark. He wished a boat would go by. He sorely wanted to be distracted from his thoughts. He was disgusted with himself and ashamed of his feelings. It wasn't the car. The loss of the car was a dull ache that he had decided to ignore for now. What really hurt was a feeling he hadn't had often in his life and certainly not in many years. He felt he had failed. He hadn't been a good father to his infant son and he was no better now. Kenny was wearing him out. The police station, the suppressed anger, putting back together what Kenny had destroyed; it was getting to be too much for him.

He had let himself down, he had let Kenny down, and what was worse, the most shameful thing, he wished his son would go away. He wished he'd go back to his mother.

After the kitchen fire incident, he'd called Merle. He'd asked her if Kenny was as accident-prone at home. She'd laughed at him, the bitch. "I guess he's figured out how to get your attention," she'd said, and hung up the phone. What an outrage! She had *taken* the kids. He hadn't left them. Even after Merle had taken Tara and Kenny out to California, he had earnestly tried to see them. That last time, fourteen years ago, he had knocked on their door and Merle had shoved the squalling children toward him. "Go to your snake-father," she'd said, slamming the door, leaving one small red-faced child screaming on the steps, the other drained and flattened against the front door. God, he hadn't known what to do. She had horrified them, closed off their retreat, and left him in the gravel driveway with two children who acted as though he were actually poisonous. What could he have said to them? It's not me that's a lunatic—it's your mother? "Please," he had said, "it's just me. Your father."

After a while Merle's husband had come outside and let the tearful children into the house. The two men had sat down on the front steps. Danny, his name was, had thoughtfully smoked a cigarette while Philip concentrated on stopping the pounding of his heart.

"I'm sorry, buddy," Danny had said. "Merle's a little on the hot-headed side, but I guess you know that."

"I don't know what she wants from me. I don't understand why she's doing this."

"She's not a bad woman," Danny had said. "Temperamental, she is. Pissy, she is. But she won't let anything bad happen to those kids."

"She's turning them against their father!" he had said, shaking. "That's bad in my book."

"It's not logical, but she says you're a deserter. She says you didn't love any of them."

"Fuck it!" he had yelled, ignited by fury and frustration. "Why are we discussing this? She's a madwoman. I love my children. I wasn't with them a lot, but I loved them!"

"I know," Danny had said pleasantly, lighting another cigarette from the end of the last one. "Want one?" he had asked, tipping the pack in Philip's direction.

Philip had stared at him, stared at his pleated pants and flowered shirt, and pink-stockinged feet in huaraches. Merle had found the perfect man for her. He was imperturbable. Fighting with Danny would be a lot like punching a foam rubber pillow. Philip felt his anger ebb away. He wanted this man who was going to be living with his children to understand him. "I was working hard, trying to build something for my family. I was working," he had said. This was a lie, Philip remembered. An omission anyway. It wasn't the work. It was how much he hated being with his shrill, venomous wife that kept him away from his babies. He *hadn't* spent time with them. That much was true, and by the time they had almost reached an age where he could talk to them, they were gone. "I know this sounds feeble, but I didn't know what she was about to do. She didn't give me any warning—so let that be a warning to *you.*"

Danny had exhaled a long stream of smoke. "Listen, I don't know if this'll help ease your mind, but I like your kids. I'm going to take care of them. They'll have everything they want or need. You don't have to worry." Philip remembered how he had put his face in his hands and wept. Danny had just quietly smoked and some time later had simply said, "I guess I'll go inside now," and flipped the butt out onto the gravel. They stood and shook hands. Then Danny had gone inside a neat suburban house in Encino, California, and Philip had caught the "red-eye" flight back to New York, back to his empty seven rooms on Riverside Drive.

He *had* felt more at ease after that. He'd called, tried vainly to set up another visit, but then he had decided it would be better to stop trying to get to the kids; better to let them settle down. He'd hoped someday to be with them again, but in truth he had given up long before Kenny called at Christmas. He still could hardly believe what Kenny had told him. He wanted to see his father, spend time with him, figure out what he wanted to do with his life. Philip had responded joyfully. He had turned the library into a bedroom, told Stevie he wouldn't be able to see her so much for a while, and had tried very hard to devote himself to being Kenny's father.

For the last few weeks they had been living together in Philip's huge apartment. *Trying* to live together. Kenny had gotten his attention all right, but now that he had it, what did he want? He had thought living with Kenny would be restorative for them both, but it didn't feel that way. Kenny was driving him crazy. The truth here was apparent. Horrible, vicious Merle had been right all along. He wasn't meant to be a father, he just wasn't. He was hopelessly inept and too selfish to be a parent. Right now, he missed his former life. What he wanted to do was take the small car out of the garage and go over to Stevie's apartment. But how could he leave Kenny alone like this? Come on, Kenny, he silently urged his son. Get up and put your shoes on. Come out to dinner and be a person. "It's almost ten," Philip said.

"I don't want to go," Kenny replied.

"It would be good for you to get out and be with people," Philip reasoned.

"I don't want to go."

"Kenny, you're too old to sulk. I said we'll work this whole thing out about the car."

"I'm not sulking, Dad. I'm depressed."

Philip sighed again. If Kenny was going to be "depressed," maybe it *would* be better for him to stay home. "Fine. Stay here. I'll be home in a couple of hours," he said, looking at the clock. "I guess I'll be back some time after midnight."

"You don't have to come home. I'm not a kid, you know."

"I want to come home. I don't want you to be alone when you're feeling this bad."

"I'll be okay. I'm going to watch *Blade Runner*."

"All right, but will you make sure to eat something? There's not that much in the house. Sandwich meat and a couple of frozen dinners in the freezer."

"Dad, I'm really sorry. When I gunned it . . . I got mixed up between reverse and first."

"You told me."

"It hurt me to look at it. Like it was in pain."

"I know, Kenny, but it wasn't. It's only sheet metal."

"Do you think it can be fixed?"

"Yes, and I'm insured. So stop worrying about it. I shouldn't have let you anywhere near that car. I guess I was trying to make up to you for all the years . . ."

"Dad . . ."

"So it's not all your fault."

"I wish you'd yell at me or whatever."

Philip sighed. "Okay, what should I yell?"

Kenny took his arm away from his face and started to smile. "I think you should say something like, 'You goddamned horse's ass, I could kill you for this.'"

"Really?" Philip asked, surprised.

Kenny laughed. "Yeah," he said.

"Next time, okay? I'd like to do it spontaneously." He tapped his foot. "Seriously, this can't go on, you know. You're going to have to start thinking before you use machinery. You're a goddamned bull in a china shop. You could have killed someone today." Philip's thoughts drifted to his "playroom," the room where he kept the metal lathes and the lens grinder and the telescope he was adapting to test the ambient light filter its owner had asked him to back. If Kenny disobeyed him and fooled around in that room . . . he didn't want to consider the awful possibilities. He heard his son speaking.

"I know. I know. I terrified myself."

"Good," Philip said, nodding, slapping his thighs with his palms. "I've got to go, Ken. Stevie's waiting for me."

"You don't have to be here when I get up tomorrow, Dad. You can stay out. Really. I know you're sleeping with her."

Philip abruptly stood. Embarrassed, he brushed the creases out of his pants. Could he stop the stupid sneaking in at daybreak? "I'll give you Stevie's number," he said. He took a pencil from a cup on the bookshelf and wrote the number on a notepad in his most legible hand. "Don't lose this," he said. "I'm putting it right here next to the phone."

"Your glasses, Dad," Kenny said, pointing.

Philip put on his glasses. "I don't care how late you call or what the reason is. Just call if you need something."

"Okay, Dad," Kenny said, going to the bookshelf and removing a videocassette. Philip looked at his son, his disheveled, bulky son, and tried once again to see their resemblance. If only the kid would show some sign of affection once in a while. Kenny had already dismissed him.

"I'll see you tomorrow," he said. Kenny nodded and slipped the videocassette into the machine. Philip went to the foyer, took his raincoat and soft moleskin fedora out of the closet. He checked to see that his glasses were on his nose, and that he had the right keys, and then he left the apartment. In the common hallway, he pushed the elevator button, changed his mind, opened the front door again, went back to the room Kenny was using. *Blade Runner* theme music blared at him. "Take the aluminum foil off the food if you're going to put it in the microwave," he shouted into the din.

Philip looked haggard. Stevie had never seen him look so tired, so old. "Sweetie. You died."

"Big headache. I have a great big headache."

"Get in here. I'm going to take good care of you right now." Stevie peered around the door jamb. "Where's Kenny?"

"He's watching *Blade Runner* before he torches my apartment."

Stevie laughed. "How does a bath sound to you?"

"Are you taking one too?"

"I've taken one. Two actually. But I'll keep you company."

"Great. Shit. I forgot the french fries."

"I found some frozen squash in the very back of the freezer compartment."

"Squash?" Philip grimaced. "Okay. Whatever, as Kenny would say."

"How is he?" Stevie asked, peeling Philip's jacket from his arms, hanging it on a fat wooden hanger in the hall closet. She took his tie from him and hung that on the hanger too, and putting shoe trees in his shoes, toed them neatly next to her winter boots.

"Kenny is a mossy stone," Philip said. He squeezed Stevie with both arms from behind and, fitting his legs to the back of hers, walked her to the bathroom. Stevie turned on the hot water and poured bath crystals into the stream. Then taking him by the hand to the bedroom, she sat behind him on the bed and rubbed his shoulders as he removed the rest of his clothes.

"I've dreamed of this moment all day. I've lived for this moment."

"Want something cold to drink?"

"Yes."

"Get in the tub. I'll bring it to you."

Water crept over his hips, his chest, his shoulders. Philip sighed deeply and leaned his head against the back of the tub.

This was heaven. He took his steamy glasses off and put them on the ledge. He heard them clatter onto the floor. He didn't care. He couldn't move. What was he going to do with Kenny? Aarggh. If only his headache would go away. He felt a cool glass against his cheek.

"Here," Stevie said, handing him the glass. "And don't argue with me. Put this on your head."

"A wire coat hanger?"

"Uh-huh."

"You're joking. You're kidding. I'll look like a jerk."

"I'm not, and so what? Don't you trust me?"

"Hmmm. Yes. What do I do? How does this work."

"Like this," she said spreading the coat hanger slightly, putting the long ends over his temples. "How's your headache," she asked.

"Gone," he said, surprised. "I think it worked."

"Here are two aspirin."

"With alcohol?"

"That's ginger ale in there, fella. I had a feeling if I gave you a drink you'd go to sleep in that tub."

"Definitely. How long do I have to wear this?"

"Just until the aspirin hits. You look like a jerk, by the way," she said.

"Thank you. Thank you very much," he said, flicking water at Stevie.

"I'm going to cook now," she said, ducking. "Come out when you're ready."

Steak sizzled in the broiler. Squash bubbled happily in the sauce pan. This whole time since she met Philip was the happiest she'd ever been, Stevie thought.

"Maybe I could have something like this manufactured," Philip said, coming into the room. "A thin band without a hook. Something that doesn't look so dorky." He turned the hanger in his hand, looking at it as if he'd just seen a hanger for the first time.

"I don't know. Why not? Sit down. What would you call it?"

"The Headache Killer. Is that any good?"

"It sounds like the name of a teenage horror flick."

Philip laughed. "You're pretty funny. You should go on TV, you know that?"

"Hmmph," Stevie said, pleased.

"Something smells good."

"You're going to like this," she said, spooning vegetables onto his plate, pronging a steak with a serving fork.

"How was your day?" he asked, eyeing the squash on his fork with suspicion.

"Not too terrible. Our ratings are great, we picked up two stations this month, and Ed is relieved for exactly ten seconds, then he's the Hulk again."

"Is he trying to motivate the team or is he just insecure?"

"I don't know. Both I guess. God, I wish he'd get promoted or something. I wish he'd move to Detroit."

"Uh-huh," Philip agreed. He savored his food. As exhausted and depleted as he was, he found being with Stevie energizing. Spending easy time with someone you loved and trusted just couldn't be overrated. He was almost feeling like a person again. "How was your lunch, by the way?" he asked Stevie.

"Oh. Good. Weird. I'm not sure." She put a bite of steak into her mouth and chewed.

"Weird how? College reunion kind of stuff? How she looked?"

"A little. She looked good. Better than I remember. Better than good. Thin and rangy, if you know what I mean. Katharine Hepburn, sort of. And she has a lot of great hair. I bet she used to iron it in school—we all did that. Now it sort of billows out." Stevie chewed another bite and thought. "She's doing well; lives in Chappaqua. It sounds like she's making a lot of money. The houses are expensive there and she owns her own real estate firm."

"Uh-huh," said Philip. "What's the weird part?"

"Um. You know I used to go out with the man she married?"

"You told me. The baseball player."

"Andy. They had a little girl. Carol was pregnant when they got married."

"You knew she was pregnant?"

"Yeah." Stevie stood up and took her plate to the waste bin. She shoveled a half-eaten steak into the trash.

"Hey. You didn't eat anything."

"Oh, I had plenty," she said half-turning to Philip. "I had about three bowls of Lucky Charms while I was waiting for you. Want some ice cream? Or coffee?"

"What's wrong?" Philip stood and went to Stevie. He put his arms around her. She kissed him quickly and moved away from him. She took a sponge into her hand and rubbed intently at an all but invisible stain in the sink.

"I'm fine."

"Sure," he said, watching her. "Come back and sit down."

"It's just an old memory," she said, scraping the chair against the floor, sitting, putting her elbows on the table and her chin in her hands. "I loved him. She got pregnant."

"He was dating you both? He must have been a real nice guy."

"No. He wasn't seeing us at the same time. Her pregnancy happened before we started going out. He just didn't know it. *We* just didn't know it."

"I see."

"Anyway, they're divorced now, and Carol raised her daughter and now her daughter's almost nineteen. That, for your information, is the weird part."

"It's weird to think of yourself as old enough to have a teen-aged child."

"Right."

"That's how I feel," Philip said, taking his plate into the kitchen, returning with two coffee mugs. "About Kenny, I mean. And Tara. Wherever, however she is."

"Carol's daughter is named Lisa."

"Pretty name."

"Apparently a pretty girl. And very smart. All she has to do is speak English and wear clean clothes when she meets the personnel director tomorrow and she's got herself a summer job."

"You did that?"

"Carol asked me to help Lisa out. And frankly, I'm interested. I want to see what she's like."

"Christ, Stevie. You don't even know this kid."

"Yeah. Well." Stevie shrugged. Not knowing Lisa was the point. She wanted to know her. Had to. "I'd do as much for any friend's kid. It's no big deal."

Philip grunted. "I hope this doesn't upset you."

"It won't," Stevie said, looking at him straight on, forcing herself not to look away, firmly closing the subject.

"Are you ready for bed soon, because I'm going to drop here on the floor."

"I'm ready now," she said.

Stevie folded the silk bedspread and laid it on the blanket chest. The room smelled faintly of crushed cinnamon, roses, bay leaves. She could feel sleep gently pulling at her eyelids. The day had been so long. It must be past midnight. Still, had it really been only a day since she had slept? The bed was soft and cool. "Come here," she said to Philip, easing him to her chest, wrapping her arms around his back. She touched her cheek to his hair and took a great deep breath. She exhaled, letting the tension of the day leave her. She kissed Philip's brow.

"Oh, God," he said. "My prayers have been answered." He pressed his lips to a tee shirt-covered breast. "Mmm," he said sliding his hand under the cloth, touching warm skin, feeling her quick arousal. Sweetly, he kissed her throat, and then that kiss was followed by another kiss in the tender hollow between shoulder and neck. A thrill went through Stevie and her sleepiness vanished. She let him remove her tee shirt and then she simply succumbed to his touch. His hands skimmed across her bare skin as softly as a warm breeze, lifting tiny hairs in their wake. As Philip moved his hands over her, she curled her body around him. This is divine, she thought. *He* is divine. Philip touched her and kissed her and as she savored his kiss, she felt the whole of her body swell to meet him. It was true that time blurred memories. But she was sure, absolutely sure, lovemaking had never been like this before with another man. Her senses stirred emotions she could not name. She wanted to give him everything, blend with him so that the actual joining of their bodies was an almost incidental movement that made the exchange of their feelings possible. The warmth that started as a small pleasurable flame grew and encompassed her until she was shaken beyond her control against the man who was Philip, her love.

"That was so good, Philip," Stevie said, words slipping languorously from her lips. She held him inside her, reveling in the after-sensations of peace and quiet joy.

"I love you so much," he said. Then he separated them gently, kissed her again. He found the soft covers at the foot of the bed and covered them both, tucking the bedclothes around them. Then he took her fingers lightly into his hand. She tightened her grip and he returned the squeeze. And in moments they were both asleep.

•

*In the dream, she was cupping a ball of light in her two hands. It was a warm, shimmery little light and she wanted to capture it before it faded away . . .*

Stevie's eyes opened. What was it? A noise? She could hear only the hum of the air conditioner. She flexed her fingers, still entwined with Philip's. Philip moved, turned over, and sighed once deeply before he resumed his heavy sleep. What had wakened her? Stevie pushed her hair off her face, clasped her hands on her head. She could have a baby if she wanted to. Couldn't she? She *wasn't* too old. She was still young. She was in love with a wonderful man. If she and Philip got married, she'd still have years to decide whether or not to have a child. What if they got married and she decided she wanted a baby after all—and Philip refused? What if they didn't get married? The air in the room seemed sharp and alive. Would she be alone forever? Stevie moved closer to Philip so she could feel his body heat. He stirred. Will you give me a baby if I want one? she asked silently. There was, of course, no answer. Stevie put her fingers to the side of her throat. Her pulse was beating rapidly. What was going on? Panic. The thirty-ninth-birthday panic brought to her by its sponsor, Carol. Whew. Calm down. Calm down and go to sleep. Some time later, she did.

"You're not going to work like that?" Carol said, opening the kitchen door out to the back step and handing Lisa a glass of juice.

"What do you mean?" Lisa replied, looking down at her shirt, her jeans.

"Jeans. I mean jeans. How can you go to work on the first day of your new job in jeans?"

"Mother. I know how to dress. The personnel lady told me casual dress was fine. Don't worry. Stevie Weinberger won't think you raised a hillbilly, if that's what you're afraid of."

"I'm not worried about what Stevie thinks. What I'm suggesting here is proper office attire. Why don't you make your rigid, old-fashioned, tedious mother happy and go put on a skirt."

"If I put on *pants* will you be satisfied?"

"Put on a skirt, please."

Lisa groaned loudly and stood up, pulling open the screen door. "What do you do when I'm not around? Who do you do this to?"

"It's a problem," Carol admitted, following her daughter up the carpeted stairs to her bedroom. "Sometimes I'm reduced to wiping the faces of strange little children on the street. I've been known to straighten the ties of men at my office."

"You're joking, I hope." Lisa roughly pulled a khaki skirt from its hanger, then stepped into it and yanked closed the zipper.

"See? Doesn't that look great? Doesn't that feel better?" Carol beamed. Sitting on her bed, looking at Lisa trying on clothes in her pale blue room with its starched white bedclothes and curtains, she could almost believe her daughter was still a little girl living at home.

Lisa rolled her eyes. "I suppose you want me to wear shoes."

"I'll leave that decision up to you." Carol watched her daughter push her running shoes off her feet and root around in her closet for a pair of low heels. "Excited?" she asked.

"Uh-huh. I just hope I don't make a fool of myself."

"You? I wish I'd had half your poise when I was your age." A tenth, Carol thought. Lisa was so at ease with herself. How had she created such a girl? She smiled fondly at Lisa. "You'll do fine. You won't forget to thank Stevie?"

"I won't forget but she may not have time for me."

Carol stood and kissed her daughter's cheek. "Have a wonderful day. Do you want to have dinner tonight?"

"I'm sorry, Mom. I'm seeing Reed. But I'll call you this afternoon to talk if you want. If I can."

"Good. Okay then," Carol said hurriedly before her disapproval formed words. "I'll talk to you later."

"Good-bye, Mom," Lisa said. She listened to the sounds of her mother's departure and as the front door banged shut, she reached for the phone. She dialed the riding stable and listened as the phone rang in a fiberboard office smelling of hay and molasses and leather, twenty miles away. If the phone wasn't answered on the second ring, the office was empty. Reed was probably working Rosie. She could almost hear the squeaking tack and the grunt of the mare as Reed seemed to merely wish her into a collected gallop around the main ring. Reed said Rosie had "the legs of a stylish woman and a mouth as soft as flower petals." He was going to make a lot of money when he sold her. Oh, if Rosie were hers, she wouldn't sell her. She'd braid her and breed her and sleep on her back.

Lisa sighed and hung up the phone. What a gorgeous day for a ride. Taking an indoor job was real dedication. She had planned on working at the stable this summer. Three months was enough time to *really* get to know the animals, to work with the kids, and best of course, three months of being with Reed all day. It had taken all her willpower to do what she knew she should do. Would Marsha Norman goof off for the summer when she had a play to write? Of course not.

Lisa opened the top drawer of her old scarred-up dresser and pushed aside a mess of riding ribbons, still gilded, still crisp, locked together like fallen autumn leaves. She took a head band out of a quilted box and dragging thick hair back with its teeth, secured it on her head. She put on her mother's heavy silver chain strung with silver hearts. Taking an eyebrow pencil from a lucite sheath, she drew a line under her lashes. What was she doing? What? She looked at her image critically. She was going to look like a jerk. *Why* had she listened to her mother, the mother hen of all times? If she walked into her first day as a summer intern looking like something her mother would call a lady, she would be ruined. She would not wear make-up. No. She dipped a tissue into cold cream and erased the lines she had recently made. She removed the necklace. She took off the heels and put on her Top-Siders. Discarding the headband, she bunched her hair into a ponytail, put a rubber band around the handful of hair. Then she looked at her image with satisfaction. This is who I am, she thought.

She looked at her watch and groaned. Where were the car keys? In the jacket she wore last night? No. In her blue bag? Where was the blue bag? God-oh-God, the train left the station in twelve minutes. There. The blue bag was hanging in the closet. Lisa snagged the keys, skidded around claw-footed mahogany furniture, past walls printed in meticulous burgundy dots and blue paisleys, hauled open the heavy front door, shut it behind her and locked it.

Twelve minutes. No, ten now. She had to drive fast, but not too fast. Watch. The light. Come on, she thought, narrowing her gaze, staring down the back of the Volvo station wagon ahead of her. The streets were full of Volvo station wagons bearing business people to trains, children to school. Had she ever driven to the train at this time before? She had been an observer of the rush-hour madness before, but now she was a part of it. She was going to work. For the summer, at least, she was a commuter.

What could she expect to happen today? What would Stevie be like in real life? She was so fabulous-looking; not model-pretty, no. Pretty and real; a Carly Simon type of pretty. Did Stevie Weinberger ever screw up, talk too much, say the wrong thing? If she ever did, she probably wasn't up half the night worrying about it. It killed her how *cool* her mother thought she was. Just private school manners, Mom. That's all it is. Anyway, she liked the person she was going to be working for in the newsroom, Sarah. Sarah was just four years older than she was.

And there were some really hip-looking guys and women working there too. Dammit, she should have brought something for Stevie to read. The outline for her play. No, don't be ridiculous, she admonished herself. Stevie Weinberger is not going to read your stupid outline. Well, certainly not the first day.

Lisa speeded up to make a light, realized she was going to miss it, and braked. The Chevy rocked on its springs. Lisa glanced nervously into the rearview mirror, ascertained that a rear-end collision had been avoided, then looked at her watch. Five minutes. Plenty of time. Daddy agreed this summer job was so much more important than hanging out at Fox Hollow Farm. Much more. Just walking around with the woman from personnel had been enlightening. She was going to write the best play, she thought as she turned the car into the parking lot. Daddy was proud of her. *That* was a fabulous feeling. He said he would call at least once a week to get the latest news. He said he might even visit some time! That would be the greatest. Reed had been cool about the whole thing. "I was looking forward to working with you," he'd said, but then he had added that a summer in New York City would be a broadening experience. Well, sure. What if he had insisted that he needed her? What would she have done? Lisa shook off the brief moment of confusion, relieved that the conflict had not materialized. Her mother had beamed. Well, Mom thought she could do anything. Anything at all. Fly. Do the jitterbug. Balance the national debt. What a deal. She was actually doing something her mother wanted her to do, and she wanted to do it too. How had that happened? Lisa shook her head and nosed the car into a parking spot. For once, maybe the first time in *years*, she could do what was right for *herself* without feeling she was letting her mother down.

Lisa turned off the engine, yanked on the emergency brake, and dug in her handbag for her wallet. She had her monthly ticket, thank God. And her completed insurance forms and her hairbrush. Just remember to listen today, she lectured herself. Listen and be yourself and don't say anything stupid.

Lisa slammed the car door and locked it, then shouldered her handbag and walked quickly toward the waiting train. Squinching up her face, she thought so softly that she could get by without really acknowledging the thought at all, I'm glad I wore a skirt.

Carol listened to the squeak of her chair as she rocked it. The office was empty. Her mug, steaming with freshly brewed coffee, immodestly proclaiming her "Number One Salesman," a gift from her staff, contained not her first, but third dose of caffein. She liked seven-thirty. Seven-thirty was quiet. She could have a couple of private thoughts at seven-thirty; think about her clients, try to connect them up with a house or two. This morning she found herself wondering if she could get Malcolm to go into the city with her and see the new Hockney exhibit at the Met. Or rather, if she could get him to go without looking so pained she would give up under the guilt he induced and catch an early train home. Malcolm was sweet, and sexy, but so provincial. This relationship couldn't go much further. Carol sighed. Was she willing to go without male companionship again? It sometimes took so long to meet someone who was single and interesting. The thought of dinners for one after Lisa went back to school was depressing.

She'd better call Malcolm and see if he was free for dinner. Well, hey, if Lisa had a date, she could darn well scratch up an evening out. Lisa had suggested a double date last year. Carol shook her head involuntarily. If she had to acknowledge that Reed existed, she would, but double-date? Lisa had to be kidding.

Reed's home telephone number, written in a nearly illegible hand inside a gum wrapper, had been resting at the back of her desk for a year now, ever since that awful time she had called him. She could still remember the conversation.

"Reed, this is Carol Wilder."

"Mrs. Wilder . . . Lisa's mother?"

"Damned right. I'll get straight to the point. That you are sleeping with my daughter is revolting to me. That you are married and old enough to be her father is sickening. But that's not bad enough. She's turning down educational opportunities of a lifetime to be with you. Do you know that? Do you know you're ruining my daughter's life?"

"Hold on a minute, Mrs. Wilder. I love Lisa."

"You're ruining her life. Do you hear me?" Carol could still remember her vocal cords stretched to impossibly thin strands of glass.

"Do you think I wanted her to turn down those schools? She didn't even discuss it with me. And I'm getting a separation, you know."

"The only separation I care about is one from my daughter," she had shrieked.

"Mrs. Wilder—perhaps we could meet and talk. You're not being fair and I'd like to . . ."

She hadn't let him finish. She'd hung up on him and then she'd wept for hours. The only good thing she could say about Reed was that he must not have told Lisa about her call. Lisa would have said something and that would have been humiliating. No, in all fairness she had to give him credit for being some kind of a gentleman.

Would Stevie take to Lisa? She hoped so. Stevie Weinberger as a mentor just couldn't be improved upon: well-bred, stable, successful—and Stevie was interested in Lisa! If only there had been a role model like Stevie in her own life when she had been Lisa's age. Opening the worn cover of her listing book, she skimmed page after page of available homes. A summer job in

New York City, she thought, fingertip poised between a split ranch and a new Colonial. It was the perfect cure. After a dose of that, how was her little girl going to hold onto that romantic nonsense she wanted to call her life with Reed? No way, little girl, no way. Carol pushed a button on her phone and made the first phone call of her working day.

"Stevie, Lisa Newman is here to see you," Luann said from the doorway.

"Give me a minute," Stevie said from her desk across the room. She put both elbows on the desk and one hand to her mouth. Am I ready for this? Would it be like meeting her own daughter? Would the baby have been a girl? Yes. She had thought so. She had always thought of "it" as a girl, of herself as the mother of a girl, of Andy as the father of a girl. Well, one part of all that had come true. The proof was standing only feet away. The sound of laughter outside the room ripped into her thoughts. Two voices alternated, one, gravelly and rough, was Luann's. The other was clear, animated, sliding up and down its own musical scale. Stevie touched the cold surface of an amethyst glass paperweight; for luck? For support? Finally, she stood and walked to the door. "Hi, Lisa," she said softly. Her arm moved up from her side in slow motion as she reached out to take Lisa's hand. She saw only Lisa, not Luann, not the office around her. It was as if everything but Lisa had been turned off. What a beautiful girl, she thought, holding Lisa's hand. She looks so much like Andy. Her eyes are the same shade of blue. She has the same cheekbones, the same mouth.

"Hi, Stevie, I mean Mrs. Weinberger, I mean *Ms.* Weinberger, I mean, I'm sorry, how would you like to be addressed?" She blushed. Fool, fool, uncool fool, she scolded herself.

"Stevie, of course." She smiled. Were her hands shaking? Calm down. Your hands didn't shake like this when you met Golda Meir. "Come in. Sit down," Stevie indicated a place on the horseshoe-shaped sofa. "Would you like something? Coffee?"

"No, thank you. I don't think I can stay too long," Lisa said. "I just sort of mumbled 'ladies' room' and slipped away. I hoped I could catch you so I could thank you for doing this for me, getting me this wonderful job." Blab, blab, blab. Fewer words, please, Lisa.

"You're very welcome," Stevie said. The resemblance is so strong. Lisa could be Andy's sister. Except for her hair color, I don't see Carol at all. "Your mother says you're writing a play that takes place in a television station."

Lisa nodded vigorously. "Did she tell you the plot?" She's smaller than I thought she would be. I could pick her up. And she looks so young! How can I be nervous around someone so small and unintimidating?

"Just that it's about a married couple who co-anchor a news show and that it's a comedy."

"That's it. It's just a one-act play. I have an assortment of loose ideas," Lisa said, gathering up invisible thoughts, bundling them into a bouquet. "I know their names and that she earns more than he does, and that she's older, and that she's a Republican, and he's a Democrat, but I only have sketchy bits of dialogue as yet. And of course, the dialogue is what's *really* going to move the play." Lisa smoothed her skirt over her knees and locked her hands together in her lap. Self-centered. Jabberwocky. Talk to *her* about *her*. "Did you ever study writing?" she asked.

"No. I was a drama major. I can just about write a memo. So what do you think you'll learn here? How a news show operates?"

"Yes, and the jargon, of course." Isn't she nice? She wants me to tell about myself. *Really.* "You know, the standard advice on the subject of writing is to write what you know, and so *everyone* in my class is writing their plays about being in school and that's so *predictable*, you could just, well, I won't say it. Oh, that didn't sound very nice. But you see, there's a competition . . ."

"I know," Stevie said. "And you want to win! I think that's fine."

"Thanks for saying that. I guess it's not really considered nice to be so openly aggressive where I go to school, but I'm being honest, I have to say. *Everyone* is doing really very much the same thing so in order to separate my play from the rest I decided I ought to break from the school environment and increase what I know." Oh, that's so pretentious. Increase what I know. She must think I'm a class A prep school know-it-all.

"That makes sense," Stevie said. Was I ever that young? she wondered. Yes. "You know, a couple of my friends who work here are married."

"Uh-huh," Lisa said, not sure she understood. Figure it out. Say something smart, you fool, she commanded herself.

"To each other," Stevie explained. Is she blushing? What did I say?

"Oh, really?"

"Pam, Pamela Friedman, she's my associate producer, and B. Willy Foster, he directs the show. They met on the show and got married."

"That's *fantastic*. Perfect. Do you think they'd let me interview them?"

"They'd be flattered. The jobs they have aren't the jobs you are trying to depict, you understand . . ."

"Of course. Oh, I do. I mean, I'm writing about a married couple and actually what do I know about marriage?"

"Because your parents are divorced?" Oh, Lisa. Did the divorce hurt you very much? Stevie wanted to ask.

"Yes. I mean, I never really minded that. I see my dad quite a bit during the year and I've spent full months with him summertimes. I've just never spent time with a married couple up close."

How is your dad? Stevie wondered. What is he like? No, don't ask, she decided.

"I'll bet working together all day, I don't know, I'll bet that's got to produce some tension in the marriage, wouldn't you think? I wonder if they would tell me. Were you ever married?"

Stevie shook her head no, and smiled.

"You went out with my father, didn't you?"

In front of Stevie's eyes, a picture appeared. A black and white Andy Newman nuzzled a black and white Stevie Weinberger's neck, and she felt a chill. Stevie blinked, then laughed to cover her embarrassment. "You're not shy, are you, Lisa?"

"Oh God. I'm sorry. I am so stupid sometimes." Lisa put her head in her hands miserably and shook her head.

"Oh, no. Hey, I'm okay. You just caught me off-guard."

"I'm sorry. My mother says I have arrested development. She says I never got over the 'why' stage, not from the time I was two." Lisa pulled the rubber band from her ponytail and shook out her hair. Stevie was smiling at her. Approving of her really. Maybe she wasn't being a complete fool. Maybe Stevie liked her. "He said you were really terrific," she ventured.

A black and white Stevie turned to her lover and wrapped her arms around him. Her skirt swirled around her as he lifted her, squealing, from the ground. Stop. "I thought he was really terrific too," she said.

"It's amazing, isn't it? Fate, I mean. If you and my Dad had gotten married, I wouldn't be here." Lisa widened her eyes. "*You* probably wouldn't be here. Here, I mean. This office. Would you be living in upstate New York? Would you even be in television?"

Stevie refused the suggestive thought. She would not give it life, not now. "Lisa, that's too wild. Your father and I went out for such a short period of time. When you're in college, dating is just a fun thing to do." Wondering suddenly if she had talked down to Lisa, she added, "Well, you know what I mean."

"I suppose. I haven't dated much. I don't date in college at all. I've been seeing this one man since I was in high school."

Reed. Yes, I know, Stevie wanted to say. From the hallway she heard Pam's voice. "Is Stevie in? You look nice, Luann. Did you get a perm?"

"Yes, and somebody is with her, and don't play with me, all right, Pam-el-a?"

"What bit you on the ass, Luann? Tell her I stopped by, okay?"

"Pam," Stevie called out. "Pam, come in here. I want you to meet someone."

"Hi," Pam said, acknowledging Lisa. "What did I say?" she asked Stevie, lowering her voice, turning up her palms. "I just said I liked her hair."

Stevie shook her head. "You know. Listen, Pam, this is Lisa Newman. Lisa, this is Pamela Friedman, the friend I told you about."

"Oh, hi," Lisa said. "I'm so glad to meet you."

"Nice to meet you too," Pamela said, and turned to look at Stevie.

"Lisa is the daughter of an old college friend," Stevie explained.

"I'm working here for the summer," Lisa added.

"She's doing research for a play she's writing."

"Really?" said Pam. "What's it about?"

Stevie watched Lisa as she told Pam about her play. She could see Pam trying and failing to suppress a smile. Lisa chattered, but her audacity was so innocent, so appealing, Stevie thought. Lisa seemed both younger than her age and older at the same time.

"I have some work to do with our tape editors," Pam said to Lisa. "Do you think observing that would be of some use to you?"

"Yes, I'd love to go! Can I call Sarah and find out if it's okay? How long do you think I would need? Well I could probably stay even for a few minutes and learn something. May I use the phone?" Lisa breathlessly asked Stevie.

"My goodness," Pam said to Stevie.

"Quite something, isn't she?"

Pam nodded.

"I used to date her father when we were in college."

"Ah. This is the one. You had lunch with the mother."

"Uh-huh. What do you think of her?"

"She's very, uh, bright."

"Yes, I know. Her mother says she's a genius."

"That too, but what I meant was, around her, you need sunglasses."

Stevie laughed. "I see what you mean."

"So what do *you* think of her?" Pam asked.

"I think she's inquisitive and energetic and well-intentioned, and innocent in her way. I guess if you knew all kids would turn out like that one, having one would be sort of terrific."

"Uh-oh."

"Uh-oh, what?"

"I don't know. You got a little misty just then."

"I did not." Stevie shook her head as if to clear it, reached for a stack of papers on the coffee table. "Listen, we've got to get together after you take Lisa around. I'm feeling a little unsteady about that VP from the sperm bank. The material you gave me to read was so dry my eyeballs cracked."

Pam laughed and pulled a wisp of hair from her eyes. "I know. They certainly took the X rating out of the little fish and the little egg story. I'll write some questions up for you. Maybe we can meet before the run-through."

"It's okay," Lisa trilled exultantly from across the room. "Oh. Pardon me for interrupting," she said, coming over to Stevie.

"No, it's fine," Stevie said, resisting an urge to put her arm around Lisa. Wouldn't her own little girl have looked just like this? "We're finished."

"Stevie, thanks again for getting me this great job."

"You are very welcome. I hope you'll stop in once in a while and let me know how you're doing."

"Can I? May I? That would be so great."

"Absolutely."

"Is three o'clock okay with you?" Pam asked Stevie.

"Fine," Stevie said with a grin. She waved good-bye to Lisa and watched her until she was out of the room. When she was alone, Stevie stood in the silence. Her office felt more than quiet. It felt as though some vital element had been subtracted from the air.

# 5

Pamela Friedman watched the contact sheet floating in the tray of fixer solution. Then, with her tongs, she removed the wet paper and hung it up to dry. Blinking in the safe light, she examined the images of B. Willy playing around on his ten-speed bike; hands in the air, cross-eyed, one-handed, side-saddle, his pale silky hair blowing away from his face, the gap between his front teeth visible even in these tiny photos. He looked like a kid. A very tall, lovable little boy. The pictures were perfect. She'd enlarge that whole strip to shots of two- by three-inch size, then snip them from their backgrounds. What would be a comical backdrop for the construction? Something straight and flat. A blade. A table top. No, no, no. A ruler. Yes! Photograph a hand holding an ordinary desk ruler, enlarge it, then stick down a row of seven or eight little B. Willys on bikes riding along the ruler as if it were a road. If the black and whites worked as she thought they would, she'd shoot the whole batch again in color. Her show at the Armory was still six weeks away. There was time.

The intercom screeched and her husband's voice, crinkled by Audio Shack wiring, blatted out, "Hon, it's at the soft-crack stage. I'll need you in four minutes exactly. Zippety-zap."

"I'm through down here. I'll be right up." Was a ruler funny enough? What if the straight edge were more animated? The length of a butterfly's antennae? A single hair? Oh, that was good. An enlarged photo of the top half of Willy's head, from the eyes up, the little bikers riding across one errant wisp.

"No kidding, hon."

"Okay," she sang out. "I'm outta here." Pam turned on the ordinary light and opened the darkroom door. She lifted a small neat construction of stacked glass panes, photographic work sandwiched in between them, and maneuvered her way past the tangle of bikes, the heap of pup tents, the teepee of skis leaning against the garage wall. She still noticed the disarray. Four years of marriage and if anything, she had gotten less used to the way B. Willy organized his worldly goods. She ran her hand over the painted wall that stopped being painted halfway up the wall along the stairs. When she got to the top step, she opened the door to the kitchen.

Warm vanilla scented the room. The yellow walls, hung with a dozen glass-paned cabinets and banked with cork boards nearly hidden behind tacked-up photographs, made a cozy visual explosion after the red light in her work space. Three small color televisions were lined up on a counter, sound off, tuned to three different stations. A radio, hung from a cup hook, blew a jazzy tune into the fragrant air.

"Yummy. What a smell, Will." Pam walked over to the counter and poked a finger into the glassy glob of candy lying in a buttered pan. "I think it lives," she said, pulling her finger back quickly and sticking it into her mouth.

"Watch. It's still too hot to pull," he said. "Let me see what you did."

"Do you think she'll like this?" Pam asked, offering the artwork to B. Willy. He wiped his hands on the back of his jeans, took it reverently, and walked over to the window above the wide porcelain sink. "Like it? I should think so. It's stupendous." He turned the object to and fro in the dusky light. Pam walked to him, and tucked her hand into the back pocket of his jeans.

"It *is* good, isn't it," she said shyly.

"Honey. I don't know how you do this." B. Willy took his wife in his arms and stooping, kissed the side of her neck. The smoky mass of her hair caressed his face. The bosomy feel of her made him reluctant to release her, and yet reluctantly he did. "You are amazingly talented. I wonder if you'd bend your skills to pulling this taffy with me."

"Yes, I will. Let me wash the chemicals off my hands."

Willy slid the glistening lump from the pan and patted it into a flat ball. "How's Stevie taking this birthday?" he asked. "She's seemed nervous to me lately."

"Fine, I think. I thought. Something happened this week which I think upset her although she won't admit it." Pam took one end of the taffy ball and planting her feet firmly, pulled and resisted the opposite pull B. Willy was exerting.

"What happened?"

"She had lunch with an old college friend who apparently made some sort of remark about Stevie's age vis-à-vis having children, or rather, not having them. Then she asked Stevie to get her daughter a summer job . . ."

"You're not talking about the dishwater blond in the alligator shirts? The one in the newsroom?"

"Yeah. How do you know?"

"News, my darling, news travels fast. Every male in the station has been in the newsroom this week just to have a look. What's the problem with Stevie? Jealous?"

"No, you dope. She used to date the kid's father and then the kid shows up nineteen years later, all beautiful and smart, and don't quote me, I'm guessing by some deep sighing and some wistful looks that Stevie is reevaluating."

"Mmmm. Biology, you mean. Maternal longing."

"Something like that. Maybe."

"There's nothing so terrible about that. She'd make an adorable mother."

"Honey, she's not married."

"She could be. She will be."

"Even if she were, she couldn't do her job the way she does it and have a child. And the damned business is so fickle, a couple of months out for a pregnancy, just that, and she could lose everything."

"I don't think I agree. Our audience would love a pregnancy."

"Sure."

"They would. Steve would kick off her shoes and someone would rub her ankles, Martin Mull probably, and zingedy-zang, the audience would be curled up in her hand. But regardless. We're talking about biology, Pam. Biology doesn't give a rat's ass about her job. If you'd stop trying to suppress your own natural maternal—"

"Don't, Will. I don't want to fight about this right now. We've got to get dressed and go to dinner with them in a little while."

"I don't want to fight either. Watch what you're doing with the taffy. Here, give it to me. Will you cut up some waxed paper for me?" B. Willy handed a cardboard box to his wife. It was incomprehensible. If ever a woman was made to have children, it was Pam. She was soft everywhere. Holding her was as close to pure pleasure as he had ever imagined, more than he had ever hoped for. He could see, actually see, a smoky-haired infant wrapped in those round arms, nestled under her chin. If only . . .

Pam took the roll of waxed paper and a pair of shears to the old lion-footed oak table and pulled a length of paper from the roll.

"Hon, what do you say we try an experiment?" Willy asked her.

"Uh-oh."

"What uh-oh? It's just an experiment." Willy dug around in a drawer and produced another pair of scissors. Stretching the taffy, he cut two-inch-long sections and lined them up on a cookie sheet. "Why don't we just reverse the usual script? See how it sounds. I'll start. 'Pam, I don't want to have a baby yet. I have my work to think of and I'm not ready to take on the responsibility of a child.' "

"Terrific. I feel a lot better now that the pressure is off."

"Pam," Willy said, laughing. "Pammy, this is a game. You're supposed to say you want a baby."

"I can't. I can't say that. Not even in a game."

"Please. Just for fun."

Pam opened the scissors on the paper and pulled it toward her against the blades. She severed a three-inch-wide strip of paper neatly, then cut it into rectangles. "'I want a baa—" she said, looking at the table.

"That was good. Try it again."

"I want a banana."

"Here," B. Willy said, reaching into a fruit bowl, slapping a banana on the table. "Once more."

"I want a baboon."

"Baby."

"Baby. I don't want one."

Willy groaned, gathered spoons with a clatter, clanked pots

into the sink. He squeezed soap into the dishwater and rattled the pans. "I don't know what to do or say. I'm frustrated. If I could carry a child, I would be happy to do it. I wish I could do something, say something, to move you."

"Willy. Someday. Maybe. But I'm only thirty-four. I've got time."

"I'm *forty-four*. To me, this is someday." Willy leaned into his shoulder and wiped his face with his shirt. He continued to rattle the pans and stare out the window into an opaque, ink-colored sky.

Pam looked at his back, tensed now, at the sweet circle of scalp showing at the back of his head, watched the fierceness with which he washed the pots and pans. She was so lucky to love and be loved by this man. If only what he was asking weren't so damned much. She felt her eyes fill with tears. She walked to him and wrapped her arms around his waist, placed her cheek on his back. She squeezed him gently. The sound of clanking aluminum stopped. What could she say to stop him from hurting? I'm sorry? "I'm going to take a shower, okay?"

B. Willy nodded without turning around. Silently, Pam left the kitchen.


Philip leaned his head back into the headrest of the small Mercedes and let the music flow around him. He knew his posture would look strange to the parking attendant should he wander down to find out what had happened to him. It might look as though he were dead and frankly, the attendant wouldn't be far wrong. He felt as if he were carrying little weights under his eyes these days, little ten-pound weights. The tape finished its side and Philip stretched out his hand with effort and stabbed the button that would switch off the tape deck.

He tapped at the glove compartment and took out the package for Stevie and as he did so, a sheaf of folded paper fell to the car floor. He slipped the package into his inside jacket pocket, then bent to retrieve the papers. He unfolded them gingerly, bent them against the crease. "Information Request Form," was the heading on the first page and then line after line elicited his response to indescribably tedious questions. Did he really want to go back to school? He didn't need a degree in law, but he had been looking for something, yearning for something when he had walked into the registrar's office. It seemed to him now, as he slumped tiredly in the car seat somewhere below the building in which Stevie lived, that he had been looking for some kind of affirmation. When the lithe young man had asked his date of birth, and Philip had told him, an incredibly important retort had been missing from his questioner's response. What the young man had *not* said was, "You can't be forty-six. I would have thought you were in your mid-thirties. At the most." What he had said was simply, "The sooner you get these forms back to us, the sooner we can process them, Mr. Durfee. Next." Well. Well, well. Middle age at last. Stop feeling sorry for yourself, damn it. He opened the door and stepped out onto the concrete floor. Have some fun, Philip, he advised himself. A new part of the day was beginning. And tonight would be a celebration of Stevie. He patted his pocket, assuring himself that Stevie's gift was there and safe. He couldn't wait to give it to her; couldn't wait to see her face.

"Come in here, you," Stevie said, pulling Philip into the apartment by his waist, closing the front door behind him. "Kiss me. Quick."

Philip happily folded her into his arms, feeling the heaviness of his day fall away from him. He so loved this woman. "Love and kisses, birthday girl," he said, kissing her noisily.

"Are you staying tonight?" she asked, leading him down the corridor to her bedroom. She held her breath, but not so that he would notice.

"I can't. Don't think I don't want to."

"Kenny, something tells me," Stevie said, nudging aside her disappointment. It was her birthday! Still, Philip needed her support in his earnest attempts to father his child. If only the three of them could all be in the same place. She watched as Philip sat wearily in the chair near the window. She folded herself into a crossed-legged heap at the foot of her bed.

"He didn't show up at his job until after ten this morning. For the third time this week."

"Oh, boy. Get the rope. Find a big oak tree."

"Seriously. Mallory took him on for the summer as a favor to me. It's embarrassing."

"Philip, surely Mallory understands. He's not expecting Kenny to be like you."

"He's not supposed to have to understand anything. You hire someone. You tell him the hours. You expect him to show up."

"What did Kenny say?"

" 'No one else is there at nine so why do I have to be?' "

Stevie tightened the sash on her bathrobe and reached over the bed to the VCR. She could get him out of this funk. "Hey, I want to show you something that happened on today's show."

"Sure. Love to," Philip said distractedly. Stevie slipped a tape into the machine's mechanical maw and watched as it gobbled the tape and lowered it into its body. "Hang on a minute while I find the place."

"I'm going to have to roust him out of bed tomorrow, tie him into his clothes if I have to, and drive him to work. What if Mallory fires him? What about that? Then what am I going to do with him?"

Stevie put her hands on her lap and looked at Philip. "I don't know, sweetheart. Maybe I can get him a job."

"What a great idea. You're turning WON into a summer camp for the overprivileged."

"Hey, what's power for if you don't use it?"

"He's going to work in the shipping department at Mallory's. That's what he signed on for and that's what he's going to do. Run the tape."

Stevie pushed the Play button and after several feet of tape had been played she stopped the machine. "Did you see that?"

"Uh-huh. The door swung closed."

"Right. Now watch this." Stevie advanced the tape and played another section. "Did you see that?"

"Cue cards fell over."

"We're going to have to fire Hillary. Pam loves her, but this can't go on."

"You're right, Steve. It's sloppy."

"Right. We may not be network, but I don't see why we have to look like Made in Altoona. Honestly though, I don't think she should be in production. She's too dreamy." Stevie shook her head. "Say, did I tell you? We picked up Scranton."

"Hey—that's great, Steve. Three new stations this month," Philip said, brightening. "This is how Letterman got started. And Donohue."

"I'm pretty pleased and Ed's got a new airport ashtray for his collection. So what did you do today? Have any thoughts about getting married?" Shit. Did I say that? She stopped breathing.

Philip pulled his tie from his neck slowly and looked at the ceiling. "Let me see. I got up this morning. Had a cruller and a glass of buttermilk. Played squash with Mallory and let the asshole beat me, of course. Had lunch with the antigravity snake oil salesman. Picked up a present for my girl. Nope. I don't think I thought about getting married. Why?"

"Present? For me?"

"Wait a minute. Back up. Where did that marriage question come from?"

"The blue."

"Sure."

Stevie took a deep breath. "You remember Martha?"

"The woman who does the booking for your show. Gray hair. Ruffles."

"Yeah. She made me a birthday cake and she knit me a sweater. Wait and I'll show you." Stevie climbed off the bed and went to the closet. She took a flat box out of the closet and brought it to the bed. Removing the lid, shaking out the tissues, Stevie lifted out a frothy pink angora sweater.

"Very nice."

"I know. It's not me, but do you know what it cost to make this thing?" Stevie shook the sweater and waves of fur rippled across the garment. "A hundred and fifty bucks easy. That's what the yarn cost. And knitting angora is no day at the beach."

"Steve-o. What does this sweater have to do with getting married?"

"Oh. Martha said she wants to dance at my wedding. She never got married, you know. As far as I know, she was born, she got a job at WON in the early forties, and now she's waiting to dance at my wedding. She says I'm like a daughter to her. Philip, that kills me. I hardly know her. How can she feel that way about me?"

"A lot of people feel that way about you. You inspire a lot of fantasies."

"She's all alone. She's sixty something and she's got her job. That's it. No husband. No children. No parents. She's all alone."

"So you want to get married and adopt Martha?" Philip said playfully.

"Don't you?" Stevie responded in kind.

"Not yet," Philip said, and with unfortunate clarity the two words stood like sentinels between them. There was silence as the two looked at each other. What had he meant? Not that, both thought. Guiltily, Philip stood and pulled Stevie from the bed, holding her against him. "Hey, come on. I love you. *You're* not alone." With enormous effort, by consciously not translating the two words, by listening instead to the subsequent avowal of love and the beating of his heart, Stevie relaxed against Philip's chest. She held him tightly and they hugged for a long time. "Don't you want your present?" Philip asked at last.

"Uh-huh," she said. "Is there time? Don't we have to go soon?" In the space of a blink, in the length of an unguarded moment, the unsanctioned words intruded. Philip didn't want to marry her? "Not yet," he had said. Oh, my God, she thought. Did I want to know that?

"We don't have to be at the restaurant for over an hour."

"Okay," she said. Carol, she thought, the name calling up wordless fear.

Philip lifted his jacket from the chair and reached into the breast pocket. He handed Stevie a flat box. She took it from him and ran her hand over the silver paper. She shook the box two times, then overcarefully undid the wrappings. What would be inside? Balm? She could hope. A plain white box gave up a black satin envelope, which in turn revealed a strand of large knobby gray pearls locked with a diamond-studded clasp. Stevie gasped and stared at Philip openmouthed.

"There are thirty-nine of these," he said, reaching out a finger touching the pearls lightly. "I picked each one out myself. I bought this one from Mr. Wong. And this one from Mr. Ho." Philip smiled gently at her and collected a smile in return. "The clasp was my mother's," he said.

"Philip. I can't say . . . I don't know . . ." She handed the necklace to Philip and turned swiftly, sweeping up her hair, laying her neck bare. Philip fastened the pearls and Stevie, lifting a hand mirror from the nightstand, put her finger to her throat. "Thank you," she said in a whisper. "They're glorious. They're magnificent."

"They're yours."

"And I'm yours," she said, letting the feelings of love wash over her. She couldn't love him really if she couldn't tell him how much. "I am so in love with you," she said.

"And I, you," he said pulling her to him.

"Give me," she said pulling at his belt, tugging at his trousers. Willingly, Philip complied.

6

Slashes of light seeped from the drawn windows of the small French restaurant. Philip pushed open the oak door and once inside, handed his hat to the coat-check woman. Had his party gotten the private room he had reserved? "Durfee," he said to the maitre d'. Without consulting a large bound leather date book, he smiled and said, "Follow me, sir."

Philip trailed behind the man to the back of the room and up a winding mahogany-banistered staircase. His mind leapt ahead, anticipating the evening to come with B. Willy and Pam. He had met the pair when he had been a guest on Stevie's show and since that day, through Stevie, they had become close friends.

The maitre d' stepped to one side at the top of the landing and let Philip precede him into a small room in an interior cul-de-sac.

"Philip!" B. Willy said, standing to shake his hand. "Where'd you park that car anyway?"

"Hi," he said to the fair-haired man. "Pam," he said delightedly, kissing a soft cheek. "Some very nice garage where they promised not to let anything happen to the radio. How are you?" he asked, sitting down next to Stevie, putting his arm around her chair.

"Fine," said Pam. "Fine, if you don't mind getting pre-empted by the President."

"Oooh," said Philip sympathetically. "When did you find that out?"

"Just now," said B. Willy, poking a matchstick between his front teeth. "I checked in with Ed. My mistake."

"Maybe it's a blessing," Stevie said. "I thought the show was a little lame today. I don't know. Wolfson did part of a routine he did last time he was on, and I was a little off . . ."

"And the set almost fell down," Pam said dejectedly.

"Shhh, shhh," Stevie said. "Don't worry about that tonight."

"But you picked up Scranton," Philip said.

"So we did. Here's to Scranton, Pennsylvania," Willy said. "Home of WKZZ. Home of Themetown, USA. Home of the Scranton Pumas."

"Thanks," Philip said to the waiter who filled his wine glass. "And may I have some water? Coal capital of the state," Philip added, raising his glass.

"Nope, that's Wilkes-Barre."

"Well, here's to the Pumas, then," he said, taking a sip. He took a packet of aspirin out of his jacket.

"Headache?" Stevie asked.

Philip nodded. "It's the same headache I've had for two weeks. I hardly notice it anymore."

"I think he's developing an allergic reaction to Kenny," said Stevie, rubbing Philip's back with her hand. "Acute new daddyitis."

"Oh, right," B. Willy said. "Condolences on the Jag."

"No problem," Philip said. "It simply needs a new rear axle, a new trunk, new rear fenders, a new electrical system, taillights, shocks, transmission, and a paint job and it will be as good as new." He put his glasses on the table and rubbed his eyes, enjoying the straight face he kept as the sympathetic laughter surrounded him.

"Are you ready to order?" asked the waiter, who good-naturedly waited out the maverick hoot of laughter and then recited the specials of the evening. Orders were given and the waiter, tucking the order pad into his cummerbund, left the table. He returned repeatedly with delicate portions of pâté and greens glistening in oil. Then the entrées were served, aromatic and beautifully presented.

This is the best it has ever been for me, Stevie thought, savoring the meal and the camaraderie. It was so pleasantly normal to be having a birthday dinner with a man who liked her friends, got headaches, could drink a mediocre wine and not make a fuss. She knew this was normal because it felt so right and it was a feeling she couldn't remember having had before. If only she could be sure it would last forever. Marriage to Philip would be enough, wouldn't it? Could she live without having children of her own? Until very recently she had thought so and now this damned crack, and now another, a tiny fissure branching from the first. "Not yet," he'd said. What if Philip didn't marry her? Stop. She would be alone. Stop. Alone.

Shivering inside, unable to comprehend the surrounding conversation, Stevie smiled vaguely at her friends. She leaned into Philip's encompassing arm, gathered his warmth for reassurance, and let her thoughts spin out. The "not yet" didn't mean that he didn't love her. It meant something else. People married out of mutual need and there was no such need. The money to live separately and well was there. The sharing of intimacy was there. And so was their exclusive love.

Coming up the stairs to this room she had thought only: my birthday, my lover, my friends. At the top of the stairs were the two small rooms: the one in which they now sat, and one across the landing. The door to the other room had been open and as they stood briefly on the landing, she had peered into the other occupied space. For a small moment, part of a minute, she observed a white-trimmed tableau: a white cloth on the table, white curtains in the window, a family gathering of adults about her age. Between two of the adults was a high chair and in it, an infant in a frilly white dress. She and Philip had eaten at Jean-Jacques many times and had never seen a child, so this event must be a special one. White dresses were special, even more so for the very young. She realized now, this little girl must be having a birthday. They had been born on the same day! Stevie's sudden sense of kinship ignited a feeling as strong as desire, as inappropriate as greed. She wanted to go across the threshold of the room and take possession of the child. She wanted to bring it to their room and place it in Philip's arms.

Stevie became aware that her plate was being removed. Philip poured wine into her glass. By his inquiring look, Stevie saw that her absence had been noted, so she turned her attention to the moment. "May I open this now?" Stevie asked, eyeing a wrapped package in the center of the small table.

"I hope you like it," Pam said, before shyly passing the package to her friend.

Stevie carefully opened the paper and when the gift was revealed, stared.

"I love it. I love it," Stevie said again. She fingered the glass-and-photograph construction and swallowed. With love and care her friend had captured the essence of her life on the air. "Pam, you brilliant thing, you, this is wonderful. How in the world do you do this?"

"I hoped you'd like it," Pam said, smiling. She lowered her eyes and looked down at the tablecloth. Scrutiny was so hard for her to bear. Stevie was so natural in the spotlight, whereas Pam couldn't stand the glare. What she loved best was the background, the dark places strung with wires, fastened with gaffer's tape. And she liked small things, details, and the sense of control she felt when she had all the knowledge she needed to make a thousand small pieces form a solid, intrinsic whole. Producing "On-the-Air" was so perfect for her. Their deep friendship aside, she was forever grateful to Stevie for giving her the confidence she needed to step forward, take on more responsibility, and finally manage the production of this daily thousand-piece challenge. How had she ever been able to teach school? All of those children, all of their intricate personalities and needs, so much work done during the day, undone by their parents at night. She had tried so hard to make Willy understand what she had seen in the faces of the children she had taught, the ones who went home to empty houses, to parents too fatigued to give them the attention they needed. He insisted the two of them had enough love and time to give children, but she knew a small person with her blood and his would demand by its existence more of her than the scraps she had remaining after her intense fourteen-hour workday was over.

"I more than love it," Stevie said. "Thank you." She leaned across the table and kissed Pam on the cheek.

Pam squirmed bashfully and sought a way to get out of the spotlight. "Nice-looking pearls, by the way," she said to Philip.

"Aren't they really grand?" Stevie said, beaming. She lifted a lock of hair from Philip's nape and slid her hand there. Then she kissed his cheek.

He'd heard the expression "natural beauty" before, but Philip thought he'd never seen so clear a manifestation of that rare quality as this. It wasn't just the way she looked. Stevie had an unusual ability to put people at their ease. It was obvious both Pam and Willy would do anything for her. Pam had found a mentor and friend, and Willy, what about him? Had he had a crush on her once? Possibly. He looked at her so fondly, like a boy regarding his younger sister. Something like that. Protectiveness and affection. Why had it taken so long to find someone like Stevie? The women he had known had had impeccable taste and thin, pointed noses, like pedigreed hounds trained to search out an extravagant life. This woman was as natural as butterscotch and as real as day.

The door to the private room swung open. Sounds flooded in, obliterating the silence and the privacy. A waiter entered with a whooshing sound. A busboy followed and cleared the table. "I made this for you," Willy said, moving the wrapped can across the white tablecloth.

"Taffy!" Stevie unwrapped a piece, tentatively sucking, then biting down hard. "My favorite, and real vanilla," Stevie said through exaggeratedly clenched teeth.

"I think it could have used a few more pulls," B. Willy said, rubbing his jaw.

"It's supposed to be difficult to chew," Philip said.

"Yes," said Stevie. "I like food that gives me a hard time. No wimpy food for this crowd," she said, untwisting the paper on another piece of candy.

"Would you like coffee and dessert?" the waiter asked, glancing surreptitiously at Stevie.

"Espresso?" Philip asked Stevie.

She nodded. "It's a solvent, isn't it?" she asked Philip. " 'Cause I think my jaws are welded."

"Espresso for me too," said Pam.

"And me," said Willy."

"Espresso for four," said Philip. "I think we've got dessert covered," he added, winking at the waiter.

The busboy, opening the door with his tray, again allowed the entrance of party noises: a liquid laugh, the crystal clinking of glasses, the piercing wail of a child. "I'm sorry about the noise," the waiter said, wincing as the door closed. "Their table was reserved."

"Why in the world would someone bring a small child to a restaurant like this?" Philip asked as he listened to the child's crying, insistent even through the closed door. His headache, recently forgotten, reasserted itself.

"I'm sorry, sir, I couldn't begin to know," the waiter answered as he left the room.

"I don't know either," Philip said. "When I was a child, hell, when I was older than that, my parents routinely left me and my brother locked in the car when they went out to a restaurant." He pictured the inside of the Buick upholstered in some sort of tan nubby fabric, and himself and his brother bashing each other until exhaustion flung them into opposing corners of the car and sleep completed the separation.

"No," said Stevie, startled. "That can't be true."

"It's true. My parents didn't go out often, but when they did, there were no babysitters for us. We terrorized babysitters, so they took us and left us in the car. Stevie, don't look so worried. We weren't traumatized. We thought it was completely normal. I still do."

"I see their point," Pam said. "Aggression against the babysitter is anger at the parents for leaving. They checked in on you, I presume . . ."

Philip nodded.

Pam shrugged. "Advanced thinking, I have to say. They were ahead of their time."

"I can't believe I'm hearing this," Willy interjected. "Locking children in cars is advanced thinking?"

The door opened and the crying child sound was amplified. Philip put his hands over his ears as the coffee service was set. Stevie turned her head toward the open door and looked across to the adjoining room. The child, its face red with exertion, sat howling on a man's lap. Her father? Yes. He was jiggling her on his knee, crooning her name. "Philip, look," she wanted to say.

"Are you saying this is preferable?" Philip asked B. Willy, stabbing the air with a stiff hand. "To whom is this fair? The parents? The child? Us?"

The door closed and in the relative quiet, Philip's question was overly loud. He turned to Stevie for her customary support. After all, she would agree. An evening out was relief from the pressure of the day. That was in fact why they booked a private room wherever they could. "Stevie," Philip said. "You've gotten so quiet."

"Um. I think the party is for that little girl. I think it's her birthday too."

"What?" Philip replied irritably. What had Stevie said? He felt betrayed. He wanted her support, and he wanted her attention. She wasn't even listening to him. The door to their room opened again, and as one waiter wedged the door open, the other advanced with a birthday cake, candle burning in the center. Stevie grinned and touched her new pearls with her hand. Philip, relenting, put an arm around her and led the singing. "Happy birthday to you . . ."

"Happy birthday to you . . ." sang the two waiters who were holding the chocolate truffle cake. "Happy birthday, dear Ste-vie," joined the others.

Across the little hallway, a bare few yards away, the infant took in deep new supplies of air and wailed loudly. Philip spun in his chair and glared at the infant, then gave the woman comforting the child a furious look. The woman, evidently the child's mother, looked shocked and lifted the baby into her arms.

"God, babies," Pam said under her breath. "Babies should be in bed by now."

"You said it," Philip said, giving her an approving nod. He turned sternly to Stevie for confirmation—another chance. Stevie was conscious that Philip was looking to her for agreement, but she felt suddenly uneasy. Why was he so angry with her? Couldn't he see what she saw? Contentment. Peace. Completion. She looked at the baby, now quiet in its mother's arms, and smiled. The baby, still wet-faced, smiled back radiantly.

"Whoa. You're a natural," B. Willy said softly. "Look at that."

"Watch out, Stevie," Pam warned her. "That stuff's contagious."

Stevie didn't seem to hear her. The baby crinkled her eyes and pushed fingers in her mouth with pleasure.

"Hey, Steve. Blow out the candle," said B. Willy. "We're seconds from meltdown."

"Make a wish," Pam said, squeezing Stevie's hand.

Stevie looked past the cake, past her friends, past the table. The baby was resting her head under her mother's chin. Thumb in her mouth, she was staring beatifically into the light from the candle. What a beautiful baby, she thought. Positively divine. Stevie looked across the candlelight directly into the baby's eyes. Had she ever really seen a baby before? "I hope all your dreams come true," she heard Pam say.

Making a wish that surprised her, Stevie blew out the flame.

# 7

Lisa sat on the toilet seat top and braced her legs against the wall. "I love it," she said to her mother. She twirled her hair and braided it. Then she bit the end of the braid. "It is so, I don't know, *sensational*. Everything that happens in the world gets reported in that room. I feel so plugged in."

"Well, you certainly seem all charged up," Carol said reaching for her wine glass. She stretched out her legs in the bath water and enjoyed the sensation of warmth and weightlessness.

"And I love Stevie. Mom, she's so great. She came to the newsroom today to see how I was doing and she said she would talk to Sarah about letting me watch her show from the booth.

Mom, that's where all the action is. It's amazing in there. It's like the Starship Enterprise."

"Hmmm," Carol said, letting her thoughts disassemble. She idly sipped her wine and as she did so, she thought about the boxes of clothing down in the basement. She should sort through the whole darned pile of them for the Businesswomen's League Charity Bazaar this weekend. Thinking of the rummage sale led her to thoughts of the dance that would follow it and almost without wanting to, she thought about Malcolm and then she remembered making love with him the night before and a jolt of pure, damp, femaleness jarred her. She sank a few inches into the bathwater and moved suds toward her chest. What was Lisa saying? Stevie, Stevie, Stevie. Well, better Stevie than Reed, Reed, Reed. "I'm glad you like her, hon," she said. Mal. Bear hugs, and junk food, and a kingsize Hollywood bed. In Malcolm's warm hands, tension and stress flew far, far away. If only they could keep this relationship simple. If only she didn't have social needs. Carol wrinkled her forehead and pinched the bridge of her nose.

"What's the matter, Mom?" Carol heard her daughter asking. "I would have thought you would have loved me to spend the night with Stevie."

"What, honey? I'm sorry, I didn't hear you."

"Stevie invited me to spend the night."

"How lovely. That's very nice of Stevie, isn't it?" Carol took a large sponge and, dipping it into the bathwater, squeezed a soothing stream across her collarbones. If Lisa spent the night with Stevie, Mal could spend the night with her. "When does she want you to come over?"

"Tomorrow. Or the next night. Or whenever would be good. I thought tomorrow would be great. Is it okay?"

"Well, sure, honey. What will you do? Pack a bag and go straight to Stevie's after work?"

"Uh-huh. Do you know how old Stevie is? Well, of course

you do since you went to school with her. But she doesn't look thirty-nine, does she? They just had a birthday party for her."

Carol reached behind her neck and lifted a strand of hair out of the water and tried to snag it on the clip at the top of her head. Pulling the strand hurt. Of course Stevie didn't look her age. Did she ever have to struggle or fight for anything her whole damn life? Isn't that what aged you, wore you down? The disappointments, the compromises? Change the subject. "Lisa, you don't want those old blue ski boots, do you? And all those old clothes from high school you don't ever wear. I thought I'd take them to the bazaar."

"I don't *need* the boots, but Daddy gave them to me. I don't think I can throw them away."

"Honey, your daddy has given you lots of other things. I don't see how you can save everything he's given you."

Lisa remembered getting those sky-blue boots with the white stripes up the sides. Daddy had fitted them on her feet, and showed her how to snap them into the skis ("Squash the bug, honey"). Then, standing with his long skis enclosing her tiny, wobbly vee, they had coasted together down the little hill that had seemed so big. She could still almost hear her squeals of fear and delight, could still feel his warm cheek pressed against hers, his big hands clasped around her waist as they slid safely down the slope. Her parents were still together then. "I don't care about my high school stuff. Well, I care about the sweat-shirts. Don't give away the sweatshirts, okay? And don't give away my ski boots."

Maybe you'd like to have those boots bronzed, Carol thought. "Okay," she said. "Why don't you let me have my bath now. If you pack tonight, you'll have time for breakfast tomorrow morning."

"Are you okay, Mom?"

"Of course I am. Why do you ask?"

"I don't know. Something."

"I'm fine. I had a busy day."

"I'll go pack a few things."

Carol nodded. She closed her eyes and slipped down into the water until only her chin rested on the surface. So Stevie didn't look her age, Carol thought, mopping the sponge over her tired eyes. And she did, apparently. Well, both things were true. There were ways to look young. Everyone she knew was thinking about having this or that tucked. Eyes were supposed to be simple. She'd heard you could have your eyes done and from A to Z you'd be back to normal in two weeks, and no one would even know. Should she do it while Lisa was at home to tend her, or wait until she was back at school? Right after the surgery, there was supposedly a lot of bruising and swelling. Well, hell, this was the right season for sunglasses. Two weeks and then young woman's eyes. Then what? Her neck? Her breasts? Her belly? God. Once she started where would she stop? What would Mal think? What did men think about plastic surgery anyway? Who cared? she thought abruptly. Reaching forward, she pulled the plug. She stood and quickly draped a bathtowel around herself. She'd make an appointment with Dr. Arundel this week.

The smile would not leave her face. Stevie covered her mouth with her hand but still the smile would not disappear. Visions of the future unfurled, silk scarves in a gentle breeze. It was easy to see now how the center of her life would shift. She would cease to be who she was and would become a different version of herself, a rounder version, a fuller person. She left her desk and walked down the corridor to Pam's office. She knocked, and at the response from within, "Do it," pushed open Pam's grimy office door.

"Hey," Pam said, hanging up the phone. She was wearing an "On-the-Air" tee shirt, this one yellow, and an ammunition belt around her waist, both staple items in her daily wardrobe.

Stevie knew she wouldn't have to work to capture Pam's attention. She was fairly shimmering with excitement. Couldn't everyone see? She crossed her arms over her aching breasts and lowered herself gently into the vinyl-covered side chair across from Pam's desk. It was beginning, the exaggeratedly careful movements that showed the person she had been was becoming a different person, a caretaker, the one responsible for the vulnerable package held inside the soft covering that was her body. "Pam," Stevie said, arranging her multilayered, many-colored feelings into a simple phrase. "Pam," she said again hoping to enfold her friend, embrace her with words. "I think I'm pregnant." A smile started at one side of Stevie's mouth and traveled smoothly past the overlap of her front teeth straight across to the opposite cheek. There the smile held, displayed itself, proclaimed her unequivocal joy.

"Oh my God," Pam said sucking air. "Oh my God." You can't be, she wanted to say. It's not all right to be pregnant. You'll wreck everything. "Oh my God," she said again, her voice blurred by shock and amazement.

"I know." Stevie's grin, impossibly, widened.

Pam watched Stevie in silence. She fumbled for a response that would be a genuine expression of shared happiness. If Stevie was pregnant, there was going to be trouble. This would be the beginning of changes, unpredictable ones. Unexpectedly, she felt lightheaded, unbalanced. If Stevie was pregnant, what would happen to *her*? What would happen to Stevie? Did Stevie really want this? Did her career mean so little to her? Two months ago, Stevie wouldn't have been happy about being pregnant. She would have been horrified. "How late are you?" she asked.

"I'm not late yet, actually," Stevie said, coloring. "I, my body—my body feels differently than it has. My breasts are very sore." She touched them gently with her palms, then took Pam's hand. "We made love and the day after that I felt myself ovulate.

Sperm stay alive inside you for seventy-two hours. Isn't that right?"

"Stevie, when are you due? When are you supposed to get your period?"

"At the end of this week. I was dizzy when I got out of bed yesterday and I felt a little nauseous this morning. I know you can psychosomatize nausea, but breast tenderness? They've been this way since I ovulated."

"Steve, I don't want to be a spoilsport, but I don't think it works that way. I don't think you can be nauseous yet. I don't think you can be having symptoms yet. The egg's got to travel for a week or two before it digs in. You read the same stuff I read."

Stevie tapped the desk with her fingers. But this month her body felt different! She had held onto this feeling for eight full days without saying a word, and now she was having to defend tender breasts and a bilious taste at the back of her throat. This was how it had felt the last time, she was almost sure. "I've got an appointment with my gynecologist on Friday. Pam, I really hope I am."

"Well .. you hope so, so do I." Pam smiled faintly. She opened one of the pockets on her ammo belt and took out a pack of roll candy. She offered the roll to Stevie, who took a candy, and then Pam plunked a white circle of sweetness on her own tongue. She sucked it hard and thought. If Stevie was pregnant, Philip was going to freak out. "What did Philip say?"

"I'm not going to tell him yet. He likes 'empirical proof,' and I can't prove anything yet." What would he say? He'd be angry with her first, and that could be frightening. Consciously, he wouldn't want her to be pregnant. She'd have to be calm; get through the initial storm, take the responsibility. She was in charge of birth control and she'd flubbed it. Having that IUD taken out after all those years of not thinking about birth control at all had placed a lot of unnatural little acts and articles in her hands; so hard to use, so easy to forget. Would Philip think she'd been deliberately careless? Had she been? No more than he. In fact, just before her birthday she had made an appointment with her gynecologist to complain about the tubes and gels. She had thought surely there was something easy to use he had forgotten to recommend. Now her appointment with Dr. Wrobleski would be of a different texture. "Honey, I'm pregnant," she would say to Philip. She would say these words in a kind way, a simple way, and then she would fold her hands and wait for what followed. The rage, the discord was inevitable. That short sentence, when added to "not yet," could only produce a harsh reaction from Philip. She would loosen herself as if for a fall. She would recreate herself as a fabric with a loose weave and let his words pass through her. She would comfort him, rock him, and in the end, when his anger was spent, he would see what this new family would be like, how this union and multiplication would add richness to their lives. "After the shock wears off, Philip will be pleased, don't you think?" Stevie asked dreamily.

Pam asked skeptically, "Are we talking about Philip Durfee, the man who almost wasted a one-year-old in a party dress?"

"Come on, Pam. He had a headache and I don't blame him. Don't you see how funny and sweet he is? And how protective? A baby would fascinate him to pieces. He'd be great with a baby." Stevie imagined Philip on his hands and knees pushing a mechanical toy, warming to the giggles of a burbling child. "I think I'd be sort of good with a baby, too," she added. Now, Stevie amended to herself. She looped a thumb under her pearls and tugged gently. She fingered the clasp and stared out Pam's window. Against the gray wall of a neighboring building, another image appeared. The porch swing. She, dressed all in bulky sweaters with ribbons and silver buttons, and a long skirt with petticoats, and lace-up boots that came up to her knees. Her arm was wrapped around a small child, a little girl who, red-nosed in the cold air, was wearing woolly clothes and a knitted hat pulled down over her ears. And Philip was taking pictures.

"I don't know how great it is to get excited about all this until you know for sure," Pam said, fidgeting with a pencil, tapping it within the handle of her coffee mug.

"Boy, what a bucket of cold water you're turning out to be," Stevie said, turning toward her, staring her down.

"Sorry, Stevie. Really, I am. I'm not too sentimental on this subject. But you know I want for you what you want for you."

"Sure," Stevie said, standing, giving Pam a small smile. What was bothering her? Why wasn't she more excited? "I know."

"Keep me posted," Pam said as Stevie left her office. Stevie nodded. She was feeling a little nauseous again. She treasured the feeling.


Kenny pressed the washcloth-wrapped ice to his face and stared at Philip's lightning globe with his good eye. That bastard had really hurt him. Pushing his face to the floor and standing on his head. Plus he was out a hundred and forty bucks and his class ring and his belt, the one with the real turquoise-inlaid buckle. He reached out a hand and touched the glass globe which was filled with living lightning. With a soft hiss and crackle, a blue branch of electricity cleaved to the inside surface of the sphere following his hand as he moved it. Dad was going to kill him. The washcloth dripped water on the leather sofa and although Kenny brushed the drops away, the spots remained, chocolate brown against amber. Kenny covered the spots with his fingers, then sighed. Couches should be indestructible, he thought. Whoever heard of a leather couch? He got to his feet and, braving the headache that attacked him as he stood, he walked to his room. It hadn't been his fault. That's what he'd tell Philip. It hadn't been his fault.

•

Whistling, Philip opened the front door. God, what a gorgeous evening. Kenny had been wanting to see that Woody Allen movie and knowing that, he had picked up the tickets on the way home. They could have something quick to eat and catch the seven o'clock show. He was in the mood for spaghetti, Kenny's every-time first-choice dish. Philip went to the kitchen and tapped the larder door, which swung open. Vermicelli, linguine, pasta shells. And there were two kinds of sauce, and there was a can of corn. Pasta and a vegetable that didn't taste like one. He and Ken could have a real man's dinner.

"Kenny!" he shouted. "Ken, I'm home."

"Hi, Dad," he heard from a desultory voice.

Now what? Philip wondered. Did Ken have a rough day at the office? He lined all the cans and packages up on the counter and put a pot of water on an unlit burner. He wiped his hands on a towel and walked back to the rear of the apartment, finally knocking on the door to Kenny's room.

"Hi, son. How does a spaghetti dinner and a movie sound?" he asked, walking into the unlit space.

"I'm not hungry, Dad," Kenny said, turning his head to the wall.

What the hell was going on? Philip thought. He reached over a pile of clothes to the table lamp and turned on the light. Something about Kenny's posture looked wrong. Very wrong. A faint frisson began at his shoulders, leapt to his ears. "What's wrong," he asked quietly. Kenny turned. The flesh surrounding Kenny's eye was dull purple shot with crimson. The side of his face was scraped and raw. Kenny looked mournfully at his father and replaced the dripping cloth over his eye.

Philip felt faint. "My God!" he whispered. He strode to the bed and, taking Kenny's wrist in his hand, moved the washcloth away. The white of Kenny's eye was furiously, torridly red. "What happened? What happened to you?"

"It wasn't my fault, Dad," Kenny said softly, flinching under Philip's touch and gaze.

"Of course it wasn't your fault," Philip said. He'd been beaten up. What else could it be? He smoothed Kenny's hair away from his forehead. "Get your shoes on. We're going to the hospital."

"It's okay, Dad. It's just a black eye."

"It's not just a black eye. You've ruptured some blood vessels and that scrape needs to be swabbed out." Philip felt a tingling sensation all through his chest. His mouth was dry and his lips were numb. His son's blood was dark on the pillow. How had this happened? He was responsible for this boy and yet how was he supposed to care for him? How could he be with him every minute of the day?

"I can see fine. I don't think I really got hurt."

"St. Luke's is five minutes from here. Did someone do this to you?" Philip asked, untying a shoe lace, handing a sneaker to Kenny.

"Yeah. I guess so."

Shoes tied, Kenny stood. He held the rag to his face and let his father help him on with his denim jacket. He had a flash of pity for his father. He looked scared. If this had happened at home, Danny would have just called him an asshole. Mom would have started to cry and then she would have poured a bottle of peroxide on his face, and then he would have hung out at Fat Tony's until Moo showed up and admired his injuries. His father, this father, was worried. If he told him what happened, he'd probably have to go to the police station and look at mug shots.

"Were you in a fight? Just answer me." His son's blood. He felt like crying. This boy, this very boy, had been two feet tall once. They had walked in the park, hand in hand, Kenny pulling his quack-a-duck toy. He had watched Kenny with one eye, been alert for jostlers and thumpers and smokers and worse with the other. How was he supposed to protect his son now? He couldn't! But Jesus Christ, kids from California didn't belong in New York.

"I fell asleep, sort of, in the subway."

With a shaking hand, Philip locked the front door. He put his hand on Kenny's back and held down the elevator call button until the car arrived. The elevator, casting a thin, gray light on their faces, smoothly lowered them to the lobby floor.

"You were mugged," Philip said tensely, flagging a taxi. The two climbed into the back seat.

"Yeah. I guess so. Whatever," Kenny mumbled, resting his torn cheek against the cool glass window.

"Sit up, Ken. That glass isn't clean." Philip ached for Kenny. Crying was so hard to do. He wanted to cry himself. "Are you hurt anywhere else but your face?"

"No." Kenny tried to shake his head but the movement intensified the pain.

"Didn't anyone try to help you?" Philip asked indignantly.

"Yeah, afterward. It happened really fast."

"Go on."

"Dad."

"Go on."

"This guy. He had, like, a knife and he made me get off the train."

Philip turned to his son to stare. A knife! He could have been stabbed. He could have died!

"And so he pushed me into a corner of the station and took my stuff, and then he shoved me down. He told me not to get up until he was out of there. He stepped on my head." The words called up the sharp memory of the hard punch to his face, the gritty feel of shoeleather grinding against one cheek, the skin of the other scraping against the concrete. Despite his resolve to be strong, if only for his father's sake, tears dropped from his eyes. Danny would kick his ass for crying. Kenny gingerly dabbed at his face with his sleeve.

"Kenny, Kenny. I'm so sorry." Philip offered his son a handkerchief and when it was rejected, put his arm around Kenny and pulled him close. "We're going to the police after the doctor looks at you."

"No, Dad, forget it," he grumbled. As he disengaged himself from his father's embrace, one small, exultant part of him pondered the cause of his happiness. "I don't want to go to the police. I want to go to sleep."

The taxi wheeled into the hospital parking lot, braking gently at the emergency room entrance. Philip helped his son out of the car. "We'll talk about it later," he said. How could he protect his son from danger? Taking the handkerchief from his pocket again, he blew his nose. Then he pushed open the hospital door.

# 8

Sounds of stringed instruments wafted through the apartment in long, curling drifts. Stevie had prepared the spare room for Lisa. But somehow they had ended up in Stevie's bedroom, dressed for sleep, loosely wrapped in a silken coverlet, surrounded by heaps of soft square pillows. A heavy white platter, decorated in flow-blue glaze and piled with cheese, fruits, and sweet crackers, balanced precariously on the hills of bedcovers.

Lisa crossed her arms over her chest. She had seen this kind of luxury before in the homes of her school friends whose parents had loads of money. She knew her way around Porthault linens and Steuben glass, and didn't want this for herself. She squinted her eyes, attempting to stare down the sterling silver ice bucket. Unfortunately, she liked that bucket. It was from Tiffany, and very old. Shit. She didn't want to feel so *comfortable* ensconced in this sumptuous nest. Had she seriously hoped Stevie would have decorated with burlap and batik?

Lisa nervously returned her attention to Stevie. Her play, *Live at Five*, was in Stevie's hands. Stevie was on the last page, as a matter of fact. Would she like it? Was it any good? She had read it over so many times, none of it amused her any more. Stevie had laughed a few times, but a few cheap laughs didn't make a play great. It was too frivolous. She shouldn't have let Stevie read it. It was juvenile and sophomoric and dumb. It was too soon to be showing it to anyone. What had been her rush? Stevie was so great. Even if she didn't like the play, she would try to make her feel good, but however she tried, however gently she phrased her criticism, it would hurt knowing Stevie was trying to protect her feelings. This was it. She had finished. She was closing the cover. Lisa put a twisted bit of hair in her mouth and watched Stevie intently.

Stevie gently put the manuscript down on the bed and smiled at Lisa. "It's so good, Lisa. And it's a scream! What a funny girl you are. I really love it."

Lisa, brushing aside the balm of praise, grabbed her hair with both hands and twisted it ruthlessly into a knot. She stabbed the knot with a pencil and it held. "Really? You really like it? What parts don't you like? What's its biggest weakness? I really want you to tell me."

"Wait a minute." Stevie wrinkled up her brow as if she were concentrating deeply. "I thought I said I love it."

"Please," Lisa implored. "I can't believe it's *perfect*."

"Well, I don't know. Maybe the opening could move a little more quickly—"

"You mean at the beginning when the weather man does his report and the cameraman begins his stage-front commentary?"

"I'm not sure. Even as I'm telling you that, I don't know if that's right. That cameraman is a wonderful stroke."

"He's not too reminiscent of the stage manager in *Our Town?*"

"No. How interesting. I never saw any connection."

"Oh, good. I didn't borrow that device, at least I didn't do it *consciously*. I just got worried when I was rereading it during one of my endless revisions."

Stevie nodded as she listened to Lisa. Endless revisions over a period of what? Less than a month. Her energy was daunting. "Has anyone else seen it?" she asked.

"Well, it's really not absolutely finished. I've shown it to Reed, of course."

"And?"

"And he thought it was good too. He has been such an inspiration. Most people hear that you want to be a writer and they pat you on the head and say 'Good girl, but what do you really want to be?' But not Reed. He reads every word and is really *honest* with me. My mom loves what I write but not in a very critical way. And actually she would like my writing more if I were majoring in business administration."

"I don't get it." What a perfectionist this child was, Stevie thought with surprise. She discounts praise and adores criticism.

"Well, she won't discuss writing with me seriously. Or rather she did once or twice and when I wouldn't buy her version of how I ought to go forth into the world, the conversation about writing essentially shut down. She really can be a pain. She thinks financial success is everything and a good mile ahead of whatever is in second place."

"Are you sure that's it? I get the feeling she wants you to have every opportunity in the world."

"Yeah. That's what she calls money. Did she tell you about Reed?"

"A little," Stevie said truthfully.

"He's the most amazing man." Lisa sighed. "He's Swiss, you

know, or at least his parents were. He's very thin and hard and he has sandy-blond hair that he wears back like this," Lisa said, combing back her own hair mercilessly with her two hands. "He taught me how to ride when I was in high school." A burst of sunlight appeared before her eyes. She saw herself on Elvareen, that tricky bay, Reed snapping his crop against his leg in the center of the ring. "Mom's panicked because she thinks he's ruining my life. He's not ruining it, he's making it more wonderful." Reed. Two years and he still gave her the shivers. When she had been a student it had always been the horses first with him. He yelled at the girls, had pulled more than one from a horse if he didn't like the way she was treating it. But as stern as he was with the girls, he was so *different* with the horses. It was almost as if he had the power to see into their minds. He would slowly glide his hand over their hides, discovering bruises and scratches and knots. The horses would swing their big heads to look at him, but they let him touch them anywhere, do anything to them. How could she not have fantasized about having him touch her that way?

"Um, I don't want to be preachy," Stevie said, carefully considering each word, "but it seems to me almost any mother would panic if her daughter was having an affair with a married man, wouldn't you think? Lisa, you were in high school." What if Lisa were hers, for instance. She could imagine this Reed—lean, like his name, cruel, predatory—cheating on his soft, sweet wife, supping on this luscious . . . She would have to kill him. That's how Carol felt and she could see why.

"God. That's it. That's it exactly," Lisa said, shaking her head in disgust. "I can almost hear her voice saying that. 'My daughter seduced by a married man,' as if all married men were the same, and all of them contemptible and evil. First," Lisa said, bending back a finger, "he's getting a divorce. He was getting a divorce before we started dating. His wife is an emotional invalid. He is afraid to just leave her. He insists on leaving her in a decent way and honestly, I admire that. How could I respect any man who would walk away from a fifteen-year marriage just like that, especially when his wife doesn't work and doesn't know how to. I mean, if he would do that to *her*, wouldn't he do the same to me? Anyway, he isn't actually living with her anymore."

"When did this happen?" Stevie asked. Carol hadn't said Reed was separated.

"Last month," Lisa said defiantly, expecting response. When she got only a stare from Stevie, she continued. "So, if that still makes him a 'married man,' okay, but I think he's a separated man who will be divorced in a few months. My mother thinks this story of Reed's is all lies and that he is just stringing me along for sex. My mother is too hard on me, honestly. She's so protective, or scared or something. Maybe she's just insecure. My dad is just the complete opposite. He trusts me. He says nobody knows what's right for me more than I do. Anyway," Lisa added absently, "Reed didn't seduce me. I seduced him."

"Oh," said Stevie, suddenly embarrassed. She hadn't meant to get into this. Could she get out? She shook some crumbs from the bodice of her robe and straightened a wrinkle in the bedspread. The invocation of Andy caused Stevie to look again at Lisa, examine her for traces of a lost child. It was funny how much Lisa looked like Andy and how little she was like him. They had the same cheekbones, the same mouth, but the expressions on the two faces couldn't have been more different. He had been summer skies and mellow yellow. She was blue flame and persimmon. Lisa was a bonfire.

"I've made you uncomfortable," Lisa said, tearing the pencil out of her hair, bunching her forelock and holding it at the top of her head in a plume. Unbelievable. She could not talk about her mother's view of her life without going completely out of control. Stevie must think she was a maniac. "I'm sorry. This whole subject is one gigantic hot button with me. The *preju-*

*dice*, if you know what I mean. 'Married riding instructor seduces teenager' sounds contemptible. I'll bet Reed and I spent about a thousand hours sitting together on stable floors just talking before we ever went to bed. Reed never was the least bit aggressive. It was me. I couldn't stand it any longer. I knew I loved him, and that he loved me. Did you and Philip sit for a thousand hours talking before you went to bed?"

"No," said Stevie. Remembering that first time with Philip still made her suck in an imaginary breath. In an imperfect world, making love with Philip had been perfect. It had been very late in the night, no, the early morning of the next day, but still their third date. They had been in her living room looking out over Central Park, the mauve light of the New York City night sky outlining the rolling mass of treetops. They had been standing so close together she could not distinguish between the sound of her breathing and his. They hadn't touched at first, but still she could feel the electricity arcing between them. And then they had kissed, his lips barely brushing hers, then he had kissed her again. She had felt every part of her reaching to meet him. At their ages, anything less than everything would have been wrong. "But I'm . . ."

"Older than you," Lisa finished for her. "Oh God," she said, covering her mouth with her hands. "I'm so obnoxious."

Stevie's slow smile turned to laughter as she watched Lisa hide her head under a pillow. The funny thing was, it felt nice that Lisa could say anything to her. Didn't every mother want her daughter to feel so free? Her hand jerked suddenly at the unspoken thought. She blinked it away, made it never happen, then she playfully pulled the pillow away from Lisa's face. "Hello under there," she said. "What were you saying?"

"I forgot."

"Uh-huh."

"I did."

"I'm older than you," Stevie prompted.

Lisa sat up and sighed. She squashed a pillow into her lap. "What I was going to say in my typically understated way was that I feel old for my age. I've traveled. I've lived abroad. I've seen a lot of things. I know what I want. Reed isn't my first lover. Sleeping with Reed isn't terminal. Even marrying him isn't an irrevocable act."

Stevie sliced a pear and thought over what Lisa said. Lisa was certainly more sophisticated than she had been when she was that age. When she was that age she thought about baseball and Sigma Tau and Western Civ. And Andy. She put the pear back down on the plate and folded her hands loosely over her tummy. Hello in there, she thought quietly. The silent salutation, her first, seemed dense and real. Hello whoever you are. This is your mother. She could feel her heartbeat at her temples. She wasn't making this up, was she? She'd know soon. Tomorrow? She didn't feel crampy, but would she feel pangs tonight if she were getting her period tomorrow? She hadn't paid too much attention to her menstrual cycle in a few years, that was apparent. What was Lisa saying? Was she handling this conversation okay? Lisa seemed to be making sense.

"Mom thinks Reed is the one who is talking me into Sarah Lawrence," Lisa continued, twirling a strand of hair around her finger. "The truth is, I want to write plays, and Reed is encouraging me. I don't want to marry some businessman in a pinstriped suit and ulcerate myself to death. What I want to do with my life is first, win the Moira Glick competition. If my play is produced in New York, I will have a bona fide success behind me, and the beginning of my career. As a playwright I can live anywhere and Reed knows a place right outside Croton-on-Hudson where he can take over a stable and stock it. We can get a darling little house not too far from the stable and we can settle in. I can write and hang out at the stable, probably teach a few classes. And second, I want to have children. My mom had a very hard life raising me and working a million hours a week and honestly, she did great. No one could have done what she did. The thing is, I would like to do an even better job and I will be able to do it. We won't have a lot of money, but I'll have time to be home with my children, and that's an important difference between the way I was raised and how I would raise my own. And of course, my mother would be nearby. We could be a real family. I refuse to see what's so *awful* about all this." Again Lisa looked at Stevie again expecting combat and again receiving only a stare. Stevie was so great. She was willing to be open, to listen to her. If only her mother were so—so contemporary.

Stevie gaped at Lisa. What *was* so awful about that? She thought guiltily of Carol, who had hoped—given Stevie a mission almost—to steer Lisa onto a different path. How could she do that? Lisa wanted the little white house with a picket fence and babies. Lisa wanted the American Dream. Should she be denied that just because she possessed a genius IQ and a body like Christie Brinkley's?

Lisa's expression softened and became satisfied. "I rest my case," she said.

My God, Stevie thought. That's what I should have too. Marriage to a man I love, a baby, and my brilliant career. There wasn't even much to sacrifice. Small stuff, sure. But they both had money. She could afford as much help as she needed and Philip's apartment was like a house. Seven rooms was big enough for *three* kids. Two plus Kenny, if he wanted to stay. It was too bad Kenny was making life so difficult for Philip. Philip was beating himself up so much, he couldn't see how little he had to do with Kenny's rampage. If she told him what a great father he was and would be, he wouldn't believe her.

Stevie looked at Lisa, lying back against the pillow. How lucky Lisa was to have worked out so many of life's knots so early on. She was so wise for eighteen-about-to-be-nineteen. She was even pretty wise for forty. What do *you* think I should do about Philip, she wanted to ask. She turned off the stereo and picked up the remote control switch for the TV. "Hey, do you want to watch TV for a little while? There's a Steve McQueen movie on about now," she said. "I adore Steve McQueen, don't you?"

# 9

Philip hunched his back and tensed his muscles. He shifted his weight from one foot to the other, gathering himself, preparing himself for the furious black missile that would soon hurl itself in his direction. The ball slammed against the front wall within the red lines. Philip slapped his foot down and lunged. Good, he thought. Mallory hadn't blown a game once this week and Philip had become quite used to beating him two games out of every three they played. Mallory, that imp. He was so pleasant when he was winning; but how could he lose? He was playing squash four times a week now. Philip thought *he* could play squash four times a week if he wanted to, but this was supposed to be a game, not an obsession!

Philip blocked out the sounds that reverberated around him; the squeal of rubber heels, the smack of black balls against white walls, the curses and whoops of other players separated from his arena by thin inches. The ball came fast across the white cell, a movement more than a shape. Philip returned it with a satisfying swing, then positioned himself for the next one. Again, Mallory self-confidently smashed the ball, this time high on the left side of the front wall. Damn, Philip thought; he was having trouble returning with a tight backhand.

The ball slapped the side wall hard and hurtled toward Philip. He reached across his body, then clapped his hand to his chest, trying to contain the crushing pain that assailed him. Dimly he was aware that he had dropped his racquet, then he was on his knees, then his side, the muscles in his body paralyzed by the overpowering, immobilizing pain beneath his ribs. What had happened? What was going on? Had he been hit by the ball? He thought not. With sudden clarity, he realized that this was his heart! He was having a heart attack! Was he dying? As if from a distance, he heard Mallory questioning him. What had he been asked? I don't know, man, he answered silently, shaking his head heavily. Sure I'll lie here. I don't have anyplace to go. There was a sound, a motion. Philip turned his head. The pro was kneeling beside him murmuring reassurances. He liked Murray. He was glad Murray was here. He smiled at him. He felt someone take off his goggles. No, he thought. I can't see without those. I'll close my eyes, he decided. Someone put something under his neck. His mouth felt numb. There were little pinpricks dancing lightly across his fingertips. And the pain in his chest—it was so strong. He couldn't be dying because of a squash game. He wouldn't!

Something stopped. It was the sound, but he could not remember what it was. Air rushed around him and then new voices were there, hands handling him, one, two, three, and lift. We've got you. He opened his eyes and still everything was a blur. "I'm okay, Jimmy," he said to Mallory. "Do you want me to call someone?" he heard Mallory ask. Who? Stevie. He didn't want to scare her yet, but he needed her. Kenny would be helpless. He wanted to ask his father . . . Dad had died of a heart attack—he had died at fifty-three. Wait a minute. He had seven more years! If only he had his glasses. He could visualize his glasses in a black pouch in his locker. He felt movement, then a thud and the creak of metal doors closing. They were in the ambulance now. Ouch. "What's that?" he asked.

"It's an IV," said a raspy voice belonging to the dark-haired, bulky man-shaped blur to his right. "We just want to have an open vein if we need it."

"What?"

"Tell me where it hurts."

"Here," Philip said, lifting an arm, numb and heavy, sweeping it across his breastbone, "and I've got pins and needles. Am I, did I have a heart attack?"

"We're checking you out right now," said another voice. "Just be calm. Try to imagine the ocean, Mr. Durfee. Go to the beach, okay? I'm connecting up some electrodes here," the voice said. "You got it, John?" Philip felt a sticky sensation at his ankles and then at his wrists.

"This is going to feel a little cold," the husky voice said. "Just a little sea spray." Something wet was dotted across his chest. "When did the pains start?" a different voice asked.

"I don't know," Philip said. "Just a few minutes ago, I think." Philip listened futilely for the sounds of waves. "I wish I had my glasses," he said.

"Just relax, please, Mr. Durfee. Don't try to sit up. Have you ever had pains like these before?"

The pain, never. But the pinpricks, the numbness around his mouth. Hadn't he felt something like that after Kenny had been mugged? He thought so, but the pain? No. "Never. Is this a heart attack?"

"Well, whatever you had, you're not having it now. Okay, we're here. We're going to take you inside."

"I have to call someone."

"Sure thing. Jerry, fasten that strap down there, willya? Got him? Okay, go."

Philip felt cold everywhere. Was he going to die? What kind of way was this to go? It was a cliché way to die. It was boring. He was only forty-six! They said he wasn't still having an attack. Still, after the first one, your time was just days counting down. "I'm cold," he said out loud. Then he felt the stretcher bump, and his body lifted to a hard platform under a bright white light.

With two snaps, Dr. John Wrobleski shucked his rubber gloves and, banging open the waste bin, dropped them in. There was blood on the fingertips! It seemed to get dark for a minute, but Stevie pulled herself back into the stainless-steel-lined room. "You've begun menstruating," Dr. Wrobleski said in a quiet voice. Stevie blinked at the quilted sailboats twirling above her. "You've begun your period." Wrobleski dropped the speculum into the sterilizer. "When you're dressed," he said softly, "come into my office."

Stevie lay still for a moment watching the child's mobile bobbing overhead. She placed her hand over her stomach and held it there. How could she be so sad? This was nothing. She had thought she was pregnant for a little over a week and she wasn't. No damage was done, yet she felt so lost, so alone. Those little conversations with her "baby" were what now? Neurotic. Talking to herself. She squeezed her eyes shut. In her head, she saw the bloody gloves, so like another pair, scraping, scraping, her mind at that time spinning away from her, yet caught, a bird with its leg tied to a string.

Stevie sat up slowly and slid gingerly from the examination table. She walked into the small adjoining bathroom, innocent and white-tiled. How could she have been so wrong? She wasn't crazy. Her body had seemed so soft. And she had counted backward and forward so many times, each time adding up the right number of days. She could have conceived!

Her clothes dangled from the hooks upon which she had hung them twenty minutes before. She taped a pad to her underwear and drew her dress on over her head. She looked into the mirror hanging over the basin. She hadn't changed. She didn't look like a woman who had made up a child. She tucked a hank of hair behind her ear and pulled her pearls out from under her neckline.

She had been so certain she was pregnant, she had wanted to tell people. "Thanks for the coffee, but I don't drink caffeine anymore. I'm having a baby." "Hi, folks, before I start tonight's show, I have something to tell you. Guess what. I'm pregnant." Now she wasn't. She splashed cold water on her face and patted it dry with a paper towel that felt as if it had been peeled from a sheet of corrugated cardboard. She had felt so alive and now she felt so tired. Of course she was sad, but don't forget that silver lining, Nana would say. Okay, she wasn't pregnant this month. It was just as well. No, it was good. She stepped into one shoe and then the other. This nonpregnancy had revealed something very important to her. She wanted, really wanted, to have a baby. She wouldn't have to plunge Philip into a panic. They wouldn't have to elope. She wouldn't have to get married in a white lace potato sack. She would talk to Philip, which was really the best and only thing to do. She would tell Philip she wanted to have a baby, was meant to have one, and had to make plans. She opened the door and walked down the hall to Dr. Wrobleski's office.

The doctor's office was paneled with mahogany and the wood of his desk, too, was dark and red. She sat in a leather-padded

chair and faced him. He was toying with his glasses and looking at Stevie with a smile. "Let's see," he said, opening up the
manila folder in front of him, pressing his glasses onto the
bridge of his nose, raising his eyebrows automatically as he did
so. "I prescribed Conceptrol three months ago. And you're not
happy with it?"

"I'm sorry?" Stevie replied. She stopped staring at the doctor's face and dropped her gaze to the three-dimensional plastic
reproductive tract on the desk between them. As she watched,
Dr. Wrobleski engulfed the model with one of his large hands.
She tried to assemble her thoughts. He had never looked like a
gynecologist to her. He looked like a lumberjack with a bowtie
and someone else's doctor jacket.

"You've just had a birthday. Let's see. Nineteen forty-nine.
That makes you thirty-nine."

"Thank you," she said absently. "I don't understand. Why
did my body feel so different this month? Was I hallucinat-
ing?"

"The breast tenderness and so on?"

"Yes, mostly that, and the dizziness and nausea."

"Well, I've seen women with their stomachs out to here, and
you tap on the abdomen wall and it could be a drum. There's
nothing in there but air."

"John, I hope you aren't telling me I had an imaginary epi-
sode. I'm not the hysterical type."

"No, no. I'm sorry, Stephanie. I didn't mean to imply that.
Most likely you had a little hormonal rush of some sort. We
don't always understand the reasons for these things." Wrobleski tinkered with the model and then, as if he was still, after all
these years, perplexed, set it aside. He folded his hands and
leaned forward, resting heavily on his arms. "The stage of your
menstrual cycle can sometimes cause the symptoms you describe.
And don't bite my head off, now, but fantasizing, focusing if
you wish, can make you more sensitive to your body than you

might be otherwise. You seem to be disappointed that you aren't pregnant."

Stevie sniffed and lowered her eyes. "I'm not disappointed, just surprised. I was so sure." Stevie looked up, almost daring him to disagree.

Wrobleski leaned back in his chair. "So where do we go from here?"

Stevie didn't reply.

"What was it that you didn't like about Conceptrol?"

"John, I think I want to have a baby."

"Nothing wrong with that. Are you getting married?"

"I don't know. I want to."

"I see. I think I see. You've been seeing someone steadily."

Stevie nodded. "Yes. Seriously. I suppose I should get you to recommend something easier to deal with than what I'm using until I can speak to Philip, talk to him about . . . this. What do you think of the sponge? My best friend uses it and she likes it."

"Actually, Stephanie, preventing conception will be a good deal easier than conceiving."

"I'm sorry. What did you say?" Stevie looked around his office. There seemed to be an awful lot of diplomas in here.

"Well, your health is good. You may have some trouble conceiving, but only the normal trouble, nothing out of the ordinary."

"What do you mean, trouble?"

"Well, surely you know that as a woman gets older, she becomes less fertile."

"Yes, I suppose I knew that." Stevie grabbed a piece of her lower lip with her teeth and worried it.

Wrobleski riffled Stevie's file. "Ninety percent of all women up to the age of twenty-five are fertile. After that, the percentage decreases until at the age of forty, only ten percent of the female population can conceive."

"Forty. Actually? That number? Does your body know when your birthday is?"

"Strange but true," he said.

"Another one of those things the medical profession doesn't understand?"

"I'm afraid so."

"But why? What happens? You mean a heavy metal gate clamps down over the Fallopian tubes at forty and you don't know why?"

"It's a combination of factors, not just the age itself. It has to do with whatever time has done to the body during those forty years and the level of estrogen production and the condition of the ova. But I don't mean to worry you, Stephanie. Just call this an alert." The doctor cleared his throat. "You know we've talked about this before. You have never seemed interested in having a baby."

Stevie stared at the doctor. What color alert? Yellow. She still had time. "Well, I have some time, anyway."

"Yes, you do. And I hope this relationship works out for you. I would like very much to deliver your baby," he said, cupping his hands and drawing them to him.

Stevie's eyes flooded with tears. The sound of those words spoken out loud, overwhelmed her with longing. She could almost see those large lumberjack hands cradling a new baby, taking it from her body, bringing it into the world. Stevie blinked her eyes and plucked a tissue from a box on Wrobleski's desk.

"Should the relationship not work out, and should you still wish to have a child, we will be happy to inseminate you here."

What had he said? He would inseminate her? Oh. He meant artificial insemination. God. This was too much too soon. A half hour ago she had thought she was pregnant.

"Right here, in our offices. I enjoyed your show, by the way, the one on sperm banks."

"Thanks," Stevie said faintly. Standing, she thought about what Dr. Wrobleski had said. Artificial insemination? Surely it wouldn't come to that. She would talk to Philip. Tonight maybe. Pam was wrong about Philip. She knew him better than Pam did. She hoped. Would he bolt if she started talking about having a baby? He hadn't even said he would marry her. What he had said was, "Not yet." Maybe they didn't have the luxury of waiting until the time was perfectly right. She heard the clank of a metal gate crashing down on her Fallopian tubes and did not hear Dr. Wrobleski's farewell. She opened the office door, then closed it behind her. It was definitely time to talk with Philip.

Carol flipped through the fat copy of *Harper's Bazaar*. She couldn't look at the photos, couldn't read the tiny printed words. She had chewed her lips ragged. A cigarette, a cigarette, my kingdom for a cigarette, she thought. Dr. Arundel, a man who had been talked about in her office and around town as being awfully good, had been called into emergency surgery and here she was waiting for a Dr. Wilson, a junior associate or some damn thing, and she didn't even know what she was going to say to him. In twenty-five words or less? Make me younger. "Ms. Wilder," the chipper, overweight young receptionist called out. "Will you follow me?"

Carol stood on legs that moments before had had no problem bearing her weight, and followed the swaying form before her.

"Here we go, room one, that will be your gown on the table." She gave Carol a bright smile and spun a length of paper from a roll, fastening it to the foot end of the examination table.

"You know, I really think I ought to make another appointment with Dr. Arundel."

"Ms. Wilder, like I told you, he won't have an availability until this October and besides, you might as well talk to Dr.

Wilson. As long as you're here. He's really very nice. Now, you put the gown on and the doctor will be with you in a minute." She gave Carol a toothy smile and closed the door.

Might as well. Might as well leave and have a good breakfast, and go back to work. On the other hand, if she could look younger . . . She took off her clothing one article at a time and hung it on a peg rack. The cotton robe provided little warmth in the chilly room. Crossing her arms over her breasts, she sat awkwardly at the edge of the steel table. She was looking at the door when it opened and Dr. Wilson stepped in. His smile, his upturned, guileless smile, was the first thing Carol noticed. Then she took in his healthy pink skin and masses of uncontrollable red hair. Then she estimated his age. He was twenty-five.

"Hello," he said, pulling up a stool, swiveling it up to its highest position, and sitting on it. "I'm Stan Wilson," he said putting out his hand and shaking hers.

"Hello," Carol said faintly. He was dressed and she was wearing a thin blue nightie. She wasn't going to let this boy examine her.

"So, how do you feel?"

"I'm fine, how are you?"

Wilson laughed. "That wasn't a rhetorical question. I mean, how do you feel physically? How is your health as far as you know?"

"My health is just dandy," said Carol, "but look here. I think I'd like to wait to see Dr. Arundel. No offense. He's been recommended to me by several people and as you know, I didn't know he wouldn't be here today."

"I look too young, is that it? I should tell you that Dr. Arundel would see you and perform any surgery. I'm just filling in for now."

Carol looked down at her legs. They were swinging.

"How old do you think I am?"

"I beg your pardon. I don't know."

"Take a guess."

"Twenty."

Wilson laughed again. "I'm thirty-two and I can prove it."

Carol smiled. "I'm sorry, I must seem awfully rude." There wouldn't be any harm in just asking about her eyes. "I'd like to talk with you about my eyes."

"That will be fine, Mrs. Wilder."

"Carol."

"Carol. Let me take a look." He moved his stool closer to her and gently touched her face with his hand. He lifted her eyelids, moved the skin under her eyes, and then folded his arms across his chest. "Was that a test of some sort?"

"Pardon me?"

"I can't see anything wrong with your eyes. What did you have in mind?"

"Don't you think my eyes look awfully wrinkled? Look here," she said, pulling the skin up at the corners. "Doesn't that look much better?"

"It makes you look like you had very bad eye surgery or have a very tight ponytail."

Carol released her skin.

"Come over here," Dr. Wilson said, walking Carol over to the mirror hanging on the wall. "Look at this. These dark circles under your eyes, which is what I think you're worried about, are not surgically correctable. They're simply blood vessels under your skin, and many, many people have dark circles. Dark circles are more evident when a person is under a lot of stress and not getting enough sleep. How do you come out in those areas?"

"I'm under pressure all day and I don't sleep two straight hours the whole damned night." Carol turned from the mirror and sat again on the examination table.

"What business are you in?"

"Real estate."

"Well, it wouldn't be a bad idea to tell the boss you're ill and take some time off."

"I am the boss."

"Well, that's even simpler, then. Carol, take some time off."

"I'll think about it." The nerve. Take some time off, he said. And who would make the money to pay the mortgage and keep Lisa in school?

"I can't help but notice you are wearing one of our gowns."

"What good eyes you have, doctor."

"They are very good. And we don't ask our patients to change into them for eye examinations."

"Uh-huh," Carol acquiesced nervously. He'd better not want to see anything else.

"So I suspect you had something else on your mind."

"An overhaul, I suppose."

"An overhaul?"

"The whole damned thing," Carol said sheepishly. "Boobs, belly, and any floppy thing else."

"Hmm," Wilson said, cupping his chin with his hand. "Mind if I examine you?"

"Not at all," Carol said, "as long as you do it without looking at me."

Wilson laughed. "It's a deal," he said. "I'm just going to loosen the top of your gown, and would you mind holding this part for me?" he asked, folding the top down and putting the cloth in her hands.

Carol held her breath. Was she really letting him do this? This examination was so different from going to a GP or a GYN. He was looking at her breasts, comparing them with others he'd seen. He wasn't going to stick a stethoscope onto her ribs and ask her to cough. God, this was taking a long time. She couldn't look down. She gazed over the top of Wilson's field of curly red hair and tried thinking about her garden under the maple tree. Maybe she could try some trillium next spring. The white kind with the specks of red . . .

"All right now, I'm going to fasten this back up again," he said, and did, "and I'm just going to ask you to stand up for a second. Good. And will you help me out again and hold this?" he asked, handing her the hem of the gown.

Carol felt his warm fingers as he touched her scar at its apex. He palpated her tummy with a sure hand, then Carol felt the curtain of fabric return.

"Good, Carol, very good. If you'd feel more comfortable, put your clothes on and meet me in my office when you're ready."

Carol nodded. She hadn't been looked at by such a young man since she was thirty-two herself. She felt awkward and exposed. He must think her body hideous. With rushed movements, she dressed and with some course correction from the receptionist, she found Wilson in his office.

"I've got a few things for you to look at," he said, looking up as Carol sat down. He pushed a book toward her, a book filled with photographs of women taken from neck to waist, front view and profile, and evidently before and after. Fascinated, Carol turned the pages. In some ways it was almost prurient to be looking at the women this way. They couldn't cover themselves. Yet how interesting it was to see how her breasts compared with others. Carol turned page after page and as she did so, an idea dawned. The breasts in the before pictures seemed more distressed than hers, more in need of rescue. How could she say this? She looked up at Wilson, who was looking at her.

"Your breasts are fine," he said. "Aren't they?"

Carol nodded slowly.

"We could enlarge them, I suppose, if you really wanted us to, but your breasts are in proportion to your body shape. That scar, by the way, is that what you were talking about when you mentioned your belly?"

"Yes, isn't it awful?"

"No. You had an operation and it left a scar. Excising it would create another scar. Carol, forgive me for saying this, but you've got a strong healthy body, and there is nothing I would do to change it."

Carol blinked. He wouldn't change it. She felt relief and something that felt surprisingly like disappointment. If he wouldn't change it, how could she look younger? And if she couldn't look younger, how could she change her life?

"You know, many times when people come in for plastic surgery, they have a sort of fantasy about how their life would be if only they looked different. I know that isn't you, Carol. You've probably been influenced by this whole out-of-proportion youth mode of which our affluent society is so enamored."

Carol looked at her lap and nodded her head. "I have been feeling like I kind of looked a little bit old lately," she admitted.

"It's a damned shame," Wilson said. "I hope you'll take my advice and give yourself a rest. Will you?"

Carol nodded without looking at him.

"I don't know if this examination has made you feel better or worse, but I hope better."

Carol looked up, remembered how to smile, and said, "Much better, of course, Dr. Wilson. Stan. I feel fine now. And thank you." She stood and shook his hand, then turned and left his office.

On the street, she found the keys to her car, and once inside she put her head on the steering wheel and let the tears come. What in the world is the matter with me? she wondered, dabbing at her face, starting the car. What in the world?

Dr. Ragneesh was small, his skin the color of ripe plums. His voice was a singsong, pleasant to the ear but hard to understand. For the dozenth time, Philip wished he could see, but he knew it would be far more productive to just blow in the paper bag as he'd been told. In, out, in, out, he'd been doing this for ages while again, clammy electrodes had been pasted on his extremities.

"Very good, Mr. Durfee," the doctor crooned gently, taking the bag from Philip's hands. "I am happy to tell you you are still of this earth."

"I'm sorry," Philip began. "I'm all right?"

"Very all right, Mr. Durfee. It was not a heart attack at all," he sang, his words flowing together melodically.

Philip felt relief, then a burst of anger. "I don't get it," he snapped. Did this guy know what he was talking about?

"Please relax for a little while. Don't move yourself and I will explain. The pain?"

"Yes," Philip said. He searched, moving his hand across his chest. It was gone. "It's gone," he said dully.

"It was some hyperventilating, Mr. Durfee. You are just fine, but this anxiety was caused by something, yes? Something troubling you."

"I was playing squash."

"Yes, that I know. It was a very important game?"

"No," Philip admitted.

"Ah. You have been troubled about other things. You see I ask this because this hyperventilating, this rapid breathing, is a stress symptom, and it can cause this very frightening pain. Very common, but still very frightening."

"But I don't remember hyperventilating. I just remember a crushing pain and these pins and needles."

"Parasthesia, that is called."

"Oh," Philip said. Was he nuts? The doctor was telling him he was fine, and he was as pissed as if something had been taken from him. Thank God he hadn't called Stevie. She would have been upset and this, this stress symptom, was nothing. Embarrassing, really.

"But we shouldn't ignore this stress, Mr. Durfee. Would you

try to sit up now? Very slowly. That is good. Your body is telling you to slow down. Change something. I am going to recommend that you see your own doctor, and get a complete physical work-up. There is a slight, very slight pulse irregularity here. I would like you to have it checked over, but for now I think the best medicine is to isolate the cause of this stress, Mr. Durfee. And when you have done that, you must make it disappear."

Philip watched the doctor's hands as he tore off the sheet of cardiograph paper. Unconsciously, Philip touched his hand to his chest. Isolate the cause of his stress, the doctor had said. He could do that. It was Kenny.

# 10

Pam leaned against the inside of the bathroom door and held the vial to the light. Had the fluid changed from ruby red to a grayer tone? How could she know? Please God, no, she prayed. If she held the vial to the light, the color wasn't really red, but if she put the little glass tube in front of something white, like the bathtowel, it *was* red, damn it, red, not gray-red. How could she be pregnant? How had it happened? And yet even as she asked her incredulous self the awful question, she knew the moment, the very moment it had happened: two weeks and one, two, three nights on top of that. She and Willy had gone out with the Simons for barbecued spare ribs and beer. When they had returned to Brooklyn Heights, boozy and weak, Pam had peeled her clothing off in one piece and fallen into bed. The contraceptive sponge? The bathroom had been as far away as Kenya. Why was it that Willy liked to make love on a full stomach? "The sponge," she had sputtered, too late. "Don't worry," he had said, sated, nuzzling his face into the soft place under her ear, "I told my sperm to swim backward."

"Oh God," Pam wailed behind her hand. What was she going to do now? She snapped off the bathroom light and opened the door. Leaning in the doorway, she watched her sleeping husband in the dim light. One hand loosely fell across his chest, the other hung out of the bed. Pam clapped her hand to her face and shook her head. What was she going to do? It would be a cute baby, and Willy would be the best father. The best. And she? She would strangle her career as surely as if she took a noose to its neck.

Stevie had started out just as Pam was starting out now. It wasn't that Pam wanted to be a talk show host, not that she wanted to be on camera at all. She just wanted to produce, maybe direct. She wanted options, not just with Stevie's show, but with network shows, and you didn't get ahead in television by racing home by three to pick Chipper up from school. Pam shook her head again. It was more than wanting to be a top producer, it was wanting to be free to work all night, weekends, devote herself to her job.

Willy stirred. "Hon, is it time?"

"It's only six," she said. "Go back to sleep." She walked to the bed and placed his dangling arm back under the sheet. Willy reached for her, kissed her, and then, enveloping a pillow, rolled over onto his side.

Pam took a clean tee shirt out of a drawer and lifted her jeans from a hook behind the door. She put the clothes on and padded out to the kitchen. What to do, she thought, filling the coffee filter with coffee, running cold water into the coffee pot.

What to do. Be a part-time mom? Be a part-time mom to Chipper? Or devote herself to Chip and watch Stevie on television and be the good, how-was-your-day-honey wife when Willy came home. She took a loaf of zucchini bread out of the freezer and popped it into the microwave oven. "Bippity-bap," she said quietly, touching the buttons.

Imagine having a husband who made zucchini bread. And collected cat's-eye marbles to hold flowers, and never forgot how much she liked to be kissed just behind her ear. It almost made her cry. The best man in the whole world, and here she was pregnant with a child that would make this man's happiness complete and she was thinking of herself. Her self.

Pam tested the bread, sliced a thin piece, and brought it and the coffee to the morning-lit kitchen table. She had to think about herself. You weren't supposed to sacrifice yourself to have a child. It was supposed to be a joyful, fulfilling experience. And the child had to be considered.

A cloud of memory surrounded Pamela. She was back at P.S. 11 on West 21st Street. She could still see the tiny terrified faces so clearly, children of two-working-parent homes, dropped off at school before class started as their parents raced to their jobs, left at the school long after three, placed in "after school programs" which turned teachers into babysitters. She thought of those six-year-olds who had been "her" children, thought of the desperation so many of them felt, abandoned by their parents, scheduled into activities in lieu of backyards, cramming their needs into "quality time," the only time their mothers and fathers could find to spend with their offspring. A child should have a full-time parent, Pam had felt then and now. Quality time was an impossible goal. Quantity time was the only valid time, time to be real with a child, true to the child's needs and the parent's too. With the two of them working, Pam could only have one of those needy children and that, she felt adamantly, was unacceptable.

Damn, why had she been so stupid? The timing of this pregnancy was so wrong. She was so happy in her work finally. No more "kids," no more apprenticeship at the station, she was a professional now. People knew her and relied on her. She was getting a reputation. She was really on her way. What if she had an abortion? No one would know. Pam put the damp bread down on the plate untasted. She would know. She would know that she had killed something, someone that could positively transform her husband's life. By aborting, she would be betraying Willy, that's what she would be doing. Could she risk asking him how he would feel if she aborted? Could she risk letting this be a joint decision? She lifted the bread to her mouth and chewed as she thought.

Willy, she would say, I want you to think about what I'm going to tell you before you react. Just think. You know I don't feel ready to have a baby yet. You know that. She could imagine him tensing, the idea growing before she could even phrase the question. I'm pregnant but I'd like us to consider aborting. Ridiculous. He'd never agree. Never. And even asking him to consider would be to invite him to join the awful struggle of choosing his happiness over hers. Was it even fair to tell him? Right now, this minuscule clump of cells was an option. She could take it, or she could reject it. It was up to her.

"A pot of coffee, zucchini bread, and thou," Willy sang from the doorway. "Is it great to be alive, or what?"

Philip sat in a clothing-strewn chair in his son's room. "Your eye looks better."

"Yeah," he said. "I guess so." Kenny slid a video game into the computer and the game came on with a little tootling fanfare. "You okay?" he asked his father without looking over his shoulder.

"Yeah, I guess so."

Kenny turned a little and gave his father a sympathetic look. "Have you been working too hard or something?"

"Yup, that's what the doctor said. He said I shouldn't worry so much."

Kenny nodded, absorbed in the game. Philip stood up and walked over to the computer. Ignoring the game in progress, still trying to engage his son, he asked, "How is your sister?"

"She's okay."

"What do you think of her husband?"

"Hank? He's okay."

Philip nodded. "I wish I had a picture of Tara. I haven't seen her in so many years. Do you have one?"

"A picture of my sister?" Kenny looked incredulous. "Who has a picture of their sister? If you want to know what she looks like, just imagine a fat married lady. That's her."

Philip could not imagine the little girl he'd sired now a fat married lady. No one in his family was fat, yet Kenny hardly resembled him either. Not that he doubted his paternity; Kenny's eyes and nose were indisputably Durfee features. Philip sighed and shifted to another foot. He let his hand drape in front of the monitor so Kenny would be forced to look at him. "Stevie's coming over. We're going to make barbecued chicken."

"Dad . . ."

"I know, I know. I wish you'd change your mind."

"I just want to fool around in here for a while. Then I'm going out with the guys to *The Rocky Horror Picture Show*."

"Kenny, I want you to do me a favor."

"Sure," Kenny said, dropping his hands into his lap, looking his father full in the face.

"I want you to be scrupulously careful. No more accidents, okay?"

"Dad, they were *accidents*."

"I know, but no more. Is it a deal?"

"Deal," Kenny said. The two men shook hands. Kenny wondered once again how he was supposed to decide. His mother was nagging, nagging, nagging. Change his name. Change it to O'Brien. "Danny has been your father for your whole life," she kept saying. "Your real father deserted you." Kenny had never been sure his nutty mother had been right, but he had wanted to see. Now, after spending time with Philip, he was more confused. He appreciated Philip but he didn't feel like they were father and son. He still wasn't sure Philip even loved him. "Dad, if I don't want to go back to Encino, is it all right with you? I've been thinking maybe I could bum around at the warehouse for a while and get into school in the City in the fall." He couldn't believe he had said that. He looked nervously away from Philip's changing expressions of surprise and concern.

"Well, Kenny, sure. I mean, it's a big issue that concerns a lot of people. Your mother is still your legal guardian."

He doesn't want me, Kenny thought angrily. He should have said yes. He should have said yes, I'll take care of it.

"Let's talk about this more when we've both had time to think about it," Philip said. No, no, no, he thought. I cannot keep this boy. "Don't forget our deal," he added guiltily. Kenny nodded and restarted the video game. Philip closed the door softly behind him.

"I want you to go in and say good night to Stevie," she overheard Philip say to Kenny. Kenny was a towering hulk in the doorway, one large hand held open the door, the collar of his denim jacket was pulled up around his face.

"Dad!" Kenny protested.

"Go on," Philip insisted. "She's not going to faint."

Kenny closed the door and walked into the dining room. "Hi," he said, eyes downcast.

"Wow," Stevie said. "Some eye."

"Yeah," Kenny replied with a grin. "Spoils my otherwise totally cool looks."

Stevie smiled at him. "You'll be handsome again before you know it. Where are you off to?"

"Movie," Kenny said. "I gotta be going." He lifted a hand, a minimal wave good-bye.

"Good night, son," Philip said.

"Have fun," Stevie added. They waited until the door closed, then they looked at each other. Philip pulled out a chair and sat down in front of the remains of their meal. "It's normal for a kid his age to want to be with other kids his age," Stevie said. "This is not a rejection."

"I know," Philip said with a sigh. "What a week." ·

"Yeah," Stevie said, "but you're both all right now. Sit there. Let me take care of these," She reached for his plate to clear it from the table. "Go into the living room. Have some brandy. I'll be there in a minute." Stevie watched Philip rise tiredly and leave the room.

She brought the plates into the kitchen. This kitchen was a marvel. It was vast and well-lit, with a huge butcher-block work station in the middle of the white-tiled walls, high ceilings, every kind of pot and cooking utensil anyone could imagine. Contrasting wonderfully with the old-style charm were electronic gadgets nestled under the counters. Stevie rinsed and stacked the dishes in the dishwasher. Philip had had a rude scare and he felt so depressed. She had wanted to tell him about her appointment with Wrobleski, but the conversation could not go that way. Maybe after they had had something to drink. Maybe when the lights were out and they were touching. She turned on the dishwasher, turned off the kitchen light. Taking a lit candle in its holder from the table, she doused the dining room light too, and then joined Philip in the living room.

He was lying full-length on the sofa. A new electronic light sculpture replaced the one Kenny had broken and it was casting a soft blue light in the room. Stevie put the candle on the coffee table next to the brandy snifters, and at Philip's beckoning gesture, kicked off her shoes, snuggled beside him, and wove her arms and legs through his. They sighed together as one, looked at each other and laughed a little, hugged, and went into their own thoughts. Stevie looked across Philip's chest, past the flickering lights, to the large plate glass window which faced the river. She loved this apartment. Her own apartment was lush and modern, but Philip's seven rooms felt like a house to her, a home. His bookshelves, unlike hers, had age and permanence. The books had weathered twenty years in this one place. His carpets were old Orientals upon which his children had played. The doors closed with a heavy sound, the floors slanted in different directions, the high ceilings made the rooms feel so large. One could really imagine raising children in this apartment. There was a Mommy and Daddy room, a kid number one room, a kid number two room, and—luxury of luxuries—a maid's room to be imagined in this context as a nanny's room. "I love this apartment," Stevie said.

"Mmmm," Philip said, stroking her arm. "I'm getting a little sick of it, to tell the truth."

"You are?" Stevie asked, alarmed.

"So many rooms collect so many things. I don't know why I've kept this place so long. The river, I guess. I like the river."

"Philip. The kitchen, the fireplace. The library."

"Mmm. I think I want to move to Soho. Get a really big space, a loft, you know?"

Stevie nodded and tried to breathe. He was thinking of moving? Since when?

"Imagine three or four thousand feet, really clean space, polished floors, lots of sun. There's lots of sun downtown. I'd like that. And I could have some partitions built for storage, leave the kitchen wide open, just part of the room, and get this, Stevie. I love this idea. No bedroom. I could build the bed inside a sort of a big box with blinds and built-in electronics. Then I could put the box on wheels. I could move the bed anywhere in the space, change the view, hide it, anything. I'd get one of those industrial air cleaners to keep dust out of the air, not that there is very much dust downtown. Get up in the morning, say hello to the sun, run out to Dean and DeLuca and get baguettes and coffee beans. What do you think, honey? Doesn't that sound more like me than all of this?"

"I'm not sure. I like this."

"I bet you could like it down there too." He lifted one of her hands and matched his fingers against hers. "Instead of going to Connecticut one weekend, we'll look at lofts, okay?"

"Mmm hmm," she murmured, pushing her fingers against his, then lowering her arm, pressing her cheek into his chest.

"Hey," he said. "Is something wrong?"

She shook her head against him. Everything's wrong, she thought. A big bed on wheels? And what else? A little bed on wheels too? She took a deep breath and exhaled. Her fingers sought entry between the buttons of Philip's shirt. When they found skin, they rested. She loved this man, really loved him. If she told him what was on her mind, he would jump out of his skin.

"You're fibbing."

Stevie tapped his chest. It was unfair to unload her fears on Philip after the week he'd had. But maybe not. Maybe it was more unfair to keep everything to herself. "I thought I was pregnant," she said in a quiet voice. "But I'm not."

"Steve! Good God," he said. "You're sure you're not?"

"Yes."

"Oh. Good. Thank God. That would have about done me in, hon. A mugging, an anxiety attack, and an unwanted pregnancy in one week. Hey," he said shaking her. "Steve, are you crying?"

A wave of tremendous sadness swept over her. For a short

time she had felt so special, so privileged, to be carrying the beginnings of a precious child. The loss of that feeling had barely been absorbed and the absorption had been aided, she knew, by a fantasy: that Philip would want a baby too. Now even the fantasy was lost. Stevie pressed her face to Philip's chest and sobbed. Her sobs turned into heaving sighs as Philip rocked her. He tilted her face to him with one hand. "I wanted to be pregnant," she said thickly.

"You what? What do you mean?"

"When I thought I was, I was happy." She turned her face into his chest and sobbed anew.

"Here. Hon," he said, handing her his handkerchief, "I'm sorry. I'm so suprised. Come on now. Talk to me."

Stevie blew her nose and tried to speak. "I went to the doctor and he told me if I didn't get going I could forget about ever having a baby."

"I'm sorry, Steve, but where did this all come from? We talked about babies on about our first date, and you said you weren't interested. I remember distinctly."

"I guess I changed my mind since I fell in love with you."

"Are you sure that's it?"

Stevie shrugged and blew her nose again. The inside of her mouth was gummy and she couldn't breathe out of her nose. "I can't breathe out of my nose."

"It's okay. It's nature's way of doing something or other."

Stevie smiled. She loved him. She did. She hadn't loved anyone as much since Andy. And she had wanted to have his baby too. Love. Baby. They went together. It was a way of expressing love.

"I think you're feeling competitive with Carol."

"I am not! That's ridiculous." Stevie got up on one elbow and pushed at Philip's chest. "I love you. There's nothing too abnormal about wanting to be pregnant by the man you love."

"I'm not saying it's abnormal. I'm saying it's sudden."

"I'm not feeling competitive with Carol."

"Lie down."

Stevie complied. She crossed her feet at the ankles and folded her arms over her chest. "I can't believe you think I'm that shallow, that easily influenced."

"Okay. Maybe that's not it."

Stevie nodded, satisfied. She uncrossed her arms.

"If it's not Carol, it's Lisa."

"What? What are you saying? I'm competitive with Lisa?"

"No. I think being with Lisa has made you want to have a child of your own."

Something felt right about that. Stevie stared at the flickering of light on the ceiling. If that was right, what did it mean? "Why are we analyzing me, I want to know?" she said, thrusting out her chin, staring Philip in the face. "We didn't analyze your 'heart attack' into little tiny pieces." Philip lowered his head. She had hurt him. "Oh. I'm sorry." She hugged him. "That was mean."

"It's okay. I'm sorry too. I'm not being very sensitive, am I?"

Stevie was quiet. She was waiting. Whatever he said next would be very important.

"Having a child would be so wrong for me and I'm frightened that if you want one, we are going to have problems. I love you so much, you see." He wrapped his arms all the way around her and buried his face in her hair. She snuggled into him and held him tightly. Then she listened to the sound of her beating heart. She didn't remember closing her eyes but when morning light filled the room, Stevie found that she had slept the whole night in Philip's arms and she was even more frightened now than she had been before.

# 11

"I've got to admit, when you're right, you're right," Lisa said, getting the milk out of the refrigerator. It was such a relief that her mother had stopped giving her a hard time about things. Once she got her job at WON-TV, everything else was okay. It was sort of amazing, but their relationship was actually improving. "This job is the greatest thing I could ever have done, Mom. I'm really loving it."

"Thanks, honey. That makes me feel good." Carol poured milk onto her cereal and passed the carton to her daughter. Was she going crazy? She had woken up this morning thinking her hand was entwined in red curly hair. But when she opened her eyes her hand was simply numb from being all twisted up under the pillow. She was disappointed, but my God, what a dumb, impossible fantasy. Not only was he too young for her, he was a doctor for Christ's sake, and she was a patient. But was she really a patient? She had gone for a consultation but she hadn't been treated. What was that patient-doctor thing all about anyway? Was it illegal? Don't be ridiculous, she admonished herself. You wouldn't go to jail for going out with your doctor. Probably it was some ethical thing. Could the doctor lose his license? Stan Wilson. She sighed loudly without being aware she was doing so.

"What was that for?" Lisa asked, looking over her spoon.

"Nothing," Carol said looking up, smiling.

"Hmm," said Lisa, a look of disbelief on her face. Why wouldn't her mother ever be *real* with her? Why couldn't she treat her as an adult? "You never tell me anything," she said. "Do you realize that? I'm sure I could handle whatever is bothering you and maybe I could add something useful. Did you ever think about that?"

"My goodness, kiddo. All I did was sigh." Carol stood up and washed out her cereal bowl. She placed it in the drying rack.

"You know, you're not going to like this but I'm going to say it anyway."

Carol, resting her hands on the sink, half-turned and looked at her daughter who looked back at her. "Well?" Carol said. "Go on."

"You are the only person I know who treats me like a child. Reed and I are equals. Stevie and I are like friends. She tells me what's bothering her and she listens to me like a person. I don't understand why you can't stop being my mother and start being a person with me. It wouldn't be that hard, believe me."

"Look," Carol replied suddenly. "I *am* your mother. You may think Stevie is your friend, but in fact, my girl, you are no one to her. You're working at the station for a summer and after that you'll never see her again."

"I happen to think you're wrong about that."

"This is stupid," Carol said, washing her hands and drying them off briskly.

"It's not stupid, Mother. It's important. We are the closest people we each have and we can't be real with each other because you don't want to see me as an adult."

"I don't know what you're talking about," Carol said, shoving her chair under the table.

"Then sit down for a minute and listen to me," Lisa said. Carol reluctantly pulled out the chair and sat in it.

"What I'm talking about, for instance, is my relationship with Reed."

"We have talked about Reed," Carol said stiffly. "You and I disagree and I have nothing further to add."

"You see. That's what I mean. You've judged me and judged him, and that's the end of the story. I want you to know how happy he is making me and *you won't listen.* If something went wrong between us, how could I ever tell you?"

"Lisa, I thought you said you want me to be honest with you. I've been honest with you. I think what you are doing is a mistake you will pay for your whole entire life. I don't see how you can expect me to turn into a pal of yours, a giggly girlfriend getting all excited with you when the phone rings."

Lisa slapped the table with exasperation. "Stevie doesn't turn into a giggly girlfriend. She listened to what I said about the quality of my relationship with Reed, my plans, and based on what I said about myself she said she thought I was doing the right thing. How come *she* doesn't think I'm making a mistake?"

Carol put her head in her hands. Stevie. How easy for Stevie to commiserate with Lisa. How dare she, anyway? Stevie was supposed to be helping her steer Lisa away from that miserable

bastard. "Lisa, all I can say is, she's not your mother. I am."
How had this happened to her? How had she ended up with
this life? When she was nineteen she had fallen stupidly in
love with a smiling blond baseball player who never should
have paid her a second glance. She had shucked her drawers
too fast and for a few weeks of giddiness there were the last
twenty years to pay. Carol threw another long, unconscious
sigh. Stevie had endured the same damned childish giddiness
and had escaped. She wanted to talk with Stevie. She wanted
to talk with her very badly.

"There you go again. There you go *again*. Now I want to
know what you were thinking." Lisa fixed her mother with a
determined look.

"You want to know, Lisa? You really want to know? I'm
tired and I'm lonely and I didn't expect my life to turn out this
way."

Lisa's expression crumpled. "Mom. Lonely? Why? You have
your business and you have Mal and you have me."

"My business is my work," Carol said tiredly. "It's what I
do because I didn't get my degree and I didn't get into a profession. It's work, Lisa, and the people I see every day work
for me and that's what that is. And Mal is a nice guy and a
great lay, kiddo, and that's all. He isn't the slightest bit interesting and even he isn't marrying me and that's what that's about,
since you ask. And yes, I have you. And I love you and these
days you visit with me for a few pitiful weeks a year and when
you're here you break my heart and when you're not here I miss
you all the time . . ." Tears spilled from Carol's eyes.

"Oh, damn," she mumbled into her napkin. She dried her
eyes and blew her nose.

Lisa was stunned. Her mother had always been the epitome
of "in control of life." There had always been such unequivocal
rules around here: "This is right," and "This is wrong." Lisa
couldn't imagine how the rulemaker's own rules would ever not

work. How could she have ever believed that Mal, for instance, would be considered acceptable company. She wanted to comment on that but found herself still trying to get her mind around Mal being a "great lay." Had her mother really said that? She tried to imagine her mother taking off her clothes in front of Mal and could not tolerate the suggestion for any part of a second. What a jerk she'd been, she realized with remorse. Her poor old mother just trying to eke out a life . . . Lisa went to Carol and put her arms around her.

"Mom. I'm sorry," Lisa murmured. "I'm sorry you feel so sad, but I'm not sorry you told me."

Carol patted her daughter's arm. "I know. It's okay," she said. "I'm just going through a little bit of a bad spell. I'll be okay."

"We should spend more time together," Lisa said. "Look, why don't you drive me into the city today. Let me give you a tour of the newsroom and then you go to Bloomingdale's and I'll meet you there for lunch. Have you ever been to that neat restaurant they have at the top?"

Carol shook her head. She felt foolish and exposed. How could she have thrown her self-pitying woes in her daughter's face like that?

"You'd never believe it. It's called 'Le Train Bleu,' and it looks exactly like the dining car of a real train. The food is even good. What do you say? I'll take a cab home from the station tonight."

"I don't know, honey. I have a lot to do today."

"Mother, please. It will be fun."

"Well, all right," Carol said. "I suppose I can take a half day off once in a while." Stan had said to take time off, hadn't he? A flush suffused her cheeks. She pictured his smiling face, felt his warm touch on her belly. "I wouldn't change a thing," he had said. "Are we going to this elegant restaurant in our jeans?" she asked.

"No. God forbid," Lisa said in mock horror. "I'll be down in a minute," she said, racing for the stairs. Poor Mom, she thought. Poor Mom.

The set looked like a living room, Stevie's living room. The matching sofa and chair were upholstered in a soft peach fabric. There was a coffee table at stage-front littered with changing artifacts, a guest's novel, props. Bookshelves backed the set and there were French doors to the left and right. Stevie always sat in the chair as she was doing now, the guests sat on the sofa. Lights and microphones dangled from overhead like sleeping bats and the crew, the cameramen, their assistants, the floor manager, all wheeled and walked the apron, the outer perimeter of the stage.

B. Willy watched Stevie on the six monitors in the control booth. She looked bad on every one of them. Something was wrong; he couldn't be mistaken after all these years. She looked like she had zoned out during the show. Even when she had connected he got the feeling she was unprepared, bluffing her way through. He had never seen her do that before. She was spacey even now. "Look at her," he said to Pam, standing beside him.

"She's just fine," Pam said, her voice strained.

B. Willy swiveled completely in his chair to look at his wife. "Come on. What are you talking about? She looks like she's on something. And what's with you? You guys having your periods, or what?"

"What's that supposed to mean?" Pam snapped guiltily.

"Didn't you tell me you two are on the same schedule?"

"Jesus," she said, "the things you remember and the things you forget."

"Can you do something to her?" Willy asked, clapping his headset on over his balding pate. "Or the promo is going to suck sewage."

"Maybe. I don't think so."

"Well go down there and wake her up, okay? Stand by for promo," Willy said into his microphone. Mickey, the floor manager, waggled a finger and spoke to Willy through his microphone.

"Hang on. She needs make-up."

"Right," Willy replied. She sure does, he thought to himself. A petite blonde came onto the set and Stevie lifted her face to receive a powdering.

Stevie wanted to sneeze. No, that wasn't it. She wanted to cry. She'd been really sloppy today. Her mood was overwhelming her and she couldn't ditch it. She felt Amy brushing her bangs. Take care of me, she pleaded silently. Behind closed eyes she saw Carol and Lisa, arms linked, walking through the station. Their love for each other was almost tangible. That twenty-year-old hurt had come to life today. Meeting Carol and seeing Lisa separately hadn't pained her the way seeing them together had. They looked so close in a way only mother and daughter could be. She had wanted to save herself with a thought, she had wanted to think, I'll have a child of my own. But then she thought of Philip and last night, and the thought wilted and died.

"Give me some lip," Amy said, and Stevie automatically lifted her face. Gentle brushstrokes painted an outline, a soft finger slicked gloss on her lips. Stevie thought about Carol's invitation to lunch tomorrow. She had wanted so much to say no, but something in Lisa's face made her say yes and now, damn it, she was going to have another lunch with Carol.

"Steve, glance at the cue cards, pretty please," Mickey said. And then, in a whisper, "You okay, honey?"

"Sure, thanks," she answered, forcing herself to smile. She read the cards quickly, then read them again. On her way to the taping, she had seen Lisa in the corridor and impulsively invited her to dinner tomorrow night. She wanted Philip to meet Lisa, wanted Kenny to meet her too. She lifted her bangs, ran her hand over her forehead. It would be kind of a family dinner. Philip would be charmed by Lisa . . . what? Her reverie was interrupted. "What did you say, Pam?" she asked, irritated.

"I asked if you're all right. Willy wants to know if you're on the rag," Pam said conspiratorially, stooping beside Stevie's chair.

"For God's sake," Stevie snapped. She stood up and walked over to Mickey. "Give me that," she said, removing his headset and holding the microphone to her mouth. "Yes, I am. I am on the rag. Any other questions?" She waited a moment in the shocked silence, then shoved the headset back into a startled Mickey's frozen hands.

Pam stepped forward. "Hey, Stevie," she began.

"What, what, what?" Stevie snarled. To her amazement, Pam reddened and tears swamped her eyes. Pam turned and ran from the set. Stevie clapped her hands to her mouth. What had she done? "Pam. Pammy," she called. Stevie swung her gaze around the set. A dozen people were gaping at her, and no wonder. She was behaving hideously. "Oh, God," she said quietly. "I'm sorry, everyone," she said to the crew. "Please forgive me." She took Mickey's handset once more. "I'm sorry, Willy."

"It was nothing," B. Willy said. "Forget it. Are you going to be all right?" He watched her image nod yes in the monitor. "Are you ready to roll?"

"Yes," Stevie replied. "I have to get to Pam. Don't let her leave until I talk to her."

"I won't."

Stevie walked to her chair and arranged herself carefully. Do your job, she thought, and then you can get out of here.

"Are we ready?" Willy asked Mickey.

Mickey nodded.

"Camera one, stand by to tape," Willy said.

"Stand by, Stevie," Mickey said, holding his hand in the air, palm facing Stevie.

"Roll to record," said Willy.

"Five, four, three," Mickey mouthed to Stevie, folding his fingers down as they were counted off. "Take it," he said.

"It's the circus, tonight," Stevie said, smiling at the camera. "And we've got the inside story. Meet a lion tamer, the daring young man on the flying trapeze, a twenty-year veteran of the sideshow, and a chimpanzee who can read your mind. Or can he? Meet me right here at eleven—On the Air." She held her smile until she heard the word "Cut," then glanced up, hopefully, toward the booth. Please let the one take be enough.

Inside the booth B. Willy checked the tape. It would do. It wasn't great, but it would do. Warner was going to eat Stevie's tail tomorrow. "It's a wrap," he said. "Thank you and good night."

"All done, honey," Mickey said to Stevie.

She smiled at him, waved at the booth, and ran into the wings.

Stevie found Pam in the ladies' room. The water was running hard from both faucets and she was scrubbing her face vigorously. Stevie touched her friend's shoulder and Pam blinked at her. "Hi," she said. She toweled her face dry.

"Pam, that was awful of me. I'm so sorry I snapped like that."

"No sweat," Pam said, tossing the wad of paper towel across the room, sinking it neatly into the wastebasket. "It wasn't you, anyway," she muttered.

"It was me. I was horrible."

"You weren't that bad and anyway, you were covered. The lion tamer was a natural-born camera hog."

"I wasn't talking about the show. But that was horrible too."

"Aw, Steve. What's bothering you, huh? I've never seen you so down."

"Yeah, well."

Pam put a hand under Stevie's elbow and steered her to a cracked brown leatherette covered sofa that made the ladies' room a lounge. The two women collapsed at the ends.

"I'm not pregnant," Stevie said, hating the barren sound of the words.

Pam stared at her friend. Life was sure strange, she thought. Stevie wasn't pregnant and she was depressed. She should be celebrating. Pam tried to phrase what she would say carefully. "I'm sorry," she said. "I'm sorry because you are, but I want to say something."

"I know. You thought I was crazy."

"Listen to me, will you? Being a single mother is a rough ride. I don't doubt you could do it, but Steve, I don't think you've even thought about it."

Stevie let Pam's words sink in. She stared at the cold tile walls and absently played with her pearls. "I wasn't thinking I'd be a single mother. That never occurred to me." She swiveled her head to look at Pam. "Are you thinking Philip wouldn't marry me?"

"Honestly? I don't know. What do you think?"

Stevie shrugged then shook her head. Last week she would have said they would marry. Now? "I don't know either," she confessed. "I told him I want to have a baby." Stevie wet her dry lips, "And just as you predicted . . ."

"Doesn't want one, huh?"

"Doesn't want the ones he's got and doesn't want any new ones." She felt her nose prickle. This thing that she had said, it couldn't be true.

Pam watched her friend's misery helplessly. "Jeez, Steve. Like they say, 'Life's a bitch.' "

Stevie unfolded her legs, went into a stall, ripped off a

length of toilet tissue. Dabbing at her nose, she returned. "I've not yet begun to fight," she said.

Pam gave Stevie a smile, then she spoke. "You know this baby issue comes up fairly often in my household," she said dryly, thinking ahead to what she was going to say next. Stevie might want a baby but as best as Pam could tell, she had never even held one. She put her elbows on her knees, her chin in her hands, and spoke to her shoes. "Willy says *baby* so much, I've decided that's what the B. in his name stands for."

Stevie smiled. "Baby Willy Foster."

"Cute. Right? The word *baby* is so small and cute, I think it should be banned. This little bundle Willy wants so much comes out a baby and it stays that way for a short time and then it gets some personality and it's still small and cute. Then it needs things, mostly attention and guidance. If it gets those things, and you magically do everything right, then you've got a fifty percent chance of surviving and so has it when it gets to the next stage, the stage where it isn't cute and it will only do the opposite thing to what's good for it. That stage lasts anywhere from ten times as long as the cute stage to the rest of its life and yours. That's why I don't like the word *baby*," Pam said, looking directly at Stevie. "It's just the tip of the iceberg."

"That wasn't a lecture by any chance?" Stevie asked matter-of-factly.

"It could have been," Pam admitted. "Or else I was reminding myself."

Stevie tucked a corner of her lip into her mouth and bit it. "When I told Philip about not being pregnant, he acted surprised that I wanted to be. He said this was all very sudden, and said I was competing with Carol. I'm not doing that," Stevie said, pulling back to look at Pam, "but something about what he said felt right. Why has this maternal urge hit me so suddenly?"

Pam shrugged. "Well, your birthday, I suppose."

"Hmm," Stevie murmured. "I don't know. It's so weird. When I thought I was pregnant, I wanted to let loose, let the euphoric feeling take me over. It was like holding a helium balloon, sort of. I could feel the tug, I could have the fantasy of floating. My thoughts were, I'm pregnant, there is going to be a baby. Small and cute, like you said. I wasn't thinking, Uh-oh, the balloon could get snagged, or, It's cold up there and I'll freeze to death."

Pam grinned appreciatively. "Okay, so right now there's no balloon. Before you go for another ride, are you going to pack a sweater or what?"

"Pam, I'm tired of me, me, me. God. Every time I come to work, people applaud. I would welcome the opportunity to put this small person at the center of my life, but Pammy, even I know kittens turn into cats." She thought of Lisa knotting her hair, pulling it down, writing a play, sleeping with a man!

"Just so you know," Pam said, throwing herself back into the couch, turning her head toward her friend.

"Hey, give me a little credit," Stevie said. "A smidge."

"Oh, all right," Pam said affectionately. "So what are you going to do?"

"I don't know what I'm going to do. I'm not going to give up so fast. I love him and it's his baby that I want. I'm going to have to work on him." Would anything work? she wondered, slipping away into her thoughts. One of the things she loved about Philip was that he knew what he was about and he knew what he wanted. He wasn't intractable, but he was strong-minded, and he had said plainly that another child would be wrong for him. She heard Pam speaking.

"Want to go out to dinner with us?"

"I'm too depressed to go out."

"Willy will cheer you up."

Stevie grinned weakly. "I don't want to be cheered up. I

want to suffer. Besides, I've got to prep for tomorrow. I don't want to repeat this." She pointed in the direction of the stage.

"Do me a favor and don't worry about the show. Willy kept the cameras off you."

"Great," she said facetiously.

"You know what I mean. Watch tonight. You did fine."

Stevie nodded.

"I'd better be going," Pam said at last. "He's probably waiting for me in the car."

"I'll walk you out," Stevie said.

"Tomorrow's show is going to be a snap," Pam said, holding the door for Stevie, following her out. "Mort's been on a dozen times and he knows how to do the deal."

Stevie nodded.

"Listen. Why don't we buy each other lunch tomorrow?"

"Can't," Stevie said. "I wish I could though." This was the truth. She wanted to have lunch with Pam. How was she going to get through lunch with Carol?

# 12

Carol rested her chin on her hand, her elbow pressed into the damask tablecloth. The fingers of her other hand drummed restlessly. She hardly recognized her fingernails without polish, she thought, silencing her fingers, studying them. She had strived today for a classic understated look—like Stevie's, an inner voice remarked. She ignored her own jibe. She brushed a speck of bread crumb from her sleeve and straightened the ribbed cuff. The new cream-colored cardigan and pants had looked right when she had tried them on in the store but now she felt too understated, washed out really, and uncomfortable in slacks. She would have felt more at ease wearing a suit in

Stevie's club. She stopped drumming and signaled the waiter. "A pack of Winstons, please, Albert," she said firmly, handing him a bill.

One pack is not smoking. One pack can be one cigarette. The waiter returned with the familiar red and white package on a plate and an accompanying book of matches embossed with "The Anthony Club" in gold script. Carol ripped the cellophane strip around the top of the package and took out a cigarette. The first sulfurous taste was both familiar and dangerous, the kiss of a former and now married lover. The second puff reassured her, and the third brought her composure and control. She flicked an ash into a crystal tray, then blew a long stream of smoke into the air.

Waiting for Stevie, she thought. Waiting for Stevie again. It seemed suddenly that Stevie's presence had always lived in her mind: a small mouse, quietly chewing, until now she could no longer ignore the skittering footsteps and the teeth and the big ragged hole.

Carol had been aware of Stevie before she had even known Andy. Full images of Stevie appeared as she had been then, her cheerleader skirt swirling around her perfect legs, her picture on posters running for a class office, her name at the top of the program, female lead in the drama club production. Her poise and popularity had been daunting. Then somehow, it had been an error perhaps, or a goblin's trick, the ostrich had gone to the ball with the prince.

From the first moments with Andy, she understood that she had overreached. She was aware of every word she spoke to him, rehearsed in advance whole scripts of conversations only to have the words blow away in his presence, replaced by chattering nothings. And so she had conceived the wordless deed, never believing that it would really work. It was almost a kind of sorcery, she had thought as she circled the day.

Afterward, when the affair was over, when he had said, "Let's be friends," she had felt relief. Her classmates' pity, and with it a return to her natural un-pop status, had been more comfortable than bearing the skeptical looks that had blatantly asked, "What does he see in her?" When Andy had started dating Stevie it had seemed right that the best boy and the best girl should be together, and while Stevie hadn't stolen him, it could be said that she had, and the saying of it made it seem true. But the charm had worked. Too late, but it had worked.

Carol lit a second cigarette with the burning tip of the first. She had pretended to herself that the first missed period was a miscalculation, the second due to anxiety and also the third. The fourth missed period gave rise to a fantasy. She would move to a cool climate, New England perhaps, or Sweden, and she would have a secret child. She had been dreaming, making her plans, when her mother had poked at her belly, hauled her by her hair to the doctor. The wretched shame of it; Carol shook her head hoping to dislodge the clinging memories. She had been powerless. She hadn't even wanted to marry Andy then, he was so in love with Stevie, but trying to prevail against Daddy had been like trying to move the Sears and Roebuck building by pushing against it with her shoulder.

The wedding ceremony had been terse, the faces of their families joyless and gray. The bouquet of white rosebuds pressed into her hand by her mother and her belly bulging before her had been the only frail harbingers of hope and life. Then her darling Lisa had been born, justifying but not canceling the guilt and the hurt and the little gnawing mouse in her mind. Stevie. With them always had been Andy's living, unforgettable love for Stevie.

"Ms. Wilder?" an assertive masculine voice asked.

"Yes." She looked up at the imposing maitre d'.

"Ms. Weinberger's office just phoned. She is on her way. May I bring you something to drink?"

Carol nodded. "Thank you," she said. "A Virgin Mary." She

didn't want alcohol today. She wanted to be completely in control when she had her talk with Stevie. She was in the right, absolutely. She had been right even before this morning, but when Lisa mentioned her upcoming dinner with Stevie, fear overwhelmed her and then the anger displaced the fear. Stevie was pulling Lisa toward her like iron filings to a magnet—pulling her away from her own mother. Stevie had to admit this, back off, apologize, and what else? Carol couldn't think of anything. Suddenly everything she had thought to say to Stevie seemed lame. Stevie would deny it all and she would be left looking ridiculous. No. She would not be put off or put down. She had as much right to be in this world as Stevie Weinberger, and her rights deserved to be respected. Lisa was hers, and by befriending Lisa in this absolutely inappropriate way, Stevie was separating them. It had to stop.

Stevie slammed the car door. Sal glanced at Stevie in the rearview mirror, then edged the car out into the traffic. "What time should I pick you up?" he asked.

"Will you wait? Thanks," Stevie said. Should she have asked Carol if it was okay to invite Lisa to dinner? No. That was ridiculous. It was Lisa's responsibility to clear things with her mother, not hers. She and Lisa were becoming close and if Carol couldn't handle it, too bad. It was twelve-thirty now. They could eat, chat for an hour or so, and she would keep the time they spent very light. Then this would be it. There was no point in continuing this relationship, no point at all. She had nothing in common with Carol. They had never been friends and she had real friends she didn't have time to see. She should be having lunch with Pam.

The blue sedan nosed up to the curb. Salad and small talk and then this would be it, final, last of Carol.

"Stevie," Carol said when Stevie approached and sat down. Stevie was instantly alert. Something was bothering Carol. She was smoking and the fingers holding the cigarette were shaking. Stevie returned the greeting and ordered a glass of wine.

Stevie looked so composed, Carol thought bitterly. Her pale blue silk dress whispered respectably as she moved. Genteel diamonds reflected light as her blond hair swung around her shoulders. The cheerleader was back, the lead in the class play, the woman her husband had loved. A waiter arrived to take their order. This was going to be verbal suicide, Carol thought desperately. Why couldn't she stop herself?

"But I love the chef's salad," Stevie said to the waiter. "That's why I always have it," she smiled at him and turned back to face Carol. One more hour, she thought. In fifty-five minutes I will tell Carol my car is waiting and I will go outside and get into it. "I'm glad Lisa is coming over for dinner," Stevie said. "Philip has heard me going on and on about her and I so much want him and Kenny to meet her. I hope you don't mind."

Carol felt her pulse beat in her temples. She set her glass down on the table hard. Red liquid sloshed gently over the side of the glass, unnoticed.

"As a matter of fact, I do mind," Carol said, her voice shaking. "I mind a great deal."

"Why, Carol," Stevie said, sitting far back in her seat. "I'm sorry. I didn't think you would. Lisa didn't hesitate."

"No, I'm quite sure she didn't. If you asked her to move in with you, I'm quite sure she would pack her clothes and her stuffed animals and do that, too, but I won't let her, Stevie. Lisa is my daughter, not yours. Do you understand?"

Stevie stared at Carol. Her mouth was twisted and it looked as though she was going to cry. "No, I don't," she said quietly. "I don't understand. I thought you wanted me to spend time with her."

"I wanted you to influence her away from Reed and that was wrong of me. It was a mistake, I see it now. I should never have put the two of you together at all."

Stevie stared. She couldn't help it. Carol's chin was quivering. It was clear she had more emotion stored than could be contained. Stevie glanced surreptitiously to both sides. In any other restaurant, people would have stopped what they were doing to watch, but here, thank God, the tables were miles apart, the patrons discreet and concerned with their own affairs.

"Carol, what is this all about?" Stevie asked quietly. What crazy thing have you imagined, she thought but didn't say.

"What it's about," Carol said, "is my daughter and her life. Now that she's worshiping you, every little word you say is gospel. What right do you have, I'd like to know, to sanction her affair with Reed?"

"But I didn't," Stevie said. She acknowledged the waiter who placed the salad plate in front of her, and looked back at Carol. What had Lisa told her?

"I knew you would say that," Carol said bitterly. "I knew it." Do not give in, she said sternly to herself. "Lisa isn't one to lie."

"Nor am I," Stevie said. "Listen to me, because I don't want to fight with you. I didn't tell her to do anything. I listened to Lisa and although I neither approved nor disapproved, Carol, one thing is very clear. Lisa has both eyes open and your attempts to run her life aren't working."

"Don't twist this," Carol hissed. "I'm not trying to run her life. I'm her mother and I care deeply about what happens to her. I'm not dazzled by her false logic and her charm. I have spent half my life sacrificing so her life will be rich and fulfilling. And now you've spent a few hours with her and you think you know her. What does it cost you to 'listen' to her. Nothing. My heart is sick at what damage you may have done." No, no. This was going all wrong, Carol thought, trying not to cry, feeling all control ebb away.

Stevie looked helplessly at Carol. Had she really caused this unhappiness? She bore the awful weight of Carol's words. Had she been too accepting of Lisa's plans? She was sure she hadn't given actual approval. No. She remembered precisely. Lisa had sought her approval, built her case, which did seem to make sense, but Stevie certainly hadn't clapped her on the back and said "Go to it." They'd watched a movie on television and gone to sleep. Still, maybe Carol had a point, a small one though. "Carol, I know I didn't tell Lisa anything substantial, but if I even gave her tacit approval and it's made you this miserable, I'm sorry."

Carol shook her head. Stevie wasn't going to get off the hook so lightly. All those gnawing years couldn't be forgiven with such a little "I'm sorry." "I'm sure you are, but 'I'm sorry' doesn't fix anything," Carol said.

This was crazy. It was terrible to witness this kind of unhappiness, but it wasn't her fault and she wasn't going to put up with it. "Listen, Carol, everything that's going on with you and Lisa was going on before I met her." Could she just get up and walk out? This had been a mistake. Since her last lunch with Carol, everything in her life had been stirred up.

How easy it was for Stevie to deny everything. Single women were so glossy and so selfish. They didn't know what it meant to give to a child. "No, I'm sorry," Carol said harshly. "I'm sorry I ever expected you to understand. I guess you'd have to be a mother to feel as I do."

Stevie heard the air crackling around her ears. Carol used the word *mother* like a shield. Motherhood made Carol a saint, in her own estimation. "I wish you'd stop using motherhood as a blanket rationale for all of your feelings, Carol. Being a mother doesn't seem to me as extraordinary as it seems to you," Stevie said stiffly.

"Spoken by someone who wouldn't know," Carol said. She threw her napkin down on the table. "Can we forget this lunch ever happened?" she asked, standing. "I had hoped we would reach some sort of understanding, but I can see I was wrong."

Carol was going to walk out on her? "Fine," Stevie said. "You know, I'm starting to understand why Lisa has such trouble with you. You really are impenetrable." She stared at Carol with distaste, and then averted her eyes. If she could spot Albert, he would bring her the check, and in ten minutes this whole daytime nightmare would be over. She wished now she hadn't invited Lisa to dinner, but she would get through that too.

"Impenetrable? What do you think you mean by that?" Carol spat. She would not let Stevie have the last word.

"I mean," Stevie said, giving Carol a hard stare, "obstinate. Bullheaded. Thick as a wall."

Just like your father, Carol heard her mother's voice say. Sadness crushed her. Tears streamed from her eyes. She covered her face with one hand, reached for the chair back with the other. Blindly she sat down. She groped for the table napkin and when she found it, she put it over her eyes. She was making a fool of herself. If only she could make herself invisible and vanish. She blotted her eyes, and when she could, she lowered her hands and looked at her plate.

"I'm sorry, Carol," Stevie said, moved despite her intentions to be immovable. She had sensed from the moment she had sat down how fragile Carol was feeling and still she had lashed out. Where was her famous sensitivity? She was acting like a witch lately.

"No, no," Carol said softly. "You haven't done this to me. I've been crying for weeks now. It doesn't take anything at all to make me cry."

"Well, that makes us an ill-fated pair," Stevie said apologetically. "I've been in such a foul mood, it doesn't take anything to make me blow up."

Carol nodded, and then sobbed again. "I'm sorry, I'm sorry," she said. "I'm making a scene." If only she could get control of herself. She didn't need a plastic surgeon, she needed a shrink. She took a deep, shuddering breath and then another.

"Don't be silly," Stevie said. "I wish I could say something to make you feel better. Do you think we should get out of here?"

Carol nodded. "I feel pretty damned stupid crying in my napkin." She attempted a smile.

"How about this?" Stevie glanced at her watch. "My car is outside and we can go for a drive."

"Then maybe you could drop me off at Grand Central," Carol said. "I must have mascara everywhere," she said, peering into her compact.

Stevie signed the chit beside her plate and the two women stood, Carol on faltering legs, Stevie right beside her. The car was double-parked right outside the club. Sal was blowing sunflower seed hulls out of the window when he saw Stevie in the side mirror. He jerked open the car door, straightened his cap on his gray curly-haired head, and opened the rear door. "Sal, we want to end up at Grand Central Station," Stevie said, "but please take us the long way, through the park."

Carol and Stevie settled back into the blue velour upholstery. The dark windows, the cooled air, and the luxurious fabric enclosed them in an intimate space. Stevie felt immediately comforted. Nothing could happen to her here. It even smelled safe in this car.

Carol felt the pressure of time. Soon they would be at the station and she would climb out, say good-bye to Stevie, forever probably, and catch the 2:48 to Chappaqua. She had some fences to mend. She had attacked Stevie and embarrassed her in public. "You were right to say what you did in there, Stevie. I had made up my mind about what I was going to say to you before you arrived, and nothing could stop me. I was like a freight train running without the engineer, do you know what I mean?"

"Sure," Stevie said, reaching out a hand to touch Carol's. "That's happened to me. But why? Why were you so angry?"

Carol sighed deeply and shook her head. "It's a sad thing, you know, to look back at the whole of your life and be dissatisfied with the way it turned out and look forward and not see it getting better. I guess the only thing I think I ever did that was worthwhile was have Lisa."

"I wish you wouldn't run yourself down that way," Stevie said. Carol had created a whole life for herself and her daughter without any help. Didn't she count that for something? "Carol, you are an elegant, successful woman, and you make yourself sound like you scrub floors."

"I know it sounds pitiful," Carol replied, "but I'm trying to be honest. I was thinking before we met today how much I've thought about you over the years." Carol waved away Stevie's startled look. "Please. It's the way it is. For someone like me, you were a superwoman. You had every thing I would have wanted if I had thought about myself as someone who could rise to enjoy all the things you had. And the darnedest thing, the most awful thing, is you were always so nice. Nice to me, nice to everyone, so being jealous or wishing bad things on you made a person feel just plain mean."

Stevie looked at Carol sadly. Carol was such a handsome woman and so strong. How had she managed to maintain such a low opinion of herself? Hearing how Carol had regarded her made her cringe. She had been lucky that she had been pretty. Maybe she had been lucky that Nana had Barbie-dolled her into the college sweetheart Carol had believed her to be, but damn. From the inside, she and Carol had been the same: teenage girls figuring out how to grow up. They had even loved the same boy.

"Being with Andy, and his loving you even after I stopped loving him, was awful. That wasn't your fault, Stevie. If anything, it was my fault. I could have fought my daddy, and put my baby up for adoption, but," Carol looked at Stevie imploringly, "look what I would have lost."

Stevie nodded dumbly. She became aware that the car, stopped in traffic, was throbbing. Go, go, she wished at Sal, invisible behind a wall of black glass. Don't make me think about what you would have lost, she pleaded silently. I was the one who lost.

"Just look at her," Carol continued. "She's a miracle dropped out of heaven. I wanted to do everything for her, not just for her but for me. I had to make it up to myself, all the things I missed out on by having her, and I guess if I had to say what I wanted for her, I would have to say I wanted her to have all the things you have. I wanted her to be like you." Carol's throat hurt but she felt quiet now, at peace.

"I didn't want to have lunch with you today," Stevie said softly, "because, being with you, seeing you with Lisa yesterday, hurts me more than I want to say."

Carol wrinkled her face in consternation.

"I had forgotten about something that I did once a million years ago. You've reminded me of it and I'm glad you did even though it hurts." Stevie swallowed and tears filled her eyes. "Carol. When you were pregnant with Lisa, I was pregnant too."

Carol gasped loudly. "You were pregnant?" she asked, not yet understanding, but sensing the imminent destruction of an historical fact or an ideal she had held to be true.

Stevie nodded. She saw splinters of pictures: her attic room, the full moon in the cobalt sky, the steamer trunk under the pay telephone. "It was Andy's baby, and I didn't have it." How simple it was to say those words, how hard it had been to "not have it." In her mind, she saw an ashen younger self holding damp hands with two other girls, not knowing each other's names, not asking, the three adding up to six, all enclosed in the back of the silent white limousine. She saw the sign,

MOTEL, in flashing red letters, and the doctor's red-streaked gloves; had he been a doctor? And she saw Andy's pale face, water dripping from his hair. It had rained that night.

"Andy's baby? You were pregnant with Andy's baby?" How could that be true and she not know? She didn't love Andy anymore; didn't even like him, and still, she felt a piercing pang of jealousy. "I didn't know," Carol murmured.

"We never told anyone," Stevie said. "It was our secret until this moment. Now the three of us know."

Oh. The secret was a gift from Stevie. Carol's thoughts unfurled. Stevie had been pregnant and she had had an abortion. Her baby would have been Lisa's half-sister. Or brother. She and Stevie would have been . . . Stop this, she thought abruptly. Stop. She turned her thoughts to Stevie. "It's still a secret," Carol said, touching Stevie's fingers with hers. "What happened?" she asked quietly.

Stevie reflexively took back her hand and with the other smoothed back her hair. "He had just found out you were pregnant. He was in Baton Rouge, remember?"

Carol nodded.

"He called me from a pay phone to say you were getting married. I, I didn't have a chance to tell him, and by the time I did, it was too late. It wouldn't have mattered anyway. He couldn't have married us both, and you were so far along. I had only just missed my first period." Stevie shifted her gaze to look at the woman beside her. New tears were in Carol's eyes.

Carol tried to remember that cloudy time. Her own misery had been so large and Andy had made his seem less. He had never spoken of his pain, but she had thought she had understood. Certainly he had had enough to sadden him: losing Stevie, marrying her, unexpected fatherhood. But add all of that to this—that the woman he loved had been pregnant. My God, he had given up so much, and he had spared her. And Stevie had spared her too. Stevie could have kept her child, could have shattered their brittle marriage. "How you must have hurt," Carol said.

Stevie nodded one time. "I wasn't brave enough to have a baby alone." What would have happened, she wondered, if she had kept that baby? Her mother would have made her put it up for adoption. Eleanor would never have allowed an illegitimate child in their house. Nana would have fought with her, a little, and Granddad would have coughed and rumbled, but Eleanor's will would have prevailed. But what if somehow she had kept the baby, would she have gone back to school and graduated? No. She certainly wouldn't have come to New York. What if? What if? She had done the right thing for a twenty-year-old, but still, she had thought then she would fall in love again, marry, have other children.

"Abortions weren't legal then . . ." Carol said, her voice small, a whisper really. If it hadn't been for her baby, for Lisa, Stevie would have had a baby, not an abortion. She would have had Andy's baby, and she would have had Andy. Would Stevie have been able to make more of that marriage than she had done? No, even Stevie couldn't have turned a middle-talent baseball player with a ruined arm into an all-star. Could this pampered woman have loved life as a coach's wife in Hicktown, USA? Hardly. And if there had been no Lisa, what would she have done? I would have gotten my Ph.D. in math, she heard her inner voice retort snappily. But she had never even considered aborting. She could never have done it.

"It was pretty bad," Stevie said. She rested her head back against the seat and remembered that unseasonably cool and rainy night. In her mind, she saw the room, the plank on the bed, the light hung from the closet door. She could still hear Andy's torn voice, see his face wet with rain. That night she had said good-bye to the baby and good-bye to Andy, and she had never seen him again.

"Stevie, teenage motherhood, especially then, was abominable. You don't need me to say this, but you did the right thing."

"I think so. I thought so. Lisa is what you say, though. A miracle. I look at her and what I see makes me question what I did and makes me want a baby so much. It hurts me to know I might never have a child."

"Oh, Stevie, I could kill myself for all those things I said to you. I hate myself for being so stingy with her."

"You haven't been. Was it wrong of me to tell you about what happened? I wanted to share that story because it is me; not this superwoman you say you saw."

Carol nodded. "I'm glad you told me. I know it was hard to do."

The car lurched and stopped at a light. A crowd of pedestrians parted around the car fore and aft, some vainly peering into the glass.

"I haven't thought about all of this for a lot of years," Stevie said. "And I don't know if I would have again. I've told people for so long that I didn't want to have children, I had convinced myself. Now I feel a longing I can hardly bear. It seems nothing I have is worth much compared with having a child." It was true. The pull was becoming intolerable. It was as if all the years of shutting out the longing had intensified it and now it bore down upon her with ferocious accumulated force. She could almost hear a chant in her mind, Have a child, do it now, have a child, do it now, and that yellow alert, a light blinking on and off; her fortieth birthday, bright red, a setting sun grazing the horizon. Or was it already too late? The sounds of traffic, muted by the glass and the stream of air, became audible in the new silence.

"Why do you say you won't have a child?" Carol asked. "Damn. You are thinking about the hateful thing I said when I saw you last time. That you're too old."

"Sure, but your saying it didn't do it. I was already this old.

· 182 ·

Anyway," Stevie said brightly, "might not is not the same as definitely won't. I've got some time."

"You do," Carol said. "Does Philip want children?"

Stevie shrugged. "Not too much," she admitted.

"Oh," Carol said. "You told me he has children from a previous marriage."

"Two."

"Back in the old days, it wasn't done, but lots of women seem to be having children by themselves. At least you seem to read about it a lot. Movie stars and the like."

"Yes." *We can inseminate you in our offices*, Stevie heard Wrobleski say.

"It's the money that's the problem," Carol said thoughtfully. "Not having it, I mean. Everything costs and if you don't buy it you worry that you should have and then there's the other kids and what they have, and then there's private school, and on and on. But if you have money, and can hire people . . . Well, would you ever have a baby by yourself?"

"God. I don't know. If you were me, would you?"

"Well, I practically did. We didn't have Andy living in the house for that long. You could do it, Stevie. You should have a baby. You'd be a wonderful mother, you really would! What a lucky baby that would be."

"Yeah," Stevie said, trying out a smile. "I wouldn't be bad." She tried out an image of herself and a small child, clothed in sweaters, and no Philip taking pictures. Ouch.

"There is nothing more important you could do," Carol said with growing conviction. "My God. Having a child is an unimaginable experience. It links you to every other person who has had a child. It enlarges you, increases your capacity for love. In my case, it even makes a fool of you. If I were you, I would do it, Stevie. I wouldn't want to be childless in this big lonesome world."

Stevie nodded but she couldn't speak. Carol was sitting on

one shoulder, Pam on the other. And Philip? If he said no? Could she really do it alone? Her head was throbbing.

"Big lonesome world," Carol said again. It was almost a croon. "When they're small, you know what they're doing every minute. Then they grow up and you're lucky if you see them at all." Carol laughed self-consciously. "I've got empty-nest syndrome, and how," she said. "Can you tell?"

Stevie obligingly imagined a nest. "It's funny you should say that," Stevie said, looking at Carol. "When you said that, I saw that nest and I don't see your nest being empty. I see two grown-up birds in there, only I see the mother bird still bringing worms back for the younger one."

Carol's face darkened.

"I'm sorry," Stevie said. "That sounded wrong."

"No, go on," Carol said. "I want to know what you meant."

Stevie paused. "It's just that you keep talking about taking care of Lisa and how your life is so bleak apart from her. I was wondering just then what would happen if you stopped paying so much attention to Lisa and started paying more attention to yourself."

"I'd feel alone," Carol said.

"Maybe *alone* is the wrong word. Lisa and you are a team for life. I wish I had just a little of what you two have with my mother. Maybe *separate* is the right word."

"Separate?" Carol looked puzzled, then she smiled. Neither realized the car had stopped until the door was opened by Sal.

"I think we're here," Carol said. She didn't want to leave. She wanted to link her arm through Stevie's, go sit in the park. What an amazing story she had been told. "This was great, Stevie," she said. "And don't worry about anything this evening. With Lisa, I mean. Will you forgive me for my meanness?" she asked.

"I don't know what you're talking about," Stevie said with a wide smile.

Carol turned, hugged Stevie, and kissed her cheek. "Thank you," she said. "You've given me a lot to think about."

Stevie laughed. "I swear I was going to tell you the very same thing." Sal opened the door, and with a last squeeze of Stevie's hand, Carol stepped out into the humid day.

# 13

Stevie scraped the remains of their meal into a brown paper bag. Philip, banging more dishes on the drainboard, smiled at her but didn't say anything. She could not deny it. Dinner had been a meal and nothing more. Lisa had not seemed so charming, so beautiful, so perceptive when viewed through Philip's eyes. She had talked, talked, talked, and when she stopped talking, she beat her lashes together so rapidly a breeze was blowing in Philip's direction. The flirtation was innocent, at least Stevie assumed it was, but it had obliterated any chance of the kind of rapport that might have developed, and would have if hoping and fantasizing could determine events.

"You look tired," Philip said. He took the platter out of Stevie's hands and wrapped her in a hug."

"I guess I am.'" She rested her head against Philip's chest. She could feel his heart beating against her. She loved it when she could feel his heart. He swayed with her, a little loving dance, then he kissed her temple.

"I should drive you guys home in a little while," he said.

"What did you think of her?" Stevie asked, stepping back from Philip, turning away to put a milk carton in the refrigerator.

"Nice kid." He opened the dishwasher and restacked the dishes inside. There was a right way to stack dishes. If you aligned the big plates perpendicular to the door and the small plates parallel to the door, service for four could fit perfectly. He dusted the soap dispenser with powder and closed the trap. "A little exhausting, but nice."

Philip was right. Lisa could be exhausting. "Smart though, don't you think?"

"Mm hmm. Want some brandy or something before we go? The two of them are in his room."

"Okay. But I don't want her to miss her train."

"Don't worry," Philip said, handing her a snifter, turning out the kitchen light. "We've got time to watch the sun go down."

Arms around each other's waists. Stevie and Philip went to the sofa facing the windows overlooking the river. Philip rubbed ineffectually at a stain on the sofa and then took Stevie's hand. "This is a nice one, isn't it?" he asked, indicating the splashes of molten red tinting a salmon sky. He let the Courvoisier gently burn the tip of his tongue. The visual and physical sensations enhanced each other and pleased him. Now that he had moments like this to share with Stevie, he realized how much energy he used to expend trying to be happy alone. What he was feeling now was contentment.

"The truth is, I'm not tired," Stevie said, the need to talk compelling her more than the need to be honest. "I'm having massive anxiety and it won't go away. I feel like a flower that bloomed last week and now my petals are about to drop."

"Sweetheart, you are a nut. You look twenty-nine, tops. Flower," he laughed, and squeezed her hand.

Stevie closed her eyes and tried to feel comforted. She should drop the whole thing, for a while anyway. She shouldn't keep prodding him with this baby talk. He would buck, he would bolt, he would fly away, and she'd be standing there with her dreams in shreds and no Philip either. She felt Carol standing behind her giving her a little nudge. "I worry all the time about not being a mother, about whether I will be one. The not knowing and the tick, tick, tick, are making me frantic."

"Tick, tick, tick, huh?"

"Yeah."

"It's unsettling to me too."

"It is?"

"Sure. I care about you. How can I be happy if you're frantic about the ticking?"

Stevie closed her eyes. She was on the freight train Carol had talked about today and she couldn't get off. Good sense told her to stop talking, to wait, to discuss this issue at some other time. Nothing in her experience with people indicated you could push someone into going along with something they didn't want, yet she could not stop pushing. She had to know. "I don't want to be frantic. I just am. If I told you how much I thought about babies, you would faint. It's like I've been asleep for a couple of decades and now I've been jolted awake and it's a quarter past eleven and I'm being told that at midnight I'm going to turn into a pumpkin."

Philip leaned forward and without looking at Stevie, he put his hand carefully on the hissing globe on the coffee table. The blue branch of electricity leapt toward his fingers. He moved his fingers slightly, making the contained lightning dance. How could he say this? "Did you ever think that maybe you were never meant to have children and that this awakening is really just other people's stuff that they're dumping on you? What's her name—Martha, who wants to dance at your wedding. Carol. God knows who else. Since last month, you've gotten a whole set of new ideas, illusions I'd say, and they threaten you and me. This," he said, sweeping his hand across the sunset, "is what makes sense to me. The special time we spend in your house in Connecticut. Flying to France when we just feel like it. I want to enjoy this time, which just might be the happiest I've ever been, and first there was Hurricane Kenneth, who will not let me near him, and now there's this ticking."

"Me, you mean," Stevie said, glaring, feeling her face flush with anger.

"No! Not you. Definitely not you." He slapped the sofa hard. "This sudden urge of yours, this headlong, unbridled gallop into parenthood. I don't honestly know what it means to you, but to me it feels like a leap into oblivion." Philip took a deep breath and raked his fingers through his hair. He held his hands against the side of his head, feeling almost that if he took them away, his head would spin away from his body like a top. He slowly let out his breath. He must try to stay under control. "Steve, talking to you like this makes me feel like a beast. How *selfish* of me to talk about happiness without children. How *mean* to try and convince you to abandon your whatever it is—maternal instinct." He released his head and turned to Stevie. "Can you imagine yourself at sixty with a couple of those?" He indicated Kenny's room.

"That's horrible, Philip," Stevie said.

"I'm sorry. No, that's not true. I'm sorry about the words, but I mean them. I want you to be happy, but I want to be happy too. Kids are trouble. It sounds shitty to say it, but it's true. Kenny is hostile and dull, and that is just the truth, Stevie. I love him because he's my son, but that's why, not because he is adding anything to my life. And the other one? The one you like so much? Miss Toss-her-hair is self-absorbed and opinionated and if you didn't notice, quite a little come-on. Look at what's happening here. Telling my truth sounds hideous. Somehow it's inhuman of me to notice that these kids don't give, they take!"

Philip's voice, of its own accord, had risen to the ceiling. He heard his words ringing in the still room. God. He *was* a beast. Stevie looked pale except for a pink flush above her cheekbones. She looked as if he had slapped her. God. He hadn't meant to yell. He was taking his anger at Kenny out on her. "Stevie," he said reaching for her hand.

"Excuse me," Stevie murmured, avoiding his touch, getting off the couch. She walked quickly to the bathroom and closed the door behind her. How had she never known how much ugliness he had inside? Her head hurt to the very ends of her hair. It seemed to her that she had been wounded everywhere and by the one person she counted on to protect her. Why did Philip hate the children so much? Lisa *had* been flirting with Philip, but so what? If she didn't care, why should Philip? How could he be so intolerant? My God, poor Kenny. Maybe Merle hadn't been crazy after all. Maybe she knew things that Stevie had been too in love to see. How could she have ever imagined Philip would be a good father? She turned on the cold water and very gently splashed her face. Self-absorbed? He thought Lisa was self-absorbed? What in the world did he think he was? If something threatened to interfere with his pleasure, he wanted to eradicate it! Philip's voice penetrated the wooden door and the sound of running water.

"Steve. I'm sorry."

She carefully dried her face and hands. She wanted to stay in the bathroom but it would seem childish to linger. She opened the door. Philip stood in the doorway looking abashed.

"Lisa is going to miss her train."

"I was an ass," Philip said.

Stevie brushed past him to the hallway. "I'm going to call her, and if you don't mind, we'll catch a cab."

"Please sit for a while. I won't let her miss the train. I promise."

"I'm too rocked to talk with you. I don't think I know who you are."

"Will you please sit for a minute?"

Stevie walked to the sofa and sat on the far end. The sun had just dropped below the buildings on the opposite shore. Stevie suddenly felt exhausted. It hardly mattered what Philip said. She knew something new about him and that something was sharp and hard and as much a part of him as his eyes or nose.

"What I said was way out of line. I don't blame you for being disgusted."

She was disgusted. Stevie grunted but did not reply.

"I don't know how to convince you that I'm not a monster, but I'm not. Some people don't get along with kids. I'm one of them. I am trying with Kenny. I'm practically killing myself. Haven't you seen that?"

Stevie shrugged. She had seen that. She had seen a lot of it—that's why she was so astonished by this other Philip! Hadn't Philip put on an apron and cooked for his son, given him responsibility and respect until Kenny had made him regret his largess? Hadn't Philip hurt when Kenny was hurt? She turned back to Philip, looking for a vestige of the tender person she had loved an hour ago.

"I love you, Stevie. And this talk about children confuses and frightens me. I don't see how I fit into your plans. I don't want to be used for my seed—and cast aside. Can you understand that?"

"I would never do that," Stevie said simply. "That's not me."

"I know," Philip said as simply. Then he reached for her hand.


Lisa sat cross-legged on Kenny's bed facing Kenny's back. He was at the desk playing a computer game he had made up and programmed himself.

"You see?" he asked. "You shoot balls at the man who is at the top of the screen. These baffles are sort of like a pinball machine kind of thing which you can move by hitting these two keys. See? You score by keeping the ball in play and you get bonus points when you hit that guy, and when you use up your balls you lose your turn."

"The game is all offensive?"

"No. Look. You're not looking," he said accusingly, turning around in his chair. "The man gets his turn if you strike out."

"Uh-huh," Lisa said. She was thinking about Philip. He was so great. Just looking at him gave her a little thrill. No wonder Stevie loved him. Who wouldn't? He was clever and quirky and handsome. She created a mental image of Philip standing next to Reed. They shook hands, appraised each other, then Reed's eyes became a glassy gray. "Your dad is really neat," Lisa said, longing to say "Philip," not daring to.

"Yeah," Kenny said, beating the return bar with the side of his thumb. An electronic dot, the ball, shot upward into the maze, pinging and bonging as it ricocheted off barriers as real and as unreal as the code Kenny had punched into the disk. "Twenty-five hundred. Three thousand," Kenny called out. He jabbed a key with a forefinger.

"I bet you wish you had spent more time with him."

"I don't know," Kenny replied absently. "Hey," he shouted. "Five thousand with one ball!" He spun the chair toward Lisa. "Want to try?"

"Okay," Lisa said, uncurling her long legs. She tried to remember how she acted at dinner. She hadn't been too mesmerized by Philip, she hoped. On reflection, it seemed she had been playing to him all dinner, hoping he liked her. She felt a pang of guilt. She could hear her roommate, Margie, telling her what a flirt she was. She didn't really want Philip, she was just having a reaction! She loved Reed, she really did. And Stevie was her friend. She would check to see if Stevie acted strangely toward her, and if she did, she'd make all of her reactions to Philip bland and distinterested. God. She didn't want Stevie mad at her. That was the worst thing she could think of. She sat in Kenny's seat and flexed her fingers. "What do I do?"

Kenny explained the game and Lisa wiggled her fingers on the side of the keyboard. Then she touched the key that pulled back the electronic spring and released the ball. It bounded into the screen, caromed off the barriers, flew to the heart of the "man" as if it were easier to hit him than miss him. Lisa heard Kenny's intake of breath and released another missile. Again, the little dot sped into the frame. Numbers flicked on a meter to the side, but Lisa scarcely noticed them. The game was a breeze. She repeated the sequence of steps until she tired. Then she turned to Kenny.

"How did I do?" she asked.

"Pretty good," Kenny said, taking the keyboard out of her hand and staring at it as if he hadn't seen it before. Then he looked at Lisa. "Pretty good for a woman," he added. How could she be that good without practice?

Lisa moved back to the bed. "So what are you going to do?" she asked Kenny. "Are you going to live here, or what?"

"Nah. I don't think so," Kenny said. He lifted a Yankees baseball cap—a gift from Stevie—off the desk and put it on his head. "I've got to get back soon."

"Oh," Lisa replied. "School, huh?"

"Yeah. And my parents, you know?"

Lisa nodded. "What are they like? Your parents?"

"They're okay." Kenny spun the hat on his finger, then tossed it back onto the desk.

"Well, I guess Philip will miss you." There. She had said his name, but saying it didn't produce the satisfaction she had imagined.

Kenny didn't reply. Philip wouldn't miss him. He would go out and get some champagne or whatever and have a party. He rubbed his chest. He wished Lisa would leave now. He had this feeling if he said anything to her he'd say everything and he didn't want to. He wanted to keep his feelings to himself, where no one could see what a leftover he was.

"You're lucky," Lisa said. "Having two fathers that love you and a mother and Stevie too. Hey, you're bicoastal."

"What's that supposed to mean?" Kenny asked guardedly.

"Are you mad about something?" Lisa asked curiously, leaning toward Kenny as she spoke.

"You're crazy," Kenny said, spinning in his chair, turning on his game. "Got him!"

"Oh, I just wondered. You seem mad about something. I can usually tell these things. I'm a writer you know."

"Pow," said Kenny.

"Like the way you play that game. Like you're really shooting someone."

"Isn't it time for you to catch your train?" Kenny asked over his shoulder.

"Yeah. You ought to talk to someone, you know. You really should." Lisa found her shoes and started to put them on.

Kenny stopped his game, letting the ball bounce ineffectually to a halt at the bottom of the screen. "What's that supposed to mean?" he asked. "You know, you talk too much."

Lisa nodded. "I know. It's a really big fault. I'm all wound up inside, like this little voice is always going. I'm sorry," she said, rolling up a sock, pulling a pin out of her hair and shaking it loose. "I'm trying to work on it."

Kenny, mollified, nodded. "What did you mean, anyway?" he asked, feigning disinterest.

"Are you sure you want to know?"

"I said I did," he said vehemently.

"You seem pissed, that's all. Like you made a couple of digs at dinner and now you're firing that thing like there are real bullets in there. So that's why I wanted to know what was getting to you," Lisa said. "You didn't have to take it as an attack."

"Yeah," Kenny said, pressing a key repetitively, inattentively. "I'm trying to work out a couple of things," he said. "I didn't think I was mad."

Lisa took a breath so she wouldn't talk and just watched Kenny.

"Like, how do you know if someone loves you." He looked at her furtively and then looked back at the keyboard.

"Oh, God," Lisa said, letting out her lungful of air. "There are all different kinds of love and people have different ways of showing it. Let me think a minute . . . If a person loves you, they are who they really are with you and they accept you the way you really are. That makes the two people true friends. You know what I mean? Equal." She looked at Kenny, who was frowning at her.

"Is that it?" he asked.

"I think it's a big part of it," she said. "I think the rest of it is about, well, you know about sex, right?"

Kenny colored. "What do you think I am? Twelve?" he muttered darkly.

"I'm not sure *sex* is the right word. It's more about wanting to be physically close. Touching, eating together, talking about things, sleeping in the same bed. Are you in love with someone?" she asked.

"What? No!" Kenny barked, startled. "I'm not talking about that kind of stuff, anyway."

"Oh," Lisa said. "Good, because I don't think you're ready."

"Shows you what you know," Kenny said, bluffing, trying to pump some reality into the three paralyzing dates he had had with Rose Marie Wilcyzk before she dumped him.

"I'll bet," Lisa said knowingly.

"Never mind," Kenny said, sighing. He knew he wouldn't get anything useful out of Her Majesty. She was just like his sister, Tara. Why did women think they knew everything?

"You're not talking about your father, are you?" Lisa asked, the computer game providing her with sudden insight.

Kenny was silent.

"Oh," Lisa said. "That kind of love."

Kenny looked at her under his lashes and swallowed. Let her think what she wanted, he didn't have to say anything.

"That kind of love is different, but not *that* different. Parents find it hard to accept you the way you are and vice versa, but I think equality is still a valid concept." Wasn't that just what she was fighting about with Carol all the time? *I'm your mother*, she could hear Carol say. "They love you no matter what, according to them, but they want to change you too. Then there's the issue of putting the other person before yourself. That part is tricky though. I hear a lot from my mother about sacrifice, you know, how much she sacrificed to give me things, and I'm glad she did, you know? But I would have loved her anyway. Even if she hadn't." Lisa thought about her mother. Had she told Kenny the right thing? She wished Carol gave her more of the first part and less of the second.

Kenny thought about what Lisa had said. Did she know what she was talking about? Did he love anybody?

"So what gives?" Lisa asked.

"It's about my mother," he answered.

"Uh-huh," Lisa replied.

"She wants me to change my name to O'Brien. That's Danny's name."

"Danny?"

"My father. The other one."

"Uh-huh. Oh," Lisa said. "And you don't want to."

"I don't know."

"So what are you going to do?"

"I don't know. I'm trying to figure it out."

"Great."

"But that's why I asked you what I asked. Like, is love important? My mom says Danny loves me and Dad doesn't."

"I don't believe that. He loves you."

"How do you know?" He thought about how tight he felt whenever he was with Philip. Whenever he could, he was trying to sense Philip's feelings, but lately all he did was get Philip mad at him.

"Because parents just do. They can't help themselves."

"You can't go by that then. You have to test them, don't you see? You have to make them prove it."

"No you don't," Lisa said. "That's the last way to do it. I think you're starting from the wrong place, Kenny. Why not just assume your fathers, both of them, love you. And then be who you really are. Be honest. Did you tell your father about this name-changing thing?"

"No," Kenny said. "That would give it away." Philip had to be tested! He had to prove himself!

"Well, if you did, you might learn something," Lisa said.

"Whatever," Kenny said softly to himself. He shook his head and set up the computer game again.

# 14

Carol sat at her desk. An opulent display of summer blooms—roses, lilies, delphiniums—filled a big crystal vase. She plucked pollen-laden stamens from the lilies, then admired the bouquet again. Mal had sent them during the week and everyone had cooed and marveled. How lucky to have such an attentive man-friend. No occasion; just flowers for love. Carol shook her head. She did love the flowers but she didn't want them from Mal. She stood and opened the curtains of the window near her desk. Her prospects were due twenty minutes ago. She had hoped they would be on time; now she hoped they wouldn't show until she did what she had promised herself she would do.

She should do it now, before it was too late. There was no one around to overhear her adolescent nervousness. The sales force was out, as they should be at half past ten on a Saturday morning, with the exception of Kitty, their secretary, positioned way up at the front desk.

Carol dared herself again to make the call. She looked at the business card again. It was slightly bent, slightly grayed around the edges from lying in her wallet next to the credit cards, but the telephone number was legible and the name jumped out at her as though it were printed in three dimensions.

She had dreamed about him again. Once more she had wakened, this time her hand had been stroking red chest hairs. It was the oddest sensation. He had kissed her and she could feel the kiss on her lips when her enthusiastic response awoke her. Now she tapped her teeth with a plastic cigarette, then sucked it for its nonexistent smoke. What's the worst that can happen? she asked herself again. He'll shoot me down in the nicest possible way, that's all. She lifted the receiver and carefully tapped out the numbers. She wasn't this brave with men. This wasn't the real her. This was the kind of thing she wished she could do but had never done. She gripped the receiver with both hands as the phone in his office, only a few miles away, rang.

"Doctor's office," a cheerful voice answered. The voice instantly conjured up the image of the chubby receptionist with the Long Island twang.

"This is Carol Wilder. May I speak with Dr. Wilson?"

"Do you want an appointment to see the doctor?"

"Um, no," Carol said shakily. "I'd just like to talk with Dr. Wilson for a moment." She held her breath as the receptionist said, "I'll see if he can speak with you," and put her call on hold.

"Stan Wilson." His voice came on the line before Carol had a chance to wonder about what she should say.

"It's Carol Wilder," she said, seeing orange curls and a warm smile.

"Carol," he said. "You've been on my mind."

What did he mean? Carol thought wildly. What did he mean by that? He sounded glad to hear from her. What could she say? "Uh-huh," she said. "Well, good. I mean, I have?"

"Yes. I find myself thinking about you. You left in a such a hurry."

"Well, I was in a little bit of shock, I believe. I wasn't having one of my best days."

"I could tell," he said. "So didn't I convince you?"

"I'm sorry?" Carol answered, perplexed.

"I hoped I had convinced you not to have surgery."

"Oh, that. You did. You did convince me."

"Ah," said Stan. "So you're not calling to make an appointment."

"No, I'm not," Carol said shyly. She felt her face get warm. Oh, Lord, do what? Say what? "If you feel froggy, leap." "I guess I have to say you've been on my mind, too." She held the phone so tightly the blood stopped moving through her fingers. This was as far as she could go. If he didn't say something that was absolutely clear, she was just going to hang up, that's all.

"Carol, I just have to understand something. You aren't coming in? You aren't a patient?"

Oh no. He was going to ask her what she did want. She was going to die. "No," she croaked. She cleared her throat. "No, I'm not coming in."

"Good," Stan Wilson said, relief in his voice. "Because if you're a patient, I can't ask you out."

Carol listened to the sound of blood beating in her ears. Had he asked her out?

"Carol? Are you there?"

"Uh-huh," she whispered.

"Would you like to go out some time? Would you have dinner with me?"

"Yes," she said, life flowing back into her body. "I'd like that a lot."

Stevie called the boulder "Krypton Rock." It was a shiny, dusky-green ledge, sunk into the hillside as if thrown by a giant frisbee player or by an exploding planet. Clusters of fibrous mosses and red-tipped lichens grew in the crevices that crumbled off into the grass, but the large sunside surface was smooth and worn. Stevie bunched her denim skirt around her knees, hugging them to her chest. She turned her head to look at Philip, who lay beside her sleeping. His khaki shorts barely covered the tops of his sun-browned thighs. He had taken off his tee shirt to make a pillow for his head and his hat was shielding his face from the burning rays. Leisurely, she admired the planes of his chest, the line of his hip, the texture of his skin, and then, as if warned that this kind of appraisal was no longer her right, she turned her head to scan the pond.

Down at the end, down past the little dock and the boat house, deep in the part of the water shaded by evergreens, broken by other less spectacular lumps of "kryptonite," Kenny, lying stomach-down on a raft, paddled quietly. Stevie knew he was looking for frogs, sidling up to them silently, belching frogtalk when he had established eyeball-to-eyeball contact. She imagined Kenny teaching frogtalk to her baby—if she only had one—and then she sighed.

Having Kenny in the car last night for the drive north had helped bridge the long silences and the awkwardness she now felt with Philip. He was with her and she with him, but a shift had occurred and she could not put things back the way they were before even if she wanted to. How long could they rest at this awkward plateau before one would climb and the other would begin the journey back? She could not imagine they would go on together. So, for now, they were resting.

Stevie let her gaze range over Philip's gently breathing form again. In the last two years, she had learned his body so well she felt it was hers. She knew the way his ribcage arched out just over his diaphragm, and where the scatter of curls on his chest turned gray, and the way that scar felt when she ran her thumb across his kneecap. She knew he felt confused when he got sick, confident when he stood at the center of the stage, electric when he was peeling off the last layer of a problem he was about to solve. She knew he liked his coffee cold and the truth straight. She knew he was moral, and she knew she could depend upon him. She knew that he liked to win and that although he could accept loss, he wouldn't be content until he turned the setback into a victory. She knew that when she was with Philip, she felt more than alive; she felt connected. She knew that he loved her. Stevie knew if she added up all the things she knew about Philip they would make a man she had never dared hope she'd find, a man she wanted to be with, and plan with, do with, for the rest of her time on earth. But now she knew this one other thing. She knew Philip didn't want to have children—and this one solitary thing undid the whole so that what was left was a handful of disconnected parts.

Philip blinked in the musky dark environment of the inside of his hat. He was getting a headache. It wasn't a crusher, more like a dull ache. He could feel the sun beating hard on his chest and could see from under the hat's brim a slice of denim blue color that told him even without his glasses that Stevie was sitting beside him.

He hated this tightness between himself and Stevie. Would she get over this baby, baby, baby press? He hated his role of monster. Hated it. On one hand he wanted to give her the damned baby if she wanted it so much. God. They could afford it. He pictured coming home to his apartment and some foreign person greeting him at the door telling the household news. Mrs. Durfee and the baby were sleeping, or out, or at the doctor's. He imagined climbing into bed with his milky-blond wife and having the baby, lying between them, start to scream. The scream shifted to the seat beside him on the airplane as he became a part of the class of traveler he had always despised, the passenger with the apologetic smile. Sorry, but I can't get it to stop crying. Damn. And the rest of it. The libido that never came back after the baby. Or maybe it just didn't come back with Merle, but he'd heard the same story from other men. Women didn't want their husbands after the baby. Damn. Could his satiny Stevie become a thorny wife? Oh, he didn't want this, didn't want this at all. It was so damned unfair. He had screened for this. When he went out with women he steered far away from the nesting kind. After fifteen years of dating the mass of women who turned out to be wrong, he had found the right one, involved in her career but not obsessively so. Warm. Generous with herself. Feminine, but not overly so. Balanced. Bright, sexy, spontaneous, but rooted too. Like this house of hers. When they were here, they were living together. Separate bedrooms, of course, since Kenny, but still, hours connected by other hours, cooking, walking together, reading in separate rooms, feeling each other's presence all the time. He didn't want to change this. He wanted it to continue. He had been thinking of asking her to marry him when this damned baby stuff came up. What was he supposed to do now?

"You're going to burn," he heard Stevie say.

"Oh, thanks," he said, sitting up. He unrolled his tee shirt and pulled it on. He put his hat on his head and looked down at the pond. "He can frog forever, can't he?" he said.

"Yeah," Stevie agreed. She hated this. They were so wooden now. Even when he took her hand, like now, she wasn't comfortable.

She was so pretty, Philip thought. When he turned his head

just a little to the right of straight ahead, he could see all of her. He squeezed her hand. He couldn't think of anything to say to her anymore. He loved her, but he felt her slipping away. "What have you been up to?" he asked.

"Not much."

"Thinking?"

"Yeah. Philip, what are we going to do?"

"I don't know, Steve-o. I don't know."

"I can't," she said. "I can't just ignore the part of me that wants to be a mother. I can't explain it. I can't justify it. I can't even be sure it will make me happy. But I can't say no to it." She looked at him sadly. She could feel tears gathering in her eyes.

"Steve," Philip said helplessly, taking her into his arms. He rocked with her as she wept.

"Just tell me it's a maybe," she pleaded, drying her eyes with the hem of her skirt. "Just say maybe," she said.

Philip touched the back of her neck and looked into her eyes. He loved her. Couldn't he just say this one word? "I love you," he said.

"I know," she said. She would not release him from her gaze.

"I can't say it," he said. "I would be lying."

Stevie stood for a moment, poised on the bow of Krypton Rock. Then she turned her back on Philip and walked quickly up the hill.

# 15

"You look like you slept on the floor last night," Luann said, standing in the doorway.

"Thank you. Thank you very much," Stevie said dryly, taking a mirror out of her desk drawer. There were blue circles under her eyes. She tossed the mirror back into the drawer and slammed it. "You've noticed I've gone the whole day without mentioning whatever it is you're wearing in your hair."

"You like it?" Luann asked expectantly. She spun around and peered into the mirror hanging beside the door. She plucked at her yellow frizz.

"What is it?" Stevie asked. Some sort of wire apparatus with pinchers on the ends, wrapped around Luann's head like a turban, then snaked through the curls. It looked like a set of jumper cables.

"Jumper cables," Luann said, turning back to Stevie, crossing the field of beige carpeting to the raised work area where Stevie sat. "They add meaning to my perm, don't you think? You know. Electric."

Stevie shook her head in wonder. "I must be getting old," she said. "When I was twenty-three I wore barrettes in my hair, with maybe a rhinestone."

"Huh," said Luann, briefly imagining a twenty-three-year-old Stevie with a rhinestone barrette. She sorted message sheets in her hand. "Your grandmother called when you were exercising. You don't have to call her back," Luann said, crumpling the note and stuffing it into one of many pockets in her voluminous, iridescent rayon pants. "She said to tell you to get a haircut and she thinks Mort Salzman isn't funny, he's disgusting."

Stevie clicked her nails on the desk. "What else?" she asked.

"Some guy from Cable News wants to interview you for a piece called 'Single and Desperate.'"

"Jeez. What a creepy—. I hope you blew him off."

"I switched him to PR."

"Good."

"Pam-el-a called. Did you read the stuff she gave you to read over the weekend?"

"No. Is that all? I'll go see her now."

"Philip called."

"Okay," Stevie said. She didn't want to talk to Philip. In fact, conversation between them had gotten so strained, she had let Kenny ride in the front seat on the way home last night so she could pull her mood over her head in the back seat and sleep.

"Should I get him for you?"

"I'll call him later," Stevie said distractedly, getting up from her chair. "I'll be with Pam."

"Don't forget you've got the run-through in an hour."

"Okay," Stevie said.


"Enter," Pam called through the door. "Hi," she said when a dejected-looking Stevie flopped into the chair next to her desk. "What's the matter with you?"

"I slept on the floor last night," Stevie replied.

"You what?"

"Not really. I'm depressed. We had a rough weekend."

"What happened?"

"Same old stuff. It's getting boring to talk about it."

"Oh, Steve," Pam said, exasperation in her voice. "I wish you'd give it a rest. You don't find guys like Philip every day."

"True, true, true," said Stevie, talking to Pam's desktop. She banged a stapler with the heel of her palm a few times creating a little cache of crimped staples, then she looked up at her friend. Pam's complexion curiously matched her olive-drab tee shirt. "You don't look so great yourself, by the way."

Pam lifted frothy black bangs, and held her forehead with the flat of her hand. She looked Stevie in the eyes. "I have a little bug or something," she said. A little bug, she thought. That's original. "Did you read the stuff I gave you?"

"No. But I scanned it." Scanned the title, Stevie amended silently. The summarizing notes on the astronomical findings of the last decade had been too daunting to open.

"Steve. I don't think scanning is going to do it. Abbott Ross is a major. He could win the Nobel Prize one of these years." This was bad. Getting Abbott Ross to do "Stevie Weinberger On-the-Air" had required guts, persuasion, and her share of luck for the remainder of the year. This was the wrong day for Stevie to fake it. "If we really work at it for the next hour, I think we can rehearse your questions."

"Okay," Stevie said despondently.

"Please, Stevie. I don't want you to sound like a bimbo." Pam's stomach made a fist and acid climbed up into her throat. She clenched her teeth and tried to force the feeling away. Another wave of nausea struck. She glanced wildly at the door, realized Stevie's chair was blocking her exit, and did the only thing she could do. She pulled the garbage can out from under her desk and leaned over it.

Stevie bolted out of her chair and put her hand on Pam's forehead, bracing her against the violence of the spasms. When the heaving stopped, Stevie handed her friend a wad of tissues, then sat down across from her and stared. "You are sick," she said. "You should be home in bed."

Pam leaned back into her chair. She crossed her arms over her forehead, put her feet on the desk, and rocked the chair gently. She wasn't going to be able to keep this a secret much longer. This was the third time she had thrown up today. "I'm pregnant," she said.

"Pam!" Stevie exclaimed, responding with undiluted joy. "How wonderful!"

"Stay here," Pam said, dropping her feet to the floor. "Read this." She slapped the packet of papers in front of her friend. "I'm going to wash up."

Stevie watched Pam leave. She picked up the report and opened it to the first page. Pregnant? Oh, God, if only she were pregnant too. She read Ross's bio, then scanned the subheadings: Supernovas, Red Giants, White Dwarves, Black Holes—this didn't seem real. It was like the cast of a cosmic fairy tale. Numbers and words flickered and melted into each other.

Pam was going to have a baby! Wouldn't it be perfect if the two of them were pregnant at the same time? And then there would be six of them, the Fosters and the Durfees, on the beach at Cannes. A beach scenario sprung into her mind, complete with sound and color. She watched the salty wind whip their hair into spiky clumps, saw Philip, copper-colored, his face at peace as he watched the children play with the smooth sea pebbles, Willy with a crustacean-pink back, a waddling toddler holding the index finger of each of his hands, taking the naked babies down to the water while she and Pam smoothed oil on their topless bodies. She closed her eyes and basked in imaginary sunshine until a sharp thought interrupted her reverie. While she and Pam and Willy lolled away the summer in France, who would do her show? Some young thing who was just waiting for a chance. Someone just like the someone she used to be. She looked down guiltily at the report in her hand. She should read. She turned a page and forced herself to concentrate. The interview would be fine. And someone else was going to be on following Ross. The identity of that person hovered at the edge of her mind. The subject was something soft and furry. She would ask Pam.

Pam dragged her fingertips against the wall as she walked slowly back to her office. It had been a relief to say the words "I'm pregnant" out loud. She wanted to talk with Stevie. She pushed open the office door and slid carefully into her old desk chair. Unfortunately, Stevie was looking at her as if she were a puppy she'd just found under a Christmas tree.

"We'll just yak for five minutes, okay? Tell me what Willy said and then we'll work."

"I didn't tell him," Pam said, trying not to swivel in her chair. She looked past Stevie to the cork board, covered with overlapping black and white blow-ups of Willy: Willy in his tux, Willy in a go-cart, Willy by the ailanthus tree. She sighed. "I don't want to tell him until I know what I want to do."

"I don't get it," Stevie said, squinting up her eyes.

"I don't know if I should keep this baby," Pam said softly. "I think yes, no, yes, no, and it seems like all the yeses have to do with Willy, and all the noes have to do with me. It's driving me crazy and—" she covered her mouth and held her hand there until the tide in her stomach rolled back. "I think having a baby now would be an awful mistake."

"Pam— What are you talking about!?" Stevie nearly shouted. "You can't mean you'd have an abortion?"

By way of an answer, Pam said nothing. A metallic feeling crept up her spine: armor plating.

"I don't believe you! You're married! You're a family." Stevie watched Pam get up to close the door. She *wouldn't*, Stevie thought. She was just having a philosophical debate with herself. She would never actually have an abortion. She knew Pam and Willy so well she could visualize what their baby would look like. She could almost see Willy carrying the tiny, gummy fluffball in one of those baby holsters strapped to his stomach. She was shaking her head and staring incredulously when Pam said, "I'm thinking about it. Stevie, come on! This is the wrong time to have a baby. A couple of years from now, maybe, but if I leave the business now, I might as well forget my career. You know that."

"You can't be serious. Give up this for that? Do you know what you're saying?" Stevie sputtered. "Have you ever had an abortion?"

"No, but—" Pam began. What a mistake she'd made. She didn't want to argue with Stevie. She shouldn't have told anyone.

"Listen," Stevie said, reaching across the desk and taking Pam's wrist in her firm grip. "It's not like getting a tooth pulled. Damn it! If you have an abortion, this person," she said, pointing a shaking finger at Pam's abdomen, "will no longer exist."

"Stevie, stop," she heard Pam say, but she could not stop. She felt her thoughts tumbling backward in time. A twenty-year-old, sniffing, quaking Stevie was standing outside Sigma Tau

House and she was cold. Over her jeans, she was wearing an old yellow slicker that she'd bought for $4.95 in the Army Navy store. How could she remember that now? It was raining that night. Andy had picked her up in his sky-blue Chevy, his precious piece of junk with the rusted underbody and springs that let the car rock like a hobby horse when it braked, and that night he had been crying, hugging the steering wheel and crying, and she had never seen a man cry before. She was really cold by then. She listened to Andy cry and thought "Cry, I don't care," and told herself that he wasn't really Andy, and that if she lived through this, if she lived through this and could forget all of it, Andy and the music house and this not-a-baby-yet, she would be Stevie again. In truth, there had been a moment when she wanted to cry with him, to kiss him and be kissed, but she had frozen out those thoughts and had done what she had to do. She had turned herself to ice. "Don't touch me, please," she had said when he reached out to comfort her, "Don't," she had said.

The parking lot of the drive-in restaurant was slick black, one light nailed high above them on a telephone pole illuminating the raindrops spraying down around them. She remembered that and that Andy had cried beside her and then the limousine had nosed past the Chevy, slipping silently into a shadow. Stevie had stared at the blurry, white speck through the fan shapes left in the glass by the windshield wipers; stared and waited for the sensation to return to her hands and legs so she could open the door. And walk. Away from the Chevy. And get into . . . No.

"Stevie, stop staring at me like that," Pam said urgently. "It's a choice I have to consider. I've got to decide what to do. It's important for me to decide before it's too late." She looked at Stevie's white face. "Stevie, they're legal now. Women have abortions all the time. Be my friend, okay? I need you to be objective." I need you to tell me it's okay, she said to herself.

Stevie shook her head. Broken images, like fragments of glass, rained around her. "I don't think I can. Be objective."

"Because you want to be pregnant."

"Because I had an abortion."

"Stevie. I didn't know. When was this?"

She hadn't forgotten. It was all there just waiting for her to remember. He had followed. Andy had followed her and had opened the door to get in. "Leave me alone," she had said. "Don't do this," he had implored. "Let me be with you." The driver, a thin woman wrapped in tight black clothing, wearing heavy gold at her ears and throat, had buzzed down the electric window and had told Andy to get away from the car in a smooth skein of Spanish. And then Stevie had turned her face from him. Two girls had been in the car when, damp and shivering, she had squeezed in beside them. One of the girls had been thin, blue veins visible through the pale skin of her bare arms. The other had been large and soft. Three and three made six, she had thought. The girls with no names had spoken to her in soothing little clumps of words and she had spoken that way to them. "Are you comfortable?" "If you need to throw up, just tell her, and she'll stop the car." "Your boyfriend looked really nice," the thin girl had said. "He's not my boyfriend," she had replied.

He wasn't. He was Carol Wilder's husband.

"It's not what you think," Stevie said to Pam. "Have an abortion. Have a baby later. That's what I thought. And look."

Pam recoiled, shoving her chair back to the wall. She felt stung. Stevie was scaring her. "When did you have it?"

"When I was a kid. When I was in school."

Oh, Pam thought, understanding something now. Shocked. "Lisa's father?"

Stevie nodded. It had come out again. First to Carol, and now to Pam. The abortion had been a secret for so long and now all she wanted to do was talk about it, it seemed. Why hadn't she done so before? So she could pretend she had never wanted a baby? To whom? Two wires crossed and sparked.

"God, Stevie. You must have—that must have—" Pam touched Stevie's hand. No wonder this introduction to Lisa had thrown her so. "I don't think it's the same thing for me," she said quietly. "There will be other times."

It *wasn't* the same. She *could* have another baby. They'd been careless exactly once and it had happened. She saw Stevie pointing a finger at her abdomen. Guilt swept over her and she fought it angrily. God damn it, Stevie wasn't being fair. She romanticized everything like a goddamned storybook princess, which was exactly what you'd expect from someone who had had a princess's life. Stevie didn't need to tell her she was carrying a baby. She loved children, God damn it, but was it so wrong to want to have a child in a way that would be ideal for them all? The intercom buzzed nastily, demanding her attention. Pam stabbed the button. What time was it? Oh, for God's sake, they were taping in an hour and a half. "Okay," she said. She stabbed another button. "Ed." She reached over and tapped the notes in front of Stevie with blunt-nailed fingertips and mouthed the word "Read," then she leaned back in her chair and spun it away from Stevie.

Stevie listened briefly to Pam's end of the conversation with Ed Warner, then dropped her eyes to a page. Why didn't Pam understand how lucky she was? What wouldn't she do if she could be pregnant right this minute? Squiggly lines shifted restlessly before her eyes. There was water on the window. She rubbed it away with the back of her hand, and then saw the red light of the sign, MOTEL, flashing, lighting up the inside of the car. And then they were in a room, a bedroom, and the door opened to another room, and then, and then. Stevie squeezed her eyes closed. They had motioned to the thin girl first and she had gone into the second room. Stevie had caught a glimpse of a conical silver lamp hanging from a closet door, and then the door dividing the room was closed. A needle went into her arm and then the world stretched and expanded. Had the large girl gone next? Yes, because the thin girl was lying beside her on the bed, moaning, and then the door opened and she had seen. She had seen the doctor bending between the legs of the large girl. And the woman had said, "Shut your eyes, please" and when she opened them she was lying on the board on the table and the light was shining from the silver lamp and she had felt the scraping, scraping. Had she screamed? My Baby. The woman with the dark clothes had held her hand and then there was the blood on the rubber gloves and then she was in the parking lot at the drive-in restaurant with Andy, his face wet with rain. And then he had driven her back to Sigma Tau House. And at the door she had told him she wouldn't see him again, because she had really wanted that baby, really wanted it, and how could she have forgotten how much?

Someone called her name. She turned, still startled, to the door. It was Luann. "It's Philip," she said. "He's going out and he wants to talk to you."

Stevie stood and unconsciously straightened her clothes. She followed Luann down the corridor and, when she reached her office, went in and closed the door behind her. She hadn't known, she just hadn't, and it didn't have to be true. No one had said, If you don't have this baby there will never be another. She did not have to let this be true. "Hi," she said, feeling cold, welcoming the cold, knowing what she was going to do.

"Steve," he said, and she caught herself wanting to be in his arms, wanting to forget. He was asking her to dinner. How easy it would be to join with him in cooking a simple meal and then lie against his warm body. "I can't," she heard herself say. "I can't be with you right now."

"Do you mean tonight?" he asked.

"Not just tonight. I don't know when." Would she ever see him again? She pictured his worried face. He was her friend, her lover, part of her, but he was asking her to choose him over ever having a child! She sucked in cold air. "I can't be with you, Philip. Don't you understand? This won't go away. I want to have a baby and you don't. This isn't something that can be compromised."

"Stevie, don't do this."

There was water again. Stevie covered her silent tears with her free hand. This was so unfair. If only he could say maybe, there would be time for her to show him how simple it would be, how much more life they could have. "Philip, we're so far apart now. If only you could stay open."

"You want me to say maybe."

"Yes." Please, she thought.

"You don't mean maybe, you know. You want me to say yes."

He was telling the truth. She wanted him to say yes, and he would not! If she were ever to have a baby she would have to move on. She would have to break with Philip and find someone who wanted to have a baby too. Was there any chance she could meet someone before her body said it was too late? "We can inseminate you in our offices," she heard John Wrobleski say. Would she be able to do that?

"Didn't I get through to you? Do you understand how wrong it would be for me to be a father again?"

"I do understand," she said. "That's the terrible thing. I understand and you understand me, and there is no maybe between us."

"I love you, Steve," he said.

"I love you too," she said, her voice cracking in sadness. "But it's not enough."

Silence connected them. She could feel his presence as if he were touching her forehead with his.

Philip spoke. "Don't make this final. I don't want this to be over."

Could she have a happy life without him? She loved him so much. "I don't know yet. I don't know."

"Call me," he said. "Just call me anytime. I'll be here."

"Good-bye, Philip," she said, and not waiting to hear his reply, Stevie hung up the phone. Then, like a mechanical thing, she finished her meeting with Pam, rehearsed the show with the crew, and did her five o'clock taping.

# 16

"Boy, are you in a good mood. Sell a bunch of houses or what?" Lisa asked her mother while looking through the sheet of hair covering her eyes.

"It's all right for me to be happy once in a while, isn't it?" Carol asked, not trying very hard to conceal her smile.

"I guess so, but you can hardly blame me for calling attention to the fact that you are doing pirouettes across the linoleum."

"How do you like the juice? Is it too pulpy for you, because I can strain it a little bit, although I couldn't find the—"

"If you're looking for the strainer, I saw it out in the yard."

"Oh, Lord, that's right. I think I was sieving some . . . where is my . . . ? Oh, here it is." Laughing, grabbing up her new white silk scarf, tying it in one loose knot around her neck. "How do I look?" she asked, beaming at her daughter.

"Beautiful, Mom," Lisa said sincerely, suspicion lurking just around a bend in her mind. Her mother was never giddy in the morning. What was going on?

"But do you think the shoes work with this outfit? I'm not sure."

"They're all right," Lisa said, eyeing her mother's ballet-type flat shoes. "I hardly ever see you wearing flats." What was going on?

"But do they match?"

"Yes, they *match*," Lisa said with exasperation. "What's going on? Do you mind telling me?"

"I think maybe I'll just put a little seed in the bird feeder before I go." Carol shook some millet seed into a cup.

"You're meeting someone, a man, aren't you?" Lisa asked, scooting over to the kitchen door, standing between it and her mother and not moving. "No, no. Let me guess," she said, looking straight into Carol's radiant face. "Flats, so he's not tall. New things," she said, fingering the end of the scarf, "so he's not Mal. Wait a minute. Is this the same man as the mysterious 'I'm going out for dinner, don't wait up' of the other night?"

"Uh-huh, I've got a lunch date," Carol said gloatingly, "but ask me no questions, I'll tell you no lies. I don't want to jinx anything, all right sweetie pie? Oh, honey, run upstairs for me and get my cameo out of the blue box while I feed the chickadees, thank you."

Lisa stepped aside for Carol and stood for a moment in the doorway watching her mother walk out to the maple tree. Sunlight passed through Carol's pale pink dress, silhouetting her slim hips and long, graceful legs. Her mother looked great. It was amazing how young she looked when she was happy. Lisa grunted to herself and bounded up the stairs.

Lisa thought she remembered feeling that girlish when she was first going out with Reed. Funny thing how lately she hadn't been feeling so girlish with him anymore. She hated to think it could be because he was now separated, which would be the obvious thing anyone would say: When you couldn't have him, you wanted him; now that he's available . . . Anyway, it wasn't only that. It was that, compared with Philip Durfee, or B. Willy Foster, or even Ed Warner, he seemed so wispy, so one-dimensional. With Reed, it was the horses, and it was him. Even when it was about her, it was about him. As in, when are you coming over, and what will you be cooking for dinner? Somehow she'd gone from filly to mare since Reed moved into his own apartment, and being a filly was more fun. Maybe this was just life. Maybe this was the way all relationships went after the courtship phase was over. Lisa found the cameo brooch and clutched it in her hand. She should ask her dad about this romance/real life issue. He was in town to see her and was going to take her to lunch today. She would ask him, she thought, running down the stairs.

Luann LaPorte sat at her desk, her back against the outer wall of Stevie's office. She could hear the sound of Ed Warner's voice through the closed door, but she couldn't really make out the words. If she pushed her ear to the wall, maybe, but no, if someone walked by, and someone would, she would look really stupid. The phone rang, and she pressed a button. "Ms. Weinberger's office. No, she can't. She's in a meeting. Okay. Yes. I *said*, yes." She rolled her eyes and hung up the receiver. She scrawled a message on a pink sheet, and tried again to listen through the wall. Almost hearing was worse than not hearing at all, she decided. She was so worried. Grunch almost never just popped in on Stevie, and she could never remember him closing the door. She was really nervous for Stevie lately. The damned phone! "Ms. Weinberger's office, please hold, Ms. Weinberger's office, please hold. Ma? Hang on, Ma. Hello. Right. Ma? I can't talk right now. I did tell him. I can't talk right now, Ma, I'll call you later. You too."

Luann tuned into the rumble behind her. They were still talking in there. Ed Warner, the man of a dozen words. *Men.* Philip was a jerk for letting Stevie break up with him. Did he think he would ever find anyone else as good as Stevie ever again? That wimp. And Stevie was a mess. She looked terrible lately and she had really botched the interview with Abbott Ross last night. "Ms. Wein— Yes. No. Okay, I'll look for it when her meeting is over. The door's closed. None of your business. That's okay, don't worry about it." He wouldn't fire her, would he? That was impossible. So she messed up a little a couple of times, big deal, who didn't? Still, this was a funny kind of business. Hell, Stevie could get another job, and if she got another job, she'd take her, definitely.

At last, the door opened and Ed Warner charged out. "I'll call you if I need you," he said in parting, an ambiguous statement that defied interpretation. Luann looked up at Stevie in alarm.

"I feel scared," she said, following Stevie into her office.

"No, no," Stevie said, letting herself down into a corner of the brown modular seating. "Don't be scared."

"What did he want?" Luann asked. "He never comes down here and closes the door like that."

"He wants me to take some time off. Lu, calm down. I need the rest, I really do. I don't know if you saw the show last night."

"Of course I did. I never miss your show."

"Well, you saw."

"It wasn't that bad," she said loyally.

"It wasn't that good either," Stevie answered. "So, listen. I'm going up to my house for the rest of the week, and I'll get a lot of sleep, and read, like I'm supposed to do, and I'll probably stay next week, too, and it's all right. Even I need a vacation once in a while."

"Okay," Luann said, forcing a smile.

"So Ed's going to tell the staff I asked to go on vacation, all right? So you don't have to worry how this is going to look and anyone who wants to call me, can."

Luann resisted her desire to throw her arms around Stevie and cry, but behind her glasses, her eyes were unblinking and very round.

"And we'll rerun some top of the pops while I'm out. Now, suppose you call Sal and ask him to pick me up as soon as he can. If I leave now, I can get home before the noon rush hour." Stevie looked at her watch. "I don't have much time. I'm going to have a quick word with Pam. Lu? Do you think you could stop looking at me like you've just been told I have six months to live? Thank you. And call my garage. Hey. I'm looking forward to this," she said.

"Well then, hey, have fun," Luann replied in the most convincing tone she could muster.

Andy smiled at his daughter and helped her on with her jacket. She turned to him with her sweet smile and took his arm and together they walked out of the parking lot toward the street and WON-TV. How he loved his girl, he thought. He wanted to hug her right here on the street. Instead, he looked at her with pride.

The fascinating thing about not seeing Lisa from month to month was that on each visit he was amazed to see how much she had changed. Her beauty was constant, but her personality shifted and altered as she transformed herself from child to teenager to a woman who would do—what? Marry, get her plays produced, have kids of her own? She would let him know.

That was what was so wonderful about kids, about having a role in their lives. You could touch them, be there when they needed you, but then the best you could do for them was to step back and let them go. This situation with Reed, for instance. Last time he had seen Lisa, she had been enraptured. Now, without much advice from anyone, she was discovering how little he had to offer her. He knew she would make a decision that would be right for her. The thing was, kids were who they were going to be more or less from the moment they were conceived. Funny how few parents realized that. If their kids turned out well, they took too much credit. If they turned out badly, they took too much blame. And what about this one, this curious, effervescent soul? Maybe what she was meant to do in the world was cause change in everyone she touched. "Watch out, Bugs," he said to Lisa, who was tensing to race them across a break in the traffic. "Let's wait for the light."

"Daddy, you've got to be aggressive in New York. These drivers, they expect pedestrians in the road."

Andy laughed and squeezed his daughter's arm. "I'm not afraid to belly up to anyone, sweetheart, I just like to save it for the important events. Do you drive into the City every day?"

"No, no. I take the train. I love the train. I have time to read the paper every morning from front to back and then when I get into the newsroom, I'm already on top of things. Wait till I show you," she said over her shoulder as she led her father into the office building. Andy looked around the granite-floored, high-ceilinged lobby and allowed the sounds of rapid footsteps and conversation to impinge on his serenity. He tried to imagine why this hurry was so necessary. Thousands of people, all in a rush, scurrying toward this bank of elevators or that one, and his daughter, self-confident, completely at home in this bustle. Well, if he didn't like it, he had to at least respect it. Just the sheer size of everything was impressive. Still, didn't people in this city ever get hungry for the color green? And he didn't mean money. "You could fit the entire population of Oneonta into this building," he said appreciatively as Lisa steered him into a densely peopled elevator.

"It's something, isn't it?" she said, giving her father a grin. "Wait till you see the newsroom. Here we are," she said, the two stepping off the elevator into the plush, gray-carpeted reception area.

From the moment the doors opened, the faint tingling sensation at the periphery of Andy's mind geared up a notch. He'd gotten the buzz the moment Lisa had asked him to please come into the City and see what she was doing this summer. It wasn't too darned tough to put a name to this tingle. Its name was Stevie and he was wondering if he was going to turn his head a half-turn to the left and see her lovely self and if he did, what it would be like. He was pretty sure she wouldn't still be hard on him for the terrible way they had broken up so long ago. He hoped she wouldn't be. He shook his head almost imperceptibly. It had been nineteen years, and still he felt a soreness—like a broken bone that had never mended properly.

"You see how this works, Daddy?" Lisa said, "The weatherman stands there, right in front of that blue board, and a second camera is trained on the map, over there."

"Uh-huh," Andy said, looking from left to right.

"You see, he can't stand in front of the map or you'd never be able to light it properly or do all those special effects, so what happens is, the image of the weatherman is overlaid on top of the image of the map. It's called chroma-key . . ."

Would it be so bad, Andy wondered, if he just dropped in on Stevie? God knew he'd thought of calling her over the years. He'd turn on the TV and see her pretty face and think, "Well that's my friend Stevie." He'd think maybe there wouldn't be any harm in calling her, but then he'd think, what would she say to him? There she was with her own life, and an important one at that, and what in the world would she say to a call from an old disgraced boyfriend from the sticks? No, it had been better to think of her as someone who had loved him once and not have to hear a distant and rejecting voice on the phone. But now that he was here, perhaps only feet from where she was sitting, wouldn't it be easy and almost natural for Lisa to bring him around to say hi?

"It's pretty awesome, honey," Andy said to his daughter. "Show me your office."

"I don't have an office, actually, Dad. I have a desk over there. It's this one. Want to sit down for a while? How much time do you have?"

"Plenty," Andy said. He looked around the room next to the place where they did the taping. Dozens of gray steel desks lined up in fluorescent-lit rows. How did mammals survive in this canned air and fake light, every day, morning until night? Could this be healthy?

"Everyone around here is so nice, Daddy, you just can't believe how much I love it."

"I was wondering," Andy said, "how often you see Stevie."

"Quite a lot," Lisa said. "You know, she walks around all the time. That's one of the really great things about her. She's a real person, not stuck up or a phoney. Oh, and I spent the night at her apartment and had dinner with her twice so far. She's really great. But I guess you know that. Oh God—," she said slowly, "I'm getting an idea. When was the last time you saw her?"

"Before you were born," Andy said, looking down at his calloused hands. He was afraid if he looked up at Lisa, something in his face, or the tingle, would make itself known to her.

"Wow. What an idea. I can't believe I didn't think of this before. I'm so *mad* at myself. We could have had lunch together, the three of us. I'm so mad." She thought for a second.

Maybe it wasn't too late to do something really cool. "Do you want to see her now?" she asked breathlessly.

"Oh, she's probably too busy, Bugs. She wouldn't have the time . . ."

"Don't be ridiculous. She'd be excited to see you. I *know* she would." Lisa flipped through the telephone directory on her desk and found Stevie's listing. She tapped out the numbers and looked at her father as the phone rang. He looked so great. She was getting this terrific idea. Stevie had just broken up with Philip, so maybe it was a little soon, but wouldn't it just be fantastic if . . . "Luann, it's Lisa," she said. "I was wondering if Stevie was free . . . Oh," her voice dropped. "She's not in," she said to her father, "Oh. No, never mind. There's someone here I wanted her to meet. Yeah, thanks anyway, Bye," she said, hanging up the phone. "What a shame, Daddy," she said "I would have loved to see her face."

Andy smiled through his disappointment. So close but so far. The chance of his coming back to New York this summer was somewhere between infinitesimal and nonexistent.

"Wait a minute," Lisa said, snapping her fingers. She hoisted her big denim bag to her lap and pawed through the contents. She pulled out an address book and flopped it open at the W tab. "Guess who's got Stevie Weinberger's home phone number," she said gleefully.

# 17

Stevie leaned against the back wall of the shower and cried. She sobbed, then dried her face with a corner of a towel, then sobbed again until the warm water raining against her back had rubbed away the sharpness of the pain and the tears had stopped flowing, not because she was no longer sad, but because she had, for the moment, run out of tears. She stepped out of the shower and, as she toweled herself, she tried to sort her thoughts into small, manageable piles so she would do what she needed to do, not what she wanted to do, which was to get into her bed and sleep into the next year when she would presumably be well again.

What to wear and what to pack thoughts fell into a little pile over there. What she had left behind at the station, what she had said to Pam and Lu, what Ed had said to her, went into that little pile over there. A lump of sad, angry, abandoned feelings went into the hurting pile of Philip fragments: his voice, his crooked wire glasses, the taste of his mouth. Oh. Stevie put her hand over her mouth and squeezed her eyes tightly closed. She pressed the towel to one eye and then the other and then took a deep, shuddering breath. She missed him. Even as she cried from the loss of him, she could hear his voice in her head, comforting her, murmuring her name. How was she going to get used to being apart from him and then be with another man? That had been the idea, hadn't it? Be with another man? Oh, God, had she been crazy? No. This was the worst part, what she was feeling now.

Going into the bedroom, she turned the stereo up loud and dressed hurriedly in clothes she disliked. She snatched shirts from hangers, sending the triangles clattering against the closet walls. She hastily folded the shirts and dropped them into a duffel bag. A bundle of undergarments followed and a wad of blue jeans covered them and last, Stevie wedged a pair of worn sneakers into the ends of the duffel and zippered the bag.

She impatiently wriggled her hand through the grasping band of her wristwatch and looked at the time. The car would be ready now. If traffic wasn't too bad, she could be in Sharon in two hours. She slung the duffel bag over her shoulder, scooped up the car keys from a dish on the hall stand, and locked the front door behind her. She jabbed the elevator call button. Even as she heard the elevator grinding its way up to her floor, she heard the muffled ring of her telephone through the closed door. *Ring.* Should she go back? It might be Philip. It wouldn't be. But it might be and if it was? Would he say, "You were right and I was wrong?" Not likely. *Ring.* It might be Lu. Or Pam. *Ring.* It was Lu. "Come back. We need you." Stevie dropped the duffel and felt around in her handbag for the keys. *Ring.* She found them. Stabbing the key into the lock, she yanked, twisted the knob, and in a bound, pulled the receiver from the hook.

When she heard Lisa's voice her first thoughts were that Lisa was calling to console her and damn it, she didn't want to be consoled. If she wasn't allowed to screw up once in a while, screw them. She had a standing offer from Fox and maybe she'd damn well take it.

"Stevie, are you there?" Lisa asked.

"Sorry, Lisa, what did you say?"

"I said, I've got someone here who wants to speak with you."

At the sound of his voice, a trapdoor in the floor seemed to open and Stevie dropped through. "I don't believe it," she said finally, nearly righting herself. The dizziness would stop in a moment, she was sure. "Andy? I was just thinking about you the other day." She sat down hard on the kitchen stool.

"You sound like, like you do on television," Andy said nervously, searching to find something to say that wasn't too damned stupid, boy, and failing.

"I know," she said vaguely. It was Andy. Andy was on the phone. Could there be a worse time for him to call? There was too much for her to sort out right now without having an old bundle of hurt roll up to her door. And yet a week ago she would have been eager to see Andy. How would he seem to her now? What if she saw him as Carol described him: a dud, a loser. Wouldn't that free her from the past in some way? An image of Andy began to form in her mind and then it dissolved. He wouldn't look like that now. He would look . . . old.

"I've caught you at a bad time," he said. Her voice sounded so low. What a potato-head he'd been, even hoping she'd be glad to hear from him.

"No, no, I mean, yes," Stevie said. "I mean I was just on

my way out, but I don't want to hang up. Um. I'm surprised—how have you been?"

"Real good. Wonderful. Excuse me for a minute, Stevie," he said and, putting the receiver aside, asked Lisa if she would get him a glass of water. "I'm back," he said into the phone. "I'm sitting at Lisa's desk, and she's been perched on the edge of it like she's a sparrow and this phone's a lump of suet."

Stevie laughed. Her laugh surprised her; it almost seemed disloyal to her sadness to be laughing while her eyelashes were still wet. Andy's voice . . . "I know that look. She's curious, she says."

"Mildly put."

"She's also very special, Andy, a jewel."

"Yeah, she is. She is that," Andy said fondly. He tapped his foot on the linoleum floor and cleared his throat. It was nice of Stevie to say that about Lisa. Nice of her to be nice to her, but he couldn't say that. Hell, he was going to run out of things to say, and Stevie was going to hang up. "Listen, this is hard, you know. Asking what's new and how're you doing, after all these years have gone by. I think I want to say something with a little more meat on it, but I don't know what."

Stevie listened. Andy's voice felt like the morning sun on her face, and as if she were a flower, she found she was turning toward him.

"So, what's new and how're you doing?" he asked with a self-conscious laugh.

"Lots. Nothing. Everything," she said. "Things have been, you know, real good but," she pressed the earpiece tightly to her ear. "Oh, God. I don't know. Things have been good, but . . . I'm taking some time off. Did Lisa tell you?"

"She did. I was disappointed you weren't here. I would have liked to see you."

"Oh. Well, I would have liked that too," she said, realizing that it was true, and to her surprise, finding she was embarrassed to be saying so. Maybe the questions wouldn't have been the only reason she would have liked to see Andy. When she had thought about Andy recently, she had remembered her fantasy and she had remembered its savage dismemberment, but she'd forgotten how funny Andy had been, and how much fun. "You've still got your drawl," she said.

"Yeah, well, I had to fight to keep it. Hanging out for all these years with Yankees."

Stevie laughed.

"An' ah kin still tag a runnuh out wif a mean look, and cook up a mess a sou-ah mash that'ud fuel a sixteen wheelah fum heah t'Atlanta," Andy said, languorously spinning out his words.

"Oh, please, Andy," she said with a laugh. "They don't even talk that way in Mayberry. Have you been watching too much TV, or what?"

" 'Fraid so. Oneonta isn't New York, you know." He paused. He wanted to see her. It had been dumb to wait until the last second to see if she was around. Now she was going off somewhere and he was going to get into his truck and drive for five hours and this was going to be it. Good-bye again for twenty years. "Anyway," he said into the silence. Could he suggest they get together? What was it he wanted from her? A smile? A little squeeze of her hand so he could watch her on television and think, okay now, okay, that's my friend Stevie. We used to go together once when we were kids.

"Anyway," Stevie repeated. She looked at the clock on the kitchen wall. The second hand whirled purposefully around the dial. The car was ready for her by now, with the engine running. They didn't care so much about her celebrity status in the garage that they wouldn't snarl at her if she didn't pick up her car when she said she would. But she didn't want to hang up the phone. "What are you doing in town, by the way?"

"Came in to see my little girl." And you, he thought, fully

acknowledging the truth for the first time. He had been afraid to think it until he heard the honey in her voice.

"So you'll be back?" Stevie said. "We'll plan a get-together. We'll have lunch or something next time. I'll treat you to a pizza city-style, something very hip with capers and arugula . . ."

"Well, sure," Andy said, trying to respond in kind to Stevie's light-hearted tone. "I'd like that. We hardly ever mix our capers and our arugula upstate." Stevie laughed appreciatively, and then there was silence. He had to tell her. "Well, the truth is, Stevie, I don't get here much." Andy swept the room with his eyes. "Maybe once every hundred and fifty years. I think this was the trip."

"Oh," Stevie said, hesitating, not sure that what she was about to say was right, more afraid of some kind of opportunity about to be lost, and of the silence and aloneness she would feel when she and Andy disconnected. "Look. Maybe we can meet for a couple of minutes. There's a coffee shop next to my garage . . ."

"Just you tell me where and when," he said.

It was amazing, Andy thought, that this exquisite long-awaited meeting was taking place in such an ugly room. The coffee shop was a Formica fancier's paradise. He gazed across the orange table at the beautiful woman the girl he had once loved had become. It was impossible not to stare. "I don't mean to embarrass you," he said. "But you look beautiful." He looked at her hard, then returned to stirring his second refill of coffee in the thick cup in front of him. He lifted the cup to his mouth and sipped, grateful for something to do with his hands. What he wanted to do with his hands was put one on each side of her face and bring her mouth to his. He knew exactly how it would feel to touch her skin, to kiss her mouth; those front teeth of hers, overlapping just a little. He remembered touching those teeth with the tip of his tongue . . . Maybe it was seeing her all the time on television that made it seem like he had last seen her yesterday, and maybe it was just that he'd never stopped loving her, never stopped wondering what would have happened if Carol hadn't gotten pregnant. Hell, what was the point of holding it in any longer? They'd been small-talking for half an hour. He was going to be with her for this little bit of time and then he was going to return to the real world and think about every word they'd said to each other. What he didn't want to do any longer was hold in the words he wanted to say and later hate himself for doing so. And the truth was she was beautiful and he wanted to touch her.

Stevie felt her face warming. Every word he said was having a physical effect on her body. She was squirming and blushing and now she had crossed her thighs, hoping to dampen the heat that was starting between them. And how could he look this good? It seemed as if his good looks had doubled. His face was wider, his chest thicker, his golden hair was flecked with gray, and white lines in the tanned creases radiating out from his eyelids seemed to be put there expressly to call attention to his blue-blue eyes. "Thank you," she said, "you look terrific too." An internal alarm sounded . . . What are you doing, Stevie? she asked herself. Flirting? You just said good-bye to Philip yesterday so just stop it. She uncrossed her legs and put her feet firmly on the floor. "Do you miss playing baseball?" she asked, verbalizing the first question she could mold into words.

"Yeah. You never get over baseball," he said sheepishly, "but I would have been out of it long ago even if I hadn't torn up my arm. I like my kids. I like coaching my kids," he added, nodding his head, seeming to Stevie as if he were reassuring a generation of college students that being with them was not his second choice.

"Do you supervise all the sports or just baseball?"

"I coach half a course load of baseball, which is all I have time for with all the administrative work . . ."

"What are you thinking about?" Stevie asked as Andy's sentence trailed off.

"Oh. That I've got a lot to do when I get back and I've only got half a secretary to help me out. Where was I?"

"Half a course load of baseball," she said.

"Right. We've got forty-six teams—that's boys and girls—and so I've got some twenty-odd coaches coaching the ball-type sports. Then there's swimming, and downhill, and cross-country, and field hockey . . . Well, yeah," he said, acknowledging Stevie's open-mouthed stare, "we've got a pretty big program and I've got my hands full." He folded his hands around his coffee cup and looked at them, then looked back into Stevie's eyes. "I hope that answers all your questions about the athletic department at OSU, because after all these years I've got a few things to say to you and none of them have to do with sports. It's about some unfinished business between us."

Stevie felt a thrill and it alarmed her. Whatever was going on was crazy. She looked into Andy's face and saw the look of a man who loved her. On-air exposure could have that effect even on strangers, especially the way she was on the air, shoes off, familiar, saying whatever came into her mind; so it wasn't so incredible that coupled with events of the past, Andy could be having emotions—but she was feeling such a strong pull in return . . . Aftermath, rebound, that's all this is, she told herself. She was having a visceral reaction to an attractive, sensitive man leaping so quickly to the fore, pulling the void closed behind him. It seemed magical, yes, and unreal. It was unreal. She needed to stop this, hold onto herself, or she would forget it was clarity of purpose she wanted so badly.

"Andy, please stop," she said, risking that she would appear presumptuous, or that she might cause him to feel a fool. "I can't take too much right now. I've just . . ." Should she tell him about Philip? Over coffee? It was absurd. "I'm a little raw right now," she said. "Some things that are happening at work, and other things, and that's why I'm taking time off. I need to decompress, if you know what I mean."

"I'm sorry," he said, abashed. "My timing's not too good. Never has been."

Instinctively, Stevie reached out her hand and covered his. Their eyes met and held and then the waiter asked "Will there be anything else?" and dropped the check on the table and Stevie reached for it, and Andy said, "I've got it," and walked with her to the cash register and paid, and put two bills on the table and held the door open for her and then they were both standing on the street, leaning toward each other, each reluctant to say good-bye.

"This wasn't enough time," Stevie said. He looked pained. She had hurt him, at least a little, and the crazy thing was how much she wanted to put her arms around him.

Andy nodded.

"If I don't want to spend the whole day and night in traffic, I've got to go," Stevie said. He had pushed the blue cotton sleeves of his sweater to his elbows. Those tanned arms, muscular as they had been, reminded her of a time when she had been held in their circle. If she took just one step toward him so that he would know . . . but she shouldn't, couldn't. "Rush hour," she said. Was it that she didn't want to leave him or was it that she didn't want to be alone? Andy wasn't Philip, he was someone she hardly knew, had hardly known even *then*. Yet she was being so hard on both of them. Why? Would it really hurt too much to talk about their past, perhaps lean against him, enjoy a small amount of comfort?

"Too bad we can't put your car in the back of my truck," he said. "We're going the same way."

"But you take Route Seventeen and I take the Parkway."

"North is north," Andy said with a smile and a shrug.

"Well, maybe we'll just caravan it for a while. We can wave good-bye at the Thruway exit."

She thought she should kiss him good-bye and turn and walk down the block away from him to the garage, but her feet felt stuck to the pavement. Would it be so terrible if she stopped fighting her feelings and let herself be with him a while longer? Was there some reason why she was choosing to feel alone and bad instead of with Andy and good? "I have another idea," Stevie said. "If it's really not taking you too far out of your way, why don't you give me a lift?"

A smile shot across Andy's face, then disappeared. "But what will you do without your car?"

"I have an old beat-up Peugeot up there, the one we use . . . the one I use for running around in the country. And there's a train back . . . it's no problem."

"I've got my truck parked across the street." Andy pointed across his shoulder, afraid if he took his eyes away from her for a moment she would shimmer in the heat of the day and, like a mirage, disappear.

"Are you comfortable?" he asked.

"Sure am," she said, giving him a small smile and turning her head back to look out the window. The air blowing alongside the open window whipped her hair across her cheek.

"She's not pretty, but she's sturdy," Andy said of the Ford Bronco. "I can haul a lot of equipment in this thing."

Stevie nodded. It was easy to imagine a team of college boys swarming out of a bus and Andy, his hands on his hips, a whistle in his mouth, shepherding them, guiding them, protecting them.

"You can get that dog hair off you with a damp cloth," he said apologetically. "I cannot keep the damn dog out of here. She's a truck-riding fool."

"I wish I had room for a dog," Stevie said wistfully, holding up a pinch of fur and then letting it blow out the window. "No dogs allowed in my building anyway, even if I had time to be with one. What kind do you have?"

"A yellow Lab-type dog with a little of something else in her. She's a great old girl. Had her since she was a pup. She's twelve and still does laps with me in the morning."

Stevie thought of Andy running around a track with a yellow dog bounding at his heels, then, by comparison, she thought of Philip. She had sometimes stood in the catwalk above the squash court and watched him battle against an opponent. He was a powerful player, and fierce.

"You didn't tell me why you're taking off from work," Andy said.

Stevie filled her lungs and exhaled before answering. What was the right answer to that question? I'm heart-broken and afraid of being a barren old lady, and because I'm worrying about that all the time, I'm screwing up on the job. Yeah, she could say that if she wanted to be honest. "I'm burning out a little," Stevie said. "I just need to relax for a while."

"Vacation, then," Andy replied.

"Sort of. Mandatory vacation."

Andy turned his head to look at her and without answering turned his head back to the road. She had that look on her face that kids got sometimes. Something was bothering her and she wanted to talk about it. If he came at her too hard, she would veer away, and yet she kind of wanted to talk, wanted to be pulled at a little, coaxed. "I don't think I ever had one of those," he said.

Stevie kicked off her shoes and folded her knees, digging her toes into the edge of the seat. "I've been messing up a little lately. Really bombed last night when I had this astronomer on . . you didn't happen to see it, did you?"

"I don't think I did. What happened?"

Stevie ruefully sketched the events of the show. "Twice I

asked him questions he had already answered, and that was on top of getting the name of his university affiliation wrong, and misquoting the size of the grant, and I don't even want to remember what else. I'm only glad I remembered his name. Oh, it was amateur night, pure and simple."

"Well, you can't hit a home run every time," Andy said. "They sent you packing for that?"

Stevie shrugged. "I've been distracted lately. I mean, that was the worst show. There were others. Hey, they don't give you much margin for error in my business, and if you're going to act stupid, you're better off acting stupid without a few million people watching."

Andy grinned at her. "I've felt the same way myself," he said.

"I'm kind of glad for the time off, to tell you the truth," Stevie continued. "Weather-wise, this could be one of the best weeks of the summer. Blue skies, no haze, no rain. You get the whole summer off, don't you?" she asked, brightening her face, turning it toward him, hoping that the subject of Stevie Weinberger's career would be changed.

"A few weeks is all. School's open for summer session. Usually we go up into Canada during break, camp out in the wilderness. I like to take a couple of kids with us and teach them how to make a fire, set up a tent. Couple of weeks of eating undercooked fish and wild berries and you're glad to get back to school. But this time, we decided to hang around at home. Clean out the garage, do some ugly chores."

The word *we* hooked Stevie's attention. Her mood, which had been lightening by the minute, plummeted. Was he married? Lisa would have mentioned it . . . and he wasn't wearing a ring. "Oh. Are you married?" she asked, holding her breath.

"Divorced. Again," he said sheepishly. "I've been seeing a gal for a while, though. She teaches history up at the school."

Divorced twice? Her solid-seeming Andy with two ex-wives and a "gal"? But of course Andy would have a girlfriend and why was that so disappointing anyway? Was she building a fantasy? Yes. Somewhere in her subconscious the good prince was crashing through the forest, ready to rescue her from the forces of evil. Her imagination was out of control. Chastening herself, she sought a realistic view of her time with Andy, and found it. Andy was having a reunion with an old girlfriend. Maybe she hadn't even interpreted his look accurately. Maybe she was sizzling all by herself.

Andy wrinkled his brow as he pretended to concentrate on his driving. He hadn't wanted to mention Penny and yet that *we* had jumped smack into the conversation. Hell, not mentioning her would have been dishonest. Why had he felt like being sly? Penny and Dixie and the white farmhouse with the two-car garage were aspects of his real life and Stevie was a glamorous apparition from his past. So. He wanted to dwell, for the next two hours at least, in the land of make-believe. That was dangerous and he was fixing to get himself hurt. "So, is there someone special in your life?" he asked, ignoring the irrational hope for the answer to be no.

"There was," she said sadly. "We just broke up. Yesterday, as a matter of fact."

"I'm sorry," he said, reaching across the expanse of seat between them and touching her shoulder. "I'm real sorry."

"Me too," she said, her mouth smiling, her eyes pained. "Does your radio work?" she asked. Not waiting for a reply, she switched the knob to On.

"I want to hold your han-n-nd. I want to hold your hand," they sang in unison, then laughed together.

"Did we ever dance to that?"

"We tried," he said. "It makes for better singing than dancing."

"Andy, this is it," Stevie said, leaning forward and pointing the way. "It's the next turn on your right."

Andy swerved the truck onto a dirt road that cut through a lightly wooded patch, crossed a brook, and terminated at the side of a frilly, gingerbready Victorian house.

"They didn't build houses like this one off the road," she explained. "The people I bought it from found it in a little town a few miles down and had it moved. They put it on a truck," she said, "and drove it here. I still can't believe it."

Andy pulled up the hand brake and shut off the ignition. The delicious sounds of the birds and the brook were welcome after the long drive. And the house was a pretty thing, dainty and solid at the same time. Like Stevie, he thought. This house was like Stevie.

"I'm so happy here," she said in a voice just above a whisper. She could have been saying it to herself, he thought.

"Well, isn't it a beauty!" he said appreciatively. He opened his door and stepped out into the summer day. Was she going to invite him in, or was she going to say, "So long and thanks for the lift?" He walked around the side of the truck and opened the door for Stevie. "The latch sticks a little bit," he said, jerking at the handle, swinging open the grudging door.

"I'll just get my bag," she said, reaching behind her. He was so close, she could hear the sound of his breathing. Could he hear the sound of hers?

"Let me take that for you," he said, hefting the duffel down with a fluid motion. Her fragrance, as light and as fresh as that of the green tree-scented breeze, tugged at him. He wanted to put his hands on her waist and swing her down. He wanted to bury his face in her hair, and pull her body close to him, but he held out his hand to her instead. She took it but, not willing to risk looking in his eyes, dropped her gaze to his chest. I want him, she announced to herself. She tried to swallow, but her mouth was dry. She spoke. "Wow, am I stiff," she said, laughing self-consciously, shaking out her legs.

"If you walk around for a minute, those cramps will loosen right up," he said.

Stevie took her bag from Andy, walked the few steps to the front porch, and dropped her bag on a rocking chair. From this safe distance, she turned to look at him. He was still standing beside the truck with his thumbs hooked in his pants pockets. He was looking at her, and he was waiting. Reunion was okay. Reunion was nice. He was nice. "Come on," she said, stretching out her hand, linking it through his arm when he walked to meet her. "Let me show you the lake."

Shade from the ash tree cast a dappled, moving shadow over Krypton Rock. Stevie hugged her knees, resting her chin on them, and gave the impression of a woman gazing out at the gray-green water. Andy sat both four feet to her left and right in the middle of her mind. Hugging her knees made her think of hugging him. Watching him make a whistle out of grass made her think of kissing his lips. If she kissed him, would it feel familiar, the kiss of a man she had kissed before? Or had all the years of kissing other women changed his kisses? She would like to know.

"This is a real pretty spot," Andy said. "Makes you want to take off your shoes."

"Let's," Stevie said, kicking off her sneakers, peeling off her socks. Surreptitiously, she watched Andy do the same, then she leaned back and lifted her face to the afternoon sun. "You haven't told me what happened with you and Carol," she said.

"Oh. Well, we had Lisa, which was wonderful. Then we had my baseball career, which was short. Then we got a divorce."

Stevie looked at him and then turned away. "Well, that was

the world's quickest answer to 'what's your story' I ever heard in my life."

Andy chuckled and pulled up a piece of grass.

"I'd really like to know."

"Okay, but it's not a long story. It started out good enough. Got into an A team directly after school, then a year later, I was picked up by a double A team. Different towns, you understand. Then I went with the Hawks. Triple A and I was considered very good. 'Very promising,' they said. The Hawks were home in a town about the size of a peanut somewhere at the top of Florida, I almost forget where. And Carol was trying the best she could to like this life of being on buses and dragging poor little Lisa everywhere to watch me play . . . And then there were my famous three years with the Boston Red Sox."

"Oh, I remember," Stevie said. "I remember looking for your name in the sports pages." She gave Andy a bashful smile.

"Did you? Did you do that?"

"Of course I did," she said.

Andy grinned at her and then he grew pensive. "It was a good time, Stevie. A very good time." Andy stopped talking and peeled off his cotton sweater. The tee shirt he wore underneath was emblazoned with the name and insignia of the major league team. "I grew up, of course," he said ironically.

"Does your shoulder still hurt?"

"Not too much. Sometimes if I get carried away tossing the dog around. Hell," he said, shrugging, "this is what you call an occupational hazard."

"They can fix it now," she said, touching his arm lightly, then withdrawing her hand. "I read something about laser surgery."

"Yeah, well. Listen, it's all right. I had fun. I was in the big time. I had more than my fifteen minutes of fame. There were no guarantees I would have lasted and in many ways, it was a crummy life, Stevie. Carol was right to give up on me. We didn't get along any too well, anyway."

"Andy. What rotten luck."

"Tearing the damn shoulder," he said. "One minute you're in, the next minute you're out. A business you can really build a life on," he said with a rueful laugh. Then his eyes saddened. "After the Red Sox, I felt so, I don't know, homeless. When I got the offer from OSU, I just grabbed it. It was a real good deal. Good money. Nice campus. Free house. Wholesome kids. And they really wanted me. I needed to be needed. Carol never took to campus life and being there just tore it. Whatever was left of us." Andy paused. "It killed me when she took Lisa down to Chappaqua, but . . ." he sighed. "But the school was only four hours away, so . . . Anyway."

Silence drifted over them. Suddenly Andy turned to Stevie. "Hey, let's go down there and throw some rocks. I got such an urge to chuck a few stones."

She gave him a surprised look. "But I thought . . ."

"Underhand," he said.

"Follow me," she said, picking her way down the slope to the water.

The boat house was dank but the moist, cool air was refreshing. Together they untied the dinghy and jumped in. Andy took the oars and with sure strokes, pulled until the boat was in deep water, then rested back crosswise in the boat. "Is there anything better than cloud watching?" he asked. The soft afternoon light glinted off the water and the breeze brought with it the doughy smell of "cooking" vegetation. "When you're watching clouds, you can just sort of turn your thoughts loose. This is what we do in the sticks instead of going to psychiatrists," he said.

Stevie laughed appreciatively. That's what she ought to do

when she got back next week. Find a shrink and go for a while. People had always told her how well-adjusted she was, and maybe she had taken too much pride in that. Take a look, Steve, she thought to herself. You're a mess. "Clouds, huh? Maybe, but maybe I need the real thing. I'm thinking about it."

"You've never been shrunk?"

"Nope."

"No kidding? I thought everyone in New York went about eight times a week. I've gone. Yes, I did," he said in response to Stevie's surprised look. "I went for a couple of months when Donna and I were breaking up. We went to one of those marriage-counselor type of shrinks. Didn't do much good but it wasn't the shrink's fault."

Stevie let her eyes wander over Andy's face and then down to his tee-shirted chest. It was strange. She recognized parts of him. The short-bitten nails, the freckles on his forearms, his profile and the shape of his nose, but most of his body was a mystery to her. With a shock she realized they had only made love with most of their clothes on and always in the dark. A flash of desire temporarily blinded her. She shifted in her seat and searched her recent memory. What had he just said? "Donna? Was she your second wife?"

"Yup," he said. "We were married for about a minute and a half."

"Come on."

"A year and a half," he admitted. "But it was a short year and a half. She didn't tell me until after we were married, and then I couldn't get her to change her mind. My God," he said suddenly, raising himself up on one elbow, turning to face Stevie, who sat clasping her knees, her back to the bow. "What am I doing, running off at the mouth like this? I must be starved for adult company."

"What didn't she tell you?" Stevie said, leaning forward. "That she was a gun-runner? That she was planning a sex-change operation? If you stop this story now, you're going for a swim, I warn you."

Andy rearranged his sweater, which had been serving as a pillow, and reclined again. Stevie could see he was arranging his thoughts at the same time.

"It was real important to me at the time. I really felt lost without Lisa . . . and when Donna and I got married, we were what? Thirty? When we got married, I just assumed . . ."

Stevie caught her breath and fastened her gaze on Andy's face. The sun was going down over the lake and the pink light softened his features. He looked thirty still. His chest rose and fell with his breathing and Stevie, when she checked the rhythm of her own breathing, found they were breathing together. "She was a stubborn little thing, that Donna," he said. "She didn't call it stubborn. She called it, 'she didn't want to do what she didn't want to do.' Seemed real clear to me at the time. She didn't want kids and I did. The only thing to do was split up."

Stevie swished the bristle brush over the dinner plate and forced herself to focus her attention on the sensation of warm water on her hands. Something had changed in the last hour but she didn't know precisely when. Until then, she had been feeling that their time together was limited, that each moment had to be weighed, each word measured, each expression controlled, all transactions gently censored so that the boundaries of their reacquaintance would be held intact toward its predetermined end. Now, Andy was bringing dinner dishes from the table and she was washing them and he was putting things in the refrigerator not as if he had just met this refrigerator, but rather as if he had moved things around in it many times before and would in all probability be removing leftovers from it for years to come.

The change must have happened in the orchard. After they

had tied up the boat in the fading light of day, they had walked up the slope, collected their shoes, and continued up past the house to the orchard. She knew she was still thinking in the orchard that in a short while she was going to walk Andy down to the truck and kiss him good-bye. She had been imagining that kiss: a kiss on the cheek or a peck on the lips given through the window so she wouldn't want too much. And then she had been showing him the tree that was just a shell really, a husk of apple bark filled with crumbling brown compost, that perversely, stubbornly, produced leaves and apples every year. Philip had named that tree "Never say die," and he visited it first, sometimes before the groceries were in the house, just to see what the tree had done while they had been away. So there she had stood at Philip's tree with Andy, and her feelings were moving again from should to shouldn't. Up to down. Do to don't. And then she had run her hand up the shell of a tree and felt the change. From the moment Carol had first phoned, not very long ago, she had been hammered relentlessly by the events of the past and by a frightening vision of the future. And so maybe Andy was balm. Maybe his presence was a gift that shouldn't be questioned, just accepted. She had turned to him and he had held out his hand and she had taken it. His hand was warm and dry. It asked nothing, demanded nothing, it simply felt like the right place for her hand to be. Together, they had walked down the grassy hill to the house.

Once inside, her new-found calm was lost and sentences crumpled by anxiety were blurted. Hers: "Isn't it late? To be driving so far?" His: "It sure has been a long time since that cup of coffee." Hers: "Spaghetti. Do you like spaghetti?" His: "Maybe I could use the phone." Hers: "The towels are in the closet in the guest room. The blue room. Up the stairs on your left . . ." And he had stirred the spaghetti sauce with her hand-carved maple spoon, and she had made a salad with greens from the lettuce garden by the porch steps, and just beneath the assurance of doing familiar tasks, they both had trembled with something less than certainty, something more than hope.

Over dinner he had asked her to tell him about Philip. And finally, she had told him. She told him about the love and the tearing pain when she decided to break with Philip and how she thought about the baby she hadn't had. And then to brush the words away she had risen from the table and flooded the sink with hot soapy water. And now he stood just behind her, not letting her retreat, and she felt his presence palpably, like a shawl made of something living draped across her shoulders.

"That night. That last night was awful," he said sadly. "I've never forgotten it. I've never felt so helpless since."

"I had to shut you out." She plunged her hands back into the water and shook her head as if a cloud of gnats had gathered around her face.

"I didn't blame you for hating me, but I always wondered if you knew how deeply I wanted you and our baby."

Stevie placed her hands on the sides of the sink and held on. She was tumbling again. She was afraid to speak, afraid to turn. If she did she might become a butterfly, or she might die.

"Did you know?" he asked. He had placed his hands on her arms just below the shoulders. He held her lightly, but she could feel each of his fingertips on her bare skin. "I was like a cat in a box. I couldn't find a way out. I had to marry her. But I don't think I ever stopped—" And then he turned her gently toward him. Unguarded, she felt desire, tenderness, and now some kind of hopeless hope. The feelings merged and fused.

She lifted her face and he bent to her and then he touched her lips with his. She raised her arms and wrapped them around his neck and gratefully pressed against him. He held her tightly to him and whispered her name. When they broke their embrace, he kissed her again, and she felt him hard

touching her with just the tip of his penis. "With a million buttons . . ."

Stevie groaned and pulled him to her. "And I want you just as much now," he said, sinking into her. Each of his movements pierced her with pleasure and separated her more from herself until she felt the only hard part of her body was the part that was him. She felt like liquid spilling over the edge of a glass as she gave herself over to one orgasm and then, quickly, another, and then her emotions flowed too. She held her tears until Andy too was depleted, and then she cried from relief and love and a thousand hurts that were blessedly gone.

"I love you," he said, holding her and rocking her. She touched her lips to the soft skin of his neck, and although it was dawn, they both fell again into slumber.

*In the dream she was cupping a ball of light in her two hands . . .*

Stevie's eyelids flew open. She knew this dream. This dream was about the baby. She disengaged herself slightly from Andy's arms and reached down between her legs. She felt the thick wetness that was Andy's seed. She looked at him, at his sweet face. Andy had said that he still loved her. And wasn't it true that she still loved him? Could it be that this was fate or destiny, the way her life was supposed to be if it hadn't been wrenched off the rails so long ago? Maybe they were meant to re-create . . . She straightened the covers and turned her head to look at Andy's sleeping face again. "We have all the time in the world," he had said last night. But that wasn't quite true. She didn't have a lot of time—unless this was the dream fulfilled, unless Andy could give her back the baby she had thrown away.

# 18

"Sell the house? Sell this house? I don't believe you." Lisa threw herself onto her mother's bed and pounded the pillows until she had made a nest for her fulminating mood.

Carol regarded Lisa's reflection as she stood before the full-length mirror that backed her bedroom door. "Good Lord, Lisa, I haven't done anything yet. I'm just mentioning it. I want you to think about it because it's something I want to do."

"I *hate* this. I hate this conversation."

"The first time you said 'I hate this conversation,' you were about four. What were we talking about? I can't remember, but you said 'I hate this conversation,' and you put your hands

over your ears and shook your head, your little pigtails swinging against your cheeks until we couldn't talk anymore, we
were laughing so hard. Oh, I remember, it was closing time at
the zoo and you didn't want to leave." Carol laughed and
turned to Lisa, hoping she would be laughing too. She was
scowling. "Honey, try to see it from my point of view, okay?
You don't live here anymore." Carol turned again to the mirror,
slipped out of the black and white blouse for the second time,
and reached for the cream silk. She tucked the blouse into the
waistband, then pulled at it to soften the line. The black skirt
was perfect. It skimmed her slim hips and thighs, then flared
out in a flirtatious little flounce at her calves. The problem was
the blouse. The cream blouse with the shawl collar was either—
and she didn't know which—dead elegant or too plain, and
while the black and white print that came with the skirt looked
great on the hanger, when she put it on, all the color drained
right out of her face.

"The cream blouse, Mother. No contest," Lisa said flatly.

"You're sure it's not too plain."

"No. It's not. It's perfect. Wear your pearls. Listen to me.
I'm here now, aren't I? And I live here in my head when I'm
at school."

Carol turned her back on Lisa and rummaged in her underwear drawer. Please let them be there. Yes, in the back was the
cellophane-sealed pair of French lace pantyhose which had
been waiting for this two-hundred-dollar-pair-of-shoes opportunity. She sat down at the edge of the bed, rolled the hosiery
into two crinkly little pats, and stretched them over her legs.
Then she went to the closet and found the shoes still housed
in the clean white box, wrapped in crisp layers of tissue, their
new-shoe aroma smelling every cent of the fortune they had
cost. She stepped respectfully into the low-heeled black pumps,
torn between wanting to preserve their maidenhood and wanting to tame them, break them, claim them as her own. She

walked daintily back to the mirror, the pristine soles barely touching the floor at all.

"Those are nice," Lisa said, rolling onto her side, examining her mother's feet. "When did you get them?"

"Thanks, honey," Carol replied. "I was in White Plains last week and I stopped in at I. Magnin."

Lisa rolled back onto her pillow-nest, her mother's shoes already forgotten. "Were you listening to me?" she asked querulously. "Did I reach you? This is my house too!"

"I know it is. I know that. I know you have an attachment to it, and I understand it's a certain kind of comfort to know that your mother is still living in the house where you grew up. But Lisa, honey, this house is too big for one person and it's too dark. I've just been tolerating this darkness for I don't know how long and being alone in this big, dark house makes me feel lonely."

"Lonely? Since when? You're never home! All you do is work, shop, and go out with Stan. When are you lonely, can you tell me that?" Lisa stared angrily at her mother's back. Primp, primp, preen, preen. It was sickening. An idea struck. "Wait. Don't tell me. I'm a little slow tonight. These are clues. You're lonely and you're selling the house. This isn't some subtle way of telling me you're moving in with Stan and getting married, is it?"

Now wouldn't that be nice? Carol thought. She walked to her dresser and pulled a long strand of pearls from a box. She slipped the strand over her neck and centered the clasp. "You're being ridiculous," she said mildly.

"Hmm. I'm not so sure."

"Is something eating you, hon, or are you just going through an obnoxious phase?"

"Gosh, Mom," Lisa said, her voice saturated with sarcasm. "What in the world is the matter with me? You want to sell the only house I ever lived in—"

"That's not true."

"You said you want to sell it!"

"It's not true this is the only house you ever lived in."

"Excuse me, the only house I *remember* living in, and you're out every night with a thirty-two-year-old—"

"Ah-hah," Carol said, waggling her finger. "That's it, isn't it? I don't know why, but I was waiting for this." Carol looked at her daughter's seething expression. "I was wondering when you were going to say something about Stan's age."

"Good. Well, I'm saying it."

"What are you saying exactly?"

"It's not right. It doesn't feel right."

"To whom?"

"Mother. Be serious. He's seven years younger than you. You should be going out with someone in his *fifties*. Stan's practically an *intern*."

"Lord, Lisa, when did you get so conventional," Carol said, turning to the mirror, brushing her hair. "I can hardly believe all this 'should' stuff is coming out of you."

"And he looks like a nerd."

"Stop it," Carol said sharply. "That's absolutely enough. It would be nice if you liked Stan, but you don't have to. I do like him, and quite a bit I might add, and I don't want to hear any more ugly talk out of you."

Lisa threw herself back into the pillows with an exasperated sigh, stretched both arms out to the side, and stared up at the ceiling. The only sound in the room was that of a hairbrush crackling through Carol's hair followed by small sharp clicking sounds as Carol opened and shut little cases of eye and cheek color. "I'm sorry," Lisa said at last. "It's your life, I guess."

"Thank you."

"What time will you be coming home?"

"I don't know. We're going out with a colleague of Stan's and his wife and we may go to a club after that. Why?"

"Haven't you noticed we never have time to talk anymore? I think I spoke to you more when I was calling you up from school."

Carol turned around and walked to the bed. Was she crazy or had she and Lisa exchanged roles somehow? Yes, back at the beginning of the summer when Lisa had been out every night with Reed . . . She sat down and looked at Lisa, who was about to twist her hair clean off her head. "What's the matter, kiddo? Is something wrong between you and Reed?"

"I wondered if you were ever going to ask."

"Hey, would you mind giving the old witch a break?" She shook Lisa's arm affectionately until she seemed to relent. "Well?" Carol asked again.

"He's acting weird. I don't know. I don't know if I even love him anymore."

"What do you mean, weird?"

"Well, like if you love someone, you try to put their interests first, right?"

Carol shrugged. "Yes. A qualified yes."

"Well, I got offered a job at WON—"

"Lisa!" Carol exclaimed. "Not a full-time job!"

"No, no. Part-time, at night. But it's a real job in news. And, Mom, I love it there. It's not that hard to imagine that I could have a career in television—" Lisa broke off and rolled over onto her stomach. "Oh, I don't know," she said into the pillows. "I just don't know anything anymore."

Carol jostled her arm affectionately. A night job in New York? Reed wouldn't like that. Hooray. "Is Reed trying to discourage you?"

"Yes. He said it would just sidetrack me away from—"

"Will you turn over so I can hear you?" Carol asked.

Lisa complied, punched the pillows, crossed her arms over her chest. "He said this part-time job would just sidetrack me away from my writing, but I don't see that, Mom. I could transfer to NYU, get into their creative writing program, and work at night in this great job; and everything Reed says to discourage me sounds so phony. Do you see what I mean?"

"I'm listening," Carol said carefully.

"I guess I could understand it if he said he was sorry he wouldn't see me so much, but he doesn't say that. He says Sarah Lawrence is a better school. He says I'm going to miss my friends. He says New York City is a warped environment and that I'm being seduced by the electronic media. I don't know. Is he right? If he is, why don't I see it? I think this job could be important to me whatever I do. Don't you think?"

Carol watched her daughter run through a riff of nervous gestures. Twist, wrinkle, chew—and still she was a beauty. It seemed clear, she thought, that Reed could see he was going to lose her and he was starting to play dirty. It was equally clear that Lisa had all the facts and a strong inclination. "Honey, having a whole lot of options can sometimes feel confusing, especially if different people are telling you different things. I don't think anything I could tell you would mean as much as you figuring out the best road for yourself, and I think you've got a real good fix on the situation, I really do."

"But, Mom," Lisa protested.

"When do you have to give the station an answer?"

"I already did. I told them yes, but it was a quick reaction. I could always tell them I changed my mind."

"Okay, then. You've got time, so take it and give all of this a real good think. Whatever you decide, you really can't lose." She clapped her hand on Lisa's blue-jeaned thigh, gave her an assuring little wiggle, then stood. "Help me find my handbag, will you? The black one with the stitching across—"

"Mom! What do you think I ought to *do*?" Lisa demanded. "Why are you being evasive? What is this, some sort of game?"

"No, it's not," Carol said from inside the closet. Damn. Was that the doorbell? "Honey, let Stan in. Tell him I'll be right down."

"It's something," Lisa insisted. "Since you started seeing Stan, it's like you don't care about me anymore."

Carol stepped out of the closet and turned off the light. "Don't, Lisa. That's not it at all," she said gently. "It's just that I had a sudden realization that you've been right all this time about me, you know, telling you how to run your life."

"What are you talking about!?" Her mother was driving her crazy. First she was all over her about everything from her clothes up and now when she needed real advice she was slipping and sliding and throwing her clothing all over her room like a, a, kid. And no matter what she said, Stan Wilson was sucking up every bit of Carol's attention and it was unbecoming. It was just disgusting for her mother to be acting like a lovesick teenager.

"Honey, will you let Stan in? Never mind. I'll do it myself."

"Go ahead," Lisa said, standing aside to let her mother pass. "Oh, by the way I forgot to tell you."

"Hurry, Lisa. Poor Stan is—all right, what? What did you forget to tell me?"

"I forgot to tell you that after Daddy took me to lunch last week he went out with Stevie and neither one of them has been home since."

Carol felt flushed, then fluid, then cold. She gripped the door jamb so that she wouldn't fall, barely registered Lisa walking out of the room past her, then, wanting to hide herself in darkness, she snapped off the light. So, the story was going to end this way after all. Stevie was going to get her man, Andy was going to get his woman, the whole awful accident of her interference in their could-have-been-perfect lives was being erased. Lord, how could it still hurt to think of them together? But it did hurt. Somehow in the arms of beautiful, unimpeachable Stevie, Andy changed from the dull little boy who had never grown up into the prize of a man she had been unable to hold.

She looked down at her new shoes and in the dim light they seemed pathetic—pitiful little props to make her think she was worthy of a sexy younger man. Had she really thought she could transform herself . . . She heard the doorbell ring again, its cheery chime breaking into her disconsolate thoughts. That chime made her think of Stan, not just his presence on her doorstep but his presence in her life. It was amazing to her and a blessing that such a wonderful man liked her, gloomy side and all. But it was true. Stan was real and warm and he cared about her. And she was crazy about him. When she was with Stan she felt whole and happy, confident that she was liked as is, the way she was. Being with Stan Wilson made her feel good, so why, she wondered, a sharp ray of reason illuminating her murky thoughts, why was she letting her spoiled, jealous little girl hurt her so much? So Stevie and Andy went out together. So what if they screwed until they welded together? Stevie and Andy were old, old news. There was a darling, lovable man downstairs just waiting for her to fly into his arms. She refocused her vision and watched as Lisa plodded down the stairs. "Hold it," she said, her voice ripe with anger, bursting with it. "Just you hold on."

Lisa turned, one hand on the banister. "But Mom, poor Stan—"

"That was wicked and it was cruel. I want an apology and I want it now."

Lisa felt the room shift. Her former relationship with her mother became something else, something that swooped and dipped and raised the hair on the backs of her arms. She was frightened. She had gone too far, played too rough—but wait a minute. *She* was the injured party! *She* was the one who was being neglected. She deserved more from . . . No. No, no, no. What she had done was unjustifiable. She had been vicious, and the worst thing was, she had meant to be. The banister felt slick beneath her hands and the words, "You were wrong," stamped themselves immutably across her conscious mind. She was worse than wrong. She was an ungrateful little bitch. Her mother should have her put to sleep. "You're right, Mom. That was inexcusable. I'm so sorry, I could die."

Carol grunted and walked down the stairs. Lisa caught her hand as she passed. "Mom, wait. Please don't go yet. I don't want you to leave this mad at me."

"Lisa, if I could send you to your room without supper and cut off your privileges for a month, I would. That was a hateful, hateful thing to say."

"I know. If I said nothing but 'I'm sorry' for the rest of the year I still wouldn't be telling you how sorry I am."

"Okay, then."

"Will you forgive me?"

"Yes."

"Really?"

"Yes. Yes. I said yes," Carol said angrily.

The two women walked down the rest of the stairs together. "If you hadn't said it that way, Lisa," Carol said, "like a bullet."

"I know," Lisa said mournfully.

"I mean, why shouldn't they spend time together? For God's sake. I haven't felt love for your father for fifteen years."

"Mom," Lisa said, putting her hand on Carol's arm as she went to the door. "It's just that I feel so alone lately. Like everybody is leaving me. You and Daddy and Reed, and now the house . . ."

Carol looked at her daughter's face. The confident, mature, sophisticated Lisa had been stripped away, leaving a child of six who was lost in the supermarket. Her anger disappeared and concern enveloped her. It had been weeks since they had shared more then a rushed meal together. Maybe it had been longer than that. "I'm not leaving you, honey," Carol said. "I'm not leaving you in any way. Stay here for a minute. I'll ask Stan to wait in the car."

Lisa leaned against the wall. What had her mother said? About confusion and options? If this was good, why did she feel so awful? She heard Carol speaking with Stan outside the door and then the door opened and Carol came back inside.

"Is it okay?"

"We'll only be a few minutes late." Carol sat on the stairs and made room for Lisa beside her. "I've been thinking about what you said."

"About Daddy? Please, Mom, I wish with all my heart I could take that back."

"No, not about your father. About your feeling left."

"Yeah."

"I *have* been preoccupied lately. It's true. And I guess I haven't been listening to you with both ears all the time and thinking about you every minute like I used to."

Lisa tapped her sneaker toe on the floor but didn't speak.

"I haven't been in love in a long time, honey. And it feels so good, I just want to drink it."

"Yeah," Lisa said softly. "I remember the feeling."

"Oh, sweetie," Carol said, putting her arm around her daughter's shoulder. "I'm not much of a fortune teller, but I suspect you'll be in love again."

"Yeah," Lisa said with a small smile. They sat together quietly, their knees and shoulders touching. What a selfish little pig I've been, Lisa thought. "I don't like what I've been saying and thinking lately," she said quietly.

"It's okay," Carol said, patting Lisa's knee. "You said you're sorry. It's okay."

"Not just now. For a while. Stan's not a nerd, Mom. He's really not. I'm just so used to having you all to myself."

"Shh, shh. I know."

"I'm a brat."

Carol laughed and, putting her arm around Lisa's shoulder, squeezed her affectionately. Lisa leaned into her mother's shoulder and savored the feeling of being hugged by the person she felt closest to in the world. "You have to go," she said at last, stoically breaking away.

"You're right," Carol said, standing, brushing the creases from her skirt. "Is my lipstick on straight?"

"You look fabulous. You look like a million."

Carol smiled and turned the doorknob. "If I don't see you later, I'll see you at breakfast."

"Mom?"

"What is it, honey?"

"What we were talking about before. Could you just tell me one or the other? What should I do?"

Carol smiled. "You're going to push me to the wall, aren't you?"

Lisa nodded.

"Well," Carol said, opening the door a crack. "I don't know what *you* should do. But I guess I can say what I'd do if I were in your spot. If it were me I'd take the job."

Lisa walked to her mother and hugged her. "Thanks, Mom," she said in a very small voice. "I really love you."

"I love you too, my darling girl."

Pam planted herself in the doorway of the control booth. "I can't leave with you tonight," she said to B. Willy. "I've gotta take this guy out for a drink and interview him."

Willy spun his chair toward her. "Got a second to talk?"

"Sure," she said.

He got up and steered her across the corridor into his office, then shut the door. The small room was windowless, every ugly surface piled high with videocassettes, the whole junkyard mess illuminated by a forty-watt bulb in an ancient goosenecked lamp. Two gray chairs faced each other, the corner of a gray metal desk interposed between them.

"You're working too hard," he said when they had both sat down. "That's what I want to tell you. We planned one lousy evening out this week, in a real restaurant with tablecloths and someone to cook the food and wash the dishes, and now you're ditching me to interview someone who could probably have gotten his ass in here during the day."

"Will, he couldn't. He's a talent agent and he would only see me if he could stay plugged into his phone. He's in from L.A. for one day. He's leaving tonight at nine."

Willy leaned back and crossed his arms behind his neck. "You look like hell, you know."

"Thanks," Pam said mildly, looking down at her knees.

"I'm only telling you this because I love you."

"I'll go wash my face. Put on some suntan."

"Don't get up. You have time."

Pam looked at her husband, who was simply staring at her. "What? What, Willy? Why are you staring at me like that?"

"Because I'm waiting for you to tell me what's going on."

"Nothing. I told you. I have to work late. Jesus Christ, you work late and I don't give you the third fucking degree."

"Well, that was passionate. I mean the words were there, but you didn't even raise your voice. You can't, can you? Too tired to even raise your voice. Yeah, that's better. A little fire in your eyes. Go ahead, hit me as hard as you can," he said, throwing out his arm, inviting her punches.

Pam flailed at him with soft fists. "Leave me alone," she said, punching his arm.

"No," he said, capturing her and pulling her down into his lap. He wrapped strong arms around her and hugged her tightly to him. Instantly, the struggle left her and she molded herself to his body, allowed herself to be rocked. "Will, please."

"No, I won't. I won't let you melt yourself down to a puddle because of this job. It's just a job, Pam. It's not worth killing yourself for a job."

"I love my job," she said into his neck.

"Love it all you want, but don't let it eat you up. You're putting in ridiculous hours. I've watched you standing at the sink at ten p.m. pushing food into your mouth and not even knowing that you are eating. I come down to see you at lunch and you're sleeping on your floor. What happened to the cozy little home life we used to have? We don't eat together. We haven't made love since I don't know when. You don't even look me in the eyes anymore."

"I'm sorry, honey. I'm pregnant."

"What?!"

Pam still couldn't look at him. She hugged him tighter, tried to bury herself in the thin folds of his polo shirt, resisting his attempt to pry her loose so he could look in her face. She hadn't meant to blurt it out that way, but now that she had she was relieved. Whatever the worst was, it would happen now and she wouldn't have to bear the secrecy any longer.

Willy insistently unclasped her fingers and arms and forced her into an upright position until he was holding her, still on his lap, but holding her hard by the shoulders. "You're kidding me, right? You're kidding me."

"No," she said, shaking her head, then putting her arm around his neck and melting back into his embrace.

"Pammy, Pammy, Pammy," he said, crooning her name and rubbing her back. "You're going to have a baby. We're going to have a baby. Oh, God, I can't believe it. I'm going to be so happy when I stop being mad at you. How long has this been going on?" He felt little heaving hiccoughs against his chest and the underside of his jaw was warm and wet. "Oh, no. Fuzzy Puss. Baby. Are you crying? What is it? Talk to me." He held her and moved the cloud of black fluff away from her face. "Talk to me," he said again.

"I love my job," she said thickly.

"I see."

"You do?"

"I think so."

"What then?"

"That's why you've been killing yourself: doing twice the job because after you have the baby, you'll have to quit."

Pam nodded vigorously against his shoulder and tears engulfed her again. So many feelings struggled for supremacy she could not order them; relief joined with intimacy, anger gave way to sadness, surrender consumed all. The days and nights of anguishing alone hadn't altered the things that had been true from the start. She couldn't give up this baby and even Willy knew she would have to give up her work. She reached over his shoulder and plucked a tissue from a box half hidden by a plastic shark and a box of doughnuts. Maybe in a few years she could start again. She had started over before. She wiped her eyes and blew her nose and looked her husband right into his gentle blue eyes. "I'd like to be the first to congratulate you," she said.

"And I you," he said, smiling broadly.

"On a great shot. One shot. What luck!"

"Oh, yeah? When was this?"

"Remember the night we had dinner with the Simons? And drank all that beer?"

"Do I? No kidding. I remember that night. I remember all of it," Willy said with a grin. He put his hand on Pam's belly and marveled. That one reckless act of boozy love and now he was going to be a father! He looked again at his beautiful, bountiful wife. "Hey, we should name the kid after that beer. We'll call him Bud."

"If memory serves me, we were drinking Heineken," she said dryly.

"Fine. Why quibble? What's in a name?"

Pam laughed and pinched his arm.

"Ouch," he said. "What was that for?"

"For having your way with me."

"I would do it again. Kick me, beat me, gouge out my nose."

"Oh, Willy," she said, shaking her head. "Willy, Willy, Willy."

"Pammy, Pammy, Pammy," he said, smacking his lips, running a hand across her breasts.

"Stop," she said, slapping his hand away. "Someone's going to come in here."

He grinned at her and folded his arms around her back. "I can't tell you how happy I am. I could dance. I could sing." He grinned at her some more. She returned a half-smile, a comma of a smile. Willy would be the king of all daddies. It was so easy to imagine all six-foot-three of him, impossibly folded into a child's Cookie Monster chair, some little mouth-breathing angel twisting damp fingers around his as he did all the pig voices and the wolf, huffing and puffing.

"Did you tell your mother? You didn't tell anyone, right? You're going to cancel your drink date right now, aren't you, so we can celebrate." B. Willy freed his arm, plucked the phone off his desk, and pushed it toward her.

"No. Now listen, I'm working until I go into labor, do you hear me? And don't you dare bully me."

"You don't have to quit your job after you have the baby," he said.

"What?" she said. "I do. I don't want to have one of those waif children, one of those kids sitting on the back stoop waiting his whole childhood for Mommy and Daddy to come home from the office."

"What if he only has to wait for Mommy to come home from the office?"

"What, Willy?"

"Maybe it will be a girl, not a boy, but either way this hair is dominant." He combed her hair gently with his fingers. "Yup. He or she is going to be a real furball like its mom."

"What did you say? Before that."

"I'm going to stay home with our kid. You are going to work, and I'm going to quit. Zippety-zap. I quit. I'm outta here."

"Will! What are you saying? We can't afford—"

"Details. Details."

"But—"

"Pam, I've had fantasies about this. I've thought this out in the privacy of my own head. I'm primed for this moment." Willy looked at the stunned expression on Pam's face. He gently closed her jaw with a forefinger under her chin and continued. "Listen, you'll stay out for a few months and we'll get everything ready. Then you'll give birth to the furball and then we'll all cuddle together until you're ready to go back. Then you'll go back. I won't."

"I can't do that! You can't do that!"

"Why not?"

"Because you can't quit your job. You love your job."

"No, sweetheart. *You* love *your* job. I work. I've been at this a lot longer than you have, and I'm tired of this crap myself, babe," he said, stretching out his arms to emphasize the squalor of the office. "I've put in a lot of years in this room and the other one with all the little monitors."

"You're great at this. You're famous for this."

"I'm not bad."

"You would miss this."

"Honey, please believe me. I could stop directing in a second with no regrets. What I'd really like to do is make baby food. I'd like to go to the park. I'd like to fix up the house and the backyard. I'd like to read a few books."

"Willy, you are nuts. You can't just retire at the age of forty-four and become Mr. Mom. I can't let you do that even if you think you want to. How long do you think you're going to be able to get off on straining peas?"

"For a while. A long while. When the furball goes to school, I'll do something else. I'm a very resourceful guy."

"Willy, we can't afford to live on my salary."

"We can too. We'll scrimp a little. You'll stop going pig wild on clothes." He plucked at her promotional tee shirt.

"I will if you will," she said, sticking her finger through a hole in his faded polo shirt. Could Willy be right? Could they really do it? Money, money, money. If she got a raise, that would help, and maybe they could rent out the top floor of their brownstone. It would be a lot of work to fix it up and would require some money up front, but maybe they could get an equity loan . . . But even if they could manage it financially, wouldn't Will go berserk at home with an infant? "I think we should talk about this some more," she said, her voice, despite her reservations, lifting with hope. "I think you're having some weird kind of stroke."

"I'm of sound mind and body. Very. You just make the baby, okay, honey?" he said softly. "Leave the details to me."

Could she do that? If she could, it would be such a wonderful thing. A tiny sprig of possibility opened and expanded, and became a probability. In her mind, she saw Willy and a child wound so close together they would have to be pried apart if the child were ever to walk. "Oh, Willy," she said, hugging him tightly around the neck. "If you were an animal, you'd be a mother kangaroo."

"There are worse things," he said, chuckling happily, rubbing her back.

"Why didn't I tell you sooner?"

"Yeah. Why didn't you? You should have."

Instead of answering she curled tightly into his arms, dropped her head on his shoulder.

"I think you're getting heavier," he said, shifting her weight a little on his lap.

"Well, if I am it's not the furball," she said "Three weeks isn't heavier."

"Listen you," he said, hugging her. "The crazy hours are going to stop now, right?"

She nodded.

"You're going to sleep and eat regularly,"

She nodded.

"And you're going to start now by calling that asshole agent and breaking your appointment."

"I can't, but this is the last time, Will."

"Swear?"

"Yeah." She looked at his doubting face. "Scout's honor," she said, holding up her fingers. "Honey, the funniest thing."

"What's that?" He kissed her forehead.

"I'm happy."

"Of course you're happy. You're the girl with everything."

There was a pause as Pam considered Willy's pronouncement. He was right, absolutely right. "What do you know?" she said, straightening up, sliding one leg then the other off his lap and standing. She touched his bald spot fondly with her hand, then smoothed down his soft blond hair. He wrapped his arms around her waist and pressed his face to her bosom. She put her arms around his shoulders and hugged him closer. It was all going to happen, but not in the scary way she had imagined. She was going to have their baby, and she was going to have her career too, and suddenly it seemed so simple she could hardly believe she had imagined it any other way. "What do you know?" she said again. "I can hardly believe it, but I really am. I'm going to have a baby," she said as if she were realizing it for the first time. She was going to have a baby! "Thank you, my love," she said, with more gratitude than Willy would ever understand. She kissed him. Then she darted out of his office and down the hall.

As Andy stumble-walked down the hill, he plucked his damp shirt away from his body and let the air play over his chest. His thighs hurt. His calves hurt. His lungs hurt. Even his eyebrows hurt. Running four miles up over the ridge was the first good workout he'd had in a while and it was taking so long for his breathing to return to normal again. It was shocking how fast his body went to hell when he missed a few days of exercise, but between love, food, and the heat of the sun, he simply hadn't been inclined to work out. God, this had all seemed like a bubble in time, a period so magical, so extraordinary, the normal rules simply hadn't applied. To begin with, each morning he'd awakened to the sight of blond hair splayed out over the pillows, the covers and the borders of the sheets all lace-edged as if some old grandmother fairy had crocheted her little heart out. Then he'd look up at the light in the windows, and the white curtains would puff into the room and the mourning doves would say "Who, who, lucky you," and then he'd touch Stevie; just her hand or her cheek and she'd wake up with a smile on her face that would say how happy she was to see him. Sometimes he looked at her and saw three different women he knew as Stevie and wondered at the strangeness of that.

One Stevie was the first girl he had ever loved. This Stevie was like the curtains in the window: airy, and light, and so very young. He saw her sometimes when she licked her fingers, or *eeked* when a spider climbed out of the sugar jar, or looked away when he shucked his drawers, the way she had when they'd made love in the grass. He had known that Stevie for such a short, sweet time. Those days had been sunshine, baseball games, studying together in the student lounge. Sugar, uh-uh, uh-uh, uh-uh, oh honey, honey . . .

And then there was the second Stevie, the public Stevie.

This Stevie was like tart cherry pie. He had watched her sparring with politicians, teasing movie stars, pulling a little to the left, shoving a little to the right. Music played when they said this Stevie's name. Watching her through the one-way glass box made him feel that he knew her very well, better than her public, because there had been a time when her words and thoughts had been all for him. But even as he had turned off the TV at night, puffed up with his I-know-the-real-Stevie knowledge, turning in the dark to some other person lying beside him, he had known that he was just shitting himself. For all his knowledge of this TV Stevie, she wasn't his.

And now there was a third Stevie. She didn't open at his touch the way she once had, didn't move to his lead. She held onto her thoughts and to her feelings so that when she did invite him in, what he touched was self-possession. And she wanted him because what she saw and felt pleased her; not as it had been, the cheerleader and the baseball player. This Stevie was a generous woman. A wrong thing could be said by him and she would not need to challenge it. A wrong thing could be done, and it was overlooked. And also, a certain stiffness of bearing and of form had been softened by time.

These mornings when he looked at her and then reached out a still hardly believing hand to touch her, he found curves, not angles; cushions, not planes; and then she'd smile at him, that easy, contented, I-love-you smile, and reach her arms around his neck, lace falling from her shoulders. And then he would fall into her, and as he did, for a moment at least, the three images of this woman would stand apart, and he would try to know which one of them he really loved; the virgin ingenue, the out-of-reach celebrity conquered, or a woman he hardly knew who said she loved him and whom he said he loved, who had floated off with him in this bubble of time and promised to love him forever; this woman who was different from any other, and who lay soft, soft in his arms.

And so these past mornings he and Stevie had made love, then they had made breakfast, and then it was hot, too hot to run. Even now, the sun wasn't down yet and it was after eight. Right now Stevie would be in the kitchen making something delicious out of lamb or some kind of cold soup with flower petals in it and then she might excuse herself when he came into the kitchen as she had been doing every night and go sit up in the swing that was hanging from an apple tree so he could call Penny.

Lying to Penny was the only bad thing about this whole wonderful, eventful time. She meant too much to him for him to tell her on the phone that he and Stevie were getting married, and he was too entranced to drop Stevie off his lap, drive like a mad person up to school, tell Penny the bad news, and race back. Well, maybe he could do it now. Maybe he could drive up tomorrow morning. He took a deep breath and let it out loudly, a little groan hitching itself to the tail of his breath and resonating in his chest.

God. Facing Penny was going to be awful. He had never promised her anything but he hadn't broken off with her either. It was more than that he hadn't wanted to hurt her, although there had certainly been a large element of that. Also, he liked her. Also they got along real well. It had been mostly good, and very comfortable, and out of cowardice and laziness and fear of being alone he had let eighteen months accumulate, and during that time, Penny had gathered up a heap of uncontradicted hope. And now he was going to have to hurt her real hard and real bad and apart from the fact that he'd never committed himself to her, she would have no way of expecting a breakup, none at all. It wasn't fair what he was going to do to Penny and yet how could you stay with a person out of being fair? He had tried staying with Carol to be fair and he'd hurt them both and lost Stevie too.

The dirt road wound through a place shaded by a thicket of trees. Dappled light danced in the waning sunlight. Andy pushed the hair back from his face and thought. If he got up tomorrow morning real early, and drove hard . . . maybe he could catch her before her first class. She'd be staying at his house, taking care of Dixie. Would morning really be the right time? Yes. He'd have to make sure she was awake, not in bed. Maybe he could somehow do this at the kitchen table, Penny sitting across from him, all bright and serious and trusting, with her short brown hair and wide smiling face. She'd be wearing some kind of cotton shirt and a plain skirt, a little on the short side so you could see she had the greatest legs in the business. Those dimples in her knees. And Penny did have the nicest way about her. She actually loved those damned faculty barbecues and cocktails. She made it easy for him to socialize, have a life besides the dog and the kids and the TV. So of course everyone thought and couldn't resist saying what a perfect couple they were. And then there was the way she just naturally took care of everything, buttons jumping back onto his shirts, Mr. Clean showing up under the sink. Penny was a neat, predictable, no-fuss Nebraskan girl and it was a damned shame he just didn't love her. Correction, he loved her, he just didn't love her the way he wanted to love her—the way he loved Stevie.

Stevie. His heart was just wide open to Stevie. Thinking about her with her blond hair splayed out all over the pillow made his heart lurch and his pants tighten. The days had progressed like years: flirtation, seduction, domesticity, commitment. Two birds flew across his vision, landed in a tree, took off again together. Like that. We are like that, he thought. He thought about Stevie, lying in his arms talking about babies, wanting to have a baby. It would be a damned shame if this woman didn't have a child. She should have one, should have had one, his. It was late in his life for him to be thinking of diapering again, and having a baby crying in the night, and going to Sunday school plays. But hell, if she wanted a baby, he owed her that. And she would be a terrific mother. Terrific.

Stevie's house came into the view below as he cleared the thicket of aspens and yellow birch trees he had been walking through. It sat all small and white on its mirror of a lake, its little twiggy orchard stuck up behind like something you'd get with your train set. It was too bad, he thought, they couldn't live in this house or a house like it. How was he going to survive in New York? Concrete everywhere and noise all the time and no dogs allowed. Well, Penny would take Dixie. That would be okay. He would miss OSU and his kids, especially Russo, who had been halfway to being a junkie and now three years later wanted to coach baseball and spent half his waking hours following him around everywhere. Too bad Stevie couldn't—don't think it, he cautioned himself. Stevie would die in Oneonta, just die. She was making a couple of hundred thousand a year and was a television star and he wouldn't even think of asking her. She thrived on the stress threshold, just look at her. On the phone constantly, packages being sent to her by Federal Express. What would she do in Oneonta after she'd conquered the mall? The idea of her standing around a faculty barbecue with all those professors clinging to her like flies on a sticky bun and the wives all clumped up at the fringes saying spiteful things . . . No, even if she would do it, moving her to Oneonta would fill him with guilt every day.

No, the thing to do was for him to move. He should be able to take his pick of job offers with his experience, and close to the City he'd make a lot more money too. He wouldn't have to work in New York. He could find a slot in the suburbs and commute into New York at night. Sure, maybe he'd look for something in Westchester. He'd see grass during the day and a lot more of Lisa. And at night he'd be with the woman he loved. God. Yes, God. He'd nearly lost her forever and now

God was giving him back his chance to be with the woman who all along was meant to be his wife.

Andy touched her mailbox lovingly as he turned into her drive. It was settled, then, he thought. Get to bed early and get up early tomorrow morning. Drive home, tell Penny, start lining up a replacement for himself at the school for the fall term. Jennings was just about ready. He could do it.

An inviting aroma wafted toward him as he climbed wearily onto the porch steps. Oh, yes. Shower, food, then bed with Stevie. That would be enough to keep him happy forever.

Philip opened his desk drawer and took out the leather-framed photograph of Stevie, the one he'd taken of her standing under the magnolia tree that first weekend in May. He had told her he loved her and then, her face blank with surprise, he had kissed her and mussed her hair and steered her in her pink dress with the white collar and the row of pearl buttons down the front, steered her and parked her under the magnolia tree. She'd posed under the tree; it, gaily arrayed in its gang of pink and white buds; she, crossing and recrossing her arms, trying to strike a casual pose while at the same time trying to exert some control over the elated and still self-conscious smile that was causing her eyes to squint and pulling her mouth into a huge, happy grin.

Now Philip looked at the picture of Stevie, pink and white and in love, and it hurt him. She loved him. He loved her. But they were apart. He put his hand over the phone and then he moved it away. He had called her this morning. He had known he shouldn't call because she had made it so clear that he wasn't to and he had made it so clear that she could any time. But he had called her anyway, his fingers blatantly ignoring his explicit command to desist. He was connected with her office whereupon Luann told him Stevie had gone to her country house and could she give her a message? And he said, airily, he hoped, "No, no. Thanks, anyway, I'll call her there." But he had taken her absence as a sign to leave things as they were, for a while anyway. Because he hadn't anything to add to what he had said. I love you. I don't want to have another child. So he shouldn't stir her up, shouldn't pull at her. He shouldn't even look at her. He put the picture back in the drawer, face down, and closed the drawer firmly. So intent was he, he never heard Kenny enter the room.

"Don't you want some light in here, Dad?"

"Oh. I didn't realize. The darkness crept up on me," Philip said, feeling somehow guilty as if he had been caught at something. He found his glasses, bent the earpieces around his ears, and switched on the nice old green-shaded desk lamp his father had left him. "When did you get in? I thought you were out with your friend."

"No, he had to help his dad at the store."

"Oh. Did you eat?" Philip looked at his watch. "It's almost nine. Are you hungry?"

"I had some bananas."

"That's not dinner." Kenny needed a haircut and some new clothes, Philip thought. His Video World sweatshirt was ready for the shoe polish box. "How about a sandwich?"

"I'm not really hungry."

"Well, I could use something. Want to keep me company?"

"Okay."

The two walked to the kitchen, Philip turning on lights as he went. In the kitchen, Philip tossed a damp pile of banana skins into the trash, perused the refrigerator for something interesting, found the half-eaten carcass of a broiled chicken, a dish of pasta salad, and some greens in a refrigerator bowl. He placed the dishes on the old pine table and looked to see if Kenny was going to take out the tableware. When he didn't, Philip did. "Will you help me with some of this food?"

"Okay," Kenny said blandly, pulling back a chair.

"Why don't you pour us something to drink?" He watched as Kenny wordlessly backed out of the chair, swung wide the refrigerator door, slamming it closed with his heel, and clunked a bottle of soda and two glasses onto the table.

"How about some ice?"

Kenny repeated his movements, again wordlessly, and as Philip watched, a little burr of irritation germinated and began to grow. Clunk, bang. Did he have to be so graceless? And why was it so damned hard to talk to this kid? Kenny acted as if each word he spoke cost him a hundred dollars. "I played squash with Jimmy the other day," Philip ventured, deciding to abandon the irritation rather than give it life, "and he says you're doing a great job. He says he really depends upon you."

"I just pack crates."

Philip mentally threw up his hands. He wouldn't say anything until Kenny did. It was childish but it was childishness in self-defense. He sliced off a slab of chicken, placed it on his plate beside the wilted pile of salad greens, and began to eat. As he ate he let his thoughts scurry around in his brain. The contract on his desk, the one he had been reviewing for signature when the absence of Stevie's picture forced his hand into the drawer, that contract would need refinement. Stevie. He wanted to be with her. He would have liked to put his hands to his head and groan, but Kenny was across from him chewing and gulping. What was she doing in Connecticut? Was she missing him as much as he was missing her? She had to be.

He had put the picture away in the drawer, so that he wouldn't think of her every minute. He had folded up her robe and her Yankees sleep shirt, the WON-TV mug she kept in the cupboard, the vitamins and the chamomile shampoo and the face cream with a dozen kinds of herbs and a scent he knew as "Stevie-in-bed." He put all of these things in a cardboard box marked "Xmas Ornaments," and put them in the top of the closet in the library. Former library. Kenny's room.

Kenny still had not said a word, but from the way he was gnashing his food and furrowing his brow, he looked as though he wanted to. "What are you thinking about, son," Philip said, putting aside his reverie and his self-imposed rules. Predicting Kenny's reply, he said "Nothing," and as Kenny did in fact say "Nothing," they said the word in unison, and that made them laugh.

"Gotcha," Philip said.

"Yeah," Kenny agreed good-naturedly, and then he smiled at his father and put pasta salad in his mouth.

"So how about it? What's going on in your mind these days?"

Kenny chewed and appeared to be organizing his thoughts. "I was thinking about how I didn't get to do any surfing this summer."

"Well, maybe we could get out to the beach this weekend. We could stay at an inn in the Hamptons. Rent you a surfboard. I could use a change of environment myself. How would you like that?"

"I was, uh, thinking more about Malibu."

"Oh," said Philip, his mind darting ahead, seizing on the conclusion that would take Kenny a half hour to verbalize. "Are you thinking about going back? I thought you were going to stay through September. At least."

"I know." Kenny scratched his jaw and shifted in his chair. His brown eyes flicked warily from Philip's face to the glass of cola and then back again. "I'm getting bored," he said.

"Homesick, you mean," Philip said quickly. Did he have to feel bad that his son was bored? He'd taken him to Connecticut, he'd taken him to Boston, he'd practically taken him on his back everywhere. Was it his fault he couldn't find the key to waking Kenny up?

"Whatever," Kenny said. He scowled at his glass and rubbed out the trails left by moisture beads traveling down its side.

"When are you thinking of leaving?" Philip asked quietly.

Twin feelings burgeoned. One was sorrow. The other was relief. He focused intently on his son, who would no longer look at him.

"Dad, I want to change my name."

"To what?" Philip asked in surprise. He left the homesick arena and gamely followed Kenny to the next one, scattering his previous thoughts behind him. Was changing one's name a new something kids were into? Did Kenny think if he changed his name to Fury or Savage he would get some energy? He'd like to recommend a few names if that were the case. Like Happy or Wunderkind.

"O'Brien," Kenny said.

Philip's body registered what had been said before his mind comprehended it. For a part of a moment, Philip only knew that something was being taken away. He blinked his eyes. O'Brien? That was Kenny's stepfather's name. He wanted to change his name from Durfee? "That's Danny's name."

Kenny nodded.

"Why? Would you spell it out for me?" Philip asked, although even as he did, he knew that what Kenny was about to do was inevitable. Unconsciously, he put his hand to his chest.

"Mom's been after me."

Merle. Philip could almost hear her, her voice the sound of ripping fabric.

"She's been saying how Danny's my real father and all, since he raised me."

Philip stared at his son. Yes, *his* son! Not O'Brien's! He wanted to quench the dryness in his mouth but he could not lift his hand to the glass. "But you know I'm your natural father, Kenny. And I'm alive. I'm sitting in front of you." Philip heard the desperation of his voice, but it could not be helped.

"I know," Kenny said miserably. "I've been meaning to tell you, only I didn't want you to feel bad."

"I do feel bad: I feel wronged and I feel guilty. Maybe I should have done more for you than I've done."

Kenny was shaking his head. "It wasn't you, Dad. I know you're my real father."

Philip found tears of frustration and pain gathering in his eyes. This was so unfair. He hadn't been warned. He wasn't being given a chance to dispute this decision. How could his son disown him like this? He watched blindly as Kenny scraped his plate into the garbage can, noisily dropped it into the sink, and walked to the place where the kitchen ended and the hallway began.

"It's not because of you, Dad. You were great to put up with me and all. I just want to go home now." Kenny opened his mouth and, as though he had exhausted his supply of words, closed it again. Then he turned to walk down the hallway to his room.

"Ken, wait a minute," Philip said testily, watching as Kenny half-turned, a look of apprehension in his eyes. "Is this why you came to stay with me this summer? To check me out? Was this a trial of some sort and now you're telling me I lost?"

"No, Dad. I just wanted to see you."

Philip held Kenny with his gaze, held it until he could hold no longer. "Okay," he said, at last releasing him. Visibly relieved, Kenny Durfee, soon to be Kenny O'Brien, left his father's presence. Philip moved the salt shaker to the center of the table, then he took his dishes to the sink. He opened the dishwasher and, in the precise way he had, a way that he thought best and the way that comforted him, Philip stacked the dirty dishes into the machine. Had Kenny told him the truth? He didn't know. If he was lying, it was to protect his feelings and frankly, Philip thought, they needed protection. He carefully filled the little drawers with blue powder, shut one, and closed the dishwasher. One thing he did know. The idea of Kenny leaving made him feel more alone than he had felt before Kenny arrived.

Philip dropped tiredly onto the long leather sofa. He picked the remote control device up from the coffee table, and without thinking, he turned on the television. The picture came on, the stream of music came up—the strings and woodwinds that announced "Stevie Weinberger On-the-Air." Then a voice said that this was a rerun, that Stevie Weinberger was away on vacation.

Philip folded his arms above his head. The show—Stevie interviewing a tennis player who had won the tournament he was telling Stevie he hoped he would win—had been taped before he met her, and it was eerie to watch. A video-taped Stevie, especially a version he had not met, seemed a fabrication, the creation of a talented television performer, not flesh and blood at all. Yet she did exist, and she had been part of him. And she had severed him from her as Kenny was doing. Had he ever felt so alone in his life? Once maybe. When Merle had taken off with the kids. When he had watched a five-year-old Tara and a two-year-old Kenny scream, red-faced, in a gravel driveway in California. Could he talk Kenny into staying longer, giving them another chance? Even as he asked himself the question, he knew that Kenny's visit had been a romantic contrivance on Kenny's part, a sincere yet unrealistic attempt to reconnect with the man who had given him life. Kenny must have been as frustrated as he had been when he found he could not do what he had set out to do. Maybe he'd felt loving his father would be disloyal to his stepfather. Yes, that made sense, Philip thought. Maybe Kenny had actually set out to prove to himself that he loved Danny more, and so had sabotaged every chance of closeness. If that was true, it explained why getting close to Kenny had been impossible. It was an odd kind of thing, their relationship. Their love for one another was both there and not there, real and imaginary.

But what of his love for Stevie? He had loved her, cared about her, respected her. And she had felt the same way. Had he tried hard enough to keep them together? His need to speak to her overpowered his earlier self-admonitions. Maybe she had changed her mind, and if she hadn't, damn it, he wanted to plead with her to reconsider her decision. Kenny was in his room. Was he packing? He had never said when he was leaving. What was Stevie doing? Would she be sitting in the dark on the porch swing, listening to the frogs? Would she be thinking of him? He should call her. He should tell her at least that he missed her.

Philip went to the desk and picked up the receiver, started to tap the buttons that would bring Stevie to him. As he brought the earpiece to his ear, tinny voices emanated from it: Kenny. And a girl. He put the phone down and looked out the window. Below him, almost soundlessly, cars sped by. Across the avenue, the Hudson River, flecked with light, flowed past without breaking. Philip marked off the time in his head. One minute. Two. Four. Was Kenny through using the phone? He lifted the receiver and again heard Kenny's voice. Wouldn't he get off? Would he have to go into his room and tell him to hang up?

"Dad, it's for you," Kenny said from the doorway.

"For me?" Philip asked, startled.

"I'll hang up the phone in the other room," Kenny said, disappearing.

"Hello?" Philip heard a young woman say. He had never heard this voice before. "Hello," he said back.

"Hi. Don't faint. It's Tara."

There was silence as Philip put the name and the voice together. His daughter! "Tara! How are you?"

"I'm fine. Better than fine. Oh, I'm nervous. This is so strange! I don't know what to call you." She laughed. "I don't think I can call you Philip. And not Daddy. I already—how about Father? What if I call you Father?"

"That would be wonderful," he said. Fourteen years. That's how long it had been since . . . He tried to imagine what she would look like now. She was wearing something blue, he was sure of it. He wanted to ask her but it would sound crazy. He pressed the receiver hard to his ear. If only she were here where he could see her. How could a conversation like this be anything but strained? "What do you look like?" he blurted. "Kenny didn't have a picture of you."

"A picture of his sister? Please," she said lightheartedly.

"That's what he said," Philip responded.

"I have a picture of you," she said.

"You do?"

"I cut it out of *People* magazine, a couple of years ago. That space program thing."

"Oh, yes," Philip said. "The food container. The squeezy jar."

"That's it. I thought you looked great. I carried that picture around for a long time. In my wallet. Did the picture look like you?"

"Close enough. I don't always look that serious."

"Of course not. Kenny has been calling and telling me how great you are, and about how he wrecked your car and started a fire in the kitchen, and why you haven't just put him in the mail and sent him home is a mystery to all of us."

"It hasn't been that bad," Philip said, pleased at Kenny's report, perhaps more pleased with Kenny than he had been for months. Maybe Kenny loved him a little? "Well, once I did take him to the post office and had him weighed, but I couldn't go through with it," he joked, delighted at the ease he was feeling. Wasn't Tara terrific? Wasn't she fun?

"God, aren't you great to be so nice about him? Mom and

Dad just want to shoot him. Mom likes to say that before she goes to bed at night she prays that when she wakes up in the morning, Kenny will be in college."

Philip laughed, and Tara laughed too. So it wasn't just him! "How is your mother?" he felt obliged to ask.

"Oh, she's fine. You know. Still crazy after all these years."

There was absolutely nothing to say to that, Philip thought. He wouldn't even try. "Kenny tells me you're married."

"He said fat and married, didn't he?" she said laughing. "That's what he tells people. I think he's embarrassed to say pregnant."

Philip juggled the images. Married. Fat. Not fat. Pregnant. "You're pregnant?"

"Not anymore. That's my news. Oh, how do I say this? This is going to sound sappy, but it's true." Tara clucked her tongue. "I've missed you. I have."

Philip cleared his throat. He could not speak. "Tara," he managed to say.

"I have a baby girl, Father. Her name is Sophie. Sophie Lynn. I want her to know her grandfather."

Philip felt a wall inside him crumble; all the years of holding himself taut, protecting himself from the hurt and the rejection, had also protected him from this, this vulnerable state— loving a child. How many times had he listened to those little children screaming; relived his guilt, his failure. Water fell from his eyes, and he put his hand to his face. "I remember when you were just born," he said. She had been so small and perfect. Five, five, five, and five. He had counted all those little digits a hundred times. Even then, he had heard this same baby-finger-counting story from his friends, but when it was his own daughter, he had at last understood the miracle. They had wrapped her in a pale yellow blanket with satin binding and taken her out to the car. And they had simply sat in the car for the longest time, just sharing the love for their new child. "She looks like you." "No, you." And it was strange that he could remember it now, but he'd had a fantasy then. He had thought about giving her a beautiful wedding. And now he had missed that. "You were the most perfect little thing," he said. "All pink with the most amazing head of hair."

"It stood up, right? That's why you called me Fuzzy."

"How did you know that?"

"Mom. In one of her more generous moments."

Had it been as momentous when Kenny had been born? He and Merle had been battling. Kenny's conception had occurred during a moment of truce in a war zone. Still, he had been proud to have a son. Kenneth, after his father. "How am I going to see my grandchild?" he asked.

"Can you come out here? We live in Santa Barbara. Hank and I. We have lots of room."

"I'd love to. Will you send a picture of all of you and your address and tell me when would be good for you?"

"Sure thing. Father."

"This was wonderful, Tara." There was silence as the two prepared themselves to say good-bye. "What are you wearing, I wonder," Philip said finally.

"What am I wearing?" she asked. "I'm wearing jeans and a big blue shirt. It's Hank's. Why?"

"Crazy thought I had. I thought you were wearing blue."

"You're psychic!" she exclaimed. "Me too. A little."

"I don't know," he said fondly. "I don't know if I am. I just imagined you in blue. I can't wait to see you."

"I feel the same way."

And then Tara and Philip said good-bye and Philip put down the phone. He kept his hand on the receiver for just a little while, reluctant to part from this warm feeling. When he looked up, he realized how dark it had become. Why was it so damned dark in here? Kenny must have turned out the lights and gone to bed. Philip looked at his watch. Midnight! Kenny leaving. Tara returning. It was a lot to think about and he was wide awake. It was too late to call Stevie now, he decided. What he needed was some Cognac to relax him.

He poured a small portion of drink into a glass and warmed it in his hands. He swirled the liquid around and it seemed his thoughts were swirling too. He had a granddaughter. A brand-new baby had come into the world, a child of his blood. He ached to see her and hold her, to be part of a family. Why had he been so damned inflexible with Stevie? All she wanted was a baby—and that didn't seem so frightening anymore. His children had been stolen from him and, with the loss of them, he had lost most of what it meant to be a parent. Even with their return, he was still essentially childless. Like Stevie. To be childless felt hollow. The word *hollow* resonated. He saw himself blowing up like a balloon and floating away. No wonder Stevie felt such a strong pull. Stevie. The idea of her with a baby at her breast, all smiles and tenderness for him, and for their child, moved him. Couldn't he do it? Couldn't he do it right this time? And if he could, wouldn't his life be full?

Philip walked tiredly to his room. He took off his clothing, turned down his bed, and gratefully slipped between the sheets. He tapped a stick on the nighttable and the lights went off. He fluffed his pillow, and then put his hand beside him, wishing Stevie's hand would close on his. He didn't want to be a hollow man, a lonely man. He would call Stevie tomorrow. He had something to tell her now. Better than call her, he would see her. He would get up very early and drive. If he left at six, he could be there at eight. Philip's last conscious thought was wordless. He imagined himself holding Stevie in his arms.

# 19

The first sound she heard was the cooing of the mourning doves. Stevie listened to the doleful sound of the birds and looked into the pale light of the west-facing windows. It was seven, maybe just before. She didn't want to reach across Andy's body to take her watch into her hand, didn't want to wake him. He was sleeping so peacefully, so nicely, she thought. Andy was a very pleasant sleeper. He didn't toss or sweat or snore. He just lay on his back, his arms folded politely over the blanket, his lashes not even fluttering. Did he dream? It was said that everyone did, but if Andy did, he must dream of clouds.

Cloud therapy, she thought. Maybe it had worked. A brief time that had begun with tension so bright it had been nearly visible to the naked eye, had closed with a sort of mellowness and hominess she had thought achievable by two people only after months together. At the beginning, their passion had been a wild, searching thing: all need and fear and discovery and revelation. With the passing of leisurely days and gentle nights, normal sensations had returned so that she felt his legs against hers as mortal legs, not as lightning offshoots of an electric storm. It had surprised them both that in the center of this calm comfort, she had cried last night. The tears had rolled out from the sides of her eyes right into her pillow. She had told him she was feeling vulnerable and he had soothed her until, in fact, she felt soothed. But she had thought the sadness more than the effects of vulnerability.

Perhaps it was a kind of fear of the unknown. Or what happened when a person got what she wanted. Or maybe it was just a sort of motion sickness. She had been shaken and shifted so much. How would one normally respond to having everything, then nothing, then everything again unless it were with tears? Reflecting upon the sum of her days with Andy, it seemed to her as though time had stopped, rewound itself, re-created the extraordinary joining that happened a generation ago. But with that re-creation came the constant presence of a third party, an invisible, voiceless spirit, reminding her that she was being given the rarest of gifts: another chance. Her last chance, she thought. Last chance before the thruway. Last chance to have a baby of her own.

It was funny how it happened. It had been Andy who had been saying they should take things slowly, his cautionary words honing her fear that with the passing of time he would, without warning, be transformed from destined true love into someone horribly, awfully wrong. Either that or he would continue to be sweet and loving and then he would button his fly and say, "Thanks for a great time. You keep in touch, you hear?" But neither had happened. Instead, he had blown out the candle beside the bed the night before and after some pause had said three words. "Stevie, marry me." She had gasped and he had taken her hand in the dark, squeezed it. "We'll have as many babies as you want, darlin'," he'd said. And she'd said, "Oh, Andy. Andy." "Is that a yes?" he'd wanted to know. "Yes," she'd said. And then she had cried, the source of her tears as unknown to her as the purpose of sadness in the world at all. For a woman in love, who was about to be married, about to embark on familyhood, she was certainly crying a lot, she thought. She felt like crying now. She eased herself quietly out of the bed. She put on her old cotton bathrobe, a blue plaid man's robe that she'd bought once on whim at a tag sale, and crept out of the room, shutting the door behind her.

The old stairs creaked their familiar response to her tread and as she ran her hand over the satiny wood of the banister she wondered how much longer she would be coming here. There, she thought, gathering to her all of the sensations, textures, and feelings she associated with this house before they disassembled. There was a reason for sadness. If she moved up north with Andy she would have to close up the house, maybe sell it, and if there was a place in the world where she felt completely whole it was in this house, not the apartment, not the place where she grew up. This house was her home.

Sighing, she went into the kitchen, now bright with morning light. Giving up the house is a small sacrifice, Stevie, she admonished herself, very small when compared with what she would gain. And, she reminded herself, it was she who had turned this house into an object of love. She could do the same with another house. She filled the teakettle with water, coaxed the stove's stubborn flame by blowing softly into the gas ring, and dropped loose breakfast tea into the hand-made blue crockery teapot. Then she parted the lace curtains in the window above the sink and looked up into the orchard. The sun coming up behind the apple trees was showering them with gentle particles of light. Ripening fruit glistened and leaves fluttered in the breeze that was tumbling down the hill. She could see Philip's tree from here. It was bent downward into a curve, determined shoots growing up from the top of the bend, up toward the sun. She missed Philip, she acknowledged sadly, and then the kettle whistled into the middle of her incomplete thought. Stevie cocked the whistle back and closed down the flame.

She carefully poured hot water into the teapot and took her favorite teacup down from a shelf. The dining table was at the far side of the room, facing down toward the lake. Stevie brought her steaming cup of tea and a box of biscuits to the table and settled into the worn old chair at its head. While her tea cooled she stared out at the lake. The wind was pushing at the water, fanning the surface in wide crescents away from her, bowing it out into belly shapes, a shape she longed to have. So why this sadness, this elusive pulling sorrow? What she was feeling was loss, she realized, and although she immediately tried to eradicate the thought, it was as easily erased as a large tree fallen across the road.

Andy was not Philip. He was not as smart, not as complex in any way. Philip's personality was founded on this complexity and yet those same intricate turns of mind that made him interesting and interested had produced the fear in Philip that prevented him from seing beyond his miserable experiences with his first family. Andy was, she hated to even think the word, more simple. If it came across the plate and it looked good, he swung at it. And so it followed. He loved her. She loved him. She wanted a baby, and so he would give her what she wanted. While this was gratifying, his thoughts about their future seemed innocent, too innocent. Andy wouldn't fit in in New York. He would never be comfortable there. Forcing him would be like shoving a handful of wildflowers into a cut crystal vase. He would feel like her consort at media events, dinner parties. Her weekly schedule of awake at six, office at eight, work through lunch, tape until six, prepare for her next day's show until nine, eat, sleep, left little time for a commuting athletic director husband, and no time for a child. Even if she simply quit her job and let Andy uproot himself and commute several hours a day as he had convinced himself he would do, he would find little comfort at the end of the long day in a concrete cell in a concrete city. To live with Andy in New York City would be pointless and warped.

So it would be she who would have to change, move, say good-bye to all the familiar places and things. And she would have to say good-bye forever to Philip and his quirky, intricate mind, and the way he loved her, and the kind of life they had had, and all of the fantasies of the life they could have had in the future.

If it hadn't been for Andy's sudden intervention, would she have called Philip? She wondered. Would she have given up her longing for a baby? Would he have changed his mind? No and no. It was time to snuff out the useless wondering about what might have been. She had tried. Philip had been clear. He was gone from her, so of course she was missing him. It was the finality that was causing the tears. This new, overlapping love for Andy had not canceled out her love for Philip. It seemed as though she had room for both.

Stevie smoothed a wrinkle in the cotton tablecloth she had bought with Philip when they had been in France. She lovingly traced the floral design with a fingertip, her mind reliving a sunny day, a small shop, her awkwardness and Philip's laughter as she tried to cope with the language and the difference between yards and meters, francs and dollars . . . Stevie caught herself wandering down a path that could only bring her to a wall. She wrenched herself into the present.

Today Andy was driving home to sever some strings, tie others up. She would have to talk to him before he left, persuade him that it must be she who made the move to a new city, a new life. She hoped it would be easy to convince him of that. A protracted discussion over a period of time would only wear her down. It would be best to act quickly now that she had decided.

A picture of Luann's dour expression flashed into her mind; Luann, her own pit bull terrier, lunging against her chain, terrorizing forces from without. She would miss Lu. And Willy and Pam, and her chauffeured car and all the trappings of her job and the reality of her work; the access she h^d to interesting minds, the daily opportunity she had to probe those minds, speak her own. She often made light of what she did for the kind of money she made, but underneath her words and self-mockery there was a confidence that came from being good at what she had chosen to do. But she wanted a family more, she reminded herself. With luck, next year at this time she could be a mother!

Stevie sipped her tea and started, recoiling at the bitter taste. She added sugar to the cup and as she stirred she stared out at the windblown lake. She did love Andy. He was a good man, and funny and wise in his way. He went straight to the center of any issue, found its truth. She admired that. He believed in children and in God and in good food and exercise, and what in the world was wrong with that? He was a marvelous lover and an old friend. He wanted a good family life and so did she. And so sacrifice was the price. She would shake off this sadness soon, when she felt the commitment, not just spoke of it. She would move to Oneonta. She would make new friends. She would get a news show; there was no question. She'd be snapped up in a second. And she would have their baby, maybe two. There was time. And as soon as she began her new life, as soon as she got started, she would begin to feel happy again.

Andy opened his eyes. He had the kind of dreadful feeling he had when he'd left the keys in the truck by accident, or something worse. He searched gingerly for the source of his dread, knowing all the while it was close to the surface and was harder to avoid than to seize. Then he remembered. He was driving home today to tell Penny he was getting married and leaving the school. God help him, what was the time? Quarter to eight! What happened to six? Lord. He could see patrol cars lining up along both sides of the highway just waiting to slap speeding tickets on him. Andy counted to ten and threw back the covers. There was time to shower at least. He could have a cup of coffee out on the porch with Stevie. And then he would have to drive.

He walked across the hall to the bathroom. There were so many things he had to do. Get a real estate agent. Sell his furniture. Organize the schedule. God knew what the dean would expect from him, and whatever it was he would try to do it. He would damned well need some good will if he was going to relocate to another school so fast. Wouldn't want anyone to think he'd been thrown out. Whatever it was and whatever it took, Stevie would understand and be patient! You wouldn't think a woman so used to having instant everything would be so good. But she was. She was a good woman, and he loved her. She was a fighter and she was strong. They were a lot alike in that way. Look how she was protecting him from her sadness, putting away little pieces of Philip that she found around the house, not saying a word about what she was feeling. And she must be feeling a lot of things. Women didn't go from one man to another too easily and he hadn't given her any time to grieve. A week or so without him would probably be good for her;

give her a chance to settle down. Andy turned on the water in the shower and stepped in, enjoying the heat and the pounding of the spray.

He wished he had a little something to give her, a memento to seal their commitment, but the only ring he had on him was a key ring. He'd take care of that tomorrow, get down to the mall. God. Another wife and another baby. He had never even heard of something happening like this. It could be a movie. Starring Kathleen Turner as Stevie. And who would play him? Bob Redford for sure. It was strange how the decision seemed to almost make itself. He'd almost felt like someone else when he had said, "Stevie, marry me." And then she'd said yes. This lovely woman said yes. Uh-huh. What would Lisa say? He wished he could see Lisa's face when he told her he was marrying Stevie. Just thinking about that made him smile.

Andy soaped his body, lathered his hair. Soon, soon. He'd call Stevie tonight and he'd be back in New York in about a week. They'd waited nineteen years to be together. He guessed another week was manageable. The sooner he left, the sooner he'd be back, Andy thought, rinsing himself. He could be on the road in a couple of winks.

There was a blue truck in the driveway that Philip didn't recognize. A workman, he supposed, but where was Stevie's car? Maybe he should have called. Maybe she wasn't even here. But when could he have called? Last night had been too late and this morning had been too early. And besides he was more filled with the need to act than caution would have allowed. He adjusted the crown of his hat, resting his finger in the indentation for a reassuring moment, settled his glasses on his nose, then opened the door.

Where would he find Stevie? In the basement with the workman, examining valves? Or would there be no Stevie at all, just a man in paint-spattered overalls drinking coffee over the sink? He knocked twice on the screen door and walked into the kitchen. He scanned the kitchen work area, swinging his gaze at last to the far side of the room, and there at the table sitting in the armchair was Stevie. She didn't move and the expression on her face was something between shock and fear. He understood. He felt the same way himself. "Steve," he managed to say.

"Philip," she said in return. She could feel her heart thumping in slow, booming beats. Was it really Philip? He looked so dear, so sad, so much the man she loved, she wanted to go to him, be held by him—and at the same time she was feeling so drawn toward him, she wanted to shout at him, "Go away." He shouldn't be here, shouldn't be anywhere near here, she thought desperately. The water had stopped running upstairs and Andy would be coming down very soon and she couldn't bear to think of what she would say or do then, couldn't bear the thought of being in Philip's arms when Andy came into the room.

"I had to see you," he said, walking toward her, stretching out his arms to her.

"Philip, we're not alone," she said. She clasped her hands together, holding them tightly as if only they could save her.

"I know. I saw the truck," he said. She wouldn't come to him because there was a plumber here? He didn't understand. "It's all right," he said, reaching her, placing his hands on her shoulders, raising her to him.

She held him then, almost melting, but still she listened for the creak of the stairs and the entrance lines for a play that hadn't been written. Philip was kissing her neck, murmuring her name. She had to stop him. She pressed him away from her with hands flat against his chest. "Andy is here," she said. "He's upstairs."

Philip tried to read Stevie's expression but he could not. The word *upstairs* meant more to him than the word *Andy*. A man was upstairs. She had brought a man here. His mind scrambled, trying to assimilate the sense of that. The spare room? He dropped his arms. No. "Who is Andy?" he asked, his voice a whisper.

"Andy Newman. Andy from college."

The baseball player? How had they found one another? She had called him, that was how. He knew she had loved this Andy, but could that teenage love span so many years? "I love you, Stevie," he said urgently. "I have to talk to you. I came here to talk to you."

A remote tapping sound became thudding footsteps on squeaking stairs. Stevie and Philip both turned to the sound, no longer touching, but standing so close together, their embrace so recently broken, their fingerprints were almost visible on one another's arms.

"Hey," Andy said, breaking stride, stopping in midmotion, his hand stuck between the back of his shirt and the inside of his jeans.

Andy's "hey," Stevie thought, had been part conversational, part who is this?, part ready for a fight. She felt time thickening and blurring. She stepped back from Philip and stepped toward Andy so that she was halfway between them. She introduced them, guardedly handing each the other's name. Nothing she had learned from her grandmother had prepared her for this. She wanted to split herself, take each man out of the room, out of the other's way, and pledge herself to each.

Andy looked from Stevie to Philip, took them in together. There was grief on both their faces, and longing too. He could see Stevie reaching toward him with her hand while at the same time rooting herself firmly at Philip's side. It was clear now, as certain as stone. Stevie loved Philip and Philip loved her and, since that was true, everything that had happened in the time they had just spent together and anything that might ever

· 296 ·

be, was wishing, just wishing. Knowing this, Andy felt sick with loss and the loss was compounded by its exposure to the enemy, and so mortification became part of his pain. To distract himself from the pain, Andy opened himself to rage.

He could shoot himself for being so damned rash. All along while he'd been telling Stevie that they should take their time, go slow, he should have been listening to his own stupid self. Blurting out that marriage proposal after such a short time had proved what a pea-brained red-neck he really was. Had he lost his mind? Looking at Stevie now, he barely recognized her. She was as white as death, her hair hanging in strings around her face, not sweetly shining as it did after she'd showered and combed it and brushed her eyebrows up with that little tooth-brush she used and touched that shiny berry stain stuff to her lips . . . God! How could she leave him for this Philip?

Andy assessed Philip with a stony eye. Philip was one of those New York-type men, the *Esquire* Magazine variety. The man had more money in clothes on his back than he had in his whole house. Those shoes. That stupid-looking hat. The man probably ate raw fish. Damn it to hell. He couldn't believe he was going to lose this woman to a goddamned sushi eater. He wouldn't even get any satisfaction out of hitting this pansy.

Andy snorted, then nodded his head in resignation. He must have known all along. He had rushed the normal course of love because he had realized on some unconscious level that if Stevie was to be his, he would have to blow Philip out of her life by force and, while she was still dazed, steal her away. Staring at the two of them, wordless, paralyzed in this house-of-wax tableau, he could see how they matched, how they belonged together. As much as he wanted to hate Stevie for letting him get into shit up to his neck, he loved her enough to turn her loose in a civilized way.

"I think I'd best be going," Andy said, his voice louder, more jovial than he had meant for it to be. He walked to the coat peg by the kitchen door, reached for his denim jacket, and put it on. He opened the latch, pushed on the screen.

"Wait, Andy. Wait," Stevie said. She couldn't let him leave this way. This morning they had been in each other's arms. Andy half-turned, then retracted the movement. Stevie watched his broad back as he strode purposefully across the porch toward the drive. She turned to Philip and gave him a pleading look, pleading for what she did not know. His expression was blank, his complexion gray. She needed to be with Andy, and acting on that need she followed him outside.

Andy was sitting in the truck. He had gunned the engine and exhaust fumes were clouding the air. Stevie opened the truck door and hauled herself up into the cab.

"What are you doing out here wearing that thing?" he asked, folding his map away, reaching across her to put it in the glove compartment, making no attempt to touch her, not looking at her face at all. "A woman shouldn't go out of the house in her underclothes."

Stevie was afraid. The foundations of her life were heaving again after the ground had only just subsided. If only she had time to think. If only she could say "Cut," and walk away and come back when she knew what she wanted. Andy was in terrible pain and he was furious with her for causing it. She put her hand on his arm, squeezed it. She loved him. Didn't she? "Why exactly are you running out on me? I didn't know Philip was coming. I didn't call him. Nothing has changed."

Andy slapped the steering wheel and stared out through the dirty glass. He said nothing. Stevie could see him trying to swallow. "Drive out of the driveway," she said with a certainty of purpose she did not feel. "And then let's talk."

Andy put the truck in gear and drove it a hundred yards onto the dirt road, stopping in the patch of bare earth beside the mailbox. Stevie felt her pulse pounding. Her mouth was dry. "You didn't answer me. I thoug[...]

"If you could have seen yourse[...] wouldn't be asking such a stupi[...]

Stevie collapsed against th[...] her cheeks. "You're angry, [...] with the back of her hand.

Andy punched the button of [...] out some tissues, and held them out [...] slammed the compartment door shut and lea[...] against the steering wheel.

"I'm not angry. I feel like a jerk," Andy said. "That was love I saw in there. The real kind. Not fantasy land."

"Andy, don't," she whispered. His words felt like wounds. He was leaving her. But what about their baby? She slid over in the seat and put her arms around him.

"Tell me I'm wrong," he said throatily.

"You're wrong."

Andy looked at her, opened his arms and held her against him. He felt her sweet face against his neck and his anger, his thrashing, misplaced anger, dissolved, leaving behind the peacefulness of resolution. He touched Stevie's hair and in his hand, it became silk once again. "What an amazing woman you are, darlin'," he said softly, tenderly stroking her hair. "But you're lying. Now listen to me. Listen to me." He shook her gently, held her away from him. Her head remained bowed. "I'm talking to you."

Stevie lifted her tearful face to him.

"Our time together wasn't destiny, or fate, or whatever you called it. It was a lucky accident. For both of us. We've be[...] in love for a week, not grabbing at each other under some scratchy bushes out back of the music building . . ."

Stevie tried to smile, failed, sniffed loudly, then simply held the crumpled tissues against the flow of new tears.

". . . or in the old Chevy," Andy continued, "but in this

h of us with all our hair and teeth,
essing, Stevie. That's what it was.
ant to be."

n Andy's neck and shoulder
to breathe normally, but she
chance, last chance." A light
winked out. What remained in
rk truth. Andy was right, and still, she

Andy pressed his mouth to her hair, taking in for the last time the scent of her, the feel of warmth against him. "It wouldn't have worked for me either," he said sadly. Then he hugged her roughly and set her away from him. "Now, Stevie, you go on into that house and you tell that man what you want. And if he's dumb enough to let you down . . ."

Stevie looked up and saw Andy's tears. "Andy. This hurts. I hurt."

"I know." He looked hard into Stevie's blue-gray eyes. He wanted to say the words once more, wanted to say "I love you," and knew he could not. The only way this whole damned thing could get worse was if he started to cry. "Did you hear me? If that man doesn't do right by you, you call me. Understand?"

Stevie nodded. "Will you be all right?" she whispered.

"Yeah," he said. "I'll be a little better and a little worse than I was, I suppose. Or maybe a lot better and a lot worse," he said, laughing at himself, "but whichever, I wouldn't have missed this for anything."

"Me neither," and although she thought she was laughing, tears bubbled up and they went into each other's arms again. They kissed and then Andy released her, started the engine, and backed the truck into the driveway. He braked and, looking straight ahead, spoke. "Now get out of here, woman."

Stevie looked at the stern expression he had forced on himself. There was nothing left to say. She opened the door, climbed down out of the truck. "Your clothes," she remembered suddenly.

"If you think I am going to ruin this Hollywood ending for a pair of jeans and a sweatshirt . . ." Andy said, grinning.

"I'll send them to you."

He winked at her, put the truck in gear, and as she watched, he drove away.

Stevie stood until the truck disappeared over the crest of the hill and then walked slowly back to the house, each step taking her farther from Andy and closer to Philip, the man she knew as hers. She walked past Philip's car and the clump of daisies by the step and then across the porch and into the house.

Philip was sitting on the faded blue living room couch with his head in his hands. He stood when Stevie entered the room. He searched her face for an answer. What had happened? He could not tell. She looked sad, he thought, she had been crying, but she was alone.

Stevie stood in the doorway and welcomed the fine thrill of joy that coursed through her. How glad she was to simply gaze at Philip and feel again how right they were together. Philip looked tired and hurt. He was still wearing his hat but she could not see his glasses anywhere. Had he lost them again? Philip's clothes looked too big, she thought. Not oversized, but as though he had lost weight. They had both suffered terribly, had gone through so much to be brought together again. If only she could give him something to make up for the pain she had caused him. How could she have thought she could ever leave him, baby or none? How could she have thought she would be able to forget him?

Stevie walked to him and Philip took her into his arms. "I love you so much," he said.

"I love you too," she said, pressing herself to him, reshaping herself to his body. If only she could find words to explain how the sadness that had clung to her for the last week had simply, silently gone. It seemed to her in this moment that she had caused enormous discord between them; the events of the last few weeks had triggered off nineteen years of powerful feelings and she had reacted to them too suddenly and too violently in a much too compacted portion of time. Stevie held tightly to Philip and swayed with him. How could she have asked him to change everything about his own experiences—snap, like that— because she had become panicked and frightened of being childless? Whether they were to have children or not, they should decide it together. Everything would be all right now, she assured herself, treasuring the feel of his body against hers. Anything was possible and anything could be borne as long as she could be with this man.

Philip gently separated himself from her and held her out from him. She was not just his light, she was his life and she deserved the best of everything. If she would come back to him, he would do whatever it took to make her happy. "I've been so incredibly selfish. Can you forgive me?" he asked.

Stevie nodded her head, shook her head, put a finger over his lips. "You didn't do anything wrong."

He took her hands in both of his, held them. "I have things to say to you. I want to talk about getting married, about having a baby."

"Philip," she said, love suffusing her, fear releasing the last of its hold. She went back into his arms and hugged him tightly. He was willing to do this for her, but should he? "Can it wait?" she asked into the fabric of his shirt. "Can we talk later?"

Philip nodded.

"I love you," Stevie said, "and I'd like very much just to be with you."

Arms wound tightly around each other, Stevie in her robe, and Philip still wearing his hat, they crossed the porch and stepped down to a closely cropped lawn. They climbed the hill to the meadow and walked through the high grass that caressed their clothes and offered up a sweet country perfume. Philip ran his hand over the rough bark of his apple tree and then they sat together in the orchard swing and took in deep cleansing breaths of warm summer air. He moved his hand to the back of her neck and left it there. They ate the first ripe berries and talked about little things: frogs and briar roses, and the state of the mailbox. In a little while, when the sun got high and very hot, they walked down from the field, bringing with them color in their cheeks and light in their eyes. They were quiet now as they entered the cool of the house. There they kissed, and Philip closed the door behind them.

# A Selected List of Fiction Available from Mandarin

While every effort is made to keep prices low, it is sometimes necessary to increase prices at short notice. Mandarin Paperbacks reserves the right to show new retail prices on covers which may differ from those previously advertised in the text or elsewhere.

The prices shown below were correct at the time of going to press.

| | | | | |
|---|---|---|---|---|
| ☐ | 7493 1352 8 | **The Queen and I** | Sue Townsend | £4.99 |
| ☐ | 7493 0540 1 | **The Liar** | Stephen Fry | £4.99 |
| ☐ | 7493 1132 0 | **Arrivals and Departures** | Lesley Thomas | £4.99 |
| ☐ | 7493 0381 6 | **Loves and Journeys of Revolving Jones** | Leslie Thomas | £4.99 |
| ☐ | 7493 0942 3 | **Silence of the Lambs** | Thomas Harris | £4.99 |
| ☐ | 7493 0946 6 | **The Godfather** | Mario Puzo | £4.99 |
| ☐ | 7493 1561 X | **Fear of Flying** | Erica Jong | £4.99 |
| ☐ | 7493 1221 1 | **The Power of One** | Bryce Courtney | £4.99 |
| ☐ | 7493 0576 2 | **Tandia** | Bryce Courtney | £5.99 |
| ☐ | 7493 0563 0 | **Kill the Lights** | Simon Williams | £4.99 |
| ☐ | 7493 1319 6 | **Air and Angels** | Susan Hill | £4.99 |
| ☐ | 7493 1477 X | **The Name of the Rose** | Umberto Eco | £4.99 |
| ☐ | 7493 0896 6 | **The Stand-in** | Deborah Moggach | £4.99 |
| ☐ | 7493 0581 9 | **Daddy's Girls** | Zoe Fairbairns | £4.99 |

All these books are available at your bookshop or newsagent, or can be ordered direct from the address below. Just tick the titles you want and fill in the form below.

Cash Sales Department, PO Box 5, Rushden, Northants NN10 6YX.
Fax: 0933 410321 : Phone 0933 410511.

Please send cheque, payable to 'Reed Book Services Ltd.', or postal order for purchase price quoted and allow the following for postage and packing:

£1.00 for the first book, 50p for the second; **FREE POSTAGE AND PACKING FOR THREE BOOKS OR MORE PER ORDER.**

NAME (Block letters) ............................................................................................................................

ADDRESS ..........................................................................................................................................

..........................................................................................................................................................

☐ I enclose my remittance for ...........................

☐ I wish to pay by Access/Visa Card Number

Expiry Date

Signature ...........................................................

Please quote our reference: MAND